THE OATH

Frank Peretti

THE
OATH

WORD PUBLISHING

DALLAS LONDON VANCOUVER MELBOURNE

PUBLISHED BY WORD PUBLISHING,
DALLAS, TEXAS

This novel is a work of fiction. Names, characters, places, and incidents
are either the product of the author's imagination or are used fictitiously.
Any resemblance to actual events, locales, organizations, or persons.
living or dead, is entirely coincidental and beyond the
intent of either the author or the publisher.

Book design by Mark McGarry
Set in Janson

LIBRARY OF CONGRESS CATALOGING-IN-PUBLICATION DATA:
Peretti, Frank E.
The oath / Frank Peretti.
p. cm.
ISBN 0–8499–3894–5
1. Dragons—Fiction. I. Title.
PS3566.E691317027 1995
813´.54—dc20 95-14508
CIP

Printed in the United States of America
02 01 00 QKP   16

To Dan, Mike, Chaz, & Dave,

You know what? It's been great doing things that make sense—basically. Moses only had two guys to hold up his arms—I've had four. Thanks, guys.

THE OATH

Twenty-seven people died that I know of, and I can only guess that the others fled with whatever they could carry away. I could hear the screams and the shooting all night long, and I dared not venture out.

The Reverend DuBois was left hanging in Hyde Hall until this afternoon. I informed Ben and the others that I would not attend the signing of the Charter until the body was removed, so Ben ordered him cut down, taken out, and buried with the others.

By late afternoon, the men who remained in Hyde River were back in the mines as if nothing had happened, and I also attended to my business. After nightfall, we gathered in Hyde Hall under cover of darkness and signed the Charter. With the signing of our names, we took the oath of silence, so I cannot speak of these things, but only write them secretly.

The trouble is over, but I am no happier. I am afraid of what we have done. I am afraid of tomorrow.

From the diary of Holly Ann Mayfield
July 19, 1882

ONE

The Killing

SHE RAN, tree limbs and brambles scratching, grabbing, tripping, and slapping her as if they were bony hands, reaching for her out of the darkness. The mountainside dropped steeply, and she ran pell-mell, her feet unsure on pine needles and loose stones. She beat at the limbs with flailing arms, looking for the trail, falling over logs, getting up and darting to the left, then the right. A fallen limb caught her ankle, and she fell again. Where was the trail?

Blood. She reeked of it. It was hot and sticky between her fingers. It had soaked through her shirt and splattered on her khaki pants so her clothes clung to her. In her right hand she held a hunting knife in an iron grip, unaware that the tip of the blade was broken off.

She had to make it out of these hills. She knew which way she and Cliff had come and where they'd parked the camper. All she had to do was backtrack.

She was crying, praying, and babbling, "Let him go, let him go. Oh, Jesus save us . . . Go away, let him go," as she groped her way along, stooping under limbs, clambering over more logs, and pushing her way through tangled thickets in the dark.

At last she found the trail, a narrow, hoof-trodden route of dirt and stone descending steeply along the hillside, switch-backing through the tall firs and pines. She followed it carefully, not wanting to get lost again.

"Oh, Jesus," she said. "Oh, Jesus, help me . . ."

HAROLD BLY had no reputation for mercy and no qualms about dragging his whimpering, pleading wife out of the house, through the front yard, and into the street where he tossed her away with as much respect as he would have given a plastic bag filled with garbage. Maggie Bly tumbled to the street with a yelp, bloodying her palms and elbow on the rough asphalt. Hurt and afraid, she righted herself and sat there, a blubbery, blue-jeaned mess, her tousled blonde hair hanging over her eyes. With the back of her hand, she swept her hair aside and saw her enraged husband walking away from her, a silhouette against the porch light that formed a glaring, dancing streak through her tears.

"Harold!" she cried.

Harold Bly, a tall, barrel-chested man, turned, one foot planted on the top porch step, and deigned to look upon his wife one more time. There was no pity in his eyes. In his mid-forties and twenty years her senior, he was and had always been a boss man who did not take kindly to betrayals. He'd enjoyed throwing her into the middle of the street. In fact, he wished she would get up so he could do it again. "It's all over, Maggie," he said with a slight shake of his head. "It's a done deal."

Her eyes widened in terror. Gasping and whimpering, she struggled to her feet, then ran to him. "Harold, please . . . don't. I'm sorry, Harold. I'm sorry."

"You think you can go two-timing on me and then just say you're sorry?" he shouted, then pushed her down the porch steps with such strength that she fell again, letting out a cry the neighbors could hear.

"Harold, please don't make me go. Please!"

"Too late, Maggie," he said with a wave of his hand as if passing sentence on her. "It's only a matter of time now, and there's nothing I can do to stop it. Now you'd better get out of here, and I mean get way out of here." He turned to go inside, then added, "I don't want you around me when it happens. Nobody does."

"But where can I go?" she cried.

"Well, you should've thought of that a lot sooner."

Across the narrow street a lace curtain was pulled ever so slightly open, and the wife of a mining company foreman watched the drama while her children watched cartoons on a satellite channel. Two doors down and opposite the Blys' large, brick home, a miner and his wife cracked open their front door and listened together.

"Harold," they could hear Maggie almost screaming, "don't leave me out here!"

He was just opening the front door, but he turned once more to stab at her with his finger. "You stay away from me, Maggie! You come near here, and I'll kill you, you hear me?"

The front door slammed, and now Maggie was alone in the dark.

I hope she doesn't come here, the foreman's wife thought and quickly let go of the lace curtain. The miner and his wife looked at each other, then closed their door quietly, hoping Maggie wouldn't hear the sound.

Maggie wiped away the tears that blurred her vision and looked around the neighborhood for any haven, any sign of welcome. Maybe she could go to the Carlsons . . . No. She saw the parlor curtains of their turn-of-the-century home being drawn across the windows. The Brannons, perhaps? No. Across the street, she saw the porch light, then the living room light, of their white house blink out.

It was a clear July night, and Maggie realized that most of the neighborhood must have heard the argument. None of the neighbors would open the door to her; they wouldn't risk Harold's wrath.

Despite the warmth of the evening, Maggie felt cold, and she folded her arms close to her body. She looked down the steep hill toward the rest of the little, has-been town and felt no warmth from the tight rows of metal-roofed homes and aging businesses. The rooflines with their chimneys looked like night-blackened sawteeth against the moonlit mountainside beyond. There was hardly a light on anywhere.

Suddenly Maggie realized she was a stranger now, and to any stranger, Hyde River could be a cold and sharp-edged place.

She wandered fearfully down the hill toward the highway that ran through town, her hand going to her heart as if feeling a deep pain. She looked behind, then ahead, then into the black sky, where stars twinkled benignly between the high mountain ridges. She stared for a long moment at the Hyde Mining Company, an immense concrete citadel just across the river, now black against the sky. In her terror-crazed imagination, the windows of the old building were eyes and the huge doors mouths, and it was sizing her up for a meal. She was sure she even saw it move. She quickened her step, looking over her shoulder, then toward the sky again, as if some unseen monster lurked there.

She came to the Hyde River Road, the narrow, two-lane highway that ran through the core of the town and meandered south through thirty miles of deep valley to the town of West Fork, and beyond that, to the outside world. Just a few blocks up the highway, the town put on its best face. There, young businesses clustered around a four-way stop. Down the highway in the opposite direction was the old part of town. It had been through a lot more winters, had hung tough through a century of booms and busts, and made no apologies for its age. Maggie hurried up the highway, toward the newer section of town, through the four-way stop and past the small businesses, the True Value Hardware and the Chevron station, Charlie's Tavern, still open, and Denning's Mercantile. Beyond these, the town was a steadily decaying parade of ramshackle homes, boarded-up storefronts, dismembered pickup trucks, and rusted mine equipment. Finally she came to the McCoys' mobile home, a windowed, metal shoebox with no wheels, perched and sagging on pier blocks and concrete-filled oil drums, the ruined roof now supplemented by heavy blue tarpaulins. Maggie could see Bertha McCoy peering out at her through her kitchen window. When their eyes met, Bertha's face quickly disappeared.

Maggie approached the toy-strewn front yard. Griz and Tony, the McCoys' two mongrels, barked at her, which set the other dogs in the neighborhood barking. A knock on the door by this time would be only a matter of courtesy; the McCoys had to know someone was there.

Maggie knocked, just a few timid taps, and Bertha called from inside, "What do you want?"

"Bertha? Bertha, it's Maggie."

"What do you want?"

Maggie hesitated, flustered. What she wanted was nothing she felt comfortable shouting through a door. "Can I talk to you a minute?"

Then came a man's voice. "Who is it?" And Bertha's voice replied, "Maggie Bly."

"What's she doing here?" the man's voice asked. Then the two voices muttered in a hushed discussion while the door remained shut.

Finally the man called, "What are you doing here, Maggie?"

"I—" She looked around with fear-widened eyes. "I can't stay out here."

"Then go home."

"I can't. Harold—," She had to say it. "—Harold kicked me out."

Elmer McCoy, once a foreman for Hyde Mining, was well acquainted with Harold Bly, and Maggie could hear it in the strained tone of his voice. "Maggie, we've got no quarrel with either one of you, and we don't want one now."

Maggie pressed closely against the door as if for protection. All around, the town lay in the cold, gray colors of night, and to her, every darkened window, every shadow, seemed to be hiding something sinister.

"Elmer, if you could just let me in for a while . . ."

She could hear Bertha begging Elmer in a voice that quavered with fear. "Elmer, don't let her in here!"

"Go away, Maggie!" he yelled through the door.

"Please . . ."

Elmer's voice sounded frightened as he said, "Go away, you hear me? We don't want your trouble."

She turned away, and the dogs barked at her until she was out of sight.

EVELYN BENSON stayed on the steep trail for miles, taking step after jarring, downhill step until at last the trail emptied onto the logging road she and Cliff had followed. Having made it this far, her desperation gave way to exhaustion, her knees buckled, and she sank to the ground on the side of the road, too numb with shock to weep, too emotionally spent to pray. By now the blood that soaked her clothing had mingled with sweat, and the night wind drew heat from her body until she began to shiver.

"GO AWAY!" Carlotta Nelson hissed from behind the door of the small, one-story house.

"Please, Carlotta! Let me in. I can't stay out here!" Maggie cried, standing on the front porch and clinging to the knob of the closed door.

Carlotta Nelson and Rosie Carson, semi-cute and not quite young anymore, were still the town's favorite ladies—and determined to stay that way.

"I can't let you in here," Carlotta replied, "not if Harold kicked you out. You ought to know that!"

"Carlotta, I'm scared!"

Carlotta, her long blonde hair pulled back in a loose braid, exchanged a worried look with Rosie, a petite, freckled redhead. Carlotta had her hand on the doorknob, not to open it, but to be sure it wouldn't turn.

Rosie was near the door only because she could hide behind Carlotta. "Well—well, we're scared too, you follow?" she shouted over Carlotta's shoulder.

"Just let me in for the night," Maggie pleaded. "I'm dead if I stay out here!"

Dead? Did she say dead? Carlotta shot a look of terror at Rosie, and Rosie shot it right back: Only a wooden door stood between them and the worst kind of trouble.

"That's your problem," Carlotta said, and now her voice was quavering. "And you can take it somewhere else, you hear? Now get out of here!"

Maggie was weeping again. "Please, let me in. I'll leave in the morning, I promise!"

Her plea was met with silence.

Finally, Maggie turned and, in a stupor of fear, drifted down the porch steps to the main sidewalk, staying close to buildings, cars, and trees, continually looking over her shoulder, toward the sky and down the highway.

HAD HE not been forced to slow down due to the poor condition of the road, the trucker would never have seen Evelyn in time. As it was, he had to brake quickly when his headlights caught her, lying like a bloody corpse on the road.

He brought his logging rig to a grinding, growling halt about ten feet away from the prone body. As he eased himself down from the cab, the trucker could already feel himself starting to shake. It was dark, he was alone, and there could be more to this situation than he could see in his headlights. He approached the motionless body warily, expecting the worst: a hunting accident or a bear attack; maybe a raped, mutilated body dumped by some pervert. He glanced over his shoulder. What if the attacker was still in the area?

"Hello?" he called tentatively.

Evelyn stirred and moaned into the ground. The trucker quickened his step. Reaching her, he stooped down and gently turned her over. She was limp, her eyes closed, her face waxen. He cradled her head and felt her neck. Her pulse was strong, her breathing normal.

"Ma'am, can you hear me?"

She awoke with a start.

Evelyn was not aware of who she was, where she was, or who was holding her. All that registered in her mind were the truck's imposing grill, the rumbling diesel engine, and especially, the glaring headlights—they looked like eyes to her.

With a terrible shriek, she broke free from the trucker and leapt to her feet, staggering with exhaustion, stained with blood, her right hand wielding her knife, the broken blade flashing in the headlights. The trucker, fearful for his own safety, scrambled away from her, away from that blade. Stunned, he stood in the road watching the woman as, with crazed eyes and a cougarlike scream, she assaulted his truck with the knife, shrieking, kicking, lashing at the big machine, the blade clanging over the grill. Then realizing that she was going to hurt herself, the trucker leapt forward and grabbed her, pulling her away from the truck. She kicked and screamed and almost sliced his ear off.

VIC MOORE, tall, bearded, and burly, didn't need any trouble either. Finding work in Hyde Valley wasn't easy these days, especially for a contractor. Well, he'd managed to keep food on the table, which said something for his strength and cleverness. He'd also managed to stay married to the same woman for going on six years, which in itself was quite an accomplishment—and said something for Carlotta Nelson's ability to keep a secret. So things were going fine, thank you, and could only get better from here. At least, that was what he thought until that night.

He was just getting ready for bed, standing bare-chested in front of the bathroom sink, when he noticed what looked like a rash or some broken blood vessels directly over his heart. He leaned toward the mirror, trying to get a better angle to study the strange mark. It seemed to have a lacy, veinlike pattern to it and covered an area over his breastbone an inch or so wide and a little longer than the width of his hand. What in the world was this? he wondered.

From somewhere deep in his memory, an answer surfaced, and the heart just beneath that mark began to pound faster. Vic grabbed the edge of the sink to steady himself. His head began to swim as reason and logic fought against fear and denial. This mark, this blemish, couldn't be what he thought it might be. He didn't believe all that stuff he'd heard since he was a kid. No, he'd just pulled a muscle or something; broken a couple of blood vessels swinging a hammer or lifting a radial arm saw. He'd been working hard lately.

A loud knock at the front door made him jump. There was a moment of silence, followed by desperate pounding. Dottie, his wife, was in the shower, and he knew she couldn't hear the knocking. Vic cursed the bad timing. Who in the world—?

He had to cover himself. He couldn't let anyone see— Oh come on, he told himself, just put your shirt on. It's no big deal.

He put on his shirt, which was hanging on a hook on the back of the bathroom door. For good measure, he grabbed his robe, too.

The pounding continued, and as Vic crossed his living room toward the front door, tying his robe as he went, he could hear a voice. "Hello! Hello, please, somebody!"

Uh-oh. It sounded like Maggie Bly.

He swung the door open. Maggie almost knocked him over as she pushed her way inside and held him, practically climbed him in terror.

"Vic, let me in, let me in!"

Vic was startled, then angry. "Maggie, what're you doing? What is this?"

She held on to him, her eyes fixed on the front door as if something had chased her inside. Her words tumbled out like those of a frightened child. "Vic, you gotta let me stay here, I won't be any trouble, let me stay here please, I can't go out there!"

"Maggie, now calm down!" he hissed, forcibly breaking her hold on him. "And pipe down, will you? I've got Dottie and the kids here. You wanna get them all upset?"

Maggie tried to quiet down, but her voice was still high-pitched with terror. "Please, just don't make me go out there . . ."

Vic looked toward the hallway leading to the bathroom. He could still hear the shower running. He was getting nervous. "What's the matter? What happened?"

Maggie rubbed the area over her heart as if trying to ease a pain. "Harold kicked me out."

Vic saw what she did as he heard what she said, and he was frightened. She leaned toward him. He backed away. "Easy, Maggie, easy. Harold kicked you out? What for?"

She stood there, just crying, not looking at him.

Vic insisted, "Why'd he kick you out?"

"I've never had this happen to me before . . ." she said, sidestepping the question.

Vic got the picture, and his face tightened with fear. He stepped to the door and swung it all the way open. "Out."

Her death sentence. "Vic—"

"Out! Now!"

She clasped her hands in front of her imploringly. "Vic, don't you know what's out there?"

He lowered his voice to a whisper, hoping she would take the cue. "It's gonna stay out there. You're not bringing it in here."

"I didn't mean it—"

Vic's speech accelerated as he grew more agitated. "Maggie, whatever you're doing, it's got nothing to do with me, and it's got nothing to do with Dottie or my kids. Now get out of here!"

She hesitated, trembling, unable or unwilling to move. Vic knew he had to get her out of his house—and quickly. Reaching out, he grabbed her by the arm, then dragged her toward the door. She let out a cry.

"Shut up!" he hissed, and then he threw her out. He closed the door and bolted it.

The shower had stopped. A few moments later, Dottie, a lovely woman wearing a towel on her head and a robe, walked into the living room. "Who was that?" she asked her husband with some concern.

Vic had been standing in the middle of the room, looking at the door, waiting to see if Maggie would dare come back. As he turned to face his wife he couldn't hide the fact that he was quite upset. "Stupid kids, throwing rocks."

"What did you do?"

"I chased 'em off."

"Did you see who they were?"

"Naw, it was too dark."

She was about to ask another question, but he brushed past her, scratching an itch over his heart as he walked out of the room. He wanted to get to bed, to turn the lights out, and to put this day behind him. He didn't want to answer any more questions.

MAGGIE CAME at last to Cobb's Garage, formerly an old mining company fire station haphazardly constructed of stone and brick with two huge wooden doors on iron hinges. The lights were on: Levi was working late. She went to the side entrance and with no thought of knocking, tried the door. Finding it unlocked, she entered quickly, slammed the door shut behind her and leaned against it. Her mind was set: Levi Cobb might pick her up and throw her out, but she would not leave on her own. She would not be outside for one more moment.

A utility truck from the phone company was sitting up on jacks, and Maggie spotted Levi just beyond the back end of the truck by the cluttered workbench. A bearded, graying, heavyset fellow with wire-rimmed glasses and the huge arms of a laborer, he was holding a welding torch in one hand and just raising his welder's mask to see who had come in. At the sight of her standing against the door, holding it shut, trembling and disheveled, he cocked his head.

"Mrs. Bly?"

STEVE BENSON had gotten a call from Evelyn's mother in the middle of the night and arrived at the Clark County Medical Center in West Fork before two o'clock the next afternoon. He could sense fatigue chasing him down the hospital corridor, but he knew he had the stamina to outrun it. He strode down the hallway, weaving past patients in wheelchairs, past nurses and doctors, intent on finding Room 31. He was aware of people staring at him as he passed. A towering man dressed in rugged, outdoor clothes, he knew he looked out of place in that white, sterile environment, and yes, he did look like he'd driven half the night, his face a blackening stubble and his eyes glazed and intense. They could stare all they wanted, he thought. His priority was to see Evelyn and find out if his brother Cliff had been located.

He spotted the nurses' station and the sheriff's deputy waiting there for him—at least she was dressed like one. At the sight of her, his impatience went up another notch. What was the sheriff's department thinking, "Aw, the Cliff Benson thing's no big deal, only a minor case, send the girl"? She looked to Steve like a green-as-grass rookie: auburn hair trimmed neatly at the neck and not a hair out of place, as if she'd never done a moment's police work. Lean, fit build. A china-doll face. He also noticed she looked ill at ease, wound up, like it was her first day on the job.

Great. Just great.

She was looking his way. Don't try to stop me, young lady.

"Can I help you?" she asked, walking toward him.

"I'm Steve Benson," he said, coming to a halt to keep from running over her.

"Mrs. Benson's brother-in-law?"

"That's right," he answered, letting her shake his hand but already looking past her, toward the corridor beyond, anxious to see Evelyn.

"I'm Tracy Ellis, the county, I'm the—I'm with the Clark County Sheriff's Department," she was saying. Yeah, she was nervous all right. It was understandable. "Evelyn's mother said you were coming. So you're the brother of the—uh—"

Steve finally gave her his full attention, if only to get around her. "Cliff Benson is my brother."

She seemed to grope for her next question. "Are—are you alone? Has anyone come with you?"

"I'm alone. Let's cut to the chase here. I want to see my sister-in-law, and I want to know if you've found my brother."

She read his face and his tone, dropped her eyes for a moment, then finally said, "Evelyn is alive, safe, sedated. No serious injuries. She was cut and bruised and in shock when the truck driver brought her in, but she's resting now. She'll be all right."

Steve did not miss the fact that she'd told him only about Evelyn. But before he could speak, she touched his arm. "Could we sit down first, just for a moment?"

"What for?"

She only answered gently, "Come on," and led him to a waiting area just off the hallway, a spacious room with comfortable chairs, *People* magazines, big windows. He sank into a soft chair by the window, a chair already warmed by the afternoon sun. It felt better than he'd expected; his body was giving him hints about needing rest, hints he'd been ignoring.

Tracy Ellis pulled a chair over so she could sit opposite and close. She was holding a folder, no doubt the details of the case gathered thus far, Steve thought, but he noticed she didn't open it. Instead, she just looked—he could see she was struggling to find words.

But her expression said enough. He could read the truth in her eyes, feel it boring into his guts, overpowering his hopes, dashing his strongest desires to not believe.

"Is my brother dead?"

She still hesitated. Finally she said, "Um, we need a positive identification of the body, but . . . yes, it's almost certain that your brother Cliff is dead."

A flicker of hope returned, but only to torment him. "What—what do you mean, almost certain?"

She quickly opened the folder and scanned her notes for specific information. "Did—" She flipped to another page. "—your brother Cliff have a scar on his right leg, uh, on the side of his thigh?"

Steve took a deep breath. He could feel himself going numb.

Her face was full of apology, but she was waiting for an answer.

He nodded. "He, uh, shot himself in the leg with a pistol when he was sixteen. He was trying to show me his quick draw." He could see it all: the hand-drawn paper target tacked to the old oak tree out behind the house; Cliff, tall and gangly, with that holster tied to his leg and that drooping cowboy hat. Clint Eastwood, move over. "He was—he was a crazy kid." And I loved him for it.

"I'm so sorry."

"What happened?"

"We're not sure. Last night, a truck driver found Mrs. Benson alone on a logging road up on Wells Peak. She was in shock and incoherent, but had some ID on her. We called her home and found out from one of her sons that she and your brother had gone camping together. We found your brother's body on Wells Peak early this morning." She paused, then said carefully, "By the looks of things, we think he may have been the victim of a bear attack."

May have been? "You can't tell a bear attack when you see it?"

His tone was sharp; he was in such pain he couldn't help it. He noticed that she took it well, remaining calm and pleasant though visibly tense. "We don't have all the information yet. First of all, bear attacks, if that's what this was, are extremely rare around here, at least the reported bear attacks, and—" She hated to admit this. "—we've never established a procedure for expediting a case of this sort. In this part of the country, it takes time to gather the personnel and work out the logistics. Now, your brother's body was taken to the morgue in Oak Springs—that's over the pass, about thirty miles from here. The autopsy is scheduled for tomorrow, and we're hoping the county medical examiner can make a determination. In the meantime, we've contacted the Department of Fish and Game, and they're going to get some people out here—"

"Marcus DuFresne?"

She stopped. "Uh—excuse me?"

"The conservation officer with Fish and Game. It's Marcus DuFresne, isn't it?"

She cocked her head. "You know him?"

"We've worked together. I helped him tag some bears last year. Is he on this case?"

She hesitated just a little, but replied, "Yes, I think he is."

Nervously running his hands through his straight, black hair he said, "I'd better get in touch with him, then. We've got to get right on this before the signs fade, before we lose the evidence—"

"Well, I'm sure Mr. DuFresne is well qualified—"

"We both are. It'll take both of us." Steve was aware he was talking too loud, too fast, but he couldn't stop himself. It was as if he were putting all his pain and anger into a course of action, into something he could control.

"Mr. Benson." She raised her hand to cut him short. "Give it some time. You're too close to this—"

"We don't have time!" he snapped. "If this was a bear attack, the signs could fade within hours."

"There are qualified people working on this—"

"You want qualifications? Is that it?" Steve said, raising his voice. "Would a Ph.D. in biological science be good enough for you? How about a professorship at Colorado State University, teaching environmental science and biology? I know bears, Deputy! I've specialized in grizzly and black bear behavior for the past ten years. I've consulted with the National Park Service, I've chaired twelve boards of inquiry into bear attacks, I'm currently doing research on grizzly habitat and seasonal use in Glacier

National Park. As a matter of fact, I'm even in the process of writing down some of what I know, and you can read all about it when I finish my book, but for now, I've got a brother killed and a possible rogue bear responsible, and . . ." He stopped, exhaled a long sigh, and leaned forward, resting his head on his fingertips. He had gone too far, and he knew it.

Her calm and soothing response was much to her credit. "Dr. Benson, why don't we get you in to see your sister-in-law? We can talk more after you see her."

His tone was softer, apologetic. "I would greatly appreciate that."

SHE WAS more than just an in-law. Steve had known Evelyn long before she'd fallen for Cliff. He'd even dated her a few times himself. She was a longtime friend, a kid sister, a tease, with just enough edge to make her perfect for a guy like Cliff. As he stole quietly into her hospital room he saw her mother, Audrey Miller, sitting beside the bed, holding her hand. A bouquet of flowers was on the bedside table and classical music was playing softly from the built-in radio.

Steve didn't know what to expect, but when he saw Evelyn lying on the white sheets, pale and weak but safe and cared for, the sweet knowledge that she was alive overwhelmed him, and he began to cry.

Audrey turned and her face lit up. She spoke in a hushed, bedside voice. "Steve! Oh, hello," and then she rose and embraced him as tears filled her eyes. They held each other for as long as it took to exchange comfort, sorrow, understanding. There were no words. What could be said? Steve thought.

He looked at Evelyn. Her face was turned his way, but her expression was listless. She gave no hint that she recognized him. Audrey kept one arm around Steve as she followed his gaze to the bed.

"She's still in shock, I think."

Steve approached, bent down, and looked into Evelyn's eyes. "Evie?" he said softly. "It's Steve." For a moment there was no response. Then, like a delayed reaction, her eyes came to life and looked into his. Her lips quivered slightly, then formed a very weak and slurred "Steve . . ."

She'd been through something horrible, Steve thought. Her curly black hair was still matted with dried blood, her face and hands marred with cuts and bruises.

Gently he placed his hand on hers. She managed to wrap her thumb around one of his fingers, and then slowly she smiled. It wasn't even close to the usual Evelyn smile that could light up a room, but Steve welcomed the sight of it.

"How you doing, kid?"

For a moment it seemed she hadn't heard him. Then she said, "Cliff is dead." Her eyes grew watery, but she seemed so far away, so out of touch with her emotions and her direct situation, that her words came out in a dull monotone, a stupored statement of fact.

"Just rest, Evie. We're all here now."

She smiled weakly and gave his finger a barely discernible squeeze.

Audrey spoke in the same hushed voice. "Samuel and Travis are staying with us. They were just here. They went home with their Grampa."

Samuel and Travis, ages fifteen and eighteen. Good boys, well raised, Steve thought. Evelyn wouldn't be alone.

He patted Evelyn's hand in a gentle good-bye. "I'll be back. I'm going to go out and talk to the deputy now. You take care."

"You, too," she managed to say.

Steve and Tracy Ellis found a conference room and sat at one end of the long table.

Tracy was hesitant. "How are you doing?"

Even the thought of answering that question brought Steve's emotions to the surface. He just shook his head, afraid to answer, for fear he would lose control.

"We can wait on this."

"No." He sat up straighter and wiped away the tears that were forming at the corners of his eyes. "No, we've got to get going on it. We can't waste any more time."

She toyed with the pen in her hand and said softly, "All right."

Something about her made him ask, "And how are you doing?"

"I'm—" She opened her folder again, perhaps just for something to do. "I'm not very fine, you may have gathered."

"Well, these are not exactly fine circumstances."

She shook her head with a weak smile of agreement. "No, they sure aren't. And things are going to get rougher before they get better. I think you need to brace yourself."

"I'm working on it," he said, then changed the subject. "Has Evelyn been able to tell you anything about what happened?"

"I was going to ask you the same thing."

He shook his head. "No. She's really out of it right now."

"That's best, believe me."

Tracy had the folder open on the table and was perusing what information she had. "A truck driver found her on the logging road up on Wells Peak." She began unfolding a Forest Service map of the area. Steve pulled his chair around so they could both view it right-side up. "She was incoherent, hysterical, covered with blood. She still had a hunting knife in her hand and . . . and the truck driver says she attacked his truck, went after it with the knife."

Steve leaned forward at that. "Excuse me?"

Tracy scanned her notes and pointed to the quote from the truck driver. "'I thought she was unconscious, but then, when she saw my truck, she jumped up screaming and started attacking it, trying to stab it.'" When I talked to the trucker he was quite agitated. He'd never seen anything like it. He said he had to wrestle her off his truck and she just about stabbed him."

Steve was trying to imagine Evelyn doing such a thing. She was an even-tempered woman, mature and responsible. More importantly, she and Cliff were experienced in the outdoors. Evelyn had hunted with Cliff, had shot and dressed out game, including a large black bear during a trip in Montana. She could be quite protective of people she loved, and she was no pushover, but this reported behavior was not Evelyn.

Tracy outlined the area on the map. "He found her about here, up this logging road. That's about twelve miles above the town of Hyde River. She and her husband were camping near the ridge, right here, near the end of the Staircase Trail. No one's ever seen a grizzly on Wells Peak, but the Fish and Game people are guessing it might be a large bear . . . it's tagged, Number Three-eighteen. He's been sighted, well, not near Wells Peak at all, but—" She pointed to another mountainous area at least thirty miles to the north. "—up in here, in the North Paddox Range."

Steve studied the map. "That's not unusual. Grizzlies can travel pretty far when foraging. Does anyone know if this bear is habituated, used to people?"

"I understand he's getting that way, and that's what makes him a prime suspect. He's raided the landfill near Swiftwater." She pointed out the tiny village on the map, again, some thirty miles north of Wells Peak. "And a few homesteads there have had their garbage gone through." Tracy shook her head, her expression troubled. "But this—attack—well, nobody expected it."

"Has anyone checked the site of the attack?"

Her shoulders sagged, and she looked uncomfortable. "Sheriff Collins and I went up there this morning, first light," she said. "We didn't know what we were looking for. We knew Mrs. Benson had come down the Staircase Trail, and we knew there'd been trouble, but—" She paused. "Dr. Benson, it wasn't pretty."

He knew she was trying to protect him. But he needed to hear the truth. "Go ahead."

She fumbled just a little, leafed through her notes, and groped for words. "We found the campsite: a small tent, a firepit some distance downhill, two backpacks. The food provisions were properly stored in containers in some trees far from the camp, again, downhill."

"Hung on a rope stretched between two trees?" Steve suggested.

Tracy nodded. "That's right."

"At least seventeen feet off the ground?"

"Exactly."

Yeah, Cliff and Evelyn always did that. It was a standard method for protecting food stores—and campers—from scavenging bears. Not only was the food inaccessible, it was also far from the actual campsite and downhill, which meant downwind at night. So far, Steve thought, they'd done all the right things.

Tracy found a crude map of the site she'd made while there. She handed it to Steve. "But that's where we found your brother's body, down here near the food stores, in a grove of trees about eighty yards from the camp." The spot was marked with an X.

Both Cliff and the bear could have been at the food cache at the same time for the same reason and surprised each other, Steve thought.

"We called the coroner, and he and I packed the body out. It was transported over to Carson General Hospital in Oak Springs for autopsy. We should have the report by sometime tomorrow."

Tracy gathered up the notes, put them back in the folder, and closed it with a snap.

Steve could see that she was finished giving him information, at least for now, so he let it rest. Considering the day she'd had, the horrors she'd seen, the gruesome task of packing Cliff's body out of the mountains, he didn't blame her. She had done a good job, too. He was beginning to realize that he'd misjudged her.

"You've had quite a day," he said quietly.

"Yes sir. And I'm terribly sorry."

"Thank you." More awkward silence. "That was—that had to be quite a job, carrying Cliff out of there." Cliff was a big man, as tall as Steve and heavier.

That didn't seem to comfort her. She sat there, looking down at the folder and nervously biting her lower lip. Finally she asked, "So what are your plans?"

"I'll need to see the—" He was going to say he'd need to see the autopsy report, but this was Cliff he was talking about. Cliff's body. He didn't want to envision it. He'd seen what a grizzly could do.

He'd seen a jaw removed with one swipe of the six-inch claws, an arm torn away and eaten while the victim was still alive, a complete face lying in a bloody heap in the weeds, a child's body opened and emptied from the pelvis to the rib cage. No amount of time could dim the images, the sounds, the smells.

Cliff, dying that way? Steve had to block out any thought of it. "I—I think I'll, well, someone needs to read the autopsy report and let me know the conclusions. I might look into it myself, but right now, I just don't know." Vaguely, he noted that she seemed to be relieved to hear he didn't want to read the report. "But at any rate," he continued, "I do need to contact Marcus DuFresne. I won't be surprised if he contacts me first once he finds out who the victim was. But we'll—we'll get on with it."

She smiled at him. He was struck by the warmth, the comfort her smile gave him.

She stood and said, "If you're planning on staying in the area for a while, I could recommend the Tamarack Motel here in West Fork. It's not the Holiday Inn, but it's quaint and it's clean. I could get in touch with Marcus and let him know you're here, and then if you'd like, I could take both of you up to the site tomorrow, let you look it over."

But Steve was thinking about the passage of time and what that did to a trail, to signs a bear might leave behind. He was thinking about nature's way of cleaning up a campsite: rain, sun, wind, and scavenging animals, all of which could quickly erase vital clues to what had happened.

He looked up at Deputy Tracy Ellis, who appeared tired, who'd already been up to the site and back. Then he looked at his watch, considering the remaining daylight, and made a decision. "How long would it take to get up there?"

Dinner and Barn Dance
in celebration of Benjamin Hyde's birthday.
Hyde Hall
September 20, 7–10 P.M.
Music by
The Silver Settlers

Bring a hot dish and a dessert. Drinks will be provided.
So that all may take part, the second shift
will be excused at 5 P.M.

Come One, Come All!

Hyde Mining Company Flyer
September 1879

NOTICE

To the second shift foremen:

Owing to the shorter workday last week, the second shift will work a
full shift this coming Sunday. No exceptions. Regular shifts and regular
hours will resume on Monday.

Fun is one thing; production is another. All foremen will advise their
crews, and extend my thanks for the nice party.

Bulletin from Benjamin Hyde's office
September 1879

———

TWO

The Bear

Vic Moore knocked off and went home early, leaving the church roofing job undone. There's no big hurry anyway, he thought. Let Reverend Woods stew about it. The weather was supposed to be pretty good for a while, and he had other things on his mind.

Well, one thing, actually. Right now he was standing in front of his bathroom mirror again, scrubbing at the discoloration over his heart. Soap hadn't worked too well, so now he was using a petroleum-based, grease-cutting hand cleaner. He kept scrubbing and rinsing, then scrubbing again. It wasn't working, and he was getting nervous. The mark, the stain, the blemish, whatever it was, was only getting darker, and all the scrubbing was only making the area raw.

He threw down the washcloth. Now what? He looked out the bathroom window toward the mountains, the south-facing slopes with their countless regiments of pine and fir awash in the afternoon sun. A beautiful sight, but it brought only one thought: Night was coming.

They say it always happens at night.

Vic could feel fear creeping up on him, but he shook it off with angry defiance. Huh-uh, no way, he thought. Not me. This is where the rules change, folks. Nobody has to see this, nobody's going to see it, and most of all, Vic Moore is not going to cave in! I've never been afraid of anything, I've never let anybody play around with me, and I'm not starting now. With that decided, he dried his chest with a towel and put on a shirt.

He needed a tall cold one. He decided to kill some time down at Charlie's, the local watering hole. He'd kick back, shoot some pool, be with his buddies.

He went into his bedroom to get his wallet, then stopped, eyeing the small cabinet beside the bed. He walked over to it, yanked the top drawer open, and grabbed his .357. Now how could he carry it without it being seen? Carrying a gun around here wasn't so unusual. Hyde Valley was full of hunters, ranchers, and sportsmen; guns were common here. But his buddies would ask him about it, and he'd have to explain himself. They might think he was afraid of something.

He slipped the revolver into a soft leather shoulder holster and concealed it under his jacket. A jacket on these warm days was going to be miserable, but Vic Moore was going to be ready.

IT WAS three o'clock when Tracy Ellis, out of her uniform and into the same hiking gear she'd worn that morning, signed out the county's Jeep Cherokee and began the trek with Steve up to the site of the attack. The drive from West Fork up the Hyde River Road to the town of Hyde River was thirty miles and would take about forty minutes; the drive up the bumpy, rutted logging road to the Staircase Trail was twelve miles and would take another hour or so; and the hike up the trail to the campsite would take about an hour and a half. So they hoped to get to the site by a little after six, leaving them enough daylight to thoroughly investigate the site and get back down to their vehicle before dark.

As Tracy drove she gave Steve an informal tour of the meandering miles of narrow gap between mountain ranges known as Hyde Valley. He found her little history lesson helpful in clearing his mind and emotions, and for that he was grateful.

West Fork, the county seat for Clark County, was named for its location, Tracy told him. The town was first built where the west fork of the Hyde River joined up with the main stream on its rambling journey south. Once a boom town, it now struggled for a good, steady reason to exist without the mining and timber industry that had built it and kept it alive for so long. Steve noted that its downtown was turn-of-the-century brick, its sidewalks were cracked and settling, and its streets had an aggravating number of potholes. Times were good long ago, but prosperity, like a wayward lover, had fled, its promise to return never fulfilled.

"Back in her better days," Tracy said, "West Fork was a stopover for flatbottom steamboats coming up the river to pick up logs for the mills downstream and to drop off goods and settlers, and mostly prospectors. There was a real gold rush going. It's hard to believe now, but West Fork once had over twenty thousand people. Then the gold gave out in the early 1900s and people moved on."

Now, she continued, the population remained fairly steady at about three thousand, sustained by a little mining, some logging, some county government, and quite a bit of commuting the thirty miles over Johnson's Pass into the next county and to the nearest larger city, Oak Springs.

Steve and Tracy only had to drive a few blocks and cross a bridge over the Hyde River to be out of town. From there, they followed the Hyde River Road north as it followed the river into the wilderness.

So began the wilds of the north woods, a rolling riot of mountains and timber, checkered at times with clear cuts but often serene with green meadows along the meandering river. Hyde Valley was the main expanse that held the mountains apart, and from it branched other gulches, draws, and deep, shaded valleys stretching far into the hills, each one with its own namesake creek where elk and deer came to drink and coyotes prowled at night. Above the valleys, sheer rock cliffs towered, jagged and broken off by the centuries, the tenacious trees growing out of any available crevice.

There was solitude and a kind of majesty to this area, Steve reflected, what one expected to find in the wilderness.

Well, almost the wilderness. People were out here. Not civilization, exactly, but people. Every mile or so, Steve noticed another homestead, farm, or ranch belonging to the descendants of the rugged bunch who first settled there. These were people, Steve thought, who had their own way of doing things and liked to keep their distance from big towns, large groups, strict ideas. They lived in barely-hanging-on log cabins, weathered, teetering shiplapped shanties, and mobile homes crouching under added-on roofs, walls, and carports.

"What do these people do for a living?" Steve asked.

"Oh, you name it," Tracy answered. "Some logging, some mining, some commuting. Then you've got the artsy-craftsy types with cottage industries, and you have people on public assistance. But they're out here because they want to be. Hyde Valley gets in your blood; it really does."

Certainly, every resident had to have his own story, his own answer for why he was there. Steve could see several clues along the way: the vast, green pastures with century-old stumps standing black and rotten and twenty or thirty head of cattle lazily passing the day; aging logging equipment, boom cranes and log skidders; metal shops and metal garages with machines being worked on; horse barns and paddocks, their occupants free on acres of green, kicking the air, chasing the wind; satellite dishes popping up like mushrooms, facing this way and that; fire-blackened areas where the dry brush had burned away to clear the way for the spring's greening; a lumber mill half hidden behind a berm of red sawdust; a Y in the road called Able, with a dismal little tavern for sale, a gas station with one pump, and a mercantile still holding on, its Coca-Cola sign still offering Coke in glass bottles. At the Y in the road, Steve noticed an unpretentious green sign that listed Nugget 5, Yellow Knife 9, Hyde River 15, all up the left fork; a turn to the right would take them up the Nelson Creek Road to Hinders, 12. A gaudy, hand-painted sign encouraged a visit to Randy's Inn at the road's end, where you could eat the world's best hamburgers and try some fly fishing in Nelson Creek.

Then the mountains moved in, the valley narrowed, and they passed through Nugget and Yellow Knife, sorry little crackerbox towns built on hope that never paid by the stubborn souls who stayed, hidden away like woebegone weeds in the nooks and chinks of these mountains. Up the steep slope from Nugget were the mines, their dark portals punched into the mountainside and a mound of blasted and crumbled mine muck, the mountain's insides, spreading out just below them, retained with piled webs of old timbers. Yellow Knife was a tight little town wedged into such a narrow rock gorge that the buildings had to straddle the stream from which the gold came.

That's how it was with mining towns in Hyde Valley. Hemmed in by the steep mountains, these towns grew only in length, reaching up- or downstream, with room for only one winding artery to run along their spines, connecting them all to the outside world.

The last of these towns, beyond which the paved highway turned to dirt and gravel, was Hyde River.

"Around the turn of the century," said Tracy as they slowed to twenty-five and entered the city limits, "there were about two thousand people living here."

It was hard to believe, looking at the town now, Steve thought. On the outskirts, bunched together and taking up what little space there was between the road and the mountain slope, were modest dwellings, basic homes with metal roofs to shed the winter snow and makeshift ladders permanently installed to reach their chimneys. There were no yards to speak of, only open areas of gravel and mine waste wherever there wasn't a building. In front of one place, an old pickup truck sat in two halves—the rear half was now a towable trailer. The front half was . . . well, a front half was missing a rear half and a future.

Across the road, on the very brink of the river, two old storefronts sat side by side, empty shells now, sagging and baking in the sun, their windows devoid of glass, their paint peeling. One had to have been a restaurant or bar at one time, judging by what used to be an illuminated sign on its front, now reduced to a bare frame and a few jagged shards. The other could have been a grocery or hardware store. Now it was boarded up with plywood. There were no signs, no posters, not even graffiti. Perhaps no one bothered to leave a message because no one would bother to read it.

"How many people live here now?" Steve asked.

"Oh, maybe about three hundred. They're a tight little group."

"I suppose so."

The narrow valley widened, and so did the town. They drove past quaint old homes, stairstepping up the mountainside along the steep side streets. Above them all, sitting like a hen over her brood, was a small, steepled church.

Tracy pointed to the huge concrete building just across the river. "Hyde Mining Company. The reason for the town's existence."

Steve stared in surprise. The building was impressive, especially for that area. It was at least five stories tall, with ramps, tunnels, loading docks, and smokestacks. At one time, the Hyde Mining Company was obviously a going concern, but now it seemed almost deserted. "Are they out of business?"

She chuckled. "Oh, they're down but not out. The cost of mining gold and silver is putting a real squeeze on the company right now. You've got government regulations, environmental concerns, foreign competition. It's pretty hard to make a profit. But the company still owns most of the real estate around here, and Hyde River is still a company town even if there isn't much of a company."

They came to the center of town, where a few businesses clustered around a four-way stop. On the right was a small hardware store, and across the street from that, a Quik-Stop with two shiny gas pumps out front and a new Chevron sign. On the left was

Charlie's Tavern, an old bar and eating establishment that was still going strong, judging by all the pickup trucks parked outside. "Charlie's Tavern seems to be doing well enough," Steve said dryly.

"It's quitting time at the mine," Tracy explained. "Time for all the good ol' boys to stop and throw back a few."

Steve smiled as they drove through the intersection.

Next door to the tavern was Denning's Mercantile, the windows obscured with white paper and a large sign announcing a grand opening in a week. Grand opening? Well, the town couldn't be doing too bad, Steve thought, but in this little place a grand opening could prove to be a nonevent.

Beyond the businesses, set back from the main road, were houses and garages, bunched together in the limited space, separated by narrow strips of rocky ground, good attempts at lawns, and an occasional fence made of whatever was at hand, from mining timbers to oil drums. A few houses were of stone, but most were lopsided frames. Nearly all of them had metal roofs.

"I grew up here," Tracy said abruptly.

"No kidding!" Steve said, turning to look at her.

"No kidding." She pointed to a white bungalow with a red metal roof perched along the road with about five feet of front yard. "That used to be my house."

Well. A local gal.

"Where do you live now?"

"Oh, in the valley, but not here," she said, and Steve could understand her tone. "I've got a little place up the Nelson Creek Road—remember the Y at Able? Hang a right there and I'm up toward Hinders."

Then, almost as soon as it began, the town ended. The last sights Steve saw on the fading edge of Hyde River were old shacks, mining equipment, the last vestiges of railroad tracks, and some rusting ore cars lined up in a permanent, mummified formation against a mound of mine waste.

As Tracy had estimated, the drive up the rutted, bumpy logging road took about an hour. When she parked the Jeep at the base of the Staircase Trail, Steve saw his brother's pickup with the camper, still parked there.

He sighed heavily. "I hadn't even thought of the camper still being up here." Steve said, tiredly rubbing his eyes. "I'll have to make sure it's picked up."

"It's been taken care of," Tracy said as she got out of the Jeep. "Your sister-in-law's mother is making arrangements to have one of your nephews get it."

Steve looked up at the sky, double-checking the remaining daylight. "Well, grab your rifle and let's get going. I want to be sure we have enough time to check things out."

AFTER ALL the driving Steve had done, his body welcomed the leg-pumping, lung-filling exercise of climbing the steep trail to the top of Wells Peak. Both he and Tracy carried a rifle and a side arm. It was no sure thing they would encounter Number 318, but they had to be ready in case they did. As they climbed, they spoke little. They didn't want to do anything that might alert the grizzly to their approach. If 318 was in the area, they wanted him to remain there. They wanted him.

They climbed for over an hour through dense forestland until, as they approached the ridgeline, the area broke into open meadowlands and rock outcroppings. Steve looked to the south. The view of Hyde Valley was breathtaking. The valley stretched far into the distance like a deep, Norwegian fjord, fading from bright green to a distant, hazy blue-gray. There was a cool breeze blowing up the sun-heated south slope, an osprey circling lazily on the air currents, and every once in a while, in the areas still reached by the lowering sun, the Hyde River shimmered like tinsel. At any other time, Steve would have reveled in the view. Now, it was tainted by the knowledge that his brother had been violently killed in these peaceful surroundings.

"The camp's just ahead," Tracy said in a quiet voice.

They slowed their walk, listening, looking, smelling. Steve kept an eye on the ground, looking for tracks, bear droppings, claw marks, diggings, anything that would indicate a bear in the vicinity. He spotted numerous elk and deer tracks; this must be a favorite spot for them. No signs of bear, though.

A bright flash of blue caught his eye, and he looked uphill, across a rocky expanse. There was the tent, perched on the hillside, a tiny igloo of blue nylon. Steve recognized it. He'd been on several hunting trips with Cliff and Evelyn when they'd used that very tent. With sorrow coming alive at the memories, he knew he could predict the layout of the camp; Cliff always had his own tried-and-true method of doing things in the wild. Steve stopped and gave the slope a slow sweep with his eyes, moving his gaze from the tent downward toward a grove of trees below the trail. There, at least a hundred yards from the tent, were the food stores, white plastic containers slung on a rope between two trees. They were exactly where Steve expected them to be, and so far, they were untouched.

Steve took his rifle from his shoulder and chambered a round. Tracy did likewise. Number 318 might be thinking of coming back to finish his meal; he may have laid claim to the site as a food source or to the corpse, not knowing it had been removed. Without conversation they advanced slowly to a spot directly between the tent and the food. By now it was hard to tell, but Steve could guess that somewhere in here was the route Cliff had followed between the camp and the food stores. It would have been a long and meandering walk through the rock outcroppings, but the layout was well planned. Farther around the slope and over a hundred yards below the tent was a small firepit. Cliff and Evelyn had done their cooking the proper way as well: Everything having anything to do with food and its preparation was well away from the camp. The camp itself was in the open and well away from the cover of the forest, which would force a bear to leave protective cover if it wanted to snoop around. Grizzlies didn't mind that too much, but black bears were a bit more timid.

Steve looked down the hill at the food cache. It was on the edge of a grove of trees, and a bear could have been hiding there, having caught the scent of the evening meal wafting down the hill and having approached from below. He looked at Tracy and nodded toward the trees. She nodded back yes. That was where they had found Cliff's body.

It would be the first place to look, the first place one would expect to find signs of bear, clues to what happened. Steve started down the hill toward the trees, his eyes carefully surveying the ground, the surrounding forest. There were more elk tracks and droppings, but still no signs of bear.

The two trees bearing Cliff's rope stood a short distance uphill from the denser grove of trees just below. One had its top broken off, as did two other trees in the grove just below. That was strange, Steve thought. There must have been a wind storm, although it had to have happened recently, since the splintered wood was still fresh and unweathered. Steve approached slowly, listening and looking, but there was no sound, no movement.

He stopped for a moment. He could see blood on the ground and on one of the tree trunks, now dry and brown. The grass in this area was matted down, the ground clawed and disturbed.

This was where it had happened.

Steve looked at Tracy. "The body was just beyond that tree," she said quietly, pointing past the bloodied trunk.

Steve bent low and checked the ground carefully as he approached. He could make out no clear bear tracks, but apparently several animals had visited the site, sniffing and digging, overturning the sod and rocks, attracted by the blood.

He looked up. Cliff had used containers made of ABS pipe, virtually bearproof and effective in containing odors. This food cache could not have attracted the bear. Cooking, maybe; maybe just the smell of a camp and of people if the bear was habituated, but not this.

They continued to scour the area. Tracy found a jackknife Steve had given to Cliff two birthdays ago. Steve tucked it into his pocket and pushed aside the memories it brought back. There would be time for emotions later. Taking a deep breath, he forced himself to continue checking out the site.

The firepit seemed clean and undisturbed except for a few boot prints, obviously those of Cliff and Evelyn as they ate their evening meal. Up at the campsite, two backpacks remained untouched, having no food or food odors in them. Two sleeping bags were rolled out in the tent but appeared unused.

Steve sat on a log near the tent and surveyed the area once again, pondering out loud. "Okay. They cook their dinner, eat, clean up. By now it's getting dark—or maybe it isn't, we don't know—Cliff goes down to the food cache for some reason, maybe to stow the leftovers in an ABS container and hang it up on his rope. He startles the bear, the bear attacks him—" He stopped, bothered. "Then again, maybe not. The area's too open for either to surprise each other."

"Maybe he saw the bear going after the food and went down there to chase it away," Tracy suggested.

"Maybe." But he still wasn't satisfied. "No, Cliff wouldn't have gone down there and knowingly placed himself close to the bear. He's been a wildlife photographer for fifteen years. He's been in enough situations to know better."

"What if the bear charged him up here somewhere, then dragged him down there?"

"Possible. But there's no sign that anything happened around the firepit or the campsite itself, so it's reasonable to think the bear didn't charge up this way." He looked toward the grove of trees where Cliff's body had been found. "Did—" He had to force the question out "—did the condition of the body indicate . . . a scenario?"

No answer. He looked her way. She was sitting on a rock formation, cradling her rifle, looking toward the food cache. She must not have heard him.

"Do you understand what I mean?" Steve asked.

She looked at him, her expression quizzical.

He felt he needed to explain. "I'm trying to get some idea of how long the attack went on. Cliff had to have taken defensive measures, and obviously, Evie got involved at some point. It's—" He knew he was asking for information that could pain him deeply. "I guess it's time I knew the condition of the body, at least as much as I need to—you understand?"

Tracy looked at the ground. "I—I don't know if it would tell you anything . . ."

"What did you see?"

She sighed and finally looked at him. "I don't know what to tell you, Dr. Benson. I've never been in this kind of situation, investigating with someone who's so close to the victim."

"Tracy, I'm up here for a reason. I won't ask you a question if I'm not ready to hear the answer, okay? Now I need the information." Actually, he wasn't sure if he was ready to hear the answer, but he had to hear it, needed to hear it. He steeled himself.

She looked at him for the longest time and then answered quietly, slowly, "We only found half."

His thought processes stopped. He sat motionless. She was looking at him, waiting, trying to gauge his response.

His voice wouldn't engage. When it did, it came out a hoarse whisper. "Half? Only half his body?"

She nodded.

His mind filled with shocking, ghoulish questions. Which half? Which way was he divided? So where's the other half? He felt as if he might vomit. He sat there dumbly, not knowing how to proceed. He hadn't been ready to hear the answer after all.

He made a concerted effort to reorient himself and tried a re-phrased version of the question. His voice was stronger now, and he hoped it didn't betray the turmoil he felt inside. "Well," he said slowly, "I'll have to know eventually. Just tell me what you found."

He could tell this was misery for her.

"Go ahead."

Her words hit him with the force of a blow. "We found—we found the left arm detached at the shoulder, several feet away, still in the shirt sleeve—"

He felt his stomach turn. Quit it!

She slowly, reluctantly lifted her hand to her left shoulder. "And everything above this line—" She slowly traced a line downward, across her torso to her right hip. "—was gone."

LEVI COBB read the leaflet in silence, then reread it, digesting the news.

"Happened last night," said Jerry Fisk, another sheriff's deputy, "up on Wells Peak."

They were standing by the gas pumps in front of Levi's old garage. Jerry had just arrived in his patrol car and had a stack of the pink leaflets to spread around town and post in the windows of the businesses. Normally, Levi and Jerry would be telling stories and playfully exchanging insults. Today that was impossible.

"So," Jerry continued, "we're spreading the word, warning people, trying to find out if anybody's seen anything."

Levi asked, "Who was it?"

"Oh, nobody from around here." Jerry took a quick glance at some notes in his pocket. "He was a photographer from Oak Springs, a guy named Cliff Benson. He and his wife were camping up on the Staircase Trail and apparently a bear attacked them in the middle of the night. The wife tried to fight it off with a hunting knife . . ." His words trailed off.

Levi looked up from the leaflet to examine Jerry's face. There was something in Jerry's tone that didn't fit. "What?"

Jerry stuffed the notes back in his pocket just for something to do. "Oh—it was bad, that's all." He glanced around, a little short on words, then lowered his voice as if someone might be listening. "It's not my official role to be telling you this, but . . . Tracy Ellis helped bring the body down, and she says the whole upper half of it was gone. It's missing—just chomped right off."

Levi turned pale and sank into an old folding chair by the front door. He sat there, staring at the ground, muttering to himself.

Jerry didn't ask Levi to speak up. When Levi muttered, it wasn't meant to be heard. He just had to mutter.

Jerry shed his official role as a deputy for a moment. "Just between you, me, and the gas pumps, I'm having some trouble with this one, and I think Tracy Ellis is, too. We're not sure what Collins will do."

"Collins?" Levi asked, raising one eyebrow. "You think he'll want to make waves over this?"

Jerry shrugged. "We'll see. We've had people killed by bears before, maybe more than our share, but this one's pretty spectacular."

"Oh, yeah, spectacular," Levi said.

Jerry tried to soft-pedal his way out of the subject. "Well anyway, we don't want to get people all upset, so we didn't put the gruesome details in the leaflet and, uh, I'd appreciate it if you wouldn't talk it around too much." He walked over to his patrol car and opened the door on the driver's side. "But if you hear anything, if you talk to anybody who's seen anything, give me a call, will you?"

Levi answered almost absent-mindedly, "Uh-huh." Then as Jerry drove away, Levi muttered to himself, "As if anyone's gonna talk to me about this."

THAT NIGHT Steve got a call from Marcus DuFresne, and the next morning they went into the mountains as a team.

Marcus, a state game warden with silver hair and a handlebar mustache, was most familiar with 318, having patrolled the bear's favorite haunts far up the Tailor Creek drainage, some thirty miles north of Wells Peak. He even had a nickname for the bear: Herman, after his overweight and cumbersome brother-in-law. He and Herman had shared the area for several years without incident, so this hunt was nothing Marcus felt happy about. Apparently, the trouble started the way it always started, when a bear and people got a little too used to each other. Bears normally didn't want anything to do with humans, but offering a big grizzly an easy and predictable food source such as a garbage dump or unprotected trash cans could change all that. Herman had lost his fear of people and started claiming their refuse as his own, and that made him dangerous. Now the local farmers, ranchers, and homesteaders were seeing him all too often, prowling and scavenging around their homes and livestock, terrifying their children. Marcus was just planning how he would sedate the big fellow and relocate him when the attack occurred on Wells Peak. Suddenly, just moving Herman was no longer an option.

Herman's size didn't help his case any. He was at least seven hundred pounds, and the general agreement seemed to be that no smaller bear could have inflicted the extent of injury sustained by the mauling victim. It had to be the biggest bear available, and that meant 318.

By midmorning, Steve and Marcus, dressed in camouflage and carrying rifles, had reached a well-used game trail that twined across the face of the draw just above Tailor Creek. It was a path used by bear and elk alike, and recent signs indicated 318 had been in the area, making his midsummer rounds among the huckleberries, then ambling routinely down to the creek to wash it all down.

At the bottom of the game trail, alongside the creek, Steve and Marcus hoped to encounter the old grizzly. In a curious reversal of standard camping rules, they had brought two large bags of day-old doughnuts and a tub of rancid bacon grease, an odorous and tempting combination they intended to mix together and leave uncovered, open to the breeze. This time they fully intended to attract a bear.

"This'll do," said Marcus, setting down the bucket of grease and doughnuts. "We can set the bait here where he'll stumble right over it, and—" He looked uphill, where a thick growth of serviceberries formed a tightly woven thicket around the trunks of some ancient cottonwoods. "Yeah. We can set up one blind in those trees."

Steve paused to listen to the sound of the creek. It was a nice, noisy spot with lots of splashing and gurgling, enough to drown out any rustling noises he or Marcus might make from their hiding places. The wind was moving uphill, away from the bait; hopefully 318 wouldn't get a telltale whiff of their presence.

"I'll try up in there," Steve said, pointing to another thicket a little farther up the trail, in sight of the bait. "Should give me a good angle."

Marcus took a long, steady look at where Steve was indicating. "This blind here would be closer."

"It doesn't matter."

"You're going to want a good shot at him, I know."

Steve met the eyes of his hunting partner and saw no need to deny it. "I appreciate that, Marcus."

"So go ahead and take the closer one. I'll back you up from that other spot." Marcus looked up the trail and listened to the river a moment. "Maybe you won't even need me."

Steve knew what Marcus was driving at. "You are going to shoot, aren't you?"

Marcus smiled resignedly. "Don't have much choice. Around here we've got Herman, two young boars, three sows, and that's it. If there's some other nut-case bear out there, we don't know about it, we've never seen it, and we've never gotten any reports. So, yeah, it must be Herman. I just don't want to believe it, that's all."

"Maybe after today we'll know."

"Well, it's been at least thirty-six hours. And we didn't see anything in the scat." Marcus stopped speaking abruptly, aware he was on thin ice. "Oh brother, I'm sorry."

"Hey, it's all right," Steve said. He understood Marcus's dilemma. The evidence of what a bear had eaten some thirty-six hours before would most likely be a pile of scat on a game trail by now, and they both knew it. What made the matter difficult to discuss was the possibility that the pile of scat could consist of Steve's brother.

Steve reiterated what he'd said on the trail earlier. "Marcus, just standing back from it, I agree with you. After this long, we might autopsy 318 and not find a thing. And you're right, the scat we found didn't show anything either. So . . . we're about to shoot a bear on circumstantial evidence."

Marcus shrugged. "His days were numbered anyway."

Steve set to work on the baiting area. He'd said enough and heard enough.

They cleared a wide spot on the ground, dumped the doughnuts in a heap, then poured the grease over the doughnuts.

"Woo!" said Marcus. "Good stuff." It was a smell no bear could resist.

Then each man worked his way carefully through the underbrush to his hiding place, and so began the wait.

LEVI WASN'T worth much the rest of the day. He managed to carry on conversations with those who stopped by to fill their tanks, but he couldn't keep his thoughts on fishing talk or complaints about growling noises in transmissions. Whenever he was alone, his thoughts centered on what had happened at Wells Peak, and he talked about it to whatever object was available and wouldn't interrupt. First he muttered to the gas pumps as he swept around them. "Wells Peak . . . come on now, help me out. Who's been up there before that you know about and what for and when? No, I don't know. Shhh! Beats me. Don't even know who to ask . . ."

Then he discussed things with a Ford pickup while he greased the bearings. "Well, sure, somebody out there knows something, but you think they'll ever tell me? No sir, not on your life or mine or anybody's—boy, how long's it been since you've had this done? You're feeling kinda worn right here, pretty dry . . . Well, anyway, to heck with 'em. They made the mess; they can clean it up." Then he felt ashamed. "I know I shouldn't be talkin' that way, but . . ."

Then he sat at his grubby desk inside the garage and went through some bills while he talked to the tools hanging on the walls around him. "Cliff Benson. He was a photographer. Don't imagine you've ever heard of him. I sure haven't." He let the bills fall to his desk as he looked out the murky window and up the street. "It'd be nice to know what the folks in town are thinking. Betcha they're just jawin' up a storm."

He leaned back in his old wooden, wheeled office chair, his paunch hanging over his belt buckle, and asked the floor jack, "You've been around here a long time. You know people. You think that guy was the stranger Jerry made him out to be?" He snickered to himself as he clasped his hands behind his neck. "Well, yeah, you bet I'm havin' trouble with that."

Next he forced himself to work on the telephone company's ladder truck even though he could only talk about the stranger named Cliff Benson.

"I don't think an outsider would get eaten like that, you follow me?" he asked the rear axle he was working on. "Around here, you earn something like that, which means you can't be no stranger—but now don't go rollin' out of here and tellin' people I said so. Here, hold still; you think I got all day?"

The axle quit rotating, and Levi reset his wrench.

"But I can smell it. I can feel it, you know? Mr. Cliff Benson's put his big feet just one step too far into Hyde River muck." He gave a wheezy laugh and shook his head. "And now his feet are all he's got left!" Then he grew serious and thought a long time before he spoke. "Hate to think Maggie would know anything about this—or him—but—"

He cinched down the bolt and then banged it to emphasize a decision he'd just made. "All right. Tonight, as God is my judge, I'm gonna ask her! I'm gonna flush this thing out of the bushes! I'm gonna—"

"Hey, Levi, come down to earth, buddy."

Levi came back to earth, back to his old rundown garage and the wrench he was still holding in his hand. He looked out to see his old friend Ebo Denning standing outside. He crawled out from under the ladder truck, embarrassed. "Sheesh! Sorry."

"Well," said Ebo, leaning on the gas pump, "we've all got things on our minds today."

Levi started pumping gas into Ebo's old Ford pickup. Yeah, Ebo had to be under quite a load today, just like his truck. His wife Emily and his two daughters were squeezed into the cab, and the truck's bed, roof, and sides were stacked with furniture, boxes, his old lawn mower, pictures in frames, his favorite cooking pans, his old cash register. He had to be carrying out everything he owned, Levi thought, which, by this point in his long struggle, wasn't much. Yeah, Ebo Denning, a black businessman with snowy hair carpeting his head, was folding up his business and leaving town. It was over.

"Where're you gonna go, Ebo?" Levi asked.

Ebo checked all the ropes holding his load, tightening a few. "Oh, head south, I think. I got friends and family down in Sacramento, and they're into retailing. One's got a furniture store, one's got a hardware business down there. I think it'd be a good place to start over."

"Well," Levi said, glancing up the road, taking in the dismal little town, "to be honest, any move from here is probably gonna be a move for the better."

Ebo forced a smile. "Yeah, that's how I try to look at it."

Levi finished filling the tank and replaced the nozzle on the pump. "Twenty-three fifty." He would have said no charge at all, but he knew Ebo would never allow that.

Ebo dug the cash out of his pocket and counted it out. "You've been a good friend, Levi. Wanted to say that while I had the chance. And I do remember how you helped keep me in business there for quite a while."

"Well, that worked both ways."

Then Ebo said in earnest, "You take care of yourself, Levi. You know what this town can do to you."

Levi returned Ebo's serious gaze. "I know."

They shook hands. Then, as if they both felt a handshake wasn't enough, they embraced and slapped each other on the back.

"Good-bye," said Ebo, his eyes moist.

"Drive careful." He waved to Emily and the girls.

Then, with a rumble and a creaking, the old truck pulled out onto the Hyde River Road and drove off, leaving behind only the memory of Denning's Mercantile and the good family who had owned it.

Ebo was also leaving behind a problem named Charlie Mack, who was just now standing on the other side of the road, looking over at Levi but trying not to look like he was looking. Now what was he after? Levi wondered. Just trying to be sure Ebo was really leaving? Perhaps he was getting his jollies by watching Ebo drive away with just about every remaining sign of his presence, thus erasing himself from the town.

Oh, shoot, Levi thought. Charlie was crossing the street toward the garage. Levi turned to go inside, hoping Charlie was just crossing the street, that's all, and wasn't coming to see him. Even though Levi often ate lunch at Charlie's Tavern, Charlie never bought gas from Levi or brought his car over to be looked at or gave Levi any business at all that Levi could remember. So why this visit now, and right when Levi was saying good-bye to one of the few friends he had?

Levi made it to his little corner office and sat down behind his desk among the stacks of old tires, crates of motor oil, tools, and shop cloths. He picked up a pencil and a work order from the county, trying to look busy. He hoped Charlie would pass by.

No such luck. Through the grimy window he could see Charlie hurrying right between the gas pumps and toward the door.

The door was open, but Charlie stopped short of coming in and knocked on the doorpost.

Levi worked up some pleasantness before saying, "Yeah?"

Charlie poked his balding head in. He wasn't all that ugly, Levi observed, but he wasn't a pleasure to look at either. Either his thick glasses were crooked or his face was, but the two never lined up.

"Hi, Levi." His smile was a bit crooked too. "Busy?"

No, just trying to look like it, he thought. "What's on your mind, Charlie?"

Charlie stepped inside and approached Levi's desk, his hands in his pockets. For a long time he just stood there, and it was easy to see he was having a hard time getting out what he wanted to say. Levi, not feeling too gracious, didn't help him but just stared at him, waiting. You came to me, pal. The floor is yours.

"So," Charlie finally said, "how's it going?"

Levi was enjoying watching Charlie squirm, so much so that he felt a little guilty about it. In answer to Charlie's question, he just nodded his head as if to say okay. "And how's the new mercantile shaping up?"

Charlie must have sensed it wasn't a friendly question. He seemed to be having trouble answering it. "We're, uh, we're working on it."

"Got a grand opening coming up, I see."

"Yeah. Next week, hopefully."

"Guess you'll have to paint a new name on the front."

Now Charlie looked away. "Well . . . maybe. Not sure."

"Have a seat. You're making me nervous."

Charlie looked around for a chair and finally found an old metal folding chair with Cobb's Garage stenciled on the back. He pulled it up to the desk and sat on it.

"Levi . . ."

Maybe now we'll finally get down to business. "Yes, Charlie?"

"Listen, I'm not snooping or anything, you understand—"

"Mmm."

"But I hear you've been sleeping in your camper out behind your house."

Levi looked over the top of his glasses. He couldn't see very well doing that, but he felt it gave his response a nice emphasis. "If you're not snooping, somebody is "

"Hey, it's nothing like that."

"Then what's it like?"

"Well, everybody knows that once in a while, you—uh—you help people; you take them in, you know?"

Levi set down the paperwork he wasn't really working on and

leaned back resolutely. "Charlie, I've already been asked about Maggie, and I haven't had a whole lot to say to anybody."

"But I'm not snooping, Levi, I just—"

"I've got nothing to say one way or the other, but I'll tell you this: If Maggie Bly ever came to me because she had nowhere else to go, sure, I'd help her out, which is more than any of you did the other night."

That stopped Charlie cold. It took him a moment to pick himself up mentally. And boy, was he nervous! Levi thought. "Listen, Levi, I'm not really prying into Maggie's business. I'm not. But would you have any idea, I mean, just for the sake of information, would you happen to know—"

"What, Charlie, what?"

"Well, this mauling, this guy that got killed up on Wells Peak—"

Levi just stared at him.

"Was he, you know, were he and Maggie . . ."

"Now what kind of a question is that?"

"Well, she's Harold's wife."

With that, Levi almost laughed. "Charlie, are you scared of something?" Charlie said nothing, but Levi didn't think Charlie could deny it, seeing as he was hiding it so poorly. "I'm impressed that suddenly another person's problems matter to you."

Charlie was really getting flustered. "Well, I was just kind of wondering."

Levi wanted the last word at least. "Charlie, you know my message is always the same." He closed one eye and sighted down his pointed finger at Charlie's heart. "Before you start worrying about some critter in those mountains, you'd better worry about the critter you've got right in there. That's the one that's gonna kill you."

Charlie looked out the window and fidgeted in the chair. Then he muttered, "This sort of thing just hasn't happened in a long time."

Levi looked at his paperwork and said offhandedly, "Oh-h-h, it hasn't been that long, has it?"

Charlie turned from the window toward Levi. "Don't talk about it!"

Levi locked eyes with him. "No, not that long. And I guess you're afraid it might happen again. Is that it?"

"All right, fine; just forget it!" Charlie retorted. He jumped up so fast he knocked the chair over.

"Well, it might," Levi said casually, looking down at his paperwork again.

"Forget it!"

And with that, Charlie was out the door, past the gas pumps, and across the street.

Now Levi sat there alone with only the tools to talk to. "What'd I say?"

IT WAS DUSK. The mosquitoes were coming out and inquiring at every square inch of Steve's body, trying unsuccessfully to find some avenue through all that camouflage gear and insect repellent. One was buzzing right near his ear, another near his brow. But Steve did not respond. He did not stir; his powerful muscles were stone steady. The thicket of serviceberries and willow that surrounded and concealed him remained undisturbed.

He was sighting through his rifle scope, his finger tightly around the trigger. About thirty yards below him, on the game trail, a grizzly, its body thick and ponderous, its shoulder hump pronounced, had found the bait and was now pawing and clawing through the doughnuts with its long, white claws, virtually inhaling them, lapping at the grease, snorting, licking, chomping. He wasn't the biggest bear Steve had ever seen, but, at seven hundred pounds, he was impressive nonetheless. Steve was waiting for 318 to turn sideways just a little more. He was going for a shot through the chest just behind the foreleg, just below the midline, a shot through the lungs and heart that would kill the bear immediately.

The bear moved forward a foot or so, and Steve followed him through the scope. Cliff would have envied this shot, this trophy.

Had this been one of their many hunting trips together, Steve could have bragged about it just to give Cliff the old needle. It was so strange now to think that this bear had eaten—

Steve banished all thoughts except for the bear in his sights. Herman, you're going down.

The bear moved forward, pawing through the doughnuts. The chest was exposed.

Steve fired, the rifle kicking back against his shoulder. He chambered another round and had 318 in his scope again just as the bear toppled to the ground. Another round finished the kill in a matter of seconds. Somewhere in the gathering darkness he could hear Marcus hollering. The shots had been clean and true.

Steve moved for the first time, rising from the blind, his body aching and trembling. On any other hunting trip, this would have been a supreme moment. Today he felt no joy at all.

Marcus worked his way down from his hiding place, rifle ready, and approached the fallen beast. He nudged it with his rifle barrel, then stooped to read the small ear tag.

"Three-eighteen," he reported. "It's Herman."

Although Hyde Valley is best known for its gold and silver mining, the rugged trails and forestlands of Wells Peak and Saddlehorse Mountain provide a unique outdoor experience for hikers, campers, anglers, and hunters.

While Hyde Valley is rumored to have had more bear attacks per capita than anywhere else in the contiguous United States, such rumors derive more from tradition than fact and should not be taken seriously. Nevertheless, care and caution should always be exercised in the wild to prevent accidental encounters with bears. Always stay on the trails and take precautions with food.

From a local travel brochure,

circa 1970

———

There was one griz we called Old Scar, lived up above the Tyler Gorge. He ate Jack Friday, I know. Jack went up there fishin' and never came back, and all we ever found was his pole and one of his boots. Coulda been Old Scar ate Jules Howard, and maybe he ate that lady cook we had—what was her name? Nancy, I think. Somebody found her apron and part of her foot out in the woods, but nothin' else. Yeah, it's always been that way . . .

Retired miner Homer Bentlow in recorded interview, transcribed in Hyde River Memories by Jill Staten, copyright 1965

———

THREE

The Victim

Herman 318, thanks to a team of hefty volunteers and a pickup truck, was now laid out on two sheets of one-inch plywood and several sawhorses in Marcus DuFresne's garage near West Fork. Some of the volunteers wanted to hang around and see the verdict, but Marcus, being sensitive to Steve's situation, thanked them and sent them away.

The two men went about the autopsy slowly, working under the ceiling lights and also employing a mechanic's worklight at times. Just as Marcus let Steve have the first shot, he now let Steve handle the knife.

Marcus had already estimated the bear's age to be between ten and twelve years. Herman was a healthy bear with a good supply of fat under his hide, so hunger wasn't an obvious motivator for aggression. They found no significant wounds or injuries, only the bullet wounds Steve had inflicted.

As for the contents of the stomach and intestines . . .

"Well," Steve said, wiping his hands on a towel, "we weren't expecting much anyway, were we?"

Marcus shook his head. "I don't know what to say."

They found doughnuts and bacon grease, of course, but 318 had also been feeding quite well on berries, roots, and herbage. There were a few shreds of food wrappings from someone's garbage. As for flesh of any kind, there was no sign of it. Steve felt disappointed and relieved at the same time.

"He hasn't been feeding exclusively on human waste," Steve observed, "but I would say his diet suggests habituation."

"Although that's all it suggests," Marcus countered.

"I agree. We can extrapolate and infer aggression, but there's no objective evidence."

They both looked forlornly at the old dead bear, its belly opened like a broken suitcase, its innards spread out over the makeshift table.

"And you're sure you don't have some other candidates out there?" Steve asked.

Marcus gave a slight chuckle. "Well, all I can say is that Herman was the best, most likely candidate; he was the most logical candidate, and given what we know . . . I guess we got the culprit."

Steve was unsatisfied and didn't hide it. "We'll see what Evie has to say."

"How's she doing?"

"She was in bad shape yesterday, but I'm sure she'll be okay, given time. I hope she can tell us what happened."

"That would clear things up, for sure."

Then came a silence. Both men were thinking the same thing, but Marcus was afraid to mention it and Steve didn't want to talk about it.

Marcus finally gave it a try. "So when's that autopsy?"

"It was supposed to be today."

"I could give the coroner a call."

Steve checked his watch. "Kinda late."

"I can rouse him, I think." Marcus approached his next question carefully. "What—how much do you want to know?"

Steve looked down at 318, regarding the rows of teeth and the long, white claws. "Just enough, Marcus. Just enough to know for sure."

MIDWAY BETWEEN dusk and dawn, amid the silhouettes of old ruins etched in charcoal against the velvet sky, a lone figure stole silently past the old, teetering walls and crumbling foundations, his black clothing blending with the deep, angular shadows so as to make him invisible. No one would know his business; everyone else was afraid to go near this place.

With silent, feather-light steps, he entered a large ruin, letting its three remaining walls shroud him in their shadows. In the center of the collapsed and rotting structure, he knelt before a large, flat stone and placed his hands on its corners, his gaze fixed upon the stone's dim, gray image. Then he prayed, muttering his requests in a quiet monotone.

When he had finished, he drew a slip of paper from under his coat, placed it on the rock, and with a large, black pencil scribbled a name, which he repeated over and over, "Margaret Elizabeth . . . Margaret Elizabeth . . . Margaret Elizabeth . . . "

With the strike of a match, he set the paper on fire. "Time for you to die, Maggie!"

THE THIRD morning after the attack, Steve met Tracy Ellis at the Clark County Medical Center. Evelyn was coherent and recovering. It was time to talk to her about what had happened on Wells Peak.

They paused near the nurses' station to compare findings. Steve was dressed in casual slacks and shirt. He no longer looked like a grizzled, half-crazed outdoorsman. Tracy was back in her uniform, armed with a notebook and the case folder for the upcoming interview.

Tracy looked troubled. "The team finished combing the area all around the campsite, and the dogs have searched the wider area around Wells Peak." She shrugged. "They didn't find anything."

Steve only sighed. "The autopsy on 318 showed a diet consistent with habituation, but beyond that, there was nothing conclusive." He handed her a photocopy of his written report, which consisted of just a few paragraphs. "He liked berries, roots, grass, some human garbage, and the doughnuts we put out for him. But that's all we could find. My report will take about thirty seconds to read."

"So you haven't settled on 318 as the culprit?"

Steve only spread his hands. "He really is the only viable candidate, and I'm willing to accept that. I'm just saying that the autopsy couldn't establish anything one way or the other."

"Have you seen the autopsy report on your brother?"

"Marcus talked to the coroner last night, but I haven't seen the report yet. Have you?"

She nodded grimly. "Got a copy this morning." She hesitated before saying, "The bottom line is, the pathologist thinks it was a bear."

"Yeah, that's what the coroner told Marcus, and I guess I can't argue with that." Steve looked down momentarily. "Marcus and I have talked about—actually viewing the remains." He was quick to add, "But I think I'd rather have Marcus do it. I trust his judgment, his powers of observation."

Tracy thought about it, then nodded. "Have Marcus do it."

"Come on, let's see what Evie remembers."

WHEN THEY entered the room, Evelyn was sitting upright, the mattress raised and several pillows placed behind her back.

"Well," said Steve, smiling, "you're looking better."

"Half vertical, anyway," Evelyn answered with a slight smile.

"You've met Deputy Ellis?"

"I think I met her two days ago."

Tracy smiled. "You did."

"Well—hi again."

"Hi."

There were two chairs in the room, and Steve and Tracy pulled them close to the bed, then sat down. At first they talked in generalities: about Evelyn's health, her two boys, Samuel and Travis, her mother, Audrey, the care she'd received, and anything else that came to mind that would not be difficult. Steve was encouraged. Evelyn was making perfect sense, speaking coherently. She was on her way back.

"So," said Tracy, her tone and pacing signaling the approach of a tough subject, "Mrs. Benson, how comfortable would you be, talking about what happened on Wells Peak? We still have to finish our investigation. You do understand, don't you?"

"Sure."

Tracy looked toward Steve. "I'm glad Steve can be here. He's been working at his end, and the sheriff's department has been doing what it can, but without a witness, it's been tough."

Evelyn was apologetic. "Officer—uh—"

"Just call me Tracy."

"Okay. Tracy. I have to tell you, I don't remember very much."

"Well," Tracy said, trying not to be pushy, "just start at the beginning and see how you do."

Evelyn's face was troubled. She was struggling to remember but also feeling pain at every recollection. "I remember Cliff went down to put away our leftovers. We'd cooked up a meal for the evening, and—um"

"What did you have?" Steve asked, hoping to jog her memory.

"Let's see." Evelyn thought for a moment, then said, "Vegetable soup and some crackers."

"Nothing meaty? Spicy? You know, something that would give off a strong smell?"

She shook her head. "No, we try not to eat that kind of stuff if there might be bears around. Besides, if I eat rich food after hiking I want to throw up."

Steve nodded, pleased and amused. "So, okay, then what?"

"He went down the hill to where he had the food stored, and it was dark by then, so I couldn't see him very well."

By now Tracy was discreetly scribbling notes. "About what time was that?"

"I guess between nine and ten."

"Do you always eat that late at night?"

Evelyn answered, "No. We'd been doing a lot of hiking and took a long time to pick out a campsite. Then we figured we'd better get the tent up first, and by that time the sun was going down. Then Cliff wanted to rig up the food cache down in the trees while we still had some light. It all took time."

"So anyway," said Steve, "you ended up eating late."

Evelyn nodded. "And cleaning up late."

"So then Cliff went down to stow the leftovers," Tracy prompted.

"And . . ." Evelyn fumbled. "I—I just remember him going down the hill in the dark, and I couldn't see him, just his flashlight sometimes . . ." She stopped. She looked at them, and they looked back at her. Silence.

Tracy prompted, "He'd gone down the hill with his flashlight."

Evelyn just shook her head. "And then I woke up in the hospital."

Steve was disappointed—downright frustrated, actually—but tried not to show it. He looked as casually as he could at Tracy. She seemed strangely detached as she studied her notes.

Her next question had a lighter tone. "So . . . Cliff was a photographer!"

"Uh-huh. Mainly he did wildlife photography."

Tracy looked at Steve. "So this outdoors stuff must run in the family."

Steve smiled. He welcomed the lighter topic. "Pretty much."

Tracy turned back to Evelyn. "So, was that why you were up there on Wells Peak? Was he taking pictures up there?"

"No. We just wanted to get away together."

"Mmm. Just get some time away, huh?"

"Yes. He'd been working a lot of hours, and we needed some time alone. We've been out hunting in Hyde Valley before. We really like the Wells Peak area, so that's where we went this time."

"I understand your husband had been working in Hyde Valley for a few months; is that right?"

"That's right."

Hmm, Steve thought, impressed. *Tracy has been doing her homework.*

"Doing a photo shoot up and down the valley," Tracy continued.

Evelyn nodded. "He was doing local sportsman stuff. You know, hunting, fishing, that kind of thing. But he shot a lot of pictures in the old mining towns. He's always liked getting into the history and the people."

"So, he was away from home a lot?"

Evelyn hesitated just slightly before answering. "Sure. He had to go where the pictures were."

"That must have been tough."

Evelyn shrugged a little and sighed. "I took it in stride."

"But that's why you wanted to get away together? Just to spend time together for a change?"

Evelyn sounded just a little perturbed. "I believe I just said that."

"So, how would you say your marriage was going? Were you doing okay?"

Steve didn't say anything, but that question seemed a little odd. *Maybe Tracy was just making bedside conversation.*

"It wasn't a fiery romance; it wasn't a soap opera," Evelyn answered. "It was just kind of in between."

Tracy smiled. "In between."

"We got along when we were together. When we weren't together it was kind of hard to tell."

Evelyn's tone was composed, but Steve had seen that look on Evelyn's face before. *Tracy had better be careful.*

"So things were going okay, but not . . ." Tracy prodded.

"Not real okay." Evelyn went no further.

Tracy scribbled some notes then asked, "Evelyn, do you own a hunting knife?"

"Yes. Both of us did."

Steve interjected, "She and Cliff used to go hunting a lot."

"Okay," Tracy replied, jotting it down. "Evelyn, when you were found Saturday night, you still had your knife in your hand, and the blade was broken. Do you remember that at all?"

Evelyn took a moment to search her memory. "Maybe. Kind of like a dream . . . I'm not sure."

"Do you have any recollection of attacking anything, having any kind of struggle and using your knife?"

Evelyn was becoming visibly upset. "I don't know! There's just this—this—it's like a dream in my head, and I can't remember it."

Steve spoke softly, afraid he might press too far. "Evie, we're looking for a bear, okay? We figure it was a grizzly that got Cliff. Do you remember anything like that?" He was obviously leading the witness, but he didn't care.

Evelyn closed her eyes. "Steve, I can close my eyes, and all I see is a big shadow."

"Did you attack it?" Tracy asked.

"Well, I guess I did." Now Evelyn's voice had an edge to it. "Wouldn't you?"

"There was blood on your clothing and on the knife. Do you recall that at all?"

Evelyn stiffened with the memory. "I remember some blood."

"Do you remember where it came from?"

Evelyn looked straight at Tracy Ellis, tears filling her eyes. "I understand it came from my husband."

Steve could read Evelyn's face clearly: A line had been crossed, a limit exceeded. He cut in. "Evie, that's okay. You don't have to talk about it anymore."

Tracy looked his way. She obviously didn't appreciate his intruding on her investigation.

And Steve didn't appreciate her questions. He addressed

Evelyn, the one whose feelings he cared about. "This whole thing's been real tough, I know. Let's let it go for now, and you just rest up."

Tracy, to her credit, picked up Steve's cue, and relaxed. "Yeah, just rest up. I'm very sorry to have to ask you such tough questions."

Evelyn's gaze told Tracy she was not forgiven. "Just doing your job, I guess."

Steve rose to his feet. "I've got some other things I want to look into. You just get better." He bent down and kissed Evelyn on the forehead.

"Thanks for your time," said Tracy.

Evelyn turned her back to the deputy sheriff.

STEVE AND TRACY made their way to the waiting area near the nurses' station. Each had an agenda for a serious talk and couldn't wait to get started.

"I'd like to know what that was all about," Steve demanded, trying to keep his voice low.

Tracy tried the person-in-charge approach. "I knew this would be a problem, someone so emotionally involved—"

"That will be enough!" A couple who was sitting nearby looked their way. "I'll be responsible for my emotions, Deputy," Steve growled. "You'd better concern yourself with how Evie must be feeling right now and how you treated her! Couldn't you see how frail she is? How could you go in there asking questions about knives and blood and how well their marriage was doing? She just lost her husband, remember?"

Tracy purposely paused a moment to calm the situation down. Then she tried to present a rational, professional position. "I had to ask particular questions as a matter of routine. We have to cover all contingencies."

"Like how her marriage was doing? Do you think for one moment—"

"What I think is immaterial. I have a job to do." Her tone was formal as she said, "You're a professional. You know how important objectivity is in a situation like this, am I right?"

Steve wanted to lash back, but yanked his own leash and held it. She was right. He was offended and defensive for Evelyn's sake, and he was letting his feelings rule the moment. Tracy was in control; he wasn't. He took a breath and forced himself back into his professional role. It was like putting on a pair of tight shoes. "Yes. You're right. You're right, sort of."

"Sort of?"

"Personal feelings aside, the idea of complicity on Evie's part is . . . well, it's untenable, unthinkable."

"And it seems you're having trouble blaming a bear, too."

"I'm—" He wanted to deny it, but couldn't. "I'm willing to accept any hard evidence." Then he narrowed his gaze. "Which raises the question of the autopsy report . . ."

He noticed her cringe slightly. "Steve . . ."

"Is there additional evidence I still don't know about?"

She took time to formulate an answer. "Maybe you do need to read that report for yourself."

"Maybe I need to view the remains for myself."

She emphasized, "Maybe you need to read the report and evaluate it first."

He accepted that. "Do you have it with you?"

She took the report from her folder. It was a document about thirty pages thick, held together with a large clip.

He took it but didn't look at it. "I'll read it before I confer with Marcus."

"Just keep in mind your relationship to the victim."

"I'm aware of my relationship to the victim." Who do you think you are, my baby-sitter?

"All right."

"All I want is the answer to our questions—before you get any wrong ideas."

She was clearly offended. "Steve, I am not jumping to any conclusions. I do have questions, though!"

"So I observed!"

She drew a breath, held it, then gave a long sigh. "Okay, Steve, you're the expert. Tell me what happened."

"That's what I'm trying to find out."

"How is it that only Cliff was killed, and only his blood was on Evelyn's clothes, and Evelyn wasn't injured at all? If Evelyn came so close to the attack that she got Cliff's blood all over her, why wasn't she attacked as well? How did her hunting knife get broken, and how is it that she remembers everything else in such detail, even what they had for dinner, and what time they ate, and the order of events up to the crucial time in question, and then . . . ding, she's in dreamland?"

Steve had thought about that, too. "The attack was over by the time she got there. Upon finding what was left of Cliff, she went hysterical—we have the truck driver's testimony as to her disturbed mental state—and having gone hysterical, she . . . well, who knows what she may have done? Maybe she was embracing what was left or trying to put him back together; I don't know. But the hysteria is well established, I think, and explanation enough for her memory lapse. As for the knife, how do we know she didn't break the blade when she attacked the truck?"

"The driver said the blade was already broken."

"So figure she went around stabbing trees or something. She was out of her mind."

"But even your scenario puts her and her husband together at the time of death, and you'll have to admit an attacking bear isn't necessary to produce the blood on her clothes."

"Except that I don't like your line of thinking, Deputy. I can't even entertain such a possibility."

"You don't have to, Steve. You're not a cop."

"Granted." Silence. "So what's your next step?"

"I'm going to take a drive out to Hyde River and talk to some friends."

"The same friends who told you Cliff had been in the area?"

"The same. It's a small community, and word gets around."

"Well, I just might drive out there myself."

She raised her hand. "Whoa, hold on there."

"What?"

"I know Hyde River. Do we agree on that?"

"I guess so."

"So take this as wise advice from someone who knows: Don't go up there asking questions by yourself. You could get more trouble than you ever wanted."

He didn't follow her. "I only want to ask around about—"

"It doesn't matter," she interrupted. "You'd be a stranger asking questions, and that's not welcome up there."

He digested that for a moment. "So, we'll have to hope you find out something for both of us, I suppose."

"I suppose."

Steve had already decided that wasn't going to be the case when he asked, "So when do we touch base again?"

"I'll call you tonight at the Tamarack. Or you call me." She scribbled a number on a corner of a notebook page and tore it off for him. "Here's my home number. You can try me at the sheriff's department or at home. I'll let you know if I find out anything."

"All right."

She was ready to leave, and so was he.

"Steve."

"Yeah?"

She spoke carefully, "Take it slow."

MARCUS DUFRESNE came to Steve's motel room that afternoon. He looked pale and sick. He would have preferred a shot of Jack Daniels but settled for some coffee Steve had in a thermos. They sat at the small round table near the window, the autopsy report between them. For the longest time, Marcus only stared at the report, trying to find words, while Steve sat, waiting silently, giving him as much time as he needed.

"I guess—" Marcus finally began.

Steve leaned forward.

"I guess the pathologist gave it his best guess: a grizzly attack. Considering what was left of your brother, what else could he say? Have you read the autopsy report?"

"Yeah. The whole thing, this afternoon."

"Lot of technical jargon, but—"

"It was clear enough."

"Yeah. Real clear. Well, what's in that report is what I saw today." Marcus stared into space as if watching a replay of his visit to the pathology department. "One shoulder gone, no head, one arm detached. There were some ribs—" Marcus touched his own chest to illustrate. "—just sticking out of the . . . the cut, the bite, whatever you want to call it. They were just snipped off, cut right through. It was a pretty clean bite line." As Tracy had done, Marcus traced it against his own body with his hand. "It went from left shoulder to right pelvis. And—did you read about the pelvis being cut through?"

"Was it?"

"It was."

"And the rest intact?" Steve asked.

Marcus nodded. "The vital organs and the lower limbs were all there." Then he added, "And that scar from the old gunshot wound? It was there. And the fingerprints from the left arm match the prints on file with your brother's gun permit. Just so you know."

Steve nodded, then moved on to what he'd been thinking about, agonizing over, all afternoon. "No teeth marks or claw marks?"

"No. And no animal hairs." Marcus reached into his shirt pocket. "But I got some scrapings." He produced a small vial and set it on the table. "Looked like it could be dried saliva. The pathologist couldn't make anything of it, but maybe you've got some people at the university who can figure out what it is."

Steve held the vial up to the light to examine the crusty slime. "I'll FedEx it there right away."

Then there was silence again.

"So?" Steve prompted. "What do you think?"

Marcus thought about it long and hard and then shook his head. "Steve, this was one unique bear."

Steve nodded. "The soft organs were intact below the bite line—"

"Mm-hmm."

"A bear will typically go for the abdomen, for the soft organs first." He took a sip of coffee, and Marcus did the same. "A bear will bite, clamp its jaws onto its prey, tear at it, drag it . . ."

Marcus continued the line of thought. "Yeah, bears do that. So do coyotes, wolves, cougars, vultures, eagles—"

"This attack seems a little neat, if you catch my meaning."

Marcus spread his hands. "So, how do you explain it?"

Steve rested his elbows on the table, his chin on his interlaced fingers. "I think Tracy Ellis and the sheriff are already looking for another explanation. Tracy was asking Evie questions about her marriage."

"Poor Evelyn," Marcus said, disturbed by the thought. Then he offered, "I've seen a few chain-saw accidents that happened during woodcutting season. The cut in the flesh wasn't anything like that, though."

Steve could feel himself getting nauseous. He hated the question even as he asked it. "Could it have been done with a hunting knife?"

Marcus looked back at him, hating the answer. "I suppose. But it would have taken a long time and a lot of careful thought. I'd find it easier to believe a large, mechanical sawing device was used, like you'd find in a lumber mill."

"A device like that would be pretty far from the campsite."

"You're right."

"And if a human device was used, there is still the question of the missing half. If it was not consumed by an animal, then what became of it?" Steve felt bile rising in his throat. He swallowed hard. "I can't believe the things we're talking about here."

"I may not eat for days," Marcus said grimly. "But you see the problem. If we reject the whole bear idea, then we have to open up the investigation to some horrible possibilities."

"I guess that's what Tracy's doing right now."

"I guess." Then Marcus said, "But the pathologist doesn't want to go that far. He said it was a bear attack." Marcus narrowed his eyes. "But in person, off the record—talking to me, in other words—he couldn't account for the condition of the body. He couldn't say for sure what caused it."

"So we're back to where we started." Steve got up abruptly and headed for the door. "I need some air."

"I'm with you."

They stepped outside into the parking lot.

Steve's vehicle, a well-integrated truck and camper combination, was parked near the room. Marcus walked over to admire it just for something else to think about.

"Nice rig."

"Yeah, I've put a lot of miles on it. It's been to Canada, Alaska, Yellowstone—"

"Four-wheel drive?"

"Oh, yeah."

Marcus looked in the windows at the tight and efficient living environment. Then he turned. "I'd better get going. I sure hope you solve this thing."

"Oh, I'm going to solve it, all right," Steve replied, his voice strained. "Even if I have to ruffle some feathers in Hyde Valley."

Jonathan came to our home in the early hours of Wednesday, April 9th, after riding most of the night. He was badly beaten, his clothing was torn, and he was bleeding from his mouth and nose. We took him to the doctor immediately and found that his nose and jaw were broken as well as three ribs. Jonathan told us that four men from the mining company had assaulted him as he returned home from the mine, and that the attack was retribution for something he had said about the company's owner, Benjamin Hyde. When we asked Jonathan what he had said to warrant such punishment, he would not tell us for fear of being attacked again. . . .

From a letter written by Clara Beth Atkins,
Jonathan's mother, to her sister Claudia Dunsmith
of Oak Springs, dated April 12, 1880

FOUR

Hyde River

DEPUTY Tracy Ellis parked her patrol car in one of the slots outside the sheriff's department in West Fork, some pages from her notebook filled with fresh notes and her mind full of ideas. She'd just turned thirty, and although she'd gotten away from Clark County, particularly Hyde Valley, long enough to attend college and the police academy, it hadn't been long enough to lose the feel, the instinct, she had about this place. She knew the people; she'd grown up with many of them and now patrolled the valley as a deputy. Something was brewing in Hyde River. She was sure of it.

The Clark County Sheriff's Department was located in one of West Fork's vintage stone-and-brick buildings across the street and a few blocks down from the courthouse. On the main floor, just inside the front door, was the front office where the public could talk to whichever deputy was scheduled to man the front counter. Around the corner from the front office was the examining station for driver's licenses—the same deputy handled that, too. Just behind the front office was the cell block with its three jail cells, a rack of handcuffs handily located on the wall next to the steel door.

Across the room from the front counter was the office of the county sheriff, Lester B. Collins, a man known and mostly liked for his laid-back practicality. His self-written job description was to keep the peace so people could go about their business without too much commotion. That didn't mean he always enforced the laws as written, but he did keep the peace, so folks didn't mind him too much. By now, he'd been reelected so many times he'd become an institution in Clark County.

At the moment he was well-planted in his chair, reading some arrest reports and playing with a rubber band stretched around his fingers. He was still lean and fit in his early fifties, with a stony face and short-cropped hair that made him look like a marine, which he had never been. No matter. He liked conveying the image of a tough cop, a quality even his deputies were known to debate behind his back.

His office door was open as it usually was. Tracy knocked on the doorjamb, and he looked up. "Come in and close the door."

Tracy followed his order, then sat down, her notebook and case folder in her lap.

Collins was reading through a report and shared the news. "Phil Garrett got his ear nearly bit off last night. They've stitched it back on, but the doctors don't know if they can save it or not."

Tracy wasn't surprised, but she couldn't keep herself from smiling at the thought. "Well, at least it can only happen one more time—the ear part. Was it down at the Logger?"

"Where else? I've got a warrant out for—" He looked through the papers on his desk. "Ever hear of Stack Morris?"

Tracy shook her head.

Collins was bothered. "Neither have I. I'm not even sure what he looks like—or used to look like before last night."

"Phil Garrett won't be hard to spot from now on."

Collins allowed himself a quick chuckle. "Anyway, what've you got?"

Tracy referred to her notes. "A lot of weird pieces that aren't coming together. I think the bear attack theory's in trouble, and Steve Benson isn't comfortable with it either."

Collins took that news with some concern. "Why? What'd he say?"

"The autopsy on 318 was inconclusive."

Collins waved that off. "Well, what'd he expect almost two days after the mauling? That doesn't mean the bear didn't do it. The coroner seems satisfied."

Tracy gave a small sigh. Collins always preferred the easiest road. "Well, I'm not saying I won't settle for the bear theory, but there are some other matters I'd like to see resolved before I do. I talked to Evelyn Benson this morning, and she admitted she and the victim had been having marital problems."

Collins raised one eyebrow. "They'd have to be pretty severe marital problems, don't you think?"

Give me a chance to say it all, Tracy thought. "There's more. It turns out Cliff Benson's no stranger to Hyde Valley. He'd been in the valley off and on for the last three months, and he spent quite a bit of time in Hyde River, supposedly doing photo shoots."

"Supposedly?"

Tracy hesitated before spilling her next piece of news. "The night of the attack, Harold Bly kicked Maggie out of the house. I understand it was a substantial blowup."

Collins digested that a moment. "You are stretching it, deputy."

She shrugged. "It might only be coincidence, I know."

"I would say it is coincidence. Maggie and Harold having a fight is not news, it's the normal state of things."

But Tracy kept on. She had to finish. "Well, so far, nobody knows what became of Maggie, but I've gotten word that Levi Cobb is sleeping outside his garage in his camper."

Collins sat there silently, playing with the rubber band. Finally, grudgingly, he asked, "Deputy, I hope you're not thinking what I think you're thinking."

Tracy had to build up to saying it. "Sir, Maggie is Harold Bly's wife. If she was having an affair with Cliff Benson . . ."

Collins rolled his eyes. "I'd rather go with the bear theory."

"So would I."

"Then why don't you—" At the look on her face, he gave up.

He knew she would not be easily dissuaded. "All right, listen. You've got your theories, and that's fine, but give me some hard evidence. Connect at least one loose end for me, and then we can decide if you've got anything."

So he was dumping it all on her. That was easy to do from behind a desk in a town far from the problem. "Well, do you think you might talk to Harold Bly about this?"

The sheriff looked at her disdainfully. "About what? About the fact that someone's dead who his wife was rumored to be having an affair with? Now if I was an absolute moron who didn't know how to do my job and didn't care about keeping my job, then yeah, I might butt into Harold's personal business and insinuate that he's a murderer."

"I'm just trying to—"

"What you have done, Deputy, is to make assumptions that could get us all in big trouble if we don't back them up a little better." His tone was condescending as he asked, "Are you following me?"

She kept her tone calm and even, but inside she was shaking with anger. "I am trying to find connections and substance. But I have to start somewhere."

"Well, sticking my neck out for Harold Bly to chop it off is not the place to start."

"Just thought I'd ask."

He went back to his rubber band. "So before we talk about this again, get me some real information, and I mean some hard stuff. Find Maggie. Talk to her. Odds are you'll get nothing but a sob story about their marriage that doesn't have diddly-squat to do with anything."

Tracy winced. "Which means I'll have to talk to Levi Cobb."

Collins gave her a mocking smile. "Hey, this is your case, Deputy. Drop it or pursue it, it's up to you. Personally, I'm more comfortable with the bear."

Of course you are, you jerk. Then you wouldn't have to do anything. She came within a hair's breadth of saying it. Instead, she said, "But, Les, you realize Levi knows the rules out there. He isn't going to tell me anything."

"Well, I'm sure you'll think of a way to get it out of him." Tracy closed her notebook, trying not to display her frustration. "That's a good girl," he added. The only way Tracy could hide her frustration and anger was to turn quickly and get out of there.

STEVE MANAGED to arrange a Federal Express pickup of the vial of saliva—the FedEx van came right to Steve's motel room—and sent it off to a biochemist friend at the university. It would arrive the following morning, and hopefully he would get some useful information back.

Now for a visit to Hyde River. Steve got into his camper and drove out of West Fork and through the tightening valley, following the winding road as it followed the river. He passed through Able, took the left fork of the Y, drove on through Nugget and Yellow Knife, and knew he was getting close to Hyde River by the mounds of gravel tailings along the riverbed, the last vestiges of the old gold-dredging days.

It amazed him a little as he considered a sheriff's deputy like Tracy Ellis driving up into the mountains this far to do her job. Considering how far Hyde River was from the sheriff's department and how short on personnel the department seemed to be, law enforcement had to be more of a word, an ideal, than a reality.

Perhaps that explained the little sign Steve saw posted on the front of a house as he first entered Hyde River: an ominous silhouette of a revolver with the superimposed words, WE DON'T CALL 911. That about captured it, he thought. They're self-sufficient up here, to put it mildly. Everywhere he looked, he could catch the message: Mind your own business. This wasn't a place where county building codes, weed ordinances, or waste-disposal regulations carried a lot of weight. People lived as they pleased. He was reminded of Tracy's warning about strangers asking questions.

The dogs were out roaming and lying around as if the whole

town owned them. The Hyde Mining Company still cast its dismal, tombstone shadow over the town, its ramps, rails, tunnels, and towers looking like an ancient and defunct amusement ride, its old water tower now a weathered pedestal without the tank.

Steve thought he caught some stares from some of the people as he drove into town. Could be. His big camper with an out-of-state license plate virtually cried out "stranger." When he slowed down, turned off the road, and parked in front of Charlie's Tavern, he was sure he was being stared at. Well, greetings, folks. I don't want any trouble; how much do you want? He was confident he could take care of himself. He was just hoping he wouldn't have to.

He got out and stood beside his camper for a moment, trying to get a feel for the place. There were quite a few pickup trucks parked outside the tavern, every one of them standing high on big tires and sporting a rifle rack in the back window. It was after four. Quitting time at the mine and probably everywhere else. All the local boys must be gathered here: contractor types, loggers, miners, outdoorsmen. They would know these mountains, if anyone did.

He stepped up to the front door—it bore another sign advertising the grand opening of Charlie's Mercantile, the building right next door—and stepped inside, into the dimly lit den of the town's beer brotherhood. It wasn't a bad-looking place, Steve thought. The bar stretched along the entire length of the left wall, with enough stools for about ten customers; behind the bar, the bottles, neon signs, hunting trophies, and beer posters of perfect-bodied women kept the eyes busy. On the far-right wall was an impressive stone fireplace with logs smoldering, and in between were several tables, every one of them different, from a fifties-style Formica-topped kitchen table to rustic ones made from logs and elk antlers. At the far end of the room, three men in well-worn clothes, wide suspenders, and billed caps did slow, cue-chalking laps around a pool table, their beer bottles ready and waiting along the table's edges. In the far corner, a jukebox pounded out a country tune while video games bleeped and warbled.

Steve caught the eye of two men sitting at the nearest table, the younger one with his arm around a loosely behaved and tightly dressed blonde. The men were dressed in what seemed to be the Hyde Valley uniform: checked flannel shirts, billed caps with brand names on the front—usually of beer or chewing tobacco—wide suspenders, and faded jeans. They were carrying on an animated conversation until they saw him. Then they stopped talking and just stared at him. Steve returned their looks and said hi. They said hi back, but nothing else.

"Hi," came a woman's voice.

Steve looked toward the waitress behind the bar. She was plump and pleasant-faced and wearing a T-shirt that proclaimed, "Timber Dollars Feed My Family."

"Hi," he said, and fumbled in his shirt pocket for a business card. "I wonder if you might help me." Aware that the men were watching him, he stepped up to the bar and presented his card to her. "I'm Steve Benson; I'm a wildlife biologist from Colorado State University, and I've been investigating that bear attack that happened last weekend, the man killed up on Wells Peak."

She smiled as she read the card and heard his quick résumé.

The man in the thick glasses who came up behind her wasn't smiling. "What's going on, Melinda?"

She started to answer. "This is—"

"Who'd you say you were?" he demanded.

Melinda passed him Steve's card, and Steve recited the reasons for his presence again.

"Go get Paul a beer," the man ordered, and she went to serve the man seated at the opposite end of the bar. "Mr. Benson, I'm the owner of this place. You got questions, you talk to me."

Brother! It was easy to do the wrong thing in this place. "Are you Charlie?" Steve tried to sound friendly, attempting to undo his being a stranger.

Charlie read Steve's card again. "That's right. What can I do for you?" Subtitle: Whaddaya want?

"I need to talk to some people who know these mountains. You know—hunters, sportsmen. We're trying to isolate just who or what was responsible for the attack—"

"You don't know yet?" He gave Steve a skeptical look.

"Well, we're not sure."

"We've got flyers all around town that say it was a bear."

"Yeah, that's the going theory, of course."

"Who'd you say you're working for?"

"I'm not really working for anybody. I'm just here on my own."

"What for?"

"To help out with the investigation."

"A lot of help you are. They've already shot the bear, in case you haven't heard." Charlie tossed the card on the bar and turned away.

Steve called after him, "Uh, Charlie—can I call you Charlie?"

Charlie busied himself with tending the bar as he replied, "I s'pose."

"Charlie, I'm the one who shot the bear. I also did an autopsy on the bear, and the findings were inconclusive."

"Well, if you don't know what you're doing, there's nobody here that can help you."

Okay, far enough. Not another inch. "How do you know?"

"Huh?"

"I don't mean to be rude, but perhaps your patrons would like to speak for themselves."

Charlie finished pouring a beer for a customer and then returned to take another look at the business card. "So you shot the bear, huh?"

"Yes. Up along Tailor Creek. You know Marcus DuFresne?"

Now Charlie paid better attention. "Yeah. You know him?"

"Sure. We went after that bear together. He called it Herman."

Charlie was stunned. "You shot Herman?"

Steve nodded.

Charlie looked at Steve's card again. "So you really do hunt bears."

"I study them mostly. But sometimes I have to shoot one."

"How big? What's the biggest bear you ever shot?"

"Eight hundred pounds. A Kodiak in Alaska."

"Ever shot anything bigger?"

Now Steve felt he was obliged to impress this guy. "No. I think that's about as big as I've killed."

Charlie took a moment to think that over.

Steve heard a voice behind him. "You having some trouble, Charlie?"

It was one of the men from the front table, the bigger, older one, stepping into the situation. His friend and the woman were watching, and no doubt he was aware of it.

Charlie looked Steve over again as if trying to decide the answer. "Mister, are you gonna order anything?"

Steve knew he'd better answer. "Yes. A beer would be fine."

Charlie looked at the big guy standing there. "No trouble."

The big guy was still eyeing Steve suspiciously, wanting trouble. He was a rugged man with stubble on his face and beer on his breath. He was leaning close, forcing himself into Steve's space, sizing him up. Steve didn't want a fight. It was a waste of time and energy.

Charlie volunteered, "Doug, this guy studies bears. He's from a university."

At that, the man laughed. "Oh. A university." That had to mean wimp, Steve thought. "So what are you doing here?"

Charlie brought the beer. Steve paid for it and then faced the man called Doug who hadn't budged from his spot. He took time for one swallow of beer, then formally introduced himself and his reason for being there.

"It was a bear," Doug said. "It happens around here." Then he stood there, waiting for Steve to agree and leave.

"But we still need to know which bear. We shot Herman, but do you know of any bear besides Herman who might be responsible? Have you or any of your friends sighted any other bears around that aren't afraid of people or like to raid campsites?" Steve was asking about bears, but hoping some other sliver of information might come out—anything at all.

Doug just shrugged.

Steve looked at the other man, still seated with the woman. "Hi. I'm Steve."

"I'm Kyle," answered the young man. Then he gestured with his beer bottle toward the woman. "This is Carlotta."

Steve nodded toward the woman, and she cocked her head and looked him over warily. Steve turned back to Kyle. "What do you think, Kyle? Ever had anything like this happen around here before?"

Kyle seemed a bit unnerved by the subject. "Sure. I haven't seen anything, but there's plenty of people around here who have. They just don't talk about it much."

"Shut up!" Doug snapped.

"What'd I say?"

"Just don't say anything!" Doug roared, and Kyle fell silent.

Steve raised his arms slightly in quiet diplomacy. "Fine. Fine. No offense intended."

"Come on, Doug," Carlotta beckoned. "Just leave him alone." Doug rejoined her and Kyle at the table to finish his sandwich and beer but not before giving Steve a warning glare.

By now, the three men playing pool were watching to see if there'd be any action. The guy named Paul, still sitting at the other end of the bar, only stole sideways glances.

Steve asked Charlie, "May I sit down?"

Charlie shrugged. "Sit."

One of the three pool players took a shot; the balls clacked and rolled. Paul went back to his beer. Kyle and Carlotta resumed their conversation, and the jukebox kept playing. Doug kept watching Steve.

Steve chose a small, two-person table a little farther back and close enough to another patron to engage him in conversation. This guy was older, bearded, with a large, barrel-shaped body and big, muscular arms. He sat alone at a hand-hewn burl table, eating a hefty lunch and apparently having a conversation with someone who wasn't there.

Steve caught his eye and smiled in a neighborly fashion. "Hi."

The bearded fellow cocked his head and gave Steve a look that carried a lecture in itself. "Mister," he said in a low, gravelly voice, "if I were you, I'd settle for the bear."

Steve made a tiny mental note about how all these people were overstating the obvious. Then he leaned closer and spoke in a quiet voice. "But which bear? Do you know of any other rogue bear around here, some bear Fish and Game may not be aware of?"

The man had raised his hand to say hold it. "You're in the wrong place to be asking a lot of questions. If Herman did it, then let it go at that." He turned back to his lunch and prepared to take another bite of his sandwich, not looking at Steve as he said, "You push this thing any further, you'll get people riled."

"What if more innocent people get hurt?" Steve countered.

The man took a large bite of the sandwich and chewed for a moment before remarking through the wad in his mouth, "Ain't nobody innocent."

"Listen. The man who was killed was my brother!"

That registered. The man's eyes narrowed as he looked away and muttered, "Hoo boy, we're in trouble now."

Slap! Steve felt a powerful hand on his shoulder, twisting him around.

It was Doug. "I don't think he wants to be bothered."

The bearded man protested. "Doug, I can speak for myself."

"Not to him, you're not." Then Doug said sideways to Steve, "You don't want to talk to him. He's the town's nut case."

The man put down his sandwich and placed his ham-sized hands on the table, ready to get up. "Well, maybe he'd like to be the judge of that himself."

Steve stood, as tall as Doug if not taller, and this time he invaded Doug's space. "Hey. I'm not looking for trouble. I just need information, that's all, and I'll thank you to let me go about my business."

Doug had found his excuse. He grabbed a fistful of Steve's shirt and backed him up against a post, knocking a picture to the floor. "I'll give you information, Professor!"

Now the pool players were watching again, and Paul turned completely around on his bar stool.

Steve's arms came from somewhere Doug wasn't expecting and restored a comfortable distance between them, landing Doug across a table.

Doug was startled. But he got up from the table slowly, looking about, wanting to be sure the other patrons had seen it all. They had. The mood of the place shifted like the flipping of a channel.

The stranger had crossed the line. The pool game broke up as the pool players moved in, their cue sticks in their hands.

"Hey!" hollered Charlie, running from around the bar. "Now hold on, everybody!"

Doug righted himself but didn't charge. He was waiting for the reinforcements to gather.

Steve looked the pool players over, now standing with Doug, their faces full of confidence and malice.

"Now listen, there's a proper way to settle disputes," Steve said coolly.

The biggest pool player exchanged an incredulous look with the others. "I think he's telling us what to do."

Now Kyle joined up. Five to one.

DOUG ADVANCED to give Steve a shove, but Charlie stepped in. "All right, now, let's break this up."

Doug pushed Charlie away. "Stay put, Charlie. We'll be done in a second."

Steve braced himself, estimating the force of their weight against his own. He figured he would most likely lose—and it would hurt, too.

"Told you," said the big bearded man, coming alongside to stand with him.

"Stay out of this, Levi!" Doug warned. "This isn't your fight!"

Levi stood his ground, his big arms loose and ready. "Five to one is no fight at all, Doug."

Just then, the cowbell over the front door jangled as the door opened and sunlight entered the room. Doug didn't charge, and neither did Kyle. The pool players lowered their cue sticks, disappointment clouding their faces. Steve had his back to the door, and he wondered who they were staring at. But he wasn't about to turn and find out.

Then Steve heard a familiar voice. "Can't you boys play a little more quietly? For a minute I thought I heard some trouble in here."

Steve stole a glance toward the door. There stood Deputy Tracy Ellis in a casual pose, her hand on the latch of the open door, the sunlight from outside illuminating her olive uniform, her gleaming badge, and that gun on her hip.

"Hey, Tracy," Doug greeted her, his tone suddenly civil. "Buy you a beer?"

Her eyes went cold as she looked at him. "No thanks, Doug." She looked at Charlie, who had gone behind the bar again. "These guys giving you trouble, Charlie?"

Charlie looked at his regular patrons and smiled sheepishly. "Nothing out of the ordinary. Just a gentleman's dispute."

"Yeah," said Kyle, "we're okay."

"Just shootin' pool," said one of the players.

Tracy digested that a moment, carefully studying all the looks of innocence. Finally, she smiled. "Then one of you liars get me a Coke."

Laughter broke the tension. Tracy sat on a bar stool, and every man returned to his place. Levi sat down to finish his lunch, but Steve remained where he was, still in defense mode. A glare from Doug served as a reminder that the trouble, though contained for now, still remained.

Charlie brought Tracy a can of Diet Coke. She popped it open, then turned. She looked at Steve with a smile that bordered on amusement. "Why don't you have a beer, Professor Benson?"

Professor Benson? Oh. She was one of them now, and he was the outsider. "I already have one," Steve said and took his seat again, with all eyes upon him. He could see Clark County Sheriff's Deputy Tracy Ellis was enjoying this. This was her turf, her big, wide comfort zone where she knew the ropes and had the authority and Steve didn't. Well, go ahead, little lady, and play your game. I don't need to. Steve took a swallow of beer because he wanted to, not because she had suggested it.

"So, Charlie, how's the fishing?" Tracy asked, and Charlie began to report on conditions up and down the Hyde River. One of the pool players gave his input on which flies were working and where, and Paul at the end of the bar boasted about a twenty-five-inch cutthroat he'd landed just above the mill, wherever that was. Things were lightening up, and Steve could guess that was exactly Tracy's intention. She was fitting right in, deftly handling the local subject matter and even the level of the language. She and these hunks must have all gone to school together.

Doug was the only one who wouldn't join in. He downed the last suds from his beer, slammed the bottle down, got to his feet, and strode over to the cash register to settle up with Charlie. Then he left without a word or a look back. Tracy kept talking to the others, but Steve noticed that her smile seemed forced.

Then she set the Coke can down so hard it crinkled. "Back to work," she ordered herself. She got off the stool and came over to Steve, speaking in a voice all the patrons would hear. "Dr. Benson, if you've finished your beer, I'd like a word with you outside."

That seemed to have the desired effect on the pool players. Steve was in trouble, and they were smiling about it.

She turned to Levi, who was just finishing his lunch. "Levi, isn't that your Dodge truck out there?"

"Yeah, still is."

"Your license tags are expired. I'll have to proceed on that. Come on."

Levi got up from the table, left a tip, and put on his big cowboy hat.

The pool players snickered.

Tracy stopped short. "Something funny?"

They turned dumb and couldn't seem to think of a thing.

Steve and Levi went to the cash register without a word, and Charlie rang them up.

Tracy leaned close while Charlie counted out change. "Charlie . . ."

"Eh?"

Tracy stole a glance at Carlotta and Kyle. Carlotta was sitting very close to Kyle, her hand on his forearm. Tracy spoke quietly, but that didn't hide her anger. "You're the one responsible for what goes on in here. If Carlotta wants to ply her trade, then I'd better not see it, because if I see it I have to do something about it, you understand?"

That threw Charlie off balance. He looked at Tracy, then at the couple at the table, and then back again. "Uh, sure, Tracy. I understand."

"Outside, gentlemen."

They went outside.

"Steve, wait here."

So now he was Steve again. He waited by his camper. She was the cop, and after all, she'd saved him a bruising.

LEVI WALKED along not saying a word, and Tracy was glad of that, for now. She needed time to figure out how she could talk this guy out of some information, but only the information she wanted. Levi was always glad to offer information on the spiritual state of things without being asked, but certain Hyde River secrets you couldn't pry out of him. He was a product of this town, and he knew the rules and lived by them.

They came to Levi's truck, the current tags plainly visible on the license plate. Levi bent to take a close look, then tilted his hat back a little and spoke kind words to his truck. "Well now, Joseph, you haven't let me down. I knew I put those tags on there!" He patted his truck on the hood and then, having caught on to Tracy's ruse, he planted his back against the front of his truck, folded his arms, and waited to hear what this was all about.

"Levi, I've got a problem," she said, taking out her ticket book and a pen.

"Well . . . your eyes aren't too good," he said.

That irritated her. "I have to talk to you, and I needed an excuse."

Levi looked over her shoulder. "And they're watching us right now."

"Are you serious?"

"Almost all of 'em."

Tracy spun around. Charlie, Melinda, Paul, Kyle, and the pool players were all leaning out or standing totally outside the tavern door, wanting to see Levi Cobb get a ticket.

"Go on!" she hollered, waving them back. "This doesn't concern you!"

They smiled, snickered, then went back inside. They were satisfied Levi was really being ticketed. Some stole a cold glance at Steve, still standing by his camper, but nothing else developed.

Tracy kept her ticket book in her hand and pretended to scribble in it. "You know about that bear attack, I suppose."

"Oh, we all know about it. Jerry Fisk spread his pink leaflets all over town, and everybody's upset."

"Well, we're having trouble with it, Levi. We think it might be something else other than a bear attack."

He showed no response, but Tracy knew his ways. He could be unimpressed or uninformed, or he could be hiding something.

"Levi, I heard Harold and Maggie Bly have split up. Is that true?"

"Harold would be the one to answer that."

Tracy checked to see if anyone was close before she said, "He'd lie to me."

Levi thought that over and then nodded in agreement.

"I need to talk to Maggie, Levi. Do you know where she is?"

He sighed, looked at the ground for a moment, then back at her. "I can't talk about Maggie Bly."

"But you know where she is, don't you?"

He wouldn't answer. Tracy liked that. Levi couldn't lie, so his silence revealed a great deal. She hammered again, "Don't you?"

He only looked her squarely in the eye, his arms crossed, and asked, "Any other questions?"

Few people could get under Tracy's skin, but Levi seemed to have a knack for it. "Don't give me that garbage, Levi! You've been sleeping in your camper for the last several days, ever since Maggie got kicked out of her house, isn't that right?"

"If that's a crime, arrest me."

"Levi," Tracy said, her tone forceful. "I'll get right to it. That bear attack may have been a murder."

Levi looked down. All she could see now was the top of his hat.

"And as for that man standing back there by the camper who just about got his butt whipped, that's the dead man's brother."

Levi didn't look up as he said, "Yeah, he told me that."

"The dead man's wife could be a suspect, you follow me?" She wished she could see his face and get a clue as to what he was thinking. He wasn't saying anything. Maybe he was considering her words. She spoke quietly, knowing she was venturing onto thin ice. "We know Cliff Benson's been seen around here a lot the past few months. We know the Bensons were having marital problems. Now, if Cliff Benson had a particular reason for being here that Maggie might know about, then she might know something else that could keep Mrs. Benson out of a lot of trouble. Personally, I don't think she's guilty. A woman acting alone wouldn't have the strength to cut up a body the way Benson's was cut up. But she had a weapon, she had motive, and she had opportunity. So this isn't just Maggie and Harold's problem. Evelyn Benson's husband is dead, and that makes it Evelyn's problem." Then Tracy shot a glance over her shoulder at the tall professor standing by his camper. "And it makes it Steve Benson's problem too, right? Now I saw you standing by him back in the tavern. If you think you're such a great Christian, then you'd better stand by him now." Levi was a religious man—overly religious, in her book—and she was hoping she could use that for leverage.

Her challenge did seem to give him pause. He looked at her, looked at Steve, thought it over, and finally sighed resignedly. "It's gonna be up to Maggie. I'll ask her if she feels like talking, but that's all I can do."

STEVE SAW the short conference end with Levi getting into his truck and driving off without a ticket. When Tracy returned, she offered no explanation, only more orders, spoken so only he would hear them.

"Get in your camper and follow me but try not to look like it."

He replied in an equally quiet tone, "I guess I owe you some thanks."

"Try to look like I'm lecturing you, because I am. One thing you need to get straight, Dr. Benson, sir, is that I don't give warnings without a reason. I grew up here, I know the people, and I know how they think. You don't. I hope you're a little wiser now."

"Where are we going?"

"To Levi Cobb's garage. Hopefully, we'll get some information that will relate to your brother's death." Then she gave him a whimsical look. "And you'll get another glimpse of the Hyde River mentality, I'm sure. This is a different kind of place, Steve. The people can be real backward."

"Or very forward."

"And let me brief you on Levi Cobb. He seems normal enough to look at him, right? He has his garage here in town, he does contract work for the county on their trucks and heavy equipment, and he even goes to the little church up on the hill. But you're going to find out he's a little . . . off. He's a religious nut for one thing. He likes to preach, and he likes to have deep discussions with—" She hesitated. "—with cars and trucks and machinery; they're his kind of people. On top of that, he's full of the old valley superstitions."

"What superstitions?"

"You'll see what I mean. Let's go."

Tracy got into her patrol car and took off. Steve waited a minute then got into his camper and followed Tracy's patrol car as she drove past the old red brick fire station with the gas pumps out front, circled back through a narrow alley, and parked near the back door. Levi was already there, waiting for them.

Tracy stepped forward, a question on her face.

Levi answered, "She'll talk to you." He looked warily at Steve. "But you'll have to go easy. She's in a sorry state."

"We'll go easy," Tracy said, catching Steve's eyes to make sure he understood.

They followed Levi up the steep, narrow stairway to what used to be the firemen's quarters. Now it was Levi's small apartment, modestly furnished, but clean. Toward the street was a kitchen and dinette, everything neatly in place. Toward the back was a living room with sofa, two upholstered chairs and a coffee table. Steve breathed easier for the moment. He'd been expecting something bizarre.

Levi stepped to a door, apparently a bedroom, and peeked inside. Then he beckoned to them to come but put a finger to his lips. They approached quietly.

Levi eased the door open. On the bed was Maggie Bly, curled in a fetal position, her fingers in her mouth, her hair matted with sweat, her eyes wild with fear. She lurched at the sight of them.

"It's okay, Maggie," said Levi. "They're friends."

Now I am seeing something bizarre, Steve thought.

I would never raise the subject except out of my deep concern for your future happiness. I agree that James Hyde is a pleasant enough man when other eyes are watching, but it is widely believed that strange, secret practices and beliefs run in the Hyde family. I understand that Benjamin Hyde was a secretive man who long indulged in esoteric, perhaps satanic, practices, and I have no reason to doubt his son James participates in the same. You will never hear such things discussed openly in Hyde River, but they are no secret.

I hope to travel to San Francisco in the spring. If you can wait until then, I will tell you all I know, and then you can decide whether you will accept his proposal of marriage.

From a letter to Beatrice Clemens from her mother
Margaret Clemens, dated December 4, 1902

———

DECEASED—Margaret Angeline Clemens, 42, died May 18, 1903, while traveling by train to San Francisco to visit her daughter. She is reported to have fallen from the train, but there are conflicting accounts . . .

Obituary in the Oak Springs Register
May 20, 1903

———

FIVE

Maggie Bly

TRACY MOVED forward as if approaching a timid deer, her hand outstretched. "Maggie. Hi. It's Tracy Ellis."

Maggie recognized her and took her hand. "Tracy." Then her eyes looked past Tracy and Steve in horror. "Oh, my God! Close the door!"

Levi shut the door, careful not to slam it.

The room was stuffy and dark, and no wonder. The windows, even though they had blinds, were boarded up with plywood. If not for the one dimly glowing lamp beside the bed, the room would have been pitch black. The odors of the aging building, its yellowing wallpaper, dust-filled cracks, and seasonal mildew now mingled with the smell of tears, filth, sweat . . . and something else. Something dead, Steve thought, shuddering slightly.

Tracy kept hold of Maggie's hand as she looked toward Steve and spoke gently. "Maggie, this is Steve Benson. He's a wildlife biologist, and he's here to investigate what happened up on Wells Peak."

Steve tried his best not to appear threatening. He stooped down just a bit so as not to tower over the trembling woman and extended his hand to her.

She pulled away from both him and Tracy, her eyes locked on him as if he were a predator. "You're Cliff's brother!"

That threw Steve off balance. Who was this woman? "Uh, yeah, that's right." He immediately looked at Tracy, hoping for an explanation.

"How did you know he's Cliff's brother?" Tracy asked quietly.

Maggie's hand went to her mouth again, and she cried through her fingers like a child. "You're gonna hate me . . ."

Levi stepped forward and touched her shoulder. "Maggie, now, these folks don't hate you, not at all."

"They hate me."

"No, they're here to help you. We all are."

"Nobody can help me. I'm dead, I'm dead, I'm dead!"

Tracy met Steve's eyes. See what I mean? her expression said.

Steve was seeing and hearing, of course, but not understanding any of this.

"I'm no good," Maggie whimpered.

"No, now that's not true," said Levi. "You're a precious creation of God."

She recoiled at that. "No I'm not! I'm nothing!"

Levi countered, "God loves you, Maggie."

"No, He hates me!"

"God loves everybody!"

"Harold hates me! He thinks I'm ugly and filthy and dirty! He hates me!"

"Well, you don't have to listen to what Harold says. God doesn't hate you. He's here, Maggie. He wants to help."

"I'm sure He does," said Tracy, just to bring that topic to a close. "But, Maggie, we need to ask you some very important questions."

Maggie stared at them blankly.

Levi offered, "Talk to them, Maggie. It'll do you good."

Maggie calmed a little, wiping her eyes clear.

Tracy smiled to reassure her. "Some of these questions are going to be difficult, and I'm sorry, but I have to ask them, okay?"

Maggie didn't react at all.

Tracy tried the first question, asking as gently as she could. "So, Maggie, you knew Cliff Benson?"

"Yes," she answered directly. "You bet I did."

Tracy couldn't hide her surprise at such a direct answer. Steve braced himself. He could sense bad news coming.

Tracy probed for it. "Were you and Cliff . . . were you—"

"We were in love!" Maggie blurted as if defending herself. "Cliff loved me! He said he loved me! He said he'd get me away from Harold!"

There it was, just that quick, far quicker than Steve could prepare for it, much less believe it.

"It's okay, Maggie," Levi said. "You just get it out in the open. 'If we confess our sins, He is faithful and just to forgive us—'"

"Maggie," Tracy cut in, "were you and Cliff having an affair?"

Maggie showed disgust at the word. "It wasn't an affair! It was more than that. It was the most beautiful thing that ever happened to me."

Oh no, Steve thought. Not Cliff!

"How long, Maggie?" Tracy asked. "How long were you and Cliff seeing each other?"

"A couple months."

"Until Harold found out?"

Maggie said nothing. She only nodded.

"And that's why he kicked you out of the house."

"Yes." Maggie closed her eyes as if the confessions had exhausted her. "And now—now I'm gonna die."

Tracy stroked Maggie's shoulder. "You're not going to die, Maggie. We're not going to let anyone hurt you."

Maggie opened her eyes again and glared at Tracy as if she'd said something stupid. "Don't you know what happened to Cliff?"

Tracy lifted her hands. "Maggie, no, we don't know what

happened to him. That's what we're trying to figure out. That's why we're here."

Maggie sat up on the bed. "He got eaten! Eaten alive! Everybody knows that!"

"Now we don't know that for sure," Tracy said, as if Maggie had said nothing unusual.

Maggie looked toward a boarded-up window as if something lurked outside. "And now it's gonna happen to me!"

This must have something to do with the superstitions Tracy was talking about, Steve thought. And Tracy wasn't kidding. The terror in this woman was so real it chilled his blood as well.

Levi consoled her, "It don't have to happen, Maggie! You can get free of that sin right now!"

And here was Levi's religious quirk, another thing Tracy had warned him about.

"Levi." Tracy glared at the man to silence him. Then she turned back to the woman. "Maggie, do you know—"

"It was a beautiful thing!" she repeated defensively. "I don't know what I did that was so wrong! Cliff loved me and I loved him and—" she looked at Steve. "—I just wanted to be happy. I didn't wanna hurt anybody. I just wanted somebody to love me, that's all."

Tracy nodded with understanding. "I hear you, Maggie. I hear you."

Maggie softened as she saw the kindness in Tracy's eyes. "You know how it is."

"Sure I do." Tracy took Maggie's hand again. "Harold's been pretty rough on you, I know."

"I've tried to be good to Harold."

"Mm-hm."

"But he's a mean man, Tracy."

"Yes, he is."

"And Cliff made me feel good. He treated me like I was somebody, like a lady." Now Maggie looked at Steve. She was trying to make him understand. "Cliff was a good man, and he treated me right."

Trying to be helpful, Steve answered, "I'm sure he did," and then felt uncomfortable for saying it. Cliff should have been treating Evelyn right, he thought.

"I met him at Charlie's," Maggie volunteered. "He said he wanted to take pictures of the mining towns, and so I started going with him, showing him around. I liked him right away. And he kept coming back to take more pictures. Sometimes he didn't even take pictures; he just wanted to be with me."

Steve didn't know if he could listen to much more of this. Cliff and this woman. It was unthinkable. It was all he could do to hide his shock and disgust as he thought of Evelyn and the boys and what this would do to them.

But confession did seem good for Maggie's soul. She was calming down with each new piece of information she shared. Tracy knew it and was determined to draw out more.

"Maggie, where were you the night Cliff was killed?"

"At home, having a big fight with Harold."

"And that's the same night he kicked you out?"

"Uh-huh. He found out about Cliff. He was mad."

"So about what time did he kick you out?"

"I don't know. About ten." Well, that let Harold off the hook, Tracy thought. Unless he had had some of his cronies kill Benson, which would be difficult to prove.

"And that's the last you saw him?"

"Uh-huh."

"Did you ever meet Evelyn Benson, Cliff's wife?"

"No."

"So you were never threatened by her, you know what I mean?"

Maggie shook her head. "I never saw Cliff's wife."

"Did Cliff ever give any indication that his wife knew about you, or was upset about it, or might want to get even if she did find out?"

Maggie shook her head. "Tracy, Cliff's wife didn't kill him. I know."

Tracy hesitated, braced herself, and asked, "What about Harold? Did Harold say he would kill Cliff?"

Maggie shook her head.

"Did he say he would kill you?"

Her eyes became vacant, and she shook her head in despair. "He didn't have to. It's just going to happen, that's all. It's only a matter of time."

"No, it's not going to happen," said Tracy. "We're going to get you out of here, right now."

"It won't help!"

"How do you know?"

"It won't help," Levi agreed. "The problem's in Maggie's heart, so it goes with her. It don't matter where you move her."

"Well, it can't hurt to try, now can it?"

Levi shook his head in frustration. "Tracy..."

"Deputy Ellis," she corrected him.

"Deputy Ellis. That'd just be running, and you can't run from this."

"Maggie has to get out of this town before she gets hurt," Tracy said in a tone that made it an order. "Maggie, would you like to come with me? I'll get you a room somewhere safe, somewhere nobody will know about."

Maggie looked at Tracy. Maggie's expression was disbelieving.

Levi insisted, "It's in her heart, Deputy Ellis. Her sins are gonna follow her no matter where she goes!"

Tracy put her finger an inch from Levi's nose and snapped, "Shut up!"

"I'm trying to—"

"You're only filling her head with crap, Levi! Now if I'm going to help Maggie at all, it'll have to be in the real world; you got that? We're not dealing with fantasies here."

"You don't think sin is real?"

She seemed about to slap him, but reined herself in with great effort and tried to sound calm but firm. "Levi, under the present circumstances, if anybody gets her killed it's going to be you and your stories. So please, just be quiet, all right?"

Tracy took a moment just to breathe before addressing Maggie again. "Maggie, I'll get you out of the valley for a few days, take you someplace where nobody can find you."

Maggie had no answer.

"I'll come back in a few minutes. If you want to get out of here and come with me, then be ready. Levi, you help her, you understand?" He was about to protest. She nailed him with a voice that jolted Steve. "You've got another man's wife in your house, Levi, right in your bedroom! I will use that, so help me! Now help Maggie get her things together and have her ready by the time I get back. Is that clear?"

Levi looked at Maggie and spoke softly, "We better do like she says, Maggie."

Tracy rose, and following her cue, Steve went with her down the back stairs and outside.

Steve was disturbed, brooding, and bewildered all at once. "I had no idea—"

"Don't look," Tracy interrupted, "but there's a man under that lean-to over there, and I think he's watching us."

Steve didn't look as he asked, "Watching us? You mean spying?"

Tracy headed for her car, acting casual, her conversational tone covering the gravity of what she was saying. "There are people looking for Maggie, trying to keep tabs on her. Guess they'll be keeping an eye on you too—and me."

Steve managed a corner-of-the-eye glance. Across a vacant lot and under a rickety lean-to, a thin little man in blue mechanic's coveralls appeared to be working on an old Willy pickup.

"That's Carl Ingfeldt," said Tracy. "He doesn't live there, and that isn't his truck. I don't think he works for Harold Bly, but Harold's the kind of man he'd want to do favors for. It won't be good that we were seen together at Cobb's."

Tracy finally caught the little man looking their way and waved, shouting a friendly greeting, "Hey, Carl!"

Carl waved back, but not happily, and then walked away, leaving the Willy sitting there with the hood open.

Tracy sighed. "Well. They know what we're up to."

Steve paused by the patrol car.

"Who is this Harold Bly, anyway?" Steve asked.

Tracy snickered derisively. "He's the local godfather. He owns the mining company and most of the town, and there are some pretty strong superstitions about him and his family. People are afraid of him, and I think he uses that to his advantage." Then she added, "And he's not much of a husband, you may have gathered."

"So you think maybe Harold—"

"Steve," Tracy cautioned, "we'll have to talk about this later. Right now, you need to get out of town. I guess you can see, there could be more to your brother's death than a bear attack, which means I have quite a bit of work ahead of me. Now listen to me, I mean this, my job's going to be hard enough. I don't need any more skirmishes like we had in Charlie's."

"But you know what you're saying, that someone actually did that to Cliff."

"Steve, I'm not saying anything one way or the other. All I can do is try to find out what really happened and why, and—" She considered it a moment. "—no matter how it all turns out, I know it's going to be ugly through and through, and I'm not going to like it."

"Well I certainly don't like it. The whole situation is overwhelming." An understatement deserving a trophy, Steve thought.

Tracy nodded regretfully. "Just take it one step at a time. Go ahead and—I don't know, talk to Marcus again. By all means, talk to Evelyn. Maybe you'll find out something that'll change the whole picture. I really hope you do."

"But if this is the work of—of people . . ." He was trying to sort it out. "Maggie said Cliff was eaten!" Then he shrugged. "She was really out of it, though. I guess she means the bear. Levi obviously told her about it."

"We'll talk about it later," Tracy said. She opened the door of her patrol car, then looked over the roof at him. "Steve."

"Yeah?"

"Maybe it was a bear."

Steve realized there was no comfort to be found in any

possibility. No answer would ever be the right one. No answer would ever bring back his brother. "Maybe," he said, and opened the door.

"Stay out of trouble," she said, and got in her car.

They drove away in opposite directions.

EVELYN STILL wasn't all there, Steve thought. She'd seemed so well, so like herself the other day, but today she seemed vague and sketchy in her thinking and conversation.

She might have a long road back, Steve thought.

"I have dreams," she said, lying on her back and staring vacantly at the ceiling.

They'd gotten around to That Night after talking about anything and everything else. He told her he'd been to Hyde River, but he withheld more than he shared. As far as Evelyn knew, the trip to Hyde River had been unfruitful but had raised some "other possibilities" Steve was going to look into. Evelyn asked no questions, so Steve let it go. He did not tell her what he'd learned about Cliff and Maggie. He didn't know if he ever could.

Now, as Evelyn tried to recall something, anything, she began drifting between reality and . . . he didn't know what.

"I have dreams that keep coming back."

Steve stayed close, listening but expecting little.

"I keep seeing a big black thing coming out of the dark. And I hear it, I feel it thrashing around, and I feel blood splashing all over me." She shivered.

Steve asked softly, "What about people? Are there any people in your dreams?"

She continued to stare vacantly and slowly shook her head. "No. No people. Only a big black thing."

"What about your knife? Do you fight back? Do you use your knife?"

"Yes. I stab at it. I just keep stabbing and stabbing."

"Where is Cliff? Is he in your dreams?"

Tears came to her eyes as she whispered, "No. He's gone. He's gone, and all I see is a shadow where he used to be."

THE TRAVELER MOTEL on Route 16 catered to vacationers traveling south, away from Clark County and Hyde Valley. Tracy knew that few people from Hyde River would ever come this way or notice this place unless they were on vacation, so Tracy had brought Maggie here, not in her patrol car but in her own Ford Ranger. Maggie had registered under a false name.

Now they were in Maggie's room, Number 12. Tracy stood by the door in jeans and a light blue workshirt, the incognito civilian. Maggie sat on the bed. "So what now?" she asked, timid and bewildered.

"Just sit tight for a few days. Take some walks down by the lake, see a movie. You need to breathe free for a while, and I need to find out what's going on without having to worry about you."

Maggie bent just a little and looked out the window at the sky. "He might see me."

"Maggie, come on. This far away?"

"I don't know..."

"I'll be back tomorrow to check on you."

They said good-bye, and Tracy drove away.

EARLY THAT EVENING, Steve sat in a lawn chair by the little kidney-shaped pool at the Tamarack Motel, thinking, making notes, trying to clarify where things stood, and not getting very far. All he could think about was Cliff, the kid brother he would never see again; all he could see before his mind's eye were the memories, some of them so hilarious now:

The hot-air blimp Cliff tried to make out of laundry bags when he was fourteen. It flew for maybe one minute before it landed on Mr. Sorenson's barn and set it on fire.

Cliff spending all his summer earnings on a gutless Chevy with drag slicks and stuck valves; boy, it looked great, but it couldn't even climb a hill, much less race anybody. Cliff thought it would impress the girls, but it never got out of the driveway.

That stupid dock Cliff built out of inner tubes and old pallets.

It was his revolutionary design: portable, quickly assembled, quickly torn down, easy to maintain. He was going to get it patented and become a millionaire. You couldn't walk on it—it flipped over the first time they tried.

But that was Cliff, always running off half-cocked after some crazy idea and always getting a lecture from his big brother when he got back. They were a pair: the imp and the intellectual, the clown and the straight man, the kid who stayed a kid and the older brother who never got to be one.

Cliff was nine and Steve was fourteen when their folks split up and their dad moved out of state. As a result, Steve quickly found himself in the role of the father, skipping his teenage years entirely to look out for his mother and his carefree brother. Cliff almost forced it on him. Whenever he was in trouble, Cliff came to Steve, and Steve was always there for him.

But now those days of childhood were long past, Cliff was gone, killed in an unbelievably gruesome way, and Steve was left alone in the confusing, devastating present. He began to shake with emotion and turned away from the motel building so that no one would see the tears streaming down his face.

After several minutes, he sat back in the chair, wiped his eyes and nose with a handkerchief, and wondered if perhaps Tracy Ellis was right. Maybe he was too close to the situation to be investigating Cliff's death. With such a load of grief and outrage, it was nearly impossible to be objective and clear-headed, and he'd demonstrated that to himself and to Tracy Ellis despite his best efforts.

But what else could he do? With Cliff's death unexplained and unresolved, and now, with foul play being considered, he had to be here; he could do nothing less. He couldn't rest until he had the answers.

With a deep breath and a determination to press ahead despite his feelings, he referred to some notes he'd scribbled on the writing pad in his lap. He had discovered long ago that writing things down helped him organize his thoughts, helped him see what was important, and helped him find solutions. He had written down three topics:

The killing. The greatest riddle, of course. Tracking down and shooting a rogue bear would have been simple. Now he knew less and had more questions than when he'd started, and worst of all, he might be expected to trust others to solve the whole thing while all he did was sit at home fretting about it. That just couldn't happen, not as long as—

Steve jumped a little. Oh. The motel owner's big tabby cat, that's what it was, letting out a long, low growl—the strange sound that people who didn't know cats were always surprised that they made—from the bushes nearby. Steve settled back into his chair, having demonstrated to himself a secondary burden: his shattered nerves.

Next topic:

The affair. This topic could be broken down into two categories: (1) How the affair could suggest a human perpetrator in Cliff's death, unthinkable though that may be, and (2) How in the world Cliff could be so foolish as to get tangled up with that semi-deranged woman in the first place; how he could be so intoxicated that he gave no thought to what his escapade would do to Evelyn and the boys—and to Maggie Bly's husband. From all appearances, which Cliff should have seen, Hyde River was definitely a bad choice of towns for starting an affair, and Harold Bly's wife was definitely the wrong woman.

Cliff, you sure did it this time. If only I'd known . . .

He was getting upset again, so he went on to the next topic:

The myths and superstitions of Hyde River. Now here was something he knew nothing about, but apparently he'd come close to getting clobbered because of it. If there had been foul play, this would be a factor—

Crunch. Crunch. A faint sound.

Crunch.

Steve looked in the direction of the sound—and froze in horror at the sight. Under another lawn chair nearby, the big tabby crouched, his face close to the concrete. He was chomping, chewing, licking a large mouse. The lower half of the mouse sat on its haunches, lifeless, rocking to and fro with the cat's jaws. The upper half was gone, snipped off. The lower half ended in a red stump . . .

THE BARTENDER at Harvey's Restaurant and Lounge asked Steve if he'd been jogging. Steve only asked for a table in the corner and a stiff drink. He had no recollection of his long run down the road from the motel, and he wasn't entirely sure where he was.

He was sweating and breathing hard. He couldn't think.

The drink arrived and he gulped it down, the liquor burning his throat. He was still shaking. He couldn't stop.

IT WAS DARK enough to get away with spreading a little terror without being seen, so this night six huge men, all wearing black hoods to hide their faces, got together to make a few things abundantly clear to young Kyle Figgin. Kyle was bound hand and foot, kicking, squirming, trying in vain to free himself from their iron grip as they carried him like pallbearers, three on a side, his body flat out and face down. They rushed along, letting Kyle's head and face take the lead through the tall grass and prickly underbrush until they got to the edge of the river. Kyle was screaming, but his screams were only pitiful squawks through the gag they'd crammed into his mouth.

When they reached the river they didn't slow down but splashed headlong into the current until the water rose to their knees—and Kyle's face. Then they shoved him under and held him there.

Moments passed. Kyle started kicking so hard they could barely hang onto him.

"Okay," said the ringleader, who stood by Kyle's head, and they raised him just enough so he could suck some frantic breaths through his half-clogged nose. The ringleader bent to speak into

Kyle's ear. "You don't talk to outsiders, Mr. Figgin. Not a word. We just want to make you aware of that, you understand?"

Kyle didn't have time to grunt, nod, or scream an answer before they dunked him under the water again and held him there only seconds short of his life. When they raised him up again, he was pulling and snorting air through his clogged nose, desperate to stay alive.

The ringleader let go of Kyle's arm long enough to untie the gag and yank the rag from Kyle's mouth. "Don't scream."

Kyle didn't scream; he was too busy breathing—and crying, totally repentant.

"Don't feel too bad about it, son. We've all been here one time or another. Just don't forget, that's all."

With a glance from the ringleader, one of the men holding Kyle's feet cut away the ropes with a knife. Then they dropped him face first into the river and let the current carry him along as he struggled to right himself in the shallow water, his arms still bound behind him, his face dipping again and again under the rippling, splashing surface.

He was a good distance down the river by the time he finally got his feet under him and could push, kick, and half-float his way to the shore. Then he flopped on the smooth rocks and wept like a child, gasping and coughing, glad just to be alive.

By the time he'd recovered, he was alone, without tormentors but also without help. He'd washed up on the opposite side of the river. Somehow he'd have to cross again to get home, and his arms were still tied behind him.

It would be a very long night for Kyle Figgin.

NIGHT CAME, and in the vast mountainous regions beyond the city lights, the darkness was thick and absolute, enfolding the forests, blanketing the valleys, reducing the ridges to the faintest of jagged lines against the clouded sky. The air was cool and still as the sounds of night took their turns: the crickets up close and all around, the frogs farther in the distance, the coyotes howling and chattering in a faraway, other world.

Fully dressed, Maggie Bly lay on her bed in the dark, her face illuminated by the cold yellow of the motel's yardlight. She was looking out the window and listening. The light gave her a sickly complexion, but her eyes were alert and attentive. Her lips betrayed a faint smile, her first in days. She felt at ease, relaxed. Absently, she scratched at the area directly over her heart while a stain, black and odorous, began to spread in a widening circle, saturating her scooped-neck cotton shirt and blackening her fingers.

She rose from the bed and went to the window, her eyes dreamy and her smile broadening. Then she listened, as if to sweet music, her head swaying lazily from side to side. The dread, the fear, was leaving her. She couldn't help but giggle.

ELMER AND BERTHA MCCOY sat in the darkened living room of their mobile home amid TV trays, beer cans, and cigarette butts watching the late show, their stony faces lit by the bluish glow of the television. After the late show, as they did every night, they would take turns washing up in the bathroom and then go to bed. This was all in the routine, as was the two dogs out front barking at nothing in particular as they did every night.

But something was different. The dogs' barking was usually sporadic, background sound that barely registered with the McCoys. But that night the barking was louder, insistent, continuous. It was enough to force Elmer out of the soft couch and to the window. "Hey!" he yelled. "Shut up out there. Knock it off!"

But then he thought he heard singing somewhere out in the dark. Griz yapped again.

"Shut up!" Elmer turned to his wife. "Turn down the TV for a second." She pressed the mute button, and Elmer stood at the window, frowning as he tried to hear the strange sound. Even though both dogs kept barking, Elmer could still hear the singing between their barks, a woman's voice far away, barely audible, then ever so gradually, getting louder. She must be coming up the road toward their trailer.

By now Bertha was curious. "What is it?"

Elmer only motioned her to be quiet. She got up and joined him at the window.

She heard it, too. "Somebody out there singing this time of night?"

When Elmer recognized the voice, he whispered, "It's Maggie Bly."

"No, it isn't!" Bertha whispered in denial, immediately clinging to his arm.

As they stood there, the voice grew louder, moving eerily up the road.

"It's her," Elmer whispered.

Bertha clung to him tighter, hurting his arm.

It was Maggie's voice all right, a very good voice but strange and haunting. She was singing a lonesome country tune about a good man loved and lost, and love never coming again. Then, from behind the big cottonwood in their front yard, a silhouette emerged: Maggie Bly, strolling along the white center line, easy and carefree, singing her mournful song, her hands clutching her heart.

It was happening again. Bertha had never seen it; she had only heard about it. Elmer had seen it once and never wanted to see it again. But now here it was, unfolding before their very eyes, and they stood frozen, their eyes following that silhouette as it moved like an apparition up the road, the song fading like a ghost crying alone in the night.

It took only a few moments for Maggie to pass out of sight and for her song to fade. But that was enough. Elmer and Bertha moved away from the window, pulled the shade, extinguished the lights, then dropped to the floor and crawled to their bedroom to hide.

TRACY SLAMMED down the phone. She'd heard from a friend in Hyde River, and it was bad news.

Where was that phone number? She was wearing an oversized T-shirt and a pair of cutoff jeans, her favorite relax-at-home clothes. The number had to be in her uniform. She ran to the closet, groped through the shirt pocket, and found the slip of paper with the number of the Traveler Motel. She picked up the phone in her bedroom and dialed the number.

After five rings—it seemed to take forever—she heard a woman's voice answer, "Traveler Motel."

"Room twelve, please."

Tracy could hear the hesitation in the woman's voice. "Is this, uh . . ."

"This is Tracy Ellis, Sarah's friend." Sarah was the false name Maggie had used.

"She's gone, Miss Ellis. She left hours ago, and she hasn't come back yet."

"Left! Did she say where she was going?"

"No. Just walked out. I saw her hitch a ride out front."

"Did she check out?"

"No, she still has the room."

Once again, just to be sure. "She's not there?"

"No. I've been here all evening, and she hasn't come back."

"HAROLD, OH, HAROLD . . ." The voice was smooth, sultry.

Bly jolted awake, his eyes darting about, his hand moving toward the .38 revolver in the nightstand drawer. The bedroom was dark and quiet. Nothing moved.

He relaxed a little and released his held breath. The .38 remained where it was. Man, what a nightmare! That voice sounded like it was right in the house—

"Harold," came the voice again, ghostly, teasing. "Sweetheart . . ."

Bly sat up in the bed, making sure he was awake. He scanned the bedroom carefully. The dresser, the chair, his clothes slung over the bedpost, all were vague shadows in the dark. Where was she? Should he answer? Or was he still dreaming? He sat still and listened. Okay, Maggie, I'm awake now. Let's hear you talk.

She laughed loudly and mockingly. That was Maggie, all right, Harold thought. He untangled his feet from the sheets, got out of bed, and looked down from the second-story window. He caught sight of Maggie's silhouette just below the window, her hair wild and glowing in the light of the moon, her face in shadow. The sight of her made him jump, and she had obviously noticed, for she laughed even more.

She'd scared him, and now she was laughing at him. Instantly, his temper flared. He grabbed his pants off the bedpost, and, standing at the window, he hurriedly jammed one leg into the pants.

"So I caught you with your pants down, Harold?"

"Maggie, I'm gonna tear you apart!" Bly was hopping on one foot. "I'll tear you apart, you hear me?"

"Just thought I'd stop and say good-bye, sweetie!"

She disappeared. He got his pants up to his waist, zippered them, and stuck his head out the window in time to see her moving lazily toward the road. He ran downstairs, toward the front door, hitting a table in the dark, cursing.

Maggie reached the street out front and looked for any signs of life. All the old houses were dark, the occupants asleep, or at least acting like it. She stooped and grabbed a rock from the road shoulder, then pegged it at the front door of the mining company foreman.

"Hey! Wake up in there!"

No response. The house stayed dark.

She grabbed another rock and bounced it off the front door again. Now the bedroom light came on.

"You gotta hear this!"

The miner and his wife living two doors down must have heard her, too, for their front door squeaked open. She could see their faces, one above the other, peering out through the crack.

With a not-so-subtle rattling and crash, Harold Bly burst out the front door, bare-chested and powerful, holding a shotgun in his burly arms. Another light went on in a neighbor's house just down the street, and he halted at the top of the steps. People were hearing this, seeing it.

Maggie had her back to him. She was still busy rousing the neighborhood. "Hey, everybody! Wake up! I've got an announcement to make!"

Another light came on next door. Then the porch light. Mrs. Cumber, a retired schoolteacher, poked her head out the front door.

In a quick change of character, Bly stashed the gun on the porch and made his way down the stairs, reaching out toward Maggie like a loving husband should, trying to appear calm and collected. He had to get this madwoman inside before she made him look foolish. "Now, Maggie, honey, why don't you come inside and let's talk?"

She turned to face him, a carefree, cocky expression on her face, the strap of her bag over her shoulder—and a slick, black stain down the front of her blouse from her heart to her waist.

Bly stopped dead in his tracks. Then he backed up a little.

The stain was glistening, growing. He could smell the stench, like that of a dead animal. It was obvious she'd been clawing at it, for her hands were blackened, and she had black smudges where she'd touched her face.

Bly mellowed. Then he smiled a gloating smile.

"LEVI, this is Tracy Ellis. Is Maggie there?"

"No ma'am." Trouble. Levi could sense it in Tracy's voice. He could feel fear twisting his insides. "I haven't seen her tonight."

"I just got a call from somebody in Hyde River. He says he saw her on the road just a few minutes ago."

Levi held the phone to his ear and went straight to the front window to survey the road below. "Where'd he see her? What part of town?"

Tracy was flustered. "I don't know. He didn't say. He just told me he'd driven by her."

"Well, which way was she going?"

"Up the road."

That was bad. "Toward Old Town?"

"You got it."

"How long ago was that?"

"About ten minutes."

"I'm going after her."

"If you find her, just get her back to your place, all right? And do it quietly. I'm going out the door right now."

"I'll look for you."

Levi slammed down the phone and bounded for the stairway, grabbing his jacket off its hook as he passed.

LOOKING AT the black and dripping stain over his wife's heart, Harold Bly felt a wonderful sense of intoxication—power, that's what it was. Real power!

Still, he didn't approach Maggie and didn't want her approaching him either. He stood with his arms outstretched to keep her away, and spoke gently. "Now, Maggie. I think you should just move on—just, just keep going."

She cocked her head playfully to one side and said too loudly, "I showed Cliff your office at the mining company. We made love up there, Harold; you know that?"

"Maggie, now—calm down." He was acutely aware of the neighbors listening.

But she threw back her head and jubilantly shouted into the sky, "Cliff Benson was the most wonderful lover I ever had! Gentle, and kind, and—" She looked at Harold. "—a better man than you ever were, Harold Bly!"

This he hadn't planned on, and it wasn't so much what she was saying that started raising his temperature—it was that he couldn't stop her from saying it.

"We made love under the Five-Mile Bridge," Maggie announced to the world, "and up on Wells Peak. We even got a motel a few times, but that wasn't like doing it outside, you know?"

Steady, steady, he told himself, keeping his hands by his sides even as they clenched into quivering fists. He wanted to smash in that laughing, mocking face, but her face was streaked with black slime, and he dared not touch it.

She could tell. "Can't touch me, can you, Harold? Well, nobody can. Not anymore. I can do what I want, go where I want, be with whoever I want. It doesn't matter anymore, not anymore."

Harold said it quietly, but his tone was vicious. "Maggie, you shut up right now and get out of here."

She actually sneered at him. "When I'm ready, Harold. When I'm ready. Nobody tells me what to do. I'm free, Harold."

He no longer cared how much attention he attracted. He ran up the porch steps for his shotgun, grabbed it, and turned back toward the street.

But she was gone.

Across the street, the miner and his wife slammed their door shut and extinguished their porch light.

Bly went down the front steps slowly, carefully, starting to lose the resolve his anger had triggered. He looked up and down the street. There was no sign of Maggie. She might be hiding, he thought. Perhaps she'd fled. He took one step toward the street and then another, listening, peering into the dark.

He noticed Mrs. Cumber duck inside and turn off her lights. The company foreman's door slammed, and the bedroom light went out. Up and down the street, lights winked out, windows closed, doors clicked shut. Darkness and silence returned to the neighborhood.

Bly stood there alone on the dark street for a moment, suddenly realizing he should be pleased at his neighbors' behavior—the dark houses, the closed shades, the slamming doors. They really were scared, weren't they? That brought a cunning smile to his face. Sure, he thought. Maybe it was best that the neighbors heard everything. By tomorrow the messy little scene they'd witnessed would mean a whole lot more, and they'd all be talking about it. Then the talk would spread, and the whole town would get a strong message, a message they'd never forget.

From down the hill came the roar of a vehicle. Now what? Bly asked. Soon headlights appeared around the corner, sweeping across the faces of the old houses. Bly let the shotgun rest innocently at his side as he backed away from the street.

The big Dodge caught him in its headlights and rumbled to a halt right beside him. The window was rolled down.

"Evenin', Mr. Bly."

Harold's tone was not friendly. "Hello, Levi."

Levi had spotted the shotgun, of course. "Some kind of trouble?"

"No. Thought I heard some coyotes."

Levi looked up the hill toward the forest beyond the town, then back at Harold. He seemed edgy. "I—I heard your wife was out wandering through town, Mr. Bly. I was wanting to make sure she was okay."

Bly smirked at that. "So you've lost track of your roommate, is that it?"

"You know I haven't touched her, Mr. Bly, and I've tried to be careful about appearances."

"Not careful enough."

"Have you seen her tonight? Has she come by here?"

"No. I haven't seen a thing."

Levi gave him a good hard look before saying, "Then I'll be on my way." He put the Dodge into gear. "Hope you bag a coyote." The truck lurched forward, did a U-turn, and roared back down the hill toward the highway, the night closing in again behind its red taillights.

SHE'D BEEN BY her home, all right. Levi could read Harold Bly's face like a billboard, and his lies too. She had to be heading for Old Town.

Levi drove slowly, scanning both sides of the road, straining to look back into the trees. No sign of her. Either she'd made remarkably good time or she'd taken the old trail along the river instead of the main road.

One mile north of Hyde River, Levi pulled off at the Old Town turnoff, a dirt road veering off to the right. The road was now blocked by a huge berm of dirt and debris to keep vehicles out. If Levi went in there, he'd be trespassing on company land.

He had to go in. He nosed the Dodge up against the berm, shut her down, and continued on foot, flashlight in hand, climbing over the dirt pile and back down to the rutted road beyond. He swept his light back and forth across the road as he hurried along, hoping to find footprints, any sign that Maggie had been this way. So far he saw nothing. She must have taken the trail along the river, he thought. Maybe, just maybe, he could get to Hyde Hall before she did, or before—

A gust of wind caused him to halt. He clicked off his light and crouched down, looking skyward. Nothing up there but stars. He kept listening. The wind was blowing in small, intermittent gusts, and in the distance, he could hear the gentle, rushing sound of the river. He was getting close.

He started walking again, and soon he broke out of the old forest and into an open expanse where grass, berry thickets, and diseased, crooked cottonwoods barely survived amid the gutted, sagging remains of old wooden structures. Old Town. There was nothing left now but stone foundations overgrown with brush, teetering walls with no roofs to connect them, fallen piles of weathered lumber that once were homes for miners, prospectors, shopkeepers, and their families. Levi stole quietly into the town, trying to recall where everything was. He hadn't been there in a long time. Few people had.

On one side, a beam-and-plank wall with one window was all

that was left of the Gold Dust Hotel. Across the rutted and disappearing road, a crumbling foundation outlined where the tavern once stood. Levi vaguely remembered Hyde Hall being near the other end of the town, near the river. This main road should take him there.

Was that singing he heard? Or was it the wind moving through this old place, sighing through a thousand cracks and voids? He froze. He listened.

A woman's voice. A country tune.

"Maggie!" he shouted, his voice echoing down the street. "Maggie Bly!"

He heard no response but the wind. He ran in the direction of that singing, hoping to hear it again, praying it would continue. Then he heard it again, this time loud, even boisterous. It was definitely Maggie, Levi thought.

"Maggie!"

A gust of wind roared through the cottonwoods, and they swayed crazily, clapping their limbs one against another as leaves torn loose fluttered over the town. Levi crouched and covered his head as twigs and leaves rained from above him. The singing was buried under the sound.

Then Levi realized what he was hearing was not the sound of wind. No! It couldn't be what he thought it was. It couldn't be happening again!

Panicked, he ran down the road, dodging crooked trees that had taken hold in the dirt street, stepping around trenches carved by years of rain. Then he heard the singing again, and some hope returned.

"Maggie!"

Another rush of wind rolled over Old Town like a wave, bending the cottonwoods and rippling the tops of the grass beyond, on its way toward the river. Levi ignored it. He continued running in the direction of Maggie's voice.

And then, abruptly, the song ended, in the middle of a note.

"Maggie!"

Levi recognized Hyde Hall just ahead, now a cracking, overgrown foundation with three walls leaning precariously inward and no roof, no floor, no front.

Levi flashed his light here and there, sweeping through the entire structure as he approached. In the middle of the back wall, a tall stone fireplace and chimney were the only things still vertical. Berry thickets and young willows competed where the floor used to be. Levi noticed that one wall was quivering as if it had been struck. A plank near the top of the wall, loosened over the years, clattered to the ground.

He was momentarily distracted by another flashlight beam far up the road. Someone was approaching on the run. But he didn't wait to see who it was. His own beam had caught something. He stepped over the foundation wall and into the remains of Hyde Hall then waded through the tall grass to the center of the building where his light fell on a large, square stone, its top almost as flat as a table. Just beyond it, he saw Maggie's shoulder bag laying on the ground amid spatters of blood. A few yards from the bag was a running shoe, the laces still tied.

Levi sank slowly to his knees beside the bag and the shoe, and his body began to shake with weeping.

He heard footsteps hurrying toward him. A beam of light shone on his face, then on the ground, the shoulder bag, the shoe.

It was Tracy Ellis. She was too late.

"Did you see anybody?" Tracy asked.

Levi shook his head.

Tracy wasn't in her uniform, but she had her gun in her hand. "Well, come on, help me look—and get away from that bag, it's evidence!"

He wiped his nose with his hand. "There's nobody here."

She took only a moment to realize he would be no help and took off without him, shining her flashlight in every direction, searching, scrambling, tripping in the dark.

Levi just prayed. He knew Tracy Ellis would be beating around in the brush, combing over the roads and trails through Old Town, and even walking up and down the river for much of the night. He also knew she wouldn't find anything.

There were six of us altogether: myself and four men whom I will not name, and then there was James Hyde and his son-in-law, Harrison Bly. I don't know what Nelson Parmenter said or to whom he said it, but James made it clear that we'd better follow his orders, or we would end up the same way. We lashed Nelson to the old rock crusher in front of Hyde Hall, and then we took turns beating him until he was unconscious. James said to leave him there all night, so we did, and when morning came, Nelson was gone, I don't know where. Folks are saying a bear killed him while he was out hunting, but they don't know what happened the night before he disappeared. They don't know what James and Harrison made us do.

From an anonymous note found in a wall safe of the Sorenson Residence, West Fork, during demolition in 1948, and donated to the West Fork Historical Society

———

SIX

The Oath

STEVE HEARD a knock on his motel room door at nine the next morning, a knock he wasn't expecting and wasn't ready for.

He'd had a sleepless night, he'd just gotten out of bed, and the place was a mess. Maybe it was Tracy Ellis.

He opened the door. It was another sheriff. It was *the* sheriff. The small nameplate above his badge read Lester Collins.

"Dr. Benson?"

Steve was embarrassed. He hadn't shaved yet. His eyes felt swollen. Had he even combed his hair? "Uh, yes. Sheriff Collins?"

"That's right," he said, extending his hand.

"Come on in."

Great first impression, Steve thought. "Sorry about the state of things in here. I had a long day yesterday, and I'm just barely getting started on this one."

"I understand. Things have been pretty hectic for me, too. We're short of manpower, and I've been running in all directions trying to keep up. I would have met with you sooner if I could have, believe me."

Steve moved his camouflage gear off the only available chair. "Please, have a seat."

Collins took the chair. Steve sat on the bed.

"We've appreciated your help," said Collins, casting an admiring look at Steve's 30.06 leaning in the corner. He nodded at the rifle. "Is that what you used on 318?"

"That's right."

"How has it been, working with Deputy Ellis?"

Confusing, overwhelming, and frustrating, Steve thought. But he knew it wasn't really Tracy Ellis's fault. "We've done all right. As well as we've been able, anyway. There are a lot of stones unturned as yet."

"Well, then you'll be interested in the news."

"Sir?"

"That's one of the reasons I'm here." He smiled as if conveying good news. "I think the final stone has just been turned."

Steve was genuinely eager to hear about that. "Oh, really?"

"I met with the coroner and Deputy Ellis this morning, and the evidence has finally come together to our satisfaction. It was that grizzly you shot, 318. We're sure of it."

Oh, are you now? Steve was in a quandary. How could he question what the sheriff was saying without implying the sheriff didn't know what he was saying? "Did you get some new information?"

"Well, final conclusions. From the autopsy of your brother's body and the autopsy of the bear, we've been able to match things up."

"The autopsy of the bear? You mean, a subsequent autopsy?"

Collins lost momentum at that question. "Well, the autopsy."

"Sheriff, I performed that autopsy, and I didn't find anything to establish that 318 was the attacking bear. As a matter of fact, I was planning on revisiting the site of the killing today, hoping to find something I may have missed."

"Well, now you don't have to."

Steve didn't want to argue. He didn't want to be obstinate. But this was happening just a little too fast. "I'm sorry, sir, but I think I'm missing something here. Are you saying that Deputy Ellis concurred with this?"

"Of course. The coroner based his conclusion on the pathology report, and we accepted that conclusion."

The pathology report. Yes, on paper the pathologist said Cliff had died from a bear attack, but in person, when grilled by Marcus DuFresne, the pathologist had been uncertain about what had caused Cliff's death. And Tracy Ellis? Her change of mind almost smelled political. If she'd agreed to the bear theory at all, she must have been dragged kicking and screaming.

Collins pressed ahead. "Anyway, I wanted you to know right away. I knew it would be a load off your mind."

"Uh-huh." Thanks a lot, sheriff. You're really a big help. And what about Marcus DuFresne?"

"Who?"

"Marcus DuFresne, the game warden. He helped me shoot 318 and do the autopsy. Did he have something to add that I don't know about?"

"That could be."

Don't you know, Collins? "You didn't talk to him yourself?"

"No, but I'm sure Deputy Ellis did."

"Uh-huh." Steve was not at a loss for words at this moment—only words he could use.

"You seem uncomfortable."

"Well—" Choose your words carefully, Steve. "Of course, you had no real obligation to consult me before reaching your conclusion."

"Did you have another conclusion?" The question was almost a dare.

Steve had his doubts and concerns, of course. Why else couldn't he sleep last night? But he only admitted, "No. Not yet."

Collins smiled to keep things pleasant. "Well, look at it this way. We can put this whole thing behind us now. You can get back to your work at the university, just get on with your life, and most of all, your sister-in-law Evelyn can get on with hers. It's over. She's free to go her way and rebuild."

She was "free" now? Steve didn't mean to be offended, but he was. "So . . . you're saying she's no longer a suspect."

That made Collins edgy. "Right. She never was a serious suspect to begin with. It was just that we had to consider all possibilities."

"But now that you've closed the case, you say she's free to go?"

Collins looked at Steve through half-squinted eyes. "Unless you have good reason for us to reopen the case, yes."

POW!

The soft-drink can, already riddled with bullet holes, took one more bullet and flipped off the top of the log to join several others in the gravel, all bent, twisted, and ventilated.

Pow! Another can went sailing. Then another. Then another.

Tracy stood near her patrol car in the middle of an old gravel pit outside West Fork, the favorite spot of the valley's shooters and plinkers. The policy was pack it in, shoot it up, pack it out, but still the signs were everywhere: fragments of soft-drink cans and plastic jugs, bullet-riddled boxes, spent shells. Tracy had come with a grocery bag full of empty cans, set aside for moments like this. She had awakened that morning expecting a full day, but after this morning's meeting it seemed she would have time to vent some steam. And after this morning's meeting, she had plenty of steam to vent.

She was just reloading her .38 from a box of cartridges on the hood of her car when she spotted Steve's big camper lumbering down the gravel road into the pit. This guy was a hunter. He'd found her, and it hadn't taken him long. Now she'd have to talk to him, and she wasn't looking forward to it. To gain some time, she went to set up more cans.

Steve rolled to a stop by the patrol car and watched her take position and put on ear protectors. She had to know he was there, but she was plainly ignoring him. He swung the door open, hopped down from the cab, and then paused as she opened up with the revolver and another six cans; one per shot went flying.

He almost forgot his anger. She was good.

Tracy lowered the gun, removed the ear protectors, and finally turned her head to look at Steve. She must have discerned his mood. "Want to shoot a few cans?"

He hadn't given it a thought before this, but as a matter of fact, he did. It could help. Without a word, he walked to the log to set up six more targets. She went to the hood of her car to reload. When he returned, she had the gun and ear protectors ready.

"Pretend they killed your brother," she said.

Within six seconds every can had flipped and tumbled to the ground.

He handed her the gun, removed the ear protectors, and waited for her to speak.

She went to reload. "So you've heard from Sheriff Collins."

He turned to face her directly. "I want to know if you agree with him."

She flipped the cylinder open and let the shells fall into her hand. "Why do you think I'm out here killing cans?"

"So explain this to me! I don't—"

"Maggie Bly is dead."

"What?" He stared at her, disbelieving.

She slipped the reloaded gun into her holster. "She went back to Hyde River last night, and somebody killed her. We found her shoulder bag and one shoe near the river, and some of her blood, but no body—so far."

"No body! How do you know she's dead?"

"Trust me. She's dead, and she'll never be found. Just like— pardon me—the upper half of your brother's body."

Steve joined Tracy by the car just so he could lean against it. "I suppose this has something to do with the weird, backward ways of those people up there?"

"They—have their own ways of settling things."

"Then Collins lied to me."

"No, he believes what he wants to believe, and he wants to believe a grizzly killed your brother."

"So what does he think killed Maggie?"

Tracy only chuckled and shook her head. "I got Collins to drive up to Hyde River last night to help me investigate. We questioned Levi Cobb because he had arrived at the scene of the crime just before I did. But all we got was another sermon about sin and repenting. We finally ascertained that he didn't actually see what happened.

"We talked to Harold Bly—well, Sheriff Collins did—and they discussed hunting and fishing. Then Les brought up Maggie, you know, just brought her up casually, and asked him where Maggie was, and Harold said that they'd had a disagreement and she'd left him and gone to her mother's, but they were still in touch, and Les said he was sorry to hear about the disagreement, and then we left."

"That was it?" Steve asked, his tone incredulous.

"Steve, there are no witnesses and no body. Levi says he heard Maggie, but he never saw her. So if Harold Bly says Maggie is still alive, it must be true." Her sarcasm was obvious. "Case closed."

"Well, what if it is true?"

"Then nothing happened to Maggie."

"And if nothing happened to Maggie, then—"

"Then we don't have to suspect any conspiracy to commit murder, and we can fall back on the grizzly idea to explain your brother's death. Simple. Easy. Just the way Les Collins likes it. Once the coroner said it was a bear attack, Collins wouldn't hear another word."

"But why?"

"It's the whole Hyde Valley Thing. Harold Bly, the fears, the superstitions, all of it."

Steve crossed his arms. "And of course, you're finally going to explain all that to me."

"I don't suppose there's any chance you'll just leave the valley, help Evelyn get started again, and just drop this whole thing?"

He shook his head. "You should have met my brother when he was alive."

She nodded with understanding. "Just thought I'd ask." Now she drew a breath, whistled it out slowly, and tried to think of where to start. "This is going to sound so crazy."

"It's sounding that way already, so go ahead."

"Les Collins grew up in Hyde River. He's really a part of that culture. He's got a lot of that town in his blood, okay?"

"So there's a political connection of sorts."

"Well, yeah, right. Those people helped elect him, he has strong ties with them, and he respects the—" Tracy stopped and took a deep breath before saying, "Well, we call it the Oath."

"The Oath?"

Tracy looked heavenward, still groping. "It's a—oohhh—let's see. Okay, now you remember I told you there were superstitions and traditions up there?"

"Uh-huh."

"Well, I don't know exactly how this one started, but somewhere back in the town's history a bunch of the townspeople took an oath of secrecy, a pledge that they wouldn't reveal town secrets to outsiders, and that's still a town tradition. Needless to say, it makes police work difficult. We can't get witnesses, we can't get information, nobody will inform on anybody else—and there are a couple reasons for that. One, if you blab something you're not supposed to, well . . . remember what almost happened in the tavern? People have been clobbered for saying too much. Not that we in the sheriff's department ever hear about it, mind you. The other reason is—" She hesitated, then laughed nervously. "Well, you remember Maggie saying that your brother got eaten? You know, eaten up?"

"Of course. I thought she meant the bear."

Tracy shook her head. "That wasn't what she was talking about. There's a superstition that goes back as far as the secret Oath, I mean clear back to the founding of the town. There are folks up there in the valley who believe—" She hesitated, then gave a nervous laugh. "—that there's a—a big dragon lurking up in the woods, a dragon that eats people."

She looked at Steve and saw the reaction she expected: a look of total incredulity. She pressed on. "Hey, you heard Levi and Maggie talking about it. You saw how they really believed what they were saying. To a lot of the Hyde River folks, the dragon's real. They really believe it's out there."

Steve winced at the absurdity of it. "How? How can they believe such a thing?"

"You're an outsider, Steve, remember that. It's hard to understand how powerful a tradition can be if you never grew up here. I don't know how to describe it. The Irish have their leprechauns, the Scots have the Loch Ness monster, every kid grows up with the boogieman in his closet.... Listen, I can still remember my grandmother telling me that if I wasn't a good girl the dragon was going to come and eat me, and yeah, I believed it. You get that idea pounded into your head right along with Santa Claus and the tooth fairy."

"But usually we outgrow things like that."

"Santa Claus, yes. The tooth fairy, yes. The dragon . . . no way."

"But has anyone ever seen it?" Steve posed the question only to point out its obvious answer.

"Well, even if they did they wouldn't talk about it. There are the old tales, though, about people seeing it."

Steve smiled wryly. Sure. There were also people who had seen UFOs, Sasquatches, ghosts, and the Virgin Mary in the clouds, mainly because they wanted to. "Well, that doesn't prove much."

"I know," Tracy said. "But there's more to this belief. And it affects your brother's death."

"I'm listening."

"Okay. Let's say I'm Harold Bly, owner and president of the Hyde Mining Company, the company that built that town from the beginning. Now Harold's not much of anything when you measure him against the high rollers of the outside world, but in

Hyde Valley, with his land holdings and money and his family line, plus his power to provide or deny jobs, he is numero uno."

"Like you said, the godfather of Hyde Valley."

"Right. So suppose I'm Harold Bly, and I find out my wife is having an affair with some outsider, and I want to—"

"Carry out vengeance?"

"Carry out vengeance. Of course I'd want to cover it up, make it look like something else caused it."

"You're not serious—"

She knew this was going to be tough to explain. "You should try being a cop in this valley. Some things go beyond reason."

"You're actually suggesting that someone cut up my brother?"

"Steve, I'm only saying that if that is what happened, the perpetrators would have had an automatic cover-up. The Hyde River people have an Oath, especially when it comes to the dragon, and if they had any notion the dragon was responsible, you can be sure they'd never say a thing about it; they'd deny the whole thing. People are afraid up there. They're afraid of each other, and a lot of them are afraid of the dragon. And let me tell you something else: The myth isn't fading with time. If anything, the dragon is bigger now, and more hungry, and people are more scared than ever. I don't know why that's happening, but I notice it every time I go up there. You got only a small taste of it in the tavern."

Steve recalled it. "That friend of Doug's said it was something they just don't talk about, and he just about got killed for saying that much."

"And there you are." Then she added pointedly, "And Sheriff Collins knows all this. He knows the rules. So lately it's gotten tough, and kind of weird. Sometimes—if we even hear about it, that is—something shady will happen, and we won't be able to find any witnesses or evidence to build a case, and we'll end up saying, 'Well, the dragon must have done it,' meaning the case is probably unsolvable and the dragon is being blamed for it. You heard Maggie and Levi. As far as they're concerned, the dragon ate your brother. Forget human perpetrators."

"But wait a minute. You have evidence. You have my brother's body!"

Tracy brought her hands together with a clap. "Now we're up to the present, and you can see why I'm out here blasting away at cans." Her voice rose with excitement. "This is the first time an outsider has crossed somebody in that valley and gotten killed and we actually have a body left over! It's the biggest lead we've ever had, and it is definitely worth pursuing!" Then she added with exasperation, "But I am not the sheriff of Clark County! I am not bound up in politics and keeping everybody happy and getting re-elected." With that, she drew her gun and indulged in one more shot, sending a can skittering across the gravel.

She smiled in satisfaction, then said, "So if you ask me, Maggie was two-timing her husband, her husband probably had her killed, and he had it staged so people would think it was the dragon. That will be the end of it. I can assure you, Maggie Bly's body will never be found. She's gone. And if anybody wants to know what happened to her, Harold Bly will tell you she left him and ran off. There are plenty of folks up there, though, who will positively believe the dragon ate her. Trust me. I grew up there."

Steve's mouth was dry. "And in Cliff's case . . . that's what it looked like."

Tracy saw the tremor that passed through Steve's body. Her voice was quiet as she said, "It's pretty horrible but that is what it looked like, that someone left half a body to get the rumors started, to get people thinking about the dragon. Then, somehow, they did away with Maggie's body altogether—there was no need to leave part of a body. Then the word gets around the town, the people are terrified, and now I'll guarantee you, they are not going to talk to anyone. I could be wrong, but I think there's a cloud of fear and superstition up there that some very ruthless people are hiding behind."

"Harold Bly."

"Well   " She shook her head. "What can we prove? All I know is, Harold's a direct descendant of the original Hyde family, and somehow this dragon thing is connected with his family, and I think he could be using that fact to scare people, to let them think he has some special connection with the dragon. All around that town, Harold Bly's the one to know, the one to please, and whatever you do, you don't cross him and you don't talk to outsiders."

"So why does Levi talk about the dragon?"

Tracy rolled her eyes. "It's his mission in life. He's superstitious just like the others, but some years ago he got super-saved, if you know what I mean. Now the dragon's a religious thing. He sees a message in it."

"And apparently he's not afraid."

"Well, for one thing, everyone thinks he's crazy, so they stay away from him. He survives because he has no credibility—and also because he could break every bone in your body if he had to."

Steve smiled at that remark.

Tracy shrugged and sighed away her exasperation. "But anyway, here I am with my hunches and theories and not a whole lot I can do about them. You saw what happened to your brother. You saw how terrified Maggie was. This isn't something a few underpaid, low-budget, backwoods cops want to mess with, not when it's easier to just get along, let things slide. I'm sure Collins is hoping you'll just go your way, content with the bear theory, content in knowing your sister-in-law is free of suspicion." Then she added, "And that is true, you know: Evelyn is not a suspect."

"She never should have been under suspicion," Steve said vehemently.

Tracy didn't want to rehash her reasons for questioning Evelyn. "Well, she's off the list, and so you can walk away from this whole thing if you want to."

They stood there in silence, just leaning on the car and looking at the bullet-riddled cans.

"I don't know if I can do that," Steve said finally.

"You can do it, Steve, and that's what makes me envy you. Remember, you don't have to live with these people. You don't have to hold down a job as a cop in Hyde Valley where no one will cooperate with you if there's a serious crime, you don't have to try to sleep at night wondering who's out there doing this sort of thing and how they might feel about you. You can get out."

"Somebody murdered my brother, and I think you're telling me that person will go free."

"Have you told Evelyn about all this?"

He paused, then said softly, "No."

"Why not?" He didn't have to answer before she said, "Let me guess: If you tell her Cliff was murdered she'll want to know why, and she doesn't know about the affair. Right?"

Steve nodded. "And I only want her to get better, to recover her senses. I don't know what finding out about Cliff and Maggie would do to her."

"I understand," Tracy said softly. "I guess you have to decide whether it's better for Evelyn to think her husband was killed by a bear or possibly murdered by a jealous husband."

He couldn't decide. Not yet.

"I guess all I'm saying is, you can walk away, Steve. You can put it all behind you. I envy that."

She took the box of cartridges off the hood of the car. "I've got to get going. I've given you enough to think about. Don't know what else you'll do here without a bear to hunt, but you can let me know." She opened the trunk and put the cartridges away. "But, Steve, one more thing."

She waited until he looked her way, and she had his full attention. "I can't tell you what to do, but just for the record, my duty is to the law and the people of this valley. I know you have some heavy issues to resolve, but please, don't make trouble, and don't break the law. If you break the law, I'll have to do my job. Remember that."

LEVI HAD the garage doors open to let in the sunlight. The phone company truck was about finished, but Levi was still waiting on new rear springs, so it sat patiently on the right side of the garage, its rear axle dropped out. Right now, the county's backhoe needed the hydraulic pump looked at. The boom and bucket were sluggish, the operator had told him.

"Heh, sluggish for the county has to be real sluggish," Levi told the backhoe, pulling his tool chest closer and searching through a drawer for the right wrench. "So, we'll check your hose fittings and make sure they're cinched up."

He rolled under the machine on his garage creeper, seeking out the hydraulic pump. "You get those hydraulic lines sucking air, you get downright wimpy, am I right? Now hold still, this ain't gonna hurt a bit—"

"Cobb!"

"Ah. Company," Levi muttered to the hydraulic pump. He was expecting visitors today. They hadn't announced they'd be coming, but he was expecting them anyway.

He rolled out from under the backhoe slowly, careful not to bang his head. There stood Vic Moore, the contractor, with three of his buddies. One was Phil Garrett, currently in Vic Moore's employ and looking downright bizarre with a bandage covering most of his head. He'd nearly lost his ear in a barroom brawl, but Levi knew it wasn't wise to mention it. The second was Andy Schuller, unemployed miner and regular fixture around the pool table at Charlie's. The third was Carl Ingfeldt, a wiry little cuss who had an irritating way of hanging around like a black fly, just looking for morsels of information to take back to Harold Bly.

"Good morning, gentlemen," Levi said, getting to his feet.

Vic Moore stepped forward, his thumbs tucked in his pants and his fingers around his belt. Levi noticed that he smelled bad. "We hear you've been talking to the police."

Levi nodded. "Yeah, Tracy Ellis, about my license tags."

Vic looked at his three backup men, and they exchanged knowing sneers. Vic turned back to Levi. "You lying son of a—"

Levi appeared relaxed, leaning against the backhoe, but he'd drawn a hunting knife from a sheath on his hip and now held it casually, checking the edge with his thumb. "I guess you're wondering about Maggie. Ain't that right, Carl?"

Carl tried to look cool and undaunted, but he nodded.

"We want to know why you're prying into Harold and Maggie's personal business," Vic said.

Levi looked at them quizzically. "If we're talking about Harold's business, why isn't Harold here?"

"We're his friends."

"But not Maggie's? You turned her away, Vic."

Vic didn't answer. He was staring at Levi's knife.

"I've used it before," Levi answered, seeing the question in Vic's eyes. "But only 'cause I had to. He got a piece of me, but I got a bigger piece of him. Took his nose off." Phil leaned forward. "I didn't say ear." Phil glowered at him. "Anyway, let's clear the air, gentlemen, so we can all get back to work. Maggie needed a place to stay, and I put her up. Tracy Ellis came looking for her because of what happened to that photographer."

Vic bristled at that. "And you talked to her!"

Levi looked puzzled. "She's Tracy Ellis, Vic! She grew up here. She knows about all this stuff!"

"She's a cop," Vic countered. "She's working for outside people. She's working for the law."

"So what did you tell her?" Carl demanded.

Levi shrugged. "Gave her my opinion. Told her I thought the dragon got him."

That seemed to be the only word that offended these guys. Andy shoved his way toward the front. "Why you—"

Levi gestured with the knife as Vic held Andy back. "Now, come on, just take a long look at how it'll go. You know Tracy and how she feels about my opinions. You know Collins, too, and where he stands. Soon as you bring in the dragon, he pulls out. And that's what happened. I got a call from him this morning, and he wanted to be sure I got the word: They've decided a grizz got the photographer and Maggie's just taken off and Harold's in the right as always and I should just go about my business and forget about the whole thing. As for that professor, I understand he's packing up and leaving, so that's that. Sure, I took a little chance, but now the cops aren't asking any more questions, the professor's gone, and everything's over, nice and smooth."

The men looked at one another, as if deciding whether or not they agreed with Levi's actions.

"As for the widow," Levi continued in an even tone, "she's out of this thing. Maybe she'll learn what her husband was doing and maybe not, but at least she can go home and get on with her life."

Vic asked, "So what if the cops come back?"

Levi couldn't believe he'd heard such a question. "Vic, have they ever come back?"

Vic and his buddies visibly relaxed. Vic turned toward the door, then turned back as if needing to get in the last word. "Cobb, someday you're gonna say too much. You watch yourself."

"Nice talking to you," said Levi.

"JUST ONCE, just once I'd like one straight answer to a question, I'd like—I'd like—" Steve caught himself ranting out loud and stopped. He was getting as bad as Levi. He threw down his notebook and slumped in the chair by the table in his motel room. Should he just pack up, leave, and drop the whole matter? If he did, the death of his brother, and its true cause, would haunt him forever. Should he stay and investigate further? Where? What? Who could he talk to? Who would talk to him? The police were no longer with him, and the local folks had been against him from the start.

And what about Evelyn? What could he tell her, and what point would there be in doing so? He couldn't prove Cliff was killed by a bear, but he couldn't prove otherwise, so why cast doubt on the bear theory and raise all the other questions that would only hurt her? If it wasn't a bear, then Cliff was murdered. If Cliff was murdered, then there had to be a reason: the affair. But with Maggie gone, and actually, he didn't know if she was dead or alive, there was no way to prove the affair had ever happened. So why tell Evelyn when so little could be established anyway?

And what about Evelyn's memory? That might still return, and then—

The phone rang. This was either going to be the key to it all or more confusion, he thought.

He grabbed up the phone beside the bed. "Hello."

"Steve? Dan Cramer."

Steve sat on the bed. Dan Cramer was a biochemist at the university. At the sound of Dan's voice Steve remembered: the saliva sample taken from Cliff's body! In all the tangle of other information and events he'd forgotten about it. "Dan, hi. What's up?"

"Well, I don't know." Dan had a hint of laughter in his voice as if he'd just been the victim of a practical joke. "FedEx just delivered your saliva sample, and I've run some tests on it."

"Yeah?" Steve said, trying to hold back his impatience. Come on, Dan, just tell me.

"Well, first of all, we ran the electrophoresis, and it wasn't bear saliva, and it wasn't human. As a matter of fact, the bands we got ruled out any kind of mammal."

"No mammalian indications at all?"

"No. The DNA rules that out."

Great. More noninformation. "Well, is it saliva?"

"Oh, it's saliva, all right, but you're in the wrong part of the country to be sending in samples like this. Looking at the amino acids and the enzymes, I'd say you've got a reptile."

Steve's mind came to an abrupt halt as if hitting a wall. "What?"

"It's a common pattern for large lizards. The closest match would be . . . oh, black tagu, savannah monitor, something along that line." There was a protracted silence. "Steve?"

"Dan, this was my brother. I really hope this isn't a joke—"

Dan was firm. "Steve, this is no joke. I'm giving it to you straight."

"You're sure? You didn't get the samples mixed up or anything?"

"No, I gave this one priority."

"Can you fax your report to me?"

"What's the number?"

Steve realized as soon as he said it that he had no number. He didn't even know where he might find a fax machine. "I don't know what I was thinking. I doubt if they've ever seen a fax machine in this town."

"What's the address?"

Steve ran a hand through his hair. This was exasperating. "My sister-in-law is getting out of the hospital today. I was thinking of checking out of this place."

"Well, if you're through up there you can just see the report when you get back."

Steve made an instant decision. "I realize I'm not through up here yet. I might stay a little longer. Listen, as soon as I know for sure what I'm doing and where I'll be, I'll call you." Reptile? Large lizard? "I may be here awhile."

IF CHARLIE MACK was moving up in the world, he sure didn't feel like it. Sure, he was getting help from some of his patrons—the ones who didn't mind working—and Harold Bly had sent some men over. They had cut a nice-size doorway through the wall between the tavern and the mercantile. But he had really hoped Harold would help supervise the operation. Charlie was finding it almost impossible to run one business while renovating the other. He was constantly running back and forth through that doorway to keep things moving, and his feet were starting to hurt, his patience was growing short, and—

"Hey!" he shouted to two men on ladders. "Where're you going with that?"

They were trying to lower an old Indian canoe from the ceiling of the mercantile but had underestimated its weight. "Not far, Charlie."

"Well, just leave it there, leave it there."

"Thanks."

"Let's get going on the floor, guys. We have to scrub the whole thing so we can paint it."

"Where're the mops?"

"Back of the tavern."

"Where?"

He yelled, "Ask Melinda!"

Oh, well. Sure, it was busy, hectic, about to drive him crazy, but someday it would all be worth it. Someday this place would be rolling right along, doing business like it used to before Ebo Denning bought it. Someday Charlie would be able to pay Harold back, and it would all be his.

If he lived long enough.

He went behind the old oak counter and pretended to tinker with the cash register, a new digital machine he didn't even know how to operate. The thing came with instructions, but he hadn't read them. He couldn't keep his mind on it. His hand went to his chest, and he rubbed a burning itch over his heart. It was worse today. When it had first shown up a week ago, he thought it must be heartburn. But it wouldn't go away, not even with Alka-Seltzer.

It had to be nerves. Sure, that's what it was, with all the stress and the bookwork and the inventory—nerves. Stress. Hives, maybe.

Or maybe it was Harold. Harold had . . . connections. He had heard Harold could make things like this happen.

What if Harold's trying to muscle me out? He buys into the business, then gets rid of his partner, and everything becomes his, just like the rest of this town! Well, Charlie had dreams, ambitions, and they did not necessarily include Harold Bly. Harold had his empire already. Charlie wanted one of his own, even if it was a little one. He deserved it.

Charlie struck the counter with his fist. I deserve it, he thought. I deserved it when Sam Calley had this place, before he sold it to Ebo!

Sam's selling a store to Ebo Denning five years ago had erased Sam Calley from Charlie's list of friends, and it was only Ebo's leaving that finally made things right. Sure, Ebo had taken good care of the place. The mercantile was well stocked and well organized when Charlie bought it, with all the dry goods neatly arranged on shelves and the aisles clearly designated according to contents. But as far as Charlie was concerned, it was still Ebo's mercantile; it still bore his personality, his style, and Charlie couldn't stand having the slightest reminder of that black man around.

So the old photographs of miners, loggers, and pioneer families had to come down from the walls only because Ebo had hung them there; the huge whipsaw came down from the ceiling so a mural could be painted on it and it could be rehung as something new and improved and not Ebo's whipsaw. The antique tools hanging all around the ceiling, all the old hammers, saws, and plows, the wringer washer, the bunghole bore, and the blacksmith's tools could stay since they'd belonged to the original settlers of the town and the townsfolk would miss them. But Charlie rearranged them his way; they could not remain where Ebo had them. The Indian canoe would be a problem, but he'd deal with that later. Ebo's old cash register was gone, and good riddance.

"Charlie!" It was Doug, dropping by for a look-see and carrying a cold bottle of beer.

"Oh, hi, Doug. What do you think?"

"Looking good, Charlie," Doug said, clearly impressed. "I mean, like it's gonna look good."

"What are you up to these days?"

"Running the skidder for Harold. We're logging off that forty acres above Black Rock."

Charlie nodded approvingly. "Great to be working, I'll bet."

"You know it."

There was a pause. Charlie tried to sound disinterested as he asked offhandedly, "So whatever became of that bear thing?"

Doug smiled a little. "Talked to Vic Moore this morning. It's over. Sheriff settled on the bear, the grizzly they shot. So we were right. The cops are out of it, and that wimpy prof who thinks he's a hunter is packing it up and leaving."

Charlie forced a smile and leaned on the cash register. "He's going, eh?"

"Yeah, and it's a good thing for him. A guy like that just wouldn't do very well around here."

"Well, he shot Herman!"

"Hey, any one of us could have shot Herman. It don't take a college education to do that." He took another swig of his beer, then regarded Charlie. "You feeling okay? You don't look so hot."

Charlie rubbed his forehead with the back of his hand. "Just working too hard, I guess."

"Well, quit worrying," Doug said, then went over to talk to Andy Schuller and Carl Ingfeldt, who were doing the finishing work on the new doorway.

As soon as Doug walked away, Charlie hurried into the storeroom in the back, past the floor-to-ceiling shelves and into the small washroom. He closed the door and locked it, then leaned over the toilet, his arms braced against the wall, afraid he might throw up. He gasped for breath, trying to calm himself, waiting for the trembling to stop.

The hunter was leaving? The cops were dropping the whole case? So now things would go on as before. Now . . .

He went to the mirror over the sink and unbuttoned his shirt. The sore, red spot was not only still there, it was worse. The red rash had turned a dark brown, and there was an odor coming from it. He hurriedly pulled some paper towels from the dispenser, ran some cold water over them, and tried to dab the area clean. Some brown ooze came off on the towel, but the mark itself wouldn't go away. He held the wet towel there for a long moment as if the cool water would relieve the fierce burning, but there was no relief.

He began to shudder. "Oh, please. I'm only trying to survive around here. I didn't mean it—please—I swear, I didn't mean it."

One of the more bizarre incidents of the great flood of 1953 was the washing out of the Hyde River Cemetery in which some thirty-six coffins were unearthed and carried away by the raging floodwaters. Of the thirty-three coffins recovered, eighteen contained no remains and were apparently buried empty. What became of the bodies? Were there any bodies to begin with? The secret of the empty coffins was buried with them in a new cemetery and has remained a mystery to this day.

From World of the Dim Unknown: True Accounts
of the Bizarre and the Supernatural,
edited by Fraser Sullivan

———

SEVEN

Hyde Hall

THURSDAY AFTERNOON, four days after the trucker found her on Wells Peak, Evelyn was ready to go home. Her physical strength had returned; her injuries, none of them major, were well on their way to healing. Being home again with her sons, the dog, and her folks would be the best medicine.

Her son Travis, athletic and handsome at eighteen, had driven the family pickup with its camper back from the parking area at the base of the Staircase Trail. Now, with Travis driving, her mother, Audrey, sitting beside her, and her father, Elbert, following in his Ford, Evelyn stopped by the Tamarack Motel in West Fork to visit with Steve one more time before heading back over Johnson's Pass to Oak Springs and home. They met in the parking lot outside Steve's room. Evelyn wanted to be outdoors, in the sunshine. She had asked her parents and her son for a few private moments with Steve.

"You look great," Steve said, and meant it.

"I'm standing. I'm walking, I'm talking. That's got to be some improvement."

Evelyn wasn't beautiful in the traditional sense, but Steve had always thought her very attractive. She was tall and strong, normally had a mischievous glint in her eyes, and tended to face life with a patiently assertive nature and a sense of humor that he had always admired.

"So we know about me," she said. "How are you doing?"

He knew she wouldn't accept any answer but an honest one. "I'm sad, I'm angry, I'm unsettled."

"I still can't believe it," Evelyn said softly. "I can't believe Cliff's gone." Her eyes filled with tears.

"I know," Steve said softly and put his arms around her. "I know."

Evelyn leaned against him for a moment, feeling the comradeship of grief. Then she straightened. "I've still got to make the funeral arrangements, and the boys really need me right now."

"I'll be glad to help any way I can," Steve said.

Evelyn smiled. "Thanks. I really appreciate that. But you've done so much already." She nodded in the direction of her parents, who were standing by the camper talking quietly. "Mom and Dad will be helping me with what needs to be done. And I'm going to take a few weeks off from my job." Evelyn was a CPA with a firm in Oak Springs. "Tim Johnson—he's one of the partners—says he'll cover my accounts until I go back. He says I should take as much time as I need. They're a great bunch, just like family."

"Sounds like a good group," Steve agreed. "I'm glad."

Evelyn nodded. "So, as the saying goes, I'll just try to take it one day at a time." She smiled. "Or even one step at a time. I'm in God's hands. Nobody ever dies without someone questioning why, but, well, God has His ways, and we just have to trust Him."

Steve listened intently, deeply moved. Evelyn would rebuild her life; he had no doubts about that.

He thought of Tracy Ellis's words: You can walk away, Steve. You can put it all behind you. If only it were so. If only he could move on, like Evelyn, not burdened with what he had seen, what he knew, what he still needed to know. For her sake, though, Steve kept his thoughts to himself.

Then Evelyn asked Steve about his own plans. "Oh, I have a few matters to clear up here," he said vaguely, hoping she wouldn't ask him what they were.

She didn't. Instead, she hugged him once more and said, "Steve, thanks again for everything. I'll call you about the memorial service."

Tears filled Steve's eyes, and pulling back, he put his hand lightly on Evelyn's shoulders and looked directly into her eyes. "Take good care of yourself, okay?"

"I will," she promised. "You, too." Then she walked to the truck. Just before she climbed into the cab next to her son, Evelyn turned and gave him one last wave good-bye.

Steve knew she'd thanked him for killing the bear, for clearing up the whole question of Cliff's death. As far as he was concerned, her thanks were premature, and that pained him.

Evelyn, Audrey, and Travis drove away in the truck and camper, and Elbert followed. For them, Hyde Valley was history, a memory to be buried.

For Steve, Hyde Valley was still the haunting, tormenting present.

THE PHONE call came soon afterward, while Steve was studying the Forest Service maps of the area, planning his own private scouting mission on Wells Peak. To hear the phone ring perplexed him a little. As he reached for the receiver he was going down the list of people who had the number and might call: the sheriff? Doubtful. That was over. Fish and Game? Same answer. Evelyn? On the road. Dan Cramer? Steve hadn't gotten back to him yet. Tracy?

"Hello."

"*Allo,* Dr. Benson, *síl vous plâit.*"

Now this he certainly didn't expect. What was that supposed to be, a French accent? It was poorly done, whatever it was.

He answered smoothly, "This is Dr. Benson. Who is this?"

"A friend, Doctor." The voice was low, breathy, creepy. "A friend who knows what really 'appened in Hyde River."

For real? A crank? Steve was hungry for information in any case. "I'm listening."

"I have heard you are leaving, that the case is closed. That is bad, Doctor. There are th gs you still need to know."

How far should I go with this guy? How far is safe? "Well, let's see if you can tell me something I don't already know."

The voice dropped to deliver the first gem. "Maggie Bly is dead."

"Oh? Then you know of a body somewhere?"

No answer.

"I know she's missing. Some people think she's dead. What I'm asking you is, if she's dead, what happened to her body?"

The caller ignored the question. "She was having an affair with your brother."

"I know that, too."

The voice was clearly disappointed. "Oh. You already know that."

"Well, how about we get back to the question you didn't answer? If Maggie Bly is dead, where is her body?"

The voice hesitated, then tried, "You are a hunter, *oui*? You kill big game. You kill bears."

"I'm a wildlife biologist. I study bears."

"But you kill them! You killed the big grizzly who killed your brother!"

"That's what I'm told."

"Then I will tell you."

Silence. Where'd he go? "Hello? Are you there?"

"Oui. I must tell you—" It sounded very much like he did not want to tell Steve anything. Then he finally got it out. "There is a big—umm—creature in the mountains. A big creature ate Maggie Bly, and that is why her body will never be found. The creature ate your brother too."

Okay, here we go. "What kind of creature?" Steve wanted to push a little, make the guy really say it.

The voice was quite flustered. "I—I cannot say, *monsieur*. It is not good to speak of it."

"Are you talking about the dragon?"

The voice stuttered, hemmed, and hawed. Finally, "I am sorry, *monsieur*, I cannot talk about—about that. You must look into it yourself, you see?"

"Baloney. I've heard about the dragon, just like I've heard about Santa Claus and the tooth fairy. I'm looking for some hard information about who killed my brother. If you can't give me that—"

"But—" Now the voice was sounding desperate. "You must go after the dragon. You—you must kill it before it kills anyone else!"

Now this was a new twist. "You want me to kill the dragon for you?"

"*Oui, oui, monsieur.*"

"So tell me where to find it."

This guy sounded scared. "I—I cannot talk about the dragon."

Steve wanted to hang up on this jerk, but he said nothing and stayed on the line. What mattered at this point was that somebody was talking, somebody desperate.

"*Monsieur!*"

"I'm still here."

"Do you know where Old Town is?"

"Old Town?"

"*Oui.*"

"Never heard of it."

"Maggie Bly was killed in Old Town, in Hyde Hall."

Hmm. That sounded like real information. Maybe. "Hyde Hall in Old Town?"

"That is where Maggie went that night, and she was never seen again. Go there. This is where your search for the dragon begins. I will call again, *oui*?"

"I may not be at this number."

There was a long silence, and then the man asked, "You are leaving?"

"No, I'll be around a while. Please call again sometime."

"But how will I know—?"

"Call me on my car phone. Here's the number." Steve gave the phony Frenchman the number even as he doubted the wisdom of it. "If you're sincere about this, you'll reach me sooner or later."

"*Merci, monsieur.*"

"Good night."

"*Au revoir.*" Click.

Steve sat at the table a moment, reviewing the conversation. Tracy Ellis said Maggie had gone back to Hyde River, but she hadn't mentioned anything about Old Town. He looked at the Forest Service map and found Hyde River easily enough, a helter-skelter cluster of little black squares in the narrow river valley. But where was Old Town? He couldn't find it on the map. Tracy Ellis would know, but bringing her in would bring in the whole sheriff's department, and they didn't want to pursue this thing any further—if anything, they'd stand in his way. So okay. This was his investigation now.

Levi Cobb. He'd been with Maggie toward the end, lived in Hyde River, and seemed willing—or at least able—to talk. He would be a logical first step. Steve knew he might get nothing but superstition and sermonizing, but somewhere in all that gospel soup there might be morsels of truth, something he could pursue.

He started gathering up his clothes, his shaving kit, his hunting gear. He would check out of the Tamarack and get closer to Hyde River, plant himself deeper in the meandering gorge of Hyde Valley. He'd live in the camper if necessary, but he had to work himself into the fabric of the place, breathe it, smell it, get a feel for it. The truth was hiding up there somewhere, and it wasn't about to come to him. He'd have to stalk it, hunt it down.

But what about the risk, the danger? His presence would not be appreciated. He thought of the superstitions. The Oath. Cliff's body. Maggie's blood. We don't call 911.

Well, he'd just have to be ready for anything.

In a few trips, he'd loaded all his gear into the back of the camper. Then he climbed in and closed the door.

He reached into the narrow clothes closet near the door and brought out a sturdy, foam-lined case. His .357 magnum. He'd load it, and he'd wear it at all times. From a cabinet above the tiny sink he grabbed his hunting knife, in a sheath, and strapped it on his belt. It, too, would be a part of him from now on. He jammed cartridges into the 30.06 then uncased his automatic shotgun and filled the magazine. He strapped the rifle into a rack above the front bunk; the shotgun he'd keep in the cab.

The dragon. Even as he was dropping cartridges into the .357, the thought skipped lightly through his mind, What if it's real? What if there's an undiscovered life form out there? What if . . .

He strapped on the holster, dropped in the revolver, and snapped the holster shut. He was ready.

STEVE FOUND Levi Cobb outside his garage, his head and shoulders inside the engine compartment of a monstrous, articulated front-loader, a huge yellow machine with eight-foot, knobby tires, a deep loading bucket in front, and a hinge in the middle that enabled it to turn incredibly tight corners. Levi had to use a small scaffold to reach the engine compartment. Steve could hear Levi talking, but there didn't seem to be anyone else around. "You oughta see these plugs. I mean, if those county boys let 'em get this bad you should say something!"

"Mr. Cobb?"

Levi came out into the daylight, a wrench the size of his arm in his greasy hand. He took one look at the big, dark-haired man standing there with a hunting knife on one hip and a sidearm on the other, and then just sighed and leaned against the loader's eight-foot-high rear tire. "I thought you'd left." His tone said he wished Steve had left.

Steve tried to relax. He didn't want this guy to feel threatened. "Nope, I'm still here. Still hunting." He approached the loader. "I was hoping you could help me."

"Not likely."

"Mr. Cobb." Steve lowered his voice. "Is it true? Is Maggie Bly dead as well?"

Levi pulled a shop cloth from his rear pocket and started wiping the grease off his wrench. "I believe she is. There are some who say otherwise."

Steve pressed it. "How did she die, Mr. Cobb? Do you have any idea?"

"I have my views."

"Did she die the same way as my brother?"

Levi's expression was troubled, but he didn't answer.

Steve tried again. "I really need to know. I've been told there's a creature who might have killed them both. If that's true, I'd like to go after it."

Finally Levi looked up from his rag and his wrench and down at Steve with narrowed, intense eyes. "Mr. Benson, you're about a hundred years too late. I think you just need to let your brother and Maggie rest—and leave, before somebody sees you talking to me."

"I only want information."

"My information you wouldn't believe anyway."

"Let me be the judge of that."

Levi was clearly flustered and poked his head into the big machine as if to give himself time to think. When he finally spoke again, his voice was muffled inside the engine compartment. "Well, I'll tell you one thing: All that iron you're carrying ain't gonna make you one bit safer."

Steve came right back with, "I'll have to be the judge of that as well. I have a job to do, Mr. Cobb, and I intend to finish it."

Levi's head came out of the engine compartment, his bushy brows lowered over his eyes. "Benson, the creature you're after you can't kill with guns. But you listen to me. You've got an attitude that'll kill you. You'll be dead before you even know you're in trouble, and I don't want to be a part of that."

Steve looked away. Tracy had talked about Levi's sermonizing. He'd had fair warning.

So Steve switched subjects. "Then can you tell me how to get to Hyde Hall?"

Now that hit pay dirt. Levi stopped short and glared at him. Steve's tacky French tipster must have been right on the money.

The big mechanic thought the question over for a significant amount of time, then sighed resignedly and slid down the huge tire to the ground. "You can look, but you won't find anything."

"I can try."

"It's private property."

"I'll take responsibility for trespassing."

His objections answered, Levi stooped down and scratched a map in the dirt with the wrench. "Go north through town, and right past the train of ore cars. The highway'll turn to dirt road, and you'll see a grove of cottonwoods."

Steve had no trouble following Levi's directions. He came to a little gravel turnoff, which Levi had described. He put the big camper into four-wheel drive and pushed through the gravel and high grass until he found a cubbyhole behind some old firs in which to hide the camper. With the engine shut down and the door open, he could hear the sound of the river.

He slipped into his camouflage jacket, slung the 30.06 over his shoulder, and locked up the camper. From there, it was a short hike through tall grass and flood-killed snags to the bank of the Hyde River.

The river, at its summer level, was wide and slow here, with extensive shores of smooth river rock. The air was just a little breezy right now, the applause of fluttering aspen leaves and the quiet sigh of the river the only sounds. Steve sank into the tall grass near a barkless, tangled tree and surveyed the river as far as he could see in either direction, carefully scanning the foliage on both shores for movement. He listened for sounds and took several deep breaths, sorting through the smells. He remained motionless.

A familiar tension coursed through his body. It had been a long time since he'd felt this instinctive clue that there were two hunters in these woods, each hunting the other. Perhaps it was brought on by all the previous circumstances, but he went with it. He would not proceed until he knew if anything was out there and what it was.

After several minutes he'd inventoried some swallows swooping for bugs, an osprey patrolling the river for fish, and the usual flurry of insects. Still, he couldn't shake the feeling that something else was around here somewhere. With caution, his eyes making steady sweeps of the surrounding landscape, he set out along the shore, doubling back toward the town, walking on the smooth, flat rocks. He was in the open, so he did not feel safe, but he was able to cover a lot of ground quickly.

Farther down, the river narrowed, and the current became swift and deep, splashing noisily in crystalline fans over the rocks and swirling in deep green pools. It was a beautiful sight that brought thoughts of rods, flies, and lures. There could be a nice big cutthroat right over there in that deep pool below the ripple. If Cliff were here right now, he'd be setting up his camera . . .

Well, he could admire all that beauty some other time, perhaps. He kept going, hurrying over gravel spits and pushing his way through the tall shoregrass.

Then he saw a teetering structure of graying, weathered boards, obscured by willows and alders.

He thought of what Levi had said. "Old Town's just what it sounds like, an old town. It's the old Hyde River before the town moved. It's a ghost town now, and nobody goes in there."

Just ahead, old pilings jutted out of the river, the remains of the wharf where the flatbottom boats used to tie up years ago. This was it, the once-bustling mining town on the river, now silent and decaying. Steve reached the pilings and could imagine where the old road down to the river used to be. He moved inland, pushing through tangled berry thickets and grass, then climbed up a shallow bank.

When he came over the crest, he knew he'd arrived. Old Town. The ruins were a gray and decrepit scar upon the wild and beautiful setting, a dismal boneyard where progress had come to a halt and decay took it from there. He could make out the main street, mostly overgrown with grass, thistles, and serviceberries, flanked on either side with the ruins of the old buildings. Most were reduced to piles of weathered boards, fallen all over each other like jackstraws. A few brick walls remained. The foundations were visible here and there, wherever the brush had not totally engulfed them. Some tall cottonwoods still stood in what may have been the town square, but for some reason, the firs, hemlocks, and pines never got reestablished here, only the brush. Young aspens and cottonwoods had made a start in the remains of the buildings, reaching up through the floors and finding open sky where the roofs used to be. But even these trees looked weak and diseased.

Steve sank to one knee in the grass and took some time to listen, look, smell. Part of him kept pointing out how unnecessary all this caution was; it was the middle of the day, the place was quiet, and except for birds and bugs it was deserted. But another part of him felt uneasy. These old ruins had a ghostly aura about them he could feel but couldn't explain. It was as if he'd desecrated a graveyard or was treading on sacred ground.

He didn't feel alone, either. Yes, it was a deep, primitive instinct, highly subjective, but he had learned to trust it. And yet the feeling had only gotten stronger the farther he ventured into this place.

All right. Hyde Hall. Where was it?

Levi had said Hyde Hall was the second building from the river, on the south side of the road and that it was directly across from the old Masonic Lodge, which Steve would recognize by the remains of its front porch. Now he approached a large, rectangular ruin, totally collapsed, with its porch steps upended and rotting. This must be the lodge, Steve thought.

He turned and studied the overgrown foundation and the three remaining walls across the street. This had once been a large structure, about sixty feet long, maybe thirty feet deep, with a massive stone fireplace at the center of the back wall. Hyde Hall. A meeting place, perhaps? A dance hall or community hall?

He approached slowly, carefully studying the ground. Someone had been here; that was easy to see. The grass was trampled and run over in several directions. The cops, most likely, scrambling to find out what had happened.

In the middle of the street he found a large patch of bare, rain-rutted ground. It was loose, dusty, and should have had footprints. Instead, it looked raked over, the surface brushed and smoothed out. Maybe the police had been combing through the soil looking for clues; he couldn't tell.

He froze.

There went that instinct again, warning him, seizing him by the guts and yanking for his attention.

He stood still, his hand on the strap of his rifle. No sound. No smell. He was facing Hyde Hall, and the river was off to his left, barely visible below the brow of its bank. He slowly turned his head to the left, toward the river, the movement steady, smooth, robotic, as his eyes took in the surroundings in segments.

He regarded the building next to Hyde Hall. No movement.

The road? Only brush, grass, patches of bare ground from here to the river.

Across the river? He eased his body around as the rifle came off his shoulder in a steady, fluid movement. Something over there didn't look right. Get down, get down! his instinct screamed.

With three long strides he reached the cover of tall grass and dropped to the ground, his blood pulsing through his fingers as they tightly gripped his rifle. His eyes focused on a stretch of steep hillside across the river and a little upstream, a spot where the firs and pines were tall and thick.

Danger! said his instinct. His stomach, twisting into knots, agreed.

Beyond the opposite bank, where a meadow of deep grass ended and the forest began, the vertical lines in the scenery—the tree trunks, hanging limbs, tall grass—were breaking up as if Steve were viewing the scene as a reflection in a cracked mirror. When there was no wind, the scene looked normal. But then a light breeze would stir the grass or make the trees sway, and the tree trunks would seemingly break in the middle as the tops swayed gently sideways and the lower portions remained steady.

Something was over there; he could sense it.

Another puff of wind bent the trees slightly; again their trunks appeared to break in the middle.

Steve tightened his grip on the rifle. He thought he could see a shape, a curve, a barely discernible arc.

Just like a hunter in a blind, he thought. Hidden. Camouflaged. Watching me.

His heart was pounding like a drum. Fear was setting in, and he began thinking defensively. How much distance between him and whatever it was? How fast would that thing move if it charged? How far would he have to run to find cover? Would he have time to fire a shot?

With a quick, fluid motion, he chambered a round and clicked off the safety.

If only he could see what it was. If only he could pinpoint its position—

Behind him he heard the sounds of rustling brush, of swishing grass. In the silence, as tense as he was, the sound startled him as if it were thunder.

He spun around and stood, raising the rifle to his shoulder.

Up the street, two hands went up. Between the raised hands he saw a big cowboy hat, a pair of wire-rimmed glasses, and a graying beard. "Hold your fire!"

Levi Cobb.

Steve exhaled as his body relaxed and the rifle came down. His hands and arms started shaking. Elk fever, they called it, the bodily reaction you sometimes got microseconds before or after a kill.

Levi Cobb relaxed too, lowering his hands and coming forward again, moving methodically through the brush growing in the street. "Didn't mean to sneak up on you. You're a little hard to see. You're pretty good."

Steve looked across the river again. The mirage, if it was a mirage, was gone; the spell had been broken. There was nothing across the river but meadow and forest, although some trees were swaying as if something had passed through them.

He turned to face Levi and slung the rifle over his shoulder. He didn't know whether to chew out this guy or thank him for coming, so he said nothing. Steve thought Levi seemed a bit disgruntled, too.

"I don't know why I'm out here. I really don't," Levi said. He gave Steve another look over, his eyes going from the rifle to the knife to the sidearm, and then scanning the camouflage clothing. "But I got a little nervous thinking about you traipsing around out here by yourself."

Here by myself, Steve thought. Armed to the teeth, perhaps overarmed, in a strange place he knew nothing about. He could easily inventory Levi's weaponry: zero.

"Am I being foolish?" he finally asked.

The question tickled Levi, and he smiled. "Oh, not yet, I suppose. You haven't shot anybody, have you?"

Steve smiled back. Relief was beginning to set in, and it did feel good not to be alone. "No. No, I haven't even seen anybody."

"Well, good enough. So let's get this taken care of so we can get out of here." He looked toward Hyde Hall. "I see you found it. What do you want to know?"

"Tell me about the other night when Maggie Bly disappeared."

"I didn't see much."

"But you know something."

Levi nodded, then recounted the events in detail, from the phone call from Tracy to the quick conversation with shotgun-toting Harold, to the harrowing moments in Old Town. He pointed out the road he'd come down, making guesses as to which way Maggie had come, even recalling the song she'd been singing.

Then, in the middle of Hyde Hall's crumbling remains, he pointed out the spot where he'd found the shoulder bag and the running shoe.

"And where was the blood?" Steve asked.

"Right here," said Levi, waving his hand over a general area near a big, flat stone set like a monument in the center of the building remains.

Steve noticed immediately that this area, like the dirt patch in the street, had been raked over. "What is all this raking I keep seeing?"

"Cover-up," Levi said simply. "People want to put this out of their minds as soon as they can, so they come out here and clean it all up, get rid of any signs."

There seemed to be no limit to the outrageous habits of Hyde River. "You mean somebody actually sanitized the area?"

Levi answered "Yep," with a little nod.

"Brushed away any footprints, any bloodstains?"

Levi nodded again.

"Who?"

"Oh—" Levi looked toward the river and thought it over. "I don't want to put the blame on Harold Bly, but it might be some folks working for him, you never know. It depends on who gets killed out here and who wants to hide the fact." He looked at the raked ground, then surveyed the ruins. "It worked with the others, but anymore, I don't know . . ."

"There are others?"

"Were others."

Steve stared at Levi. "I don't follow you."

Levi raised his hand to call a halt. "Let's go back a bit." He looked around at the sagging walls and the big fireplace. "You know where we're standing? You know anything about Hyde Hall?"

"Nothing."

"Well, it was built by old Benjamin Hyde, the town's founder. It was a meeting hall for the mining company, and they rented it out for socials, dances, big dinners. I think there were church meetings here for awhile, but that didn't last long." He gestured with his hands as he described the place. "They had a bar downstairs during the early days and rooms upstairs so folks could stop in on their way up and down the river."

Steve looked around at the size of the building, imagining how it must have been with windows, curtains, chandeliers, maybe a wide front porch with shady overhang and turned posts. He could imagine a big log fire in the fireplace, dinner at the tables, drinks at the bar, laughter and chatter and even the plinking of an old piano. It could have been that way—or maybe he was just recalling scenes from reruns of *Gunsmoke*.

"They had some ladies for hire in the rooms upstairs, and a few hangings from a tree out back. You see, this was the hub of the town. Everything happened here first."

Levi sat on the big flat rock and removed his hat to stroke his brow. "Ehh, it was a wild town. People got real crazy, did crazy things . . ." He faltered here, uncomfortable with the subject. "In the late 1800s things got so out of control that a bunch of people got killed and some others got run out. This part of town kinda went downhill from there. It started getting a reputation. Folks got superstitious about it."

Now that was an odd thing to hear from a man given to so much superstition himself. "I have noticed some superstition around here," Steve said, his tone ironic.

"Back then," Levi continued, "this was the town of Hyde River, but over the last hundred years, the whole town's gradually moved downriver and left this place to rot. That's why they call it Old Town."

Steve took it all in: the barren, silent loneliness of the place, the absolute and total abandonment of what seemed to be good, usable real estate.

Levi continued, "Now people won't come near it, they won't build on it, they won't drive, walk, or ride through it—and they sure won't come here at night."

"What are they afraid of?"

"Oh, ghosts, spirits of the dead, all that stuff. They think the place is haunted." He looked down at the rock he was sitting on. "Some say the devil lives here, and they talk about how this is the gateway where evil comes into the world." He paused just a moment, looked around the old ruins, and then said matter-of-factly, "But most of all, they're afraid of the dragon."

Hmm, Steve thought. The dragon Tracy and the phony Frenchman had spoken about. "But you're not afraid?"

Levi shook his head. "That old lizard's got nothing on me."

"So what about the people who sanitized the area? Why aren't they afraid to be here?"

"They're here on business, helping hide the dragon, and I think helping Harold Bly hide whatever his interests are in this place. You won't see 'em here at night, though. None of 'em would ever come here alone, even in daylight."

Now Steve hesitated. Was Levi superstitious or wasn't he? Where did fact end and superstition begin in that gray head? "So tell me about the dragon, Levi. What is it, exactly?"

Levi's voice was suddenly very quiet. "We better keep our voices down. We've got company."

Steve turned and looked down the road to the edge of Old Town and caught sight of two heads just ducking behind a ruin. "Who are they?"

"The guy with the white bandage around his head is Phil Garrett. He got his ear almost bit off in a fight, and the doctor had to stitch it back on. The other one may have been Carl Ingfeldt. He looked kind of small."

"Carl Ingfeldt. He was outside your place when Tracy Ellis and I were there."

"Yeah, probably."

"What do they want?"

"Well, I'm sorry, Mr. Benson, but I think they were following me. Seems I can't go anywhere without Harold Bly knowing about it. There could be trouble now. This here is Harold Bly's land."

Steve looked at him. "What is?"

"Most all of it. It used to belong to Benjamin Hyde, and Harold's a direct descendant. He inherited all this."

"Harold Bly owns Old Town?"

"And most of the new town. Well, the mining company does,

actually, but Harold owns the mining company, so—there it is."
Levi looked in the direction where the two men had briefly appeared. "They're gone now, probably gone back to report us being here. We'd better leave." He rose from the rock, and they started making their way out of Hyde Hall and into the street.

"Levi," Steve said in a hushed voice, "I think you said others have been killed here. Did I hear you right?"

"You did."

"How many?"

"No one knows, and no one tells. But it's been going on for a hundred years."

Oh boy, here was more legend and superstition. Steve hoped he could probe around all that and get to the heart of the matter. "What about Harold Bly? Does he have anything to do with it?"

Levi winced. "Harold likes to think he's the cause of it all, that he's in charge of everything, but it's the dragon's doing, really."

It was time to humor the old guy, at least to get a few clues. "So tell me about the dragon."

They stopped in the middle of the street. If they left Old Town they would have to go separate ways, which meant Steve wouldn't get an answer to his question. Steve was willing to remain long enough to hear it, but Levi looked around, obviously a little nervous.

By now, Steve's curiosity was piqued. He prompted, "I understand the dragon is a popular superstition around here."

Levi looked at the ground, and even scraped it around a little with his toe. "No, not really."

"What do you mean?"

"There's some superstitions about it, things that might be true and might not." He looked down the road again.

"So what is it really?"

"Oh . . ." Levi could have been describing a pet hunting dog, his tone was so calm and straightforward. "It's a long, snaky, lizardy flying creature. From what I can gather, back around the turn of the century he wasn't all that big, but I guess now he's up to, oh, maybe forty, forty-five feet long if you could stretch him out, with razor-sharp teeth and a mean streak that's worse now than it ever was. He's hungrier, too. But mind you, that's only a general description."

Steve had to marvel at Levi's matter-of-fact acceptance of such a preposterous idea. "Are you kidding?"

"You asked me about Maggie," said Levi. "You were there, up in my bedroom. You heard Maggie talk about your brother getting eaten and her getting killed the same way, right?"

"Yes, I did hear that. I thought she meant the bear."

Levi shook his head. "No, she knew it was the dragon. And that's why she came here. It's part of the legend, the whole superstition. When it's your time, the dragon calls you here, and you come, and—"

"And what?"

"Well, those who believe in such things would say she came here—" He pointed at Hyde Hall. "—and went in the hall. Then the dragon dropped out of the sky, grabbed her, and carried her off to its cave and ate her." Levi could see he was losing his audience. "Now that's what those who believe in such things would say."

Steve sighed and tried to get the impatient c'mon-get-real look off his face. "So that's the traditional view, the superstition."

Levi nodded. "Hyde Hall is the traditional place where people meet the dragon. I think the dragon can take a person anywhere he wants, but tradition says it happens here."

"So Maggie, in her guilt, in her tormented state of mind, came here, thinking she had to meet the dragon, that it was—her time."

"If you don't show up when you're called, then the dragon comes after you or your family. That's part of the superstition, too." Then he added, "But I don't believe that part."

Oh. That's admirable, Steve thought. You're superstitious, but not that superstitious. Great. I was beginning to worry.

"Anyway," Levi concluded, "I figured she'd come here to Hyde Hall, and that's how I found her shoulder bag and her shoe."

And maybe you're making up this whole miserable story, Steve thought. Maybe you know good and well what happened to

Maggie Bly, and you're part of the cover-up. "Levi, tell me something. Just why is it nobody else will talk about the dragon, but you don't have any trouble talking about it?"

Levi gave a little shrug. "I'm saved, that's all."

"So with you it's a religious thing."

Levi crinkled his nose as he thought about it. "It's kind of a religious thing with everybody. They've got their dragon; I've got Jesus. Simple."

So okay, Benson, what kind of theory can you build from all this? Steve looked around the ruins and tried to apply legend to reality.

"Levi, have there been several deaths recently?"

He shrugged. "Depends on what you mean by recently."

"Oh, how about the last year or so?"

"This year we've had more than the last year—well, two already, your brother and Maggie—and last year we probably had more than the year before that. And before that—well, nobody keeps records, nobody talks, and nobody asks, but every once in a while, some people just don't show up for breakfast the next morning, you know?" Thinking about this troubled him. "Seems like it's always been that way, but it's been stacking up, speeding up, just getting worse and worse. Used to be it was legend, it was talk, it was stories from way back told by the old-timers. Now what've we got? First your brother on Wells Peak and then Maggie in Hyde Hall in just a few days, and I've got a feeling it'll get worse from there."

"But traditionally, this is where they've always come—to meet the dragon, right?"

Levi looked around at the sky. "Oh, this would be a good spot, I suppose. The trees just never do well here, so the sky's open. The dragon could drop in here easy and grab somebody."

"Uh-huh."

"It was tougher grabbing your brother, did you notice that?"

Steve was starting to lose patience. "Levi, what are you talking about?"

"The dragon had to crash through some trees trying to get at him, had to break 'em right off. I don't think he prefers to do that. It's better here."

Steve looked directly at Levi. He himself had noticed the trees the day he went to the site. "How did you know about those broken trees?" he asked slowly.

"I went up to Wells Peak and had a look."

"When?"

"Oh, right after you and Tracy Ellis came to see Maggie." Levi could tell he was shaking Steve up. "You did notice those trees? The tops broken off, the branches on the ground?" Levi looked at the sky again. "Yeah. It was tough there. Too many trees. Plus having a righteous woman there to contend with, getting in the way, fighting it off with a knife."

Steve was beginning to feel uncomfortable with this man. Levi knew things, but he could weave myth and fact together so intricately Steve couldn't be sure where one ended and the other began. "What does Evelyn's being 'righteous' have to do with it?"

Levi smiled at the thought. "She survived, didn't she?"

"I don't follow you."

Levi didn't get a chance to answer. Just then, someone else shouted at them from the end of the old street.

"Hey!"

They both turned to see Deputy Tracy Ellis coming their way.

"Uh-oh," said Levi. "We've been caught."

Tracy was looking stern, like a mother about to drag her kids home by their ears.

"What's the problem here, anyway?" Steve asked Levi.

"Harold Bly again," Levi whispered. "This land has all the people scared, so he doesn't want people like us snooping around on it."

"Gentlemen!" said Tracy Ellis, striding up to them, completely in the role of deputy. "Just what do you think you're doing here?"

"Checking out the site of Maggie's disappearance," Steve answered.

"Well, this is private property, and I've got a complaint from the owner. Levi, you ought to know better!"

"Just trying to keep this man alive," Levi said.

"Well, so am I!" she snapped back. "Now you've got one minute to vacate the premises or face arrest!"

She was sure talking loudly, Steve thought, almost as if she was performing for somebody.

Levi took one last careful look at her, then walked up the street, heading back the way he had come. Tracy stood where she was and let her voice drop to tell Steve, "Let him get ahead. I don't want you talking to him."

That was pushing it. "Does your authority extend as far as telling people who they can talk to?"

"Today it does. People are watching us."

"So we noticed. Are they the ones who called you?"

"They told Harold, and he called the sheriff. I was just a few miles up the road, and he knew it, so I had to show up. Come on, let's walk."

"My camper's the other way."

"Maybe I'll impound it. That'll keep you out of trouble."

They started up the street, well behind Levi. He was gone before they'd come to the edge of Old Town.

"So what's the game here?" Steve asked. "Are you arresting me or what?"

She was irritated and angry, and it was no act. "Steve, I told you if you made trouble or broke the law I'd have to do my job. Well, I wasn't kidding. You're trespassing, and Harold Bly has a legitimate complaint."

"I'm just trying to do my job."

"You don't have a job, Steve! Collins called it quits, remember? You're not authorized to be here, and if you come snooping around Old Town by yourself, you're going to have the whole town down your neck. Hyde Hall is off limits, it's sacred; taboo, okay?"

He stopped, indignant. "Why?"

She grabbed his arm and gave him an authoritarian push. "Keep walking!" He kept walking. "It's a long story. My prime concern right now is that you're getting people upset, which means they're going to be on my back, which means I have to be on yours." Then she added, "And especially if they see you with Levi. They don't like him, Steve."

"Well at least he'll talk to me."

"Oh, he'll talk, all right. He loves to preach."

"He wasn't preaching," Steve said, pushing his way through the tall brush. "He was telling me about the dragon."

She pushed a gnarled branch aside so she could pass. "For Levi it's the same thing."

They reached the edge of the ruins and started down the unused road toward the highway.

"So where does Harold Bly stand on all this dragon stuff?"

Tracy made sure her voice was quite low as she answered. "If people are afraid of the dragon that's fine with him."

"Especially when his adulterous wife vanishes?"

"Especially."

Steve was tossing a new theory around in his mind. "Levi said that people come here to die, to meet the dragon."

She almost stopped walking at that one. "Steve, don't believe anything Levi says! His head is full of that kind of garbage."

"But what if—" Now that he was about to voice his theory, it seemed a little silly. Maybe he had given Levi too much credence. "Just what if a predator of some kind was responsible?"

At that, she did stop. "Do dragons need firewood?"

"Excuse me?"

Tracy hesitated, then admitted, "I just came back from Wells Peak. The area's been sanitized, raked out, cleaned up. And those broken trees we saw? They're all cut up into cordwood, bucked up and stacked right there." She was incredulous. "A stack of cordwood with absolutely no way to haul it out of there!"

Steve was stunned. "Levi told me about those trees. He knew about them."

Now she was interested, even if it was Levi. "What'd he say?"

Steve chuckled a bit. "He suggested the dragon broke them off while attacking my brother."

Tracy allowed herself a small laugh. "Well, there you are."

"Another cover-up. I guess to do the dragon a favor."

She shook her head in amazement. "I can't believe how idiotic this dragon thing can get. And I grew up here!"

"This place was raked out, too."

"I'm not surprised. I'm sure it's all for the same reason. It's like I said. If someone wanted to pull off a murder, Hyde Valley has some old traditions tailor-made for the purpose."

Steve paused to think something through one more time, then asked, "So—what did break the trees off?"

"The people who killed your brother know the dragon legends. Trees broken off by the dragon would really sell in Hyde River. It would be very persuasive."

But Steve still had a problem with it. "How did they break the trees off? You're talking about snapping off an eight-inch trunk and several branches—without a machine."

She smiled knowingly. "Hey, this is logging country. Get some chain, some cable, a few come-alongs and some climbing spikes. The right people with the right tools could do it."

"So now we've got people defeating their own purpose: They break the trees off to stage a dragon attack, then cut the trees up to keep people from suspecting it was the dragon—"

She shook her head. "It's Hyde River, Steve. One thing follows another."

Steve gave her a teasing smile. "But you're still looking, aren't you? You didn't have to go back to Wells Peak, not with Collins closing the case. What were you doing there?"

Tracy shrugged off the question and said, "Let's get out of here. I still have to lecture you and take you back to your camper." They walked on. "Oh, and one more thing: Let me know if you get any weird phone calls."

The night of July 19th, we gathered with Benjamin Hyde in the main room of Hyde Hall and signed the new town charter.

We regarded ourselves as the elite of Hyde River: the owners, the businessmen, the foremen and bosses. The future was in our hands to shape as we would, and we were drunk with the possibilities.

It was to protect this future, this dream, that we swore a blood oath over the signed charter. Like everything else that had transpired in town, this was Benjamin Hyde's idea, and just as he had provided a newly written charter for us to sign, so also he provided a small basin of blood—that of the day's purged undesirables, he claimed—and required each of us to dip our fingers in it, paint a streak across our foreheads, and swear upon that blood that we would forever preserve, protect, and defend the town charter and never disclose what had happened on that day.

There were at least a hundred gathered in that room: ourselves, our wives, our children. We were devoted to Benjamin Hyde. In the light of one candle, we smeared ourselves and even our children with the blood and swore the Oath.

The Oath has been kept now for generations, by my children and their children and their children's children.

From a letter enclosed with the last will
and testament of Stephen Morrʳ Templeton, who died
in Phoenix, Arizona, on January 18, 1942,
at the age of ninety-four

EIGHT

Harold Bly

"Levi, come on, you know better than to trespass down there." Reverend Ron Woods was tall and gangly, with a large nose and sad eyes that made him look like a tortoise without a shell. He was a patient man and once again, Levi Cobb had given him occasion to prove it.

"Sure, I know better," Levi argued, "but that Benson fellow didn't. I couldn't let him go traipsing around down there by himself."

It was Thursday evening. The day was cooling down, and the shadow of the west ridge had advanced up the opposite slope and shaded half the town. Ron and Levi were walking up the street toward the old steepled church, a short climb up the hillside from the main highway. This was the part of the new Hyde River that had first sprung up when Old Town began to fade early in the century. Its original log and hand-hewn timber homes had been restored, then restored again. The matronly old church, built of logs and tilting a bit, was a centerpiece for the neighborhood, and now it too was being restored with a new coat of weather sealer and a new roof. Ron and Levi were heading up the project, and that was the real reason for their being together now. This other subject had come up out of necessity. Word had gotten around town about the Great Trespass, and Ron had gotten word—a rather strong word—that Levi needed talking to.

"But look at the cost," Ron continued, hoping reason would prevail. "Not only is Dr. Benson in trouble with the law, but we've got people upset and talking about it. Levi, it's a simple matter of respect for other people's feelings and views and keeping peace in this town."

Levi gave Ron a sideways look, signaling that a disagreement was coming. "Kind of a one-sided effort, don't you think?"

"Levi—"

"All this talk about tolerance and understanding. When do I start getting tolerated?"

Ron only smiled resignedly. He was a gentle sort, with a smooth, soothing voice. It suited his job quite well. "Maybe when you learn to keep your strong opinions to yourself."

"I can't help it. People ask me, I tell 'em."

Ron laughed. He'd learned to do that whenever he was with Levi. "Okay, Levi, okay. But you could have told him he'd be trespassing."

"I did. But he's a driven man, Ron. He's gonna find out what killed his brother or die in the attempt, I know."

"And I'll bet you told him the dragon killed his brother."

"He asked me; I told him."

Patience, Ron, patience, he reminded himself. "Well, that's something we disagree on."

"Not my fault."

"In any event," the minister continued, "you won't be doing Benson any good filling his mind with that stuff. It's the reality he needs to be informed of, like who owns that land down there and how people feel about outsiders snooping around."

"He knows now."

"So let's have a look at this roof." It was a quick change of subject, something either man could use at any time. It was one way they'd learned to put up with each other.

The old church, built in the 1920s, was looking good for its age—better and better, as a matter of fact. Since Ron had come to pastor the church some four years ago, he and Levi had repainted all the trimwork, recaulked and weather-stripped all the windows and doors, and jacked up the sagging front steps so the porch and front door lined up again. The bell in the steeple, originally from a steam locomotive, was ringing once more, thanks to Levi's machine shop and a little welding.

The problem now was the roof, or more specifically, the roofing contractor.

Levi stood with Ron along the side of the church and had no trouble spotting what Ron was upset about. "Didn't he use a chalkline?"

"Quite honestly, I don't know that he used anything—a little too much alcohol, maybe."

The first row of shingles looked all right; the second row looked a little crooked; the third row looked worse; and the fourth row looked like a desperate attempt to straighten out the error made in the first three. The rows applied above these continued to wander about the roof like a car without a driver.

Then Levi spotted something else. "Where's the shake liner?" Ron looked quizzical, so Levi explained, "He's supposed to be running a strip of felt under each row of shingles. Come to think of it, that was in his bid."

"Oh, no." More bad news.

They circled around the back of the church and found the contractor up on the roof of the back porch, slapping more shingles down and nailing them home whether they were straight or not. He didn't look up from his work when they came around, but not because he didn't see them.

"Vic!" Ron called.

Vic Moore didn't look at them. He only grabbed another shingle. "What?" His tone was so vicious it shocked them both.

"We'd like to have a word with you."

Vic kept pounding nails. "What about?"

Ron looked at Levi for help.

Levi spoke up. "You're doing a lousy job on this roof, Vic."

Vic stopped hammering and used the hammer to point at Levi. "I'm not talking to you!" He looked at Ron. "I'm not talking to him!"

Ron pressed on. "Vic, I don't see any shake liner up there. Wasn't that part of our agreement?"

Vic took a second to look at his work, then answered, "I changed my mind."

"You changed your mind about our roof?"

"You don't need any shake liner."

Levi looked at the clear sky. "Well, not today, anyway."

Vic looked as if he was ready to throw his hammer at Levi. "What's he doing here?" he said to the minister.

"He goes to this church, Vic. He's on the restoration committee."

"I don't need any direction from anybody, and I don't need him telling me how to do my job!"

"You don't huh?" Levi said. "Well, why didn't you use a chalkline on this east side? You've got the courses so crooked it makes my eyes cross."

"They're close enough."

"No, Vic," Ron said in what he hoped was a calm, rational voice. "They're not close at all."

"So now you're taking his side?"

"Vic, I'm being straight with you. This roof is costing the church a lot of money. We need better workmanship than that."

"Well, nobody's gonna see it from the street!"

Ron and Levi looked up at him, then at each other. What was wrong with the man? Vic went back to nailing, banging with more force than was needed on a little shingle nail.

Ron was hoping Vic's common sense would take hold soon. "Vic, come on, now. The inspector's going to take one look at that and—"

"I'll slip him a few bucks. He'll go for it."

Levi finally drew a deep breath, sighed it out, and nudged some gravel around with his toe as he told Ron, "Well, it's your call. You hired him."

Bang, bang, bang, bang.

"Vic, could you stop a minute?" Ron asked.

Bang, bang, bang.

"Vic, please, don't nail another shingle!"

Vic stopped, his eyes full of spite.

Ron kept his voice calm and even. "I think you should stop working until we can iron this out."

Vic considered that for maybe one second. "I've been in business in this town for twelve years. I've got friends up and down the valley who know good work when they see it, and they show me some respect! You don't like my work, you just try to get somebody else to work on your crummy little church!"

"Okay, Vic, come down," Ron said as if he were talking someone out of jumping from a ledge. "Don't nail another shingle—"

Vic burst into an adult tantrum, hurling a bundle of shingles to the ground as Levi dodged out of their path. He fired some obscenities at Levi and then translated, "You're what's wrong with this town! If you weren't around we'd all have a better time of it!"

Enough was enough, Ron thought. "Vic, that's it, it's all over," he said firmly. "Now come down from that roof and pack up your gear. You're—" The word sounded so spiteful, he dreaded saying it. "—fired."

"Well, that's fine with me!" Vic growled, going to the ladder. "You can just get somebody else, somebody you don't even know . . ." He kept muttering as he came down the ladder. "And just try to get this signed off. The inspector'll never work with anybody else; you're gonna find that out."

Vic climbed down and walked straight over to Ron. "I thought you were a better man than this, Ron! You been listening to this old idiot too long, and now you're thinking like he does!" Ron stood his ground but was wondering how bad things might get in the next few seconds. Vic was waving the hammer around like he'd love to smack somebody with it. "Well, you're not gonna make it in this town, let me tell you. Things could get real bad for you."

Ron had no interest in winning the argument. He only wanted to defuse the situation. "Now, Vic, just calm down. We can talk about this later."

Vic gathered up his tools, throwing his hammer, nails, tape measure, and shingle hatchet into a five-gallon bucket. His jacket was unzipped and hanging loose. It flopped open as he slammed his tools around.

Ron swallowed. This man was carrying a gun!

Vic grabbed the bucket and approached Levi on his way out of the churchyard. "You're dead meat, Cobb!" He put his finger right in Levi's face. "You and me, we're gonna settle this. You be ready." With those words Vic turned and stomped away toward his truck. A few moments later, they heard the truck roaring down the hill.

Ron walked over to Levi. "Don't let him upset you."

"Oh, I'm upset all right, but for him." Then Levi read Ron's face. "You're not looking so good yourself."

Ron's gaze fell to the ground. Vic Moore was gone; the confrontation was over. Now he could just be himself. "I'm upset, yeah. To be honest, I just—I just want to punch that guy!"

"Whoo! Strong words, Ron!"

The minister was apologetic. "I know, I know."

"Don't worry. We'll get the roof done."

"It's not just the roof, Levi. It's—" Then he blurted out, "What am I doing here, anyway? What's the point?"

Levi could sympathize. Vic Moore was not the first of Ron's problems in this town. "Just obey God, Ron. That's the first thing."

Ron took no comfort in that little sermon. "Obey God—fine. So where is He?"

Levi couldn't believe what he was hearing. "Ron, you haven't figured that out yet?"

Ron's abundant patience was running low. "Levi, not now."

"All right. But you asked."

"I'm sorry I asked. I was just—just spouting, that's all."

"Nothing wrong with that."

Ron looked at the tattered, ragged roof, then over the rest of the forlorn town. "I deserve better than this, you know? I'm a professional. I could really make a difference, I think, if I could just—" He was reluctant to express his feelings aloud but was in a sour-enough mood to do it. "If the placement board had a little more regard for all the training I've had, I could be somewhere else right now! I could be accomplishing something! As it is . . ."

He stared at the old church and shook his head bitterly. "I have a waking nightmare about this place. I can envision myself in my eighties, and Sue dead and the children all grown and gone, and I'm still here with no retirement, living on next to nothing, still having to do everything myself because people won't show up, still getting yelled at by all the Vic Moores, and still wedging up this old building to keep it from falling over. I didn't go to seminary to spend my life doing this!"

Levi thought it over, then said, "Maybe you're right. Maybe you need to ask God why you're here and not let go of Him until you get an answer."

It was ironic, Ron thought, that one of his own church members was giving him a sermon. But, then, Levi gave a lot of sermons. Ron relaxed a little. "What is it with people, anyway?"

Levi repeated an old theme, "You haven't figured that out yet?"

Ron waved it all aside. "I don't want to talk about it. We've got to get this roof back on before it rains."

"I've got some people I can call. Maybe they can finish the job for us."

"Great." Then Ron added, "But Levi, be careful about Vic. He's a man with a lot of anger. He could hurt you."

"I know."

Levi said nothing more, but it wasn't Vic or his threats that had triggered Levi's fears. It was the anguish he could sense in Vic's soul, the fear in the man's eyes, the gun under his jacket—and the faint stain Levi saw on Vic's shirt, right over his heart, soaking through like sweat and smelling like death.

THAT NIGHT, Vic Moore wouldn't quit talking. He was resolutely planted on a bar stool at Charlie's, throwing back beers and running down the same list, over and over.

"Now Taylor's place, that was a classic! Bid that job out at forty grand. Know how much it cost me to build it? Twenty! Taylors were happy, and you bet I was happy!" Then he couldn't help laughing. "Hope they never check the insulation under the floor—it isn't there!"

After that came the saga of Ike Buhler's cabin on June Lake, at least six inches out of level because Vic had forgotten to bring his transit but went ahead and guessed. The justification: "Aw, it's clear up there on the lake. Nobody's gonna see it."

People came and went, buying drinks, having dinner, shooting some pool, and every one of them heard at least one of Vic's stories of shoddy workmanship or shady dealing, how he'd gotten away with it, and how much money he had pocketed.

Behind the bar, Charlie was quiet, edgy, distracted. Every loud boast frayed his nerves a little more. He didn't know what to do with this guy. The other patrons were trying to ignore Vic's ramblings, but Vic was getting more pleased with himself and talking louder with each recollection he shared.

"Saved on roofing nails, saved on lumber, saved on hangers—Charlie!"

Charlie jumped a little. His hands were shaking as it was. He'd been drying glasses behind the bar just to give his hands something to do. "Yeah, Vic?"

"How many earthquakes we get around here? We get a lot of 'em?"

"No. Not very often."

Vic smiled and nodded, recalling another job. "Won't make any difference, then. Saved on labor. It'll stay there." He turned to Paul, who was in his usual spot at the end of the bar. "People trust me, you know? I've got a reputation around here."

Paul muttered without turning around, "Not after today, you

don't!" Then he went right on watching the baseball game on the television suspended above the bar.

"Yeah," said Vic, continuing his monologue as if Paul hadn't said anything, "I come up with good cost-saving ideas, so I can give people a good price." He pondered his own glory for a moment and then agreed with himself, "Yeah, I do all right." Then he turned to Paul again. "Hey, Paul!"

Paul rolled his eyes but didn't look at Vic.

"Did I ever tell you what I did to Homer Kirby? He was up there at Smyths doing that remodel, remember that? Remember how he got fired for drinking on the job?" He lowered his voice. "Hey, I was responsible for that. I waited 'til Homer knocked off for the day, and then I went up there and tossed beer cans all over the yard." He tried to take a swallow of beer but couldn't hold back a laugh, and he spit the beer all over the bar. "Wish I coulda seen old man Smyth come home and blow his stack. He sure was happy I could fit him into my schedule, let me tell you. That's what Homer gets for trying to underbid me. That don't sit too well with me, you know?"

Phil Garrett was trying to shoot pool with Kyle Figgin and Carl Ingfeldt. It was his turn to shoot, but he kept staring at Vic.

"They're never gonna get that church roof done. I've got friends, you know that? Red Johnson's my friend. He'll never sign that place off. And who's that guy at the county, you know, with the road crew? Paul? Who's that guy—"

"Wally Neddleton," said Paul without looking away from the ball game.

"Neddleton, yeah. I'll just have a little talk with him about that Levi Cobb." He took a swig of beer. "Cobb's never gonna see another county job when I get through."

Phil Garrett finally shouted, "Charlie! Make him shut up!"

Charlie was still standing behind the bar drying glasses and feeling scared. Phil's order only intimidated him further. He went to Vic and spoke quietly, "Vic, you about done with your drink?"

Vic was offended. "No, I am not."

"Well, I, uh . . ."

Suddenly Charlie found himself pulled halfway over the bar by his collar, nose to nose with Vic. "Hey, Charlie. Wanna play tough guy?"

Charlie was speechless. Vic let Charlie go with a little shove so that he almost fell backward, then laughed at him. "Whatsamatter, Charlie? I scare you?"

By now, everyone in Charlie's was watching. Vic turned and spoke to the other patrons. "Nobody—nobody—tells me what to do. I do what I want, when I want. You all know that, now don't you?"

They were silent, gawking at him.

"Well, what are you staring at?"

At the table nearest the door, a miner named Jack Carlson and his wife Amy reached for their coats. Kyle Figgin moved away from the pool table.

Vic was nonplussed. "I'm just telling you, don't take it so serious. Goodies go to the grabbers; ain't that right, Paul?"

But Paul was getting up to leave as well.

Charlie tapped on Vic's shoulder. "Vic—I got something for you."

Vic turned to see a full bottle of Jack Daniels in Charlie's hand. He got the message. He took the bottle, and got up from the bar.

"Thanks for coming in," said Charlie.

"Be seeing you," said Vic, pleased.

On his way out, Vic noticed Carlotta Nelson sitting with Andy Schuller and stepped toward her. "Hey, Carlotta—"

She cowered under his gaze. "No, Vic. Not tonight, no way."

"Aw, c'mon."

Andy spoke up, "You heard her, Vic."

Vic glowered at Andy for a moment and then he pulled back his jacket to reveal the gun. He waited until he'd gotten just the right amount of wide-eyed fear from both of them and then enjoyed another laugh as he let his jacket fall back into place. "Whatsamatter? Did I scare you?"

"That's not funny!" Andy said.

Vic only laughed at him and then went out the door.

The place was dead quiet. The video games in the corner bleeped and warbled to themselves; nobody was playing. A ball player slammed a triple on the television, but nobody noticed.

Charlie grabbed another bottle of whiskey and with shaking hands poured himself a stiff drink. He downed it in one gulp.

Andy made a face. "Shew! He smelled like a dead rat."

Charlie spoke to no one in particular, "Probably too drunk to drive."

Jack and Amy, who had their coats on now, looked out, and Jack reported, "He isn't driving. He's walking up the middle of the road."

The shot glass dropped out of Charlie's hand and clattered on the bar. He grabbed it quickly then wiped the bar frantically with a cloth.

Phil fumbled a bit with his cue stick, then tried to line up a shot. He missed by a mile.

Conversation started again. Now that Vic had gone, Jack and Amy took off their jackets and went back to their table, but Paul paid his tab and left. It was Phil's turn again, and he leaned over the pool table to sink the nine ball in the corner.

"You think maybe he's—uh—" Andy Schuller wondered.

"NO!" Phil shouted. "He's drunk. He's just drunk and that's all!"

"Well," said Carl, "it ain't me, so I ain't gonna think about it."

Phil tried the shot again and missed again.

When Charlie was satisfied all eyes were elsewhere, he ducked into the kitchen, went past the big iron sink and the hanging pots and pans, and grabbed the phone hanging on the wall by the back door. His hands were still shaking as he read the phone number off the back of a business card and tried to dial it.

STEVE HAD rented a hookup at the White Tail RV Park about ten miles south of Hyde River. It was a no-frills setup with twenty hookups and a set of restrooms with no paper towels, but almost all the spaces were filled with campers and trailers, families and groups of guys, all out to hook trout the next morning. When the cellular phone warbled from its rack above the sink, he was half expecting the phony Frenchman.

He wasn't disappointed.

"*Monsieur* Benson!"

"Well, the Frenchman! How are you?"

The man's voice was hushed, tense. "Listen, listen to me! I think there is going to be another death at Hyde Hall tonight!"

Steve sat up straight. "How do you know?"

The voice on the other end of the line was frantic, filled with fear. "He . . . was just here. He is going to Hyde Hall right now!"

"Who?"

CHARLIE KEPT his voice down and his eyes on the kitchen door. "His name is Vic Moore. He was talking crazy tonight—he is going up the road right now, going to Old Town!"

"Right now?"

"Right now! If you hurry, maybe you can catch the dragon before he gets away!"

Steve hesitated. "I'd be trespassing down there; I suppose you know that."

"If you miss your chance, you will know by tomorrow when Vic Moore is dead!"

Charlie hung up, shaking like a leaf. Enough said. Let the great hunter take it from there. Please.

STEVE BURST from the back door of his camper and yanked the power cord from the hookup. This was crazy. Risk trespassing in Old Town again, and for what? A wild tip? He hadn't resolved his argument with himself even as he jumped into the cab, cranked the engine over, and pulled out.

Should he call Tracy? he wondered. Then he realized he couldn't call her now—the phone was still in the back. He'd call her once he got there if he decided to proceed. But could he trust the tipster? He would be taking a risk, no question, but it might be worth it. He'd wait until he got to Old Town to make a decision.

He drove through Hyde River at well above the speed limit but didn't seem to draw any attention. The lights were on at Charlie's, and some rigs were parked outside. Apart from that, the sleepy little town looked deserted.

He came to the dirt road that veered off the highway just past the grove of cottonwoods. It was blocked, of course, but now he'd been back there, he knew the way, and he could make it quickly on foot. His heart was racing; he was primed. With no conscious decision to proceed he proceeded, leaving the camper beside the highway, bounding over the dirt berm and down the overgrown road to Old Town, a flashlight in one hand, his shotgun in the other, and the .357 on his hip. He'd neglected to call Tracy Ellis.

He swerved and dodged through the grass and brush. He could tell someone had passed by here recently because the tall grass was pressed down in the direction of Old Town. It could have been Levi, Tracy, or the spies for Harold Bly, or—it could be what's-his-name, if the Frenchman's tip was reliable.

He stopped to listen. Was that laughter?

Yes. A man was laughing somewhere in the dark, somewhere in Old Town. The eerie sound of it perfectly matched the surrealistic, deathlike surroundings, and Steve felt a chill.

Now the man was talking. But to whom? It was the unheard, the unseen, the unknown, that frightened him. Suddenly Levi's words, "Ghosts . . . the place is haunted . . . the devil lives here . . ." carried a lot more weight.

He extinguished his light, though he hated to do so, chambered a shell in the shotgun, then stole along in the deepening shadows of the night, his eyes finally beginning to discern the dark shapes of trees and bushes ahead of him as the grass rustled and hissed around his legs.

Yes, he could hear the man's voice plainly now, hollering and whooping as if having a one-man party. Maybe the Frenchman was right, and yet . . . this was bizarre.

What am I walking into? Steve wondered.

The wind kicked up, the first real wind of the night, rushing through the tall cottonwoods, making the leaves flutter in the dark, drowning out the man's voice. Steve kept moving. Hyde Hall. He had to get there.

Steve reached the main road through Old Town and stopped to listen, to observe. The ruins were barely visible in the dark. The trees just beyond were swaying lazily, the wind the only sound.

He heard the voice again, a little quieter but still going on and on about something. It was definitely in the direction of Hyde Hall. Steve pressed on, hoping the sigh of the wind would drown out the rustling of his footsteps.

Suddenly Steve felt a gust of wind. It was strong, forceful, rolling through the treetops and sweeping down the old street like a wave, rippling the grass, shaking the brush, and nearly knocking him over.

Then, just above the rush of that wind, came a scream. Then another scream, this one muted. Then there was a silence.

Vic Moore was definitely not alone out there. Someone—or something—had gotten him.

Steve's fear vanished. He charged like an animal, running headlong down the street, his flashlight still out.

Hyde Hall loomed up on the right. He stopped. He listened.

The wind was gone. The place was eerily quiet.

He could hear no sound except that of his own pounding heart.

He approached Hyde Hall like a hunter stalking his prey, first a step, then listen and watch, then a few more steps, then listen and watch, staying low, looking around, listening, his finger on the trigger of the shotgun.

The place was dead. Silent.

Steve reached the foundation and stepped over it. He listened again. There was no sound, so he clicked on the flashlight. The beam stunned his night-sensitive eyes, but it revealed nothing out of place. No breakage, no body, no signs of—

Wait. Here was something new. Not far from the big flat stone in the center of the building, almost in the same spot where Levi had found Maggie's purse, was a broken bottle. Steve approached and examined it in his light without touching it.

A broken bottle of Jack Daniels whiskey. The ground was wet with the spilled liquor, the smell unmistakable. He searched the immediate area for any other signs or clues. The grass was flattened all around the stone, but that was no surprise.

Steve clicked the light off and sat down on the rock, trying to figure things out. He had heard screams, yet there was no one around. The only evidence that someone had just been there was the broken bottle of Jack Daniels. There had to be—

Uh-oh. Now he heard more sounds, then saw two flashlights approaching from up the street. Harold Bly's two spies again? He immediately looked for a place to conceal himself.

The flashlights continued up the street, sweeping back and forth, searching.

He looked for a back door to this place. Funny. There were only three walls and no roof, and here he was looking for the door. Apparently it was hidden by the remnants of the fallen roof. He'd have to make a wider sweep around the rear wall to get out. He kept low and started working his way along the building.

The lights were coming closer, moving directly toward Hyde Hall. That made sense, but it wasn't good news. He recalled that his truck was still parked out on the highway like a billboard to advertise his presence. Whoever this was, they had to be coming after him. He kept a grip on his shotgun, desperately hoping he wouldn't have to use it.

"Steve!" came a voice behind one of the lights. "Steve Benson, are you out there?"

Tracy Ellis. Did that mean he was in or out of trouble? There were no more secrets; that was certain.

He called back, "Over here, in Hyde Hall!"

Now he could see the lights heading toward the old ruin. He worked his way back toward the flat rock, trying to think of ways to look innocent.

Too late. The first flashlight beam found him, and he heard the voice of Sheriff Lester Collins. "Benson! Hold it right there! Don't move!" Collins did not sound cordial. Steve didn't move. "And put down that rifle!"

This was definitely a bad development. Steve slowly set the shotgun down on the rock.

Collins and Tracy, dark shadows behind their flashlights, stepped over the foundation and into Hyde Hall.

"I've found something here," Steve said, hoping that would explain his presence.

"Drop that revolver too! Put it on the rock, slowly! And the flashlight!"

He set down the flashlight, then unbuckled his gunbelt and set it on the rock. Collins remained in front, his police revolver in his hand, while Tracy circled around behind.

Oh no, what was this?

"C'mon," said Tracy, "let's have those hands."

Steve obeyed, and Tracy put on the handcuffs.

"Mr. Benson," said Collins, "you're under arrest. You have the right to remain silent . . ."

WHEN COLLINS brought the patrol car to a halt in front of a large, brick home in Hyde River, it seemed an unexpected twist—Steve hoped it would be a favorable one.

Collins turned off his engine and looked back at Steve, still cuffed in the back seat. "Dr. Benson, I'm a practical kind of guy, and I know you are too. Now neither one of us needs extra trouble in our lives, and I'm guessing you'd just as soon get out of Hyde Valley altogether than spend time in jail. Am I correct, sir?"

"I would agree with that," Steve said. Actually, he wasn't so sure, but as the sheriff said, he was a practical kind of guy.

"All right, good. That's what I wanted to hear. Now. This is the home of Harold Bly. It's his land you were trespassing on, and he's the one who called us. He's not too happy about this, but he's a reasonable man. I'm hoping he'll be satisfied with an apology and a promise that you'll stay off his land so I won't have to take you to jail. But that all depends on you."

Tracy had pulled up in her Ranger and parked across the street. Even though she wasn't in her uniform—she was wearing an oversized shirt and jeans—when she joined them on Bly's front walk she was still acting like a cop. "Are we ready?"

"I've talked it over with him," Collins answered.

Steve glared at Tracy. He was steaming.

But so was she. "I was right in the middle of dinner!"

"You should get paid overtime," he quipped.

She just grabbed his arm and shoved him along. "Come on, let's get this over with." She led him up the front stairs, just a few steps behind Collins.

"So when do the cuffs come off?" he asked.

"We have to impress Harold first."

Harold Bly answered their knock. He was expecting them, and he looked Steve over with a sly smile. "Well, lookie here!"

Collins answered, "Harold, this is Dr. Steve Benson. I think he was trying to help us out on that bear-attack case. He didn't know he was trespassing."

"Well, we'll just see about that."

So this was Harold Bly. Tough-looking character, Steve thought, with arms that could beat a gorilla in an arm wrestle. Steve could tell Bly was enjoying this moment, this chance to be Caesar with a man's life in his hands: Thumbs up or thumbs down? You're all mine, you poor jerk. Steve knew immediately he didn't like this guy.

"Come on in," said Bly, and they followed him through the house into his living room.

The house was furnished with antiques, all vestiges of the Hyde family's glory days. In the living room, comfortable sofas and chairs were arranged on a Persian rug around the big stone fireplace. Steve noticed a handsome writing desk in one corner, and the ceiling-high bookshelves displayed antique collectibles as well as volumes of old, leather-bound books. On the mantel sat some gold nuggets in a glass case, and above the mantel was a large portrait of a distinguished-looking gentleman in suit and vest with a gold watch chain, his thumb cocked in his vest pocket, a stern, man-in-charge look on his bearded face. Maybe this was the way Harold Bly viewed himself, Steve thought.

"Come in, make yourselves comfortable," said Bly, taking the wing chair by the fireplace with the air of a king taking his throne. "Oh, and—" He waved his hand toward Steve. "—let's take those cuffs off, at least for now."

Tracy used her key and set Steve loose. He rubbed his wrists, now creased by the cold metal.

"Have a seat," Bly said. Steve sat down on the couch across the room from Bly, as did Tracy. Collins took the other wing chair near the fireplace. Now they all faced the man of the hour, ready to plead their case.

"So you're the mighty hunter," Bly said with unabashed sarcasm. "Seems the whole town's been talking about you, wondering what you're going to do next. I hear you started a big fight down at Charlie's."

Steve knew Bly was goading him, so he gave a careful, guarded response. "It was an unpleasant situation, something I neither expected nor intended. But there was no harm done." Then he added, "Just as in this situation."

"Well, I don't know that for sure, now do I? I had to have you and Levi Cobb run out of there once before, and now here you are, back again. Either I'm not making myself clear or you've got one thick head."

Steve knew this guy wouldn't be too impressed with the anonymous "Frenchman" and hot tips about a dragon, or with the notion that another person had just vanished in the same way Maggie had. "It's as Sheriff Collins was saying. I was hunting for a rogue grizzly. I had reason to believe it might be frequenting the ruins of Old Town."

Sheriff Collins piped up, "But I need to make it clear, Harold, that Dr. Benson is not working for us and never was. His actions are all strictly voluntary, and I told him this morning the case was closed. This is all his own doing, you understand."

Right, Collins, Steve thought. By all means, cover your rear.

Bly looked Steve over again and said, "I guess you don't know how folks around here feel about that place. They have a lot of strong feelings, a lot of traditions—"

"And I used to have a brother before he was horribly mutilated by—by something," Steve interrupted brusquely. "Of course I'm sorry for going on private land without permission, and I didn't mean to offend the local traditions, but I'll be blunt with you: There's a predator of some kind out there killing people, and it has to be stopped." Even if it's you and your pals, he wanted to say.

Collins piped up again, "Steve, we've been through that. You already shot the bear, and the coroner says so—"

"The coroner took the word of the pathologist, and I don't think the pathologist knew what to make of it. As for the bear, I did the autopsy on 318, and I'm not convinced it was 318 that killed my brother."

Bly waved his hand for a halt. "Hey, guys, I don't really care if it was 318 or an overgrown raccoon. It's you stomping around on my land that I care about. Besides, I don't buy this idea of a grizzly hanging around down there. Why would a bear be in that area?"

"Well, I'm working on a theory," Steve said. "It's sketchy, but—" They were waiting to hear it, and he knew he had to be very careful. He drew a deep breath. "It's, well, perhaps I could call it my Coincidence Theory. You see, I think maybe the town's superstitions could be the key to this whole thing."

Bly looked grim at that. His eyes seemed to be warning Steve to watch his step.

Steve tried to tread carefully. "If a bear finds a predictable food source, whether it's a campground, a garbage dump, or a dumpster behind a restaurant—any place where food is easily available on a regular basis, the bear will frequent that spot, it'll keep coming back. Well, if the—" Careful, Steve. "—traditions of Hyde River cause people to go out to Hyde Hall on any frequent or regular basis, then it's possible that a predatory animal of some kind, a bear, could be viewing that as an easy, predictable food source. If the local superstitions have prevailed for any length of time, there could be several bears involved, not just one." Even as this fumbling hypothesis crossed his lips, Steve knew that if he'd read it in a term paper he would have flunked it. Well, no one in the room was applauding the idea either. "Granted, what we've observed so far doesn't sound like your typical bear, but that's the theory I've been going on."

Bly seemed dumbfounded. He looked at Steve, then Tracy, and then Collins. "Am I missing something somewhere? Who's been eaten by this bear besides your brother?"

Well. Nothing like going out on a limb and having it snap off. "I was led to believe that your wife Maggie was missing, that she'd disappeared in Old Town." Steve was careful not to look at Tracy when he said that. Hopefully she'd owe him a favor.

Harold snorted. "Who told you that?"

Steve ignored the question, hoping Bly wouldn't ask it again. "And there was another person, someone named Vic Moore. I followed him into Old Town tonight. He was drunk, and I was concerned for his safety."

"So, did anything happen to him?"

"I don't know. He disappeared as well." Steve looked at Collins. "But I did find a broken whiskey bottle in Hyde Hall."

Collins laughed loudly, like he was making a point, and grinned at Bly.

Bly just shook his head. "Is that a fact? If a broken bottle means someone's been killed, ooo-weee, there's a lot of people being killed around here!"

Steve shot one quick look at Tracy. Her eyes met his, but then she turned away.

Bly was still amused as he explained, "Maggie's visiting her mother in Denver right now. I talked to her on the phone just this evening. She's fine. As for Vic Moore, listen, he does this kind of thing all the time: gets drunk, wanders off mad at the world, starts hollering and singing at the trees. Don't worry about him. A couple of days'll go by and he'll be back, groveling and apologizing and picking up where he left off. Nobody's been killed."

"There's my brother," Steve replied.

"Was your brother killed on my property? Listen, Benson. If you think someone's been killed in Old Town, show us a body. Give Maggie a call and ask if she's dead; I don't care. But she told me she's doing fine, so I figure she's still alive."

"Doing fine?" Steve asked. "According to—"

"Harold, it's Levi," Tracy cut in—finally, to Steve's relief. "Steve—Dr. Benson—has been going on information Levi gave him. That's the problem."

"Cobb!" Bly exclaimed.

"Well, you know Levi," Tracy said. "He thinks the dragon killed Steve's brother, and he thinks the dragon killed Maggie, and he's been telling Steve all his stories, and that's where Steve got his Coincidence Theory. He's trying to, you know, find some connection between the stories, the things Levi's saying and—"

Steve finished the thought, "And that's why I was in Hyde Hall. I was following a lead. I have to check out everything I hear."

Bly was not quite buying it. "I can't believe you could be that stupid. You believe all that stuff about a dragon?"

"A predator," Steve clarified. "Levi's a little off the wall; I'll give you that. To him it's a dragon. I figure it's a rogue grizzly. In any event, Levi's information on a dragon seemed to coincide with my scenario of a habituated bear."

Bly settled back in his chair. "Dr. Benson, you've got yourself a lame theory built out of nothing but lies. Anything Cobb says is worthless, understand? That guy's the biggest liar in the valley." Suddenly Bly exploded in a fresh burst of anger. "So he's got Maggie eaten by the dragon, is that right?"

Tracy nodded.

Bly's face was turning red with rage. "If Levi Cobb had his way, there really would be a dragon, and it'd be gobbling down anybody Cobb didn't agree with! My wife, eaten by the dragon. Next thing you know, he'll have the dragon eating me." Bly leaned forward and pointed in Steve's face. "Let me tell you something: That man's an ex-con; did you know that? He killed a man, right here in Hyde River, knifed him in a big fight in a bar. You think a man like that is going to tell the truth about somebody he doesn't like? Cobb's got it in for me, always has. He's a liar, Benson. He's such a big liar he doesn't even know he's lying. He believes it himself."

Steve was ready to play the reformed penitent. "Well, what can I say?" He spread his hands in a placating gesture. "I'm appalled. I'm embarrassed. I've been working with false information."

"You got that right!"

"I'm very sorry, Mr. Bly."

"You're a fool; that's what you are."

Tracy interjected, "But you see, Harold? Steve's a victim of circumstance. He wasn't aware he was on private property, he didn't know about the old traditions, and he met Levi Cobb before anybody could warn him."

Bly was calming down. Maybe it was because he enjoyed seeing Steve look stupid. He was shaking his head in disbelief and pity for the poor, duped professor. "Yeah, you sure got taken in."

"Well, Harold," Tracy said, "why don't you tell him how tough it's been on you? I'm sure he'd appreciate your feelings if he knew your situation."

Suddenly Bly noticed something, and his face lit up with mischief. "You like this guy, don't you?"

Steve hadn't noticed Tracy's hand touching his arm until she abruptly pulled it away.

But Bly had scored a bull's eye, a direct hit, and Steve found it fascinating—fun, actually—to watch Clark County Deputy Sheriff Tracy Ellis's face turn bright red.

"I think—" she started to say, then started over. "I think he just needs to learn about—about the, uh—"

Now Bly was really enjoying himself. He leaned forward to fire a bank shot off Steve, "Look out for her. She's left a trail of broken hearts all over Hyde River."

"Harold, that's enough of that!" she finally got out. "I'm only trying to help Dr. Benson out of a situation he got in quite innocently."

So I'm Dr. Benson again, Steve thought.

But now Bly was leaning back in his chair, smiling and satisfied with the success of his little stab. Steve hoped he was also appeased.

Finally Bly moved on to the subject at hand. "It's a crazy town—Steve." The first name was for Tracy's benefit. "People don't like outsiders going into Old Town. It's sacred ground to them, and all this stuff about a dragon is about to drive me crazy, but I guess we'll all just have to live with it. That's why I had that road blocked off and put up the No Trespassing signs, just to keep the peace around here."

"I'm sorry if I upset things."

"Well, people will get over it—and your leaving will help, believe me. But that land's dead weight. The people around here have such weird ideas, I can't develop it, I can't sell it. The only thing I can do is let it go back to timber again, and maybe by then the legends'll fade enough so I can have it logged."

"How did it happen, sir, if I may ask?"

"How'd what happen?"

"How did the land become linked with a dragon and with so many superstitions?"

Bly only looked away, disgusted. "We don't need to talk about that."

Tracy had had enough time to piece together her dignity and her conversational skill. "Harold, go ahead and tell him. Remember, he's been talking with Levi Cobb."

Bly had to build up to it. "Heh. Who knows how it really went." He took a moment to think, then said, "There was some kind of an Indian raid on the town back in the 1800s, and a lot of people got killed. The story goes that the land used to be a sacred burial ground and the home of the Indians' snake god. It was big medicine, and anyone who trespassed on it got a curse put on him. Anyway, those kinds of stories hang on, and get passed on, and ever since then, one story's built on another, and then another, and so now you have a big dragon living there—the Indians' snake god, I guess—and there's a curse on anybody going near the place." He sniffed in anger. "So now some folks think I've got the curse on me because it was my family that first settled this town, on that sacred ground."

Steve wanted to keep Bly talking. "I understand you're a direct descendant of the original Hyde?"

"The last of the Hyde line, as a matter of fact." Bly looked up at the painting over the mantel. "That's my great-great-grandfather, Benjamin Hyde. He started this town in the 1870s, and I'm the grandson of his granddaughter, who married a gold miner named Harrison Bly."

"Well."

"Benjamin Hyde made the original gold strike here and founded the Hyde Mining Company. So you've got the town named after him, and the river, and Hyde Hall, and who knows what else. He started everything, and he owned everything, and now I own it, or at least a lot of it." He smirked and rolled his eyes a little. "I own what used to be the town and some of what the town is now. Anymore, though, it isn't much."

Steve looked at the portrait of Benjamin Hyde. The man was standing by an old table that had been painted with an odd perspective so that a date carved in its top could be clearly seen. "July 19, 1882. What's that?"

"The date the town was officially founded. The Hyde River Charter was signed on that table in Hyde Hall, and old man Hyde was proud of that, so he posed by the table for his portrait." Then Bly pointed across the room to an old oak table on which stood a classic brass lamp. "Still got it." It was the same table, the roughly carved date plainly visible. Now that was impressive. "It's called the Founders Table. It's a great keepsake, but it has its negative side."

Steve looked at Bly, a question on his face.

Bly answered, "The family curse! The Hyde family settled on the land and founded the town, so they're the ones the evil spirits and the Indian snake god and all the curses are after. And the land's cursed too, and that's why I can't sell or develop it." Bly's face was softer now, his gaze not quite so cold, as Steve went from trespassing troublemaker to enlightened confidant. "So you see now why I don't like people venturing onto that property. I've got enough troubles as it is just trying to run a mining company that can't compete anymore. I don't need the local people climbing all over me because some outsider's going to get the dragon all upset."

"I understand, sir."

"Got things clear now?"

Steve nodded a deep nod. "Very clear, yes."

"So, do us all a favor." Bly stood, and they all stood with him. The meeting was coming to a close. "Go home. Don't make this thing bigger than it is. I'm sorry about your brother, but that's over; it's done, there's nothing else here for you to find out."

Steve extended his hand. "I greatly appreciate your indulgence, sir."

"It's all right," Bly said, shaking Steve's hand. "So how's your sister-in-law?"

"Recovering very well, thank you."

Bly looked genuinely concerned. "Great. Glad to hear it. But I heard she's blocked out the whole incident, that she can't remember anything."

"Well, yes sir, in effect."

"She doesn't remember a thing?"

"No."

"Well . . . maybe that's best."

"Maybe so."

"So why don't you all get out of here? I need to go to bed."

Once outside, Collins headed straight for his car. "You don't mind driving Professor Benson to his truck, do you, Tracy?"

"No problem," Tracy said, and she and Steve climbed into her Ranger.

"Don't worry about what Bly said," she told Steve as she turned the key in the ignition. "He does that to everybody, tries to rattle their cage."

Of all the subjects discussed tonight, Steve instinctively *knew* which one Tracy was talking about, the one that worried her and rattled her cage. He just crossed his arms smugly and replied, "Oh, it didn't bother me."

Which bothered her. "Forget it."

They drove off.

HAROLD BLY stood in the archway of his front porch, watching the red taillights disappear down the hill, his face cold again, his eyes cunning. A silent shadow emerged from the garage beside the house. Bly caught sight of it, nodded, then sat on the top step of the porch and lit a cigarette.

Phil Garrett looked to be sure the two vehicles were gone, then came up the steps to talk.

"Out kinda late, aren't you?" Bly asked.

Phil almost whispered, "We're wondering what happened to Vic Moore."

"What do you think happened?"

Phil's fear was evident on his face. "What are we gonna do?"

"Same as last time," Bly said impatiently. "Clean it all up. Put it behind us and forget it."

"But why'd you let that guy go?"

Bly took a long drag on his cigarette and smiled. "Well, who am I to stand in the way of romance?"

Phil got angry. "But he's gonna find out—"

"He's not the one to worry about!" Bly cut him off. "Steve Benson hasn't seen anything. His sister-in-law has." He looked

directly at Phil's brawl-gnarled face, making sure he had Phil's attention. "And you know what else? We're going to have to take
care of her ourselves—before her memory comes back, you follow me?"

HALFWAY BETWEEN dusk and dawn, sheltered from the light by
the leaning, decrepit ruins, a figure dressed in black came upon the
broken whiskey bottle that had once been in the hands of Vic
Moore.

Good enough, he thought. Let them find it here

He knelt before the large, flat stone in the ruins of Hyde Hall,
gripped the stone's edges, and muttered his adoration to his god.
Then he placed another scrap of paper on the stone and wrote out
two more names as he spoke them aloud, "Steve Benson, Tracy
Ellis."

With the touch of a match, the two names were consumed in
flame.

The patient complained of a burning rash over the sternum and a constant pain in the heart. Upon examination I found an open, running sore, possibly gangrenous, and recommended immediate hospitalization. Had I anticipated the dementia which apparently set in soon after, I would have taken steps to confine the patient. Unfortunately, he wandered off and has never been seen again.

In all my career I have never encountered such a phenomenon, and I regret we were never able to examine the patient more thoroughly.

From personal notes of Simon Unseth, M.D.,
who practiced medicine in West Fork circa 1895, now kept preserved
by the West Fork Historical Society

———

NINE

The Hunt

THE HENRY WEINHARD clock over the bar said half-past seven. By now, Charlie's place should have been filled with the clatter of breakfast and the usual chatter of the loggers, miners, and contractors who made this their first stop of the day. Well, most everyone had shown up, all right, but not for breakfast. What they wanted was news, information, an update. They were huddled closely around the bar, sometimes listening, sometimes talking two, three, or all at once, but always in the same, hushed tone, as if an enemy might be listening. Andy Schuller was there, and Carl Ingfeldt as well, hiding behind Andy most of the time. Big Doug stayed near the center of the group, still the alpha wolf of the pack. Doug's sidekick Kyle Figgin was still among the young and inexperienced of Hyde River, so he was wide-eyed and all ears. Even Paul Myers, who preferred his usual spot at the end of the bar, sat a few barstools closer this time so he could listen in.

In the center of the group, sitting on two barstools that had become seats of honor, Elmer McCoy and Joe Staggart were enjoying a new level of attention and respect from the others. After all, they were older; they'd been around Hyde River a long time; they'd seen things.

Elmer, retired from the mining company and the oldest man in the room, held a beer in his hand. "Oh, it's happened before. Had to be twenty years ago. Joe, you remember Max Varney?"

Joe was Elmer's white-haired and bearded fishing buddy and fellow Hyde Mining Company retiree. He carried a minimum of flesh on his old bones, unlike the full-bodied Elmer. "Yeah. Max Varney." Joe's audience leaned forward. "He was talking crazy on the second shift, talking about some guy he'd beat up on—"

Elmer added, "Killed him, I think."

Joe's eyes widened. "Oh. I never knew that."

"Oh yeah, he was bragging about it."

"I do remember him bragging and hollering. I just don't remember—"

"But the next day, he was gone. Didn't show up for work—"

"And I remember we were talking about it just like we're talking now, and there were guys out looking for him. I went with two other miners to the bottom of the mine shaft. We thought he'd fallen down there."

"But remember, Joe? Somebody—who was that—went looking over in Hyde Hall?"

The memory hit Joe like a thunderbolt. "Wasn't it Harold?"

Elmer nodded. "Yeah, I think it was Harold." Then he chuckled and shook his head in amazement. "Boy, the time goes by, don't it? Harold wasn't much more than a kid and pretty cocky."

"Just barely in his twenties?" Joe said, trying to nail it down.

"Had to be. His old man wouldn't have let him, but he snuck down there." He added a side comment. "Harold's never been afraid of Old Town, never been afraid of Hyde Hall. He's got pull down there, guess you all know that. Just like his daddy and his granddaddy. They all—well, the Hydes have always been on the inside of it, and let's leave it at that."

Joe remembered the rest of the tale. "Anyway, Harold went down there to Hyde Hall and found Max's foot, still in the boot."

As big as Andy Schuller was, he still had to clear his throat and find his voice to ask, "You mean, just the foot?"

Joe nodded. "Just the foot. Nothing else. It was clipped off clean."

Charlie maintained his position behind the bar, but he had brought a stool around to sit on. This kind of talk was making his legs shaky, and the Max Varney tale was causing the blood to drain from his face.

Kyle Figgin, much more cautious since his little lesson in the river, asked Doug first, "Did they see it?" Doug nodded toward Elmer, so Kyle asked him, "Did you see it?"

Elmer tapped the bar with his finger as he said, "Harold brought it in here and set it on this very bar. We had guys heaving up their lunch, everybody scared crazy."

Doug spat on the floor. "We'd better find Vic, that's all I've got to say." Some murmured agreement while others had no words to say at all.

"Well, what about Hyde Hall?" asked Carl Ingfeldt. "Who's gonna look down there?"

"Phil's down there now," Charlie answered, his voice weak. That brought an immediate look of horror from all of them, so he quickly added, "Harold sent him down there."

There were murmurs of relief.

"Has anybody talked to Dottie?" Kyle asked.

"I talked to her," said Andy. "Vic didn't come home all night, and she's worried sick. She says he's been acting strange."

"Man, I can't believe this," said Kyle. "This has never happened before."

Elmer was grim. "Oh, yes, it has. What do you think we were talking about?"

Joe agreed. "You might live to see it once in your lifetime, but you don't forget it, no sir."

"I can't believe it!" Kyle said again.

Elmer grabbed him by the arm to get his full attention. "Hey. What've you always been told? You see what we're talking about now, don't you?" He included the others as his narrowed eyes swept over the crowd. "It's happening. I was hoping I'd never see it again, not ever, but it's happening."

"But why?" Charlie asked.

Elmer looked at Joe. They had discussed that question. "I think it was that photographer, that Benson character." Joe nodded in agreement. "He was a wildlife photographer, right? Got into the sack with Maggie, she probably told him everything, so he started looking around, hoping for a big story to sell to the magazines, like one of those Big Foot stories. So he got taken care of, and then Maggie—"

"She talked," Joe said pointedly. "She took it outside the valley, talked to an outsider."

"But why Vic?" Charlie asked.

Elmer and Joe exchanged a glance again. Elmer could only shake his head. "Don't know if he's really gone yet, but—"

"If Vic got taken, then—"

"Then any one of us could. You go snooping after that thing, you get it riled. And someone's been snooping, all right."

Joe added, "I've never seen him take more than one. This is something else. This just isn't good at all."

"So what's he gonna do," Andy blurted, "take all of us?"

That caused a ruckus. "What for? Why us?" "Not me, I haven't done anything!" "When's enough gonna be enough?"

"Can't Harold do something?" asked Kyle. "You said he was, you know, kind of on the inside."

Elmer shook his head. "You'll have to ask him."

Oh, sure. Kyle thought but didn't say anything.

Doug asked, "So what about that professor? Is he still snooping around?"

Wiry little Carl Ingfeldt piped up. "Les Collins and Tracy arrested him last night."

Heads turned. "What?" "Where?" "What're you talking about?"

"He was down at Hyde Hall again, snooping and trespassing."

That brought some cursing and a few fists pounding the bar.

"See?" Elmer said. "You go snooping after that thing—"

Doug demanded, "So what'd they do?"

"They took him to Harold, and Harold let him go."

"What?" "What for?" "Is he crazy?" "You gotta be kidding!"

"Well, he's gone now, that's the main thing."

"Are you sure?" Doug growled.

Carl was defensive and spoke rapidly. "I've kept an eye on him. He had his camper in a space down at the White Tail RV Park, right? Well, this morning it was gone, and Sara Tyson—you know, she runs the place—said he'd left to go home. I think Harold finally talked him out of it. Either that or Collins ran him out."

Elmer was frowning. "I don't like the sound of this. How'd he find out about Hyde Hall?"

"He was following Vic, I think. Harold didn't say for sure."

Doug and the others didn't take well to that bit of information. "How'd he know about Vic?" Doug asked.

Charlie found some napkins that needed straightening and turned his back on the group.

The front door opened, the cowbell jangling. It was Phil Garrett. His bandage was gone, revealing his chewed-up ear and the jagged seam of black stitches that held it in place. He was carrying a paper bag tightly wadded shut at the top. He went to the bar and carefully opened the bag, then laid out the broken shards of a Jack Daniels whiskey bottle. "He was there all right."

Andy Schuller backed away, the blood draining from his face. Even Elmer and Joe got off their bar stools and gave the bottle some distance. Up to that moment, they'd all been talking and bickering and interrupting, but now there was an ominous silence. All they could do was stare at that broken bottle and then at each other. No one said a word.

Charlie started walking, then hurried, then ran into the kitchen, just about knocking over Bernie the fry cook, and burst through the washroom door just in time to heave his entire breakfast into the toilet.

"EVELYN?"

Evelyn could sense something in Steve's voice, even over the telephone. "Steve. Where are you?"

"I'm over in Hyde Valley, still working on some things. How're you doing?"

"I'm all right. Are you all right?"

"I'm okay, just kind of busy. Nothing to be concerned about. I just wanted to check on you."

"I'm planning a memorial service for Cliff sometime next week. I'll let you know the details."

"Okay."

Now she was ready for some straight answers. "Steve, what are you really doing?"

He evaded that question by asking one of his own. "Is anyone else there at the house?"

"Steve, stop trying to avoid my question," Evelyn said. "You keep talking about other things you have to clear up, and other possibilities. Listen, what aren't you telling me?"

He still didn't answer her question. Instead, he came back with his question again, firmly. "Do you have someone there with you?"

"Yes," she finally answered, anger in her voice. "The boys are here, and my folks."

"Okay. Good."

"Tell me what's wrong."

"Have you talked to anybody about what happened?"

"Steve! Sure, I've talked about it. I've talked to my folks, my pastor, the boys, friends—"

"But what I'm trying to ask is, have you remembered anything else that happened that night, and have you talked to anyone about that?"

She stopped to think of the right answer and said simply, "I think I do remember a little more, but I haven't talked about it. I'm not ready to talk about it."

"Well, please don't. Don't tell anybody what you saw up there, not until you tell me first."

"And why not?"

He said nothing for an awkward moment, and then replied, "I've been finding out a few things here in the valley. There are some people here with strong superstitions about how people die in the mountains and why, and they're kind of upset about Cliff and that whole thing."

"Are you going to make yourself clear sometime tonight?"

"I can't explain it over the phone. But listen, this is important; it's the main reason I called. Don't talk to anybody about this, okay? Especially if you remember anything. Tell me first. Get me on my mobile phone, and let me take it from there, okay?"

She had plenty of questions but simply sighed in frustration. "You and Cliff. I don't know why I ever put up with either of you."

"Okay?"

"Okay, Steve. Okay."

"Oh, and—"

"What?"

"Be careful."

OLD TOWN. Dusk on Friday night. The high cirrus clouds above the mountains had faded from sunset's pink to the dull gray of night, and now the first few stars were appearing. Ravens soared from treetop to treetop, then perched and cawed from the ragged outlines of the old ruins, their last call of the day. The shadows were stretching, filling Old Town, hiding the old boards, the rusted nails, the ragged, swaying grass. The bats were out, fluttering in hurried, erratic patterns, black paper cutouts against the early night sky. The ruins, arranged in single file on either side of the overgrown road, resembled monstrous, grotesque gravestones in crumbling decay, two rows of blackening monuments to fear, superstition, and now death.

Steve Benson was there, in Hyde Hall, surrounded on three sides by the creaking, leaning walls as the darkness lowered over him like a curtain and the old walls faded from dull gray to soot black. He was sitting motionless and silent on the big flat rock only a few feet from where the whiskey bottle had broken and where Maggie's shoulder bag and shoe had been found. He was dressed in black to blend with the deep shadows of Old Town, and once again he was armed with the rifle, shotgun, and sidearm. Just behind the rock was a backpack full of provisions and extra ammunition. By his side on the rock was his flashlight. He remained still, waiting.

As the darkness deepened and his watch counted out the passing of one more hour, he continued scanning the terrain around the old ruins, especially the stand of trees across the river. As it got later, the images of the ruins and the trees began to slip away and lose their forms even as he tried to keep them in focus. He knew he would be at a disadvantage.

Hopefully, he still had secrecy on his side. He'd left Hyde Valley, all right, and tried to be very visible about it. He'd paid up at the RV park and let Sara Tyson know he was leaving just in case anyone asked. Then he spent the rest of the day driving a long and circuitous route back to Hyde Valley over the mountains from the north. He had hidden the camper off an obscure logging road a few miles up the mountain slope across the river, then hiked the rest of the way, forded the river about a half-mile upstream, and reached Old Town by dusk. Hopefully, no one knew what he was up to.

Except one. She'd waited for some real dark, apparently, and now he could see brief glimpses of her light as she approached Old Town from the river, following the route he'd used the day before. Judging from her secretive approach, he wouldn't get arrested this time.

When the tiny light reached the top of the riverbank and the open field that used to be Main Street, it blinked out, no longer needed. Steve's night-adapted eyes could just barely make out her form, stealing through the grass and brush toward Hyde Hall.

He smiled, knowing the smile could not be seen.

She was silent until she'd stepped over the old foundation into

Hyde Hall and found him there on the big flat rock. Then she muttered, "I don't know why I'm doing this."

Now Steve could see her better, and he was pleased to find she was ready to spend the whole night. She was dressed warmly in hiking gear and equipped with a backpack. She was also ready to hunt—she was carrying a rifle and a sidearm.

"Well, I have my doubts as well," Steve replied, "but I also have my hunches. I want to confirm one or the other."

"It's crazy."

"Not crazy enough to keep you away."

She seemed cross as she answered, "Well, what was I supposed to do?"

"Arrest me, I suppose."

Silence. Then, "Well, just watch yourself."

"I'd like you to watch my rear, if you would "

"I beg your pardon?"

He laughed, then turned and indicated the other side of the rock and the rest of the world behind him. "I'll take 180 degrees looking this way, you take the rest looking that way."

She sat down on the rock with her back to him. "If somebody else comes along I just might arrest you—you know, to look good."

You already look good, he thought, but did not say it. Her nearly perfect silhouette had not escaped his notice. And she was strong, too. After all that hiking, carrying all that gear, she wasn't even breathing hard. "Thanks for coming, in any event."

"You're not welcome." Then, "But thanks for the call."

So they sat there, in the dark, back to back on the big flat rock, staring at the dismal, night-veiled surroundings, rifles ready, listening for sounds.

"I figured we should try a retake of last night," Steve said.

She was still acting cranky. "If you keep talking you'll scare whatever it is away."

"Maggie was singing, and Vic was hollering. Maybe that's what the predator listens for."

"You mean bear, don't you?"

"I don't know what I mean."

"This is crazy."

"Anyway, whatever attacked them, it wasn't scared off by their noise, so it won't hurt to talk."

Tracy spoke over her shoulder, "And might I ask what bait you're using?"

"Well . . ."

"Steve!"

"This—bear—doesn't seem to care for food scraps or doughnuts or grease. He goes for people."

She turned halfway around to hiss in his ear, "You brought me out here to be bear bait?"

He thought about that for a moment, then had to admit, "Yeah, pretty much."

She turned her back to him again. He just grinned.

"I'm simply trying to repeat the circumstances of previous attacks," he explained. "People alone in the woods at night. Vulnerable, easy marks."

"Baloney."

"Listen. If it was a grizzly, sure, it could have killed all the victims. In Cliff's case, food could have attracted it, but in Vic and Maggie's cases we're dealing with a creature that attacked the victims without another food source as a motivator. Only a specific rogue bear would do that. So . . . it makes sense: If I put out conventional bait we could attract anything. I'm after whatever it is that likes to kill people, where people are sufficient attractants in themselves. And this would be the most likely spot for a recurrence, given what we know."

She could only fume a moment and then repeat, "I don't know why I'm doing this."

"You enjoy my company."

That unsettled her, and she fidgeted, then stood. "That's it. I'm out of here."

"I enjoy yours."

With a mildly disgusted huff, primarily for his benefit, she sat down on the rock again, her back to his. "We are not going to find anything."

"Like you said, it's crazy."

She stubbornly kept her back to him as she said, "But about last night . . ."

"Oh, yes, last night."

Now she turned half toward him, indignant. "You have no idea how embarrassing that was for me."

He turned around to face her. "For you? Were you in handcuffs? Were you being paraded around like some kind of criminal?"

"You weren't paraded around!"

He was actually raising his voice. "I was within inches of finding out what really happened to Vic Moore. There was evidence right here that could have been gathered, but what happened? You arrested me. You—you killed the messenger!"

She could match his tone with no problem. "I didn't arrest you! Collins did that!"

He turned away, rolling his eyes. "Oh, give me a break!"

"Well, he was right there, he had his gun on you, what was I supposed to do, let him shoot us both?" She turned her back on him again, and he did the same.

They sat there silently in the dark, back to back, rifles in their hands.

Steve finally broke the silence, his voice calm, even conciliatory. "What about Harold Bly? Do you think Maggie's fine, like he said?"

Her answer was still a little curt. "I think Maggie's dead. I told you that."

"So why didn't you tell him?"

"Why didn't you?"

Silence. They sat there and listened some more.

"He had the upper hand," Tracy finally explained, her voice softening. "All I wanted to do was get you out of that mess, and that's the truth."

Steve thought it over, then sighed. "Yeah. I know."

"And now here I am, right in the middle of another mess."

"Not yet."

"Well . . ."

There was no sound but the quiet sigh of the river, no sight but the black shadows of the old buildings and the undulating outline of the trees beyond them.

"Steve."

"Yeah."

"What are you thinking really? What are you after?"

He couldn't answer.

"Don't you know?"

"I saw something yesterday," he said finally. "Something across the river. I don't know what it was, but—" He exhaled a sigh of frustration. "—but I felt it was watching me."

"What do you mean, you don't know what it was?"

Steve shrugged. "It was hiding in the trees. All I could see was some movement." He hesitated. "And there's something else: I felt like I was the one being hunted."

Tracy was quiet for a moment. The she said, "You're starting to sound scary."

"Well, sober, maybe. Cautious." Then he added, "But that's why I'm here. I have a brother dead, a woman most likely dead and her husband denying it, another victim possibly dead, a religious, superstitious Valley man telling me tales of a killer dragon—"

"Well, you can discount that."

Steve pressed on. "Plus a rather cryptic saliva analysis from the university."

"What saliva analysis?"

"Saliva taken from my brother's corpse. I had it tested back at Colorado State. They tell me it came from a reptile."

Tracy was quiet for a long moment. Then she reiterated, "Yeah, you're starting to sound scary."

"So here I am with guesses, gut feelings, hunches, and a memory, just a memory, of not quite seeing something that was watching me. Well, I want to see it again. I want it to come after me, to come right out here in the open—"

"Will you please stop it?"

"Plus your adultery-and-jealous-husband theory doesn't hold true anymore."

She turned to look at him. "Why not? It makes perfect sense to me."

He looked her in the eyes. "You're forgetting Vic Moore."

"Maybe Vic Moore is still alive somewhere," she said, although in her heart she didn't believe it.

"If he was, it'd save your theory, wouldn't it? Adultery between Cliff and Maggie can explain their deaths: They were messing around, and Harold Bly had them killed. But why Vic?"

"He could be alive," she said stubbornly. "He's gone off on drunken binges before."

"You should have heard him scream last night."

That stopped her. "You heard Vic Moore scream?"

"It sounded like he was in a terrible struggle with something— and I think he was. I think he's dead."

Tracy fingered her rifle and peered into the forest beyond the ruins. She couldn't see a thing. She didn't mean for her voice to come out in a whisper; it just did. "It may not have been an animal. Maybe Vic Moore crossed somebody just like Maggie and Cliff did."

"Maybe."

She really did not want to believe it was an animal, at least as long as she was sitting out there in the dark. "But if it's an animal, why do you think they try to hide it? You know, sanitize the attack sites?"

Steve answered in a quiet voice himself, "You'd know the answer to that better than I would. But their superstitions and their little games don't mean a thing to me. They can have them. I want the predator."

Tracy ventured, "I figure Bly's trying to fuel the superstitions. As long as people don't find out what really happened, he can go on scaring them."

"I knew I didn't like that guy. And I especially didn't like the questions he was asking about Evie."

"Mm. I caught that too."

"I called Evie. I didn't know what to tell her except to be careful, but—"

"But she could be a witness; you're right—and they know it."

"So I want to see what Evie saw."

Tracy recalled Evelyn Benson drenched in blood and crazed out of her mind, but said nothing. She just made sure her rifle was ready and her eyes wide open, and tried not to wish she were somewhere else.

IN OAK SPRINGS, Evelyn Benson slept on the left side, her side, of the half-empty bed she used to share with her husband. The lights were out, the house was dark, the sounds of night were beginning to stir: the window on the south side of the room, no longer warmed by the sun, now cooled, ticking, creaking in sporadic intervals; overhead, a roof rafter contracted with a groan; in a corner of the ceiling, tiny claws cleared a nest in the insulation.

Evelyn slept, her breathing deep and even, while the blue light of the digital alarm clock dimly illuminated her face.

Running, darkness all around, a knife in her hand. Falling, rising, screaming her husband's name over and over. The trees shaking overhead, their tops quivering, the branches breaking.

A shadow without shape, a cloud, a force, a weight, a presence.

Pushed back. Toppled. Back on her feet. Struck across the body as with a huge beam. Cliff!

The knife. Warm, sticky spattering on her arms, her neck, her face.

Cliff. She was reaching for Cliff. She could see his red shirt, half hidden in shadow. She reached for his face, tried to brush away the shadow that concealed it from her like an overhanging branch. Her hand passed through the shadow and the shadow remained. Where Cliff's face should have been, she felt cool earth. Her face contorted with horror; her mouth formed his name, but there was no sound.

She was awake, flailing her arms, groping toward Cliff's pillow, her heart pounding.

Her own room, her own house, the real world, made its way slowly back into her consciousness, and she fell silent except for the pounding of her heart. She was alone. There was no danger.

No danger? Her spirit told her otherwise.

Steve. Pray for Steve. Pray for Steve!

She tumbled from the bed and knelt beside it, not knowing what to say, reaching for God.

STEVE CHECKED his watch, the green dashes of its hands and tiny green dots of its hours glowing weakly in the dark. Just a few minutes before midnight.

"How're you doing?"

"My rear end's getting cold," Tracy replied.

"Why don't you find a place to lie down? We can sit here in shifts."

She got up slowly, stiff from sitting, and found some fallen boards, most likely a part of the roof, that seemed about the right size and angle to support her. She tested them with her hand first to see if they would move or collapse under her, then sat on them.

"Are you married, Steve?"

Well, he thought, we've talked about everything else. Why not this? "No, I'm not married."

"Were you ever?"

"Yes. For about eight years."

"Any kids?"

"No."

"Well, that's good, I guess."

"It did make for a cleaner, neater breakup, yes."

"So how long have you been single?"

"Three years."

She reclined on the boards and tried to get comfortable.

"How about you?" he asked.

"No. Not married."

"Were you ever?"

She took a moment to answer. "Depends on how you look at it. It wasn't much of a marriage to begin with. It never should have happened, but—I was young, he was a hunk, and he made me lots of promises, you know?"

She was young? "So how old are you now?"

"Thirty. And wiser." Then she added, "Maybe."

"You don't seem too sure."

"I'm still stuck in Hyde Valley, aren't I? If I was smart I would have found a job somewhere else, anywhere else. Love can make you do stupid things."

"Yes, it's a strong emotion, all right. It can be downright devastating."

He stopped. She waited.

Then she finally prompted, "Were you devastated when your marriage broke up?"

Now we're really going to get into it. "I've survived."

"Do you mind if I ask you what happened?"

He thought it over, then replied, "Her name was Jennifer, and she left me for a friend of mine."

"I am sorry."

"Thanks," he said. "It's taken me a long time to come to this conclusion, but I realize now that both of us were at fault. There were things that each of us could have done differently."

"I know what you mean," Tracy said, her tone both solemn and sincere.

Steve tried to lighten up the conversation. "So, anyway, I've tried to be more careful since then, just keeping my eyes open, putting survival first and, well, keeping the whole concept of love confined to its biological context."

"What do you mean?"

"Love is like everything else. It's a product of evolution, a higher level of neurological and chemical responses—"

"Do tell," she said archly.

Steve laughed. "Look, don't get me wrong. All I'm trying to say is, keeping love in its true context makes it easier to understand. Also, you keep it in control, in check."

She sat up on the old boards. "Baloney."

"What do you mean, 'baloney'?"

"Is that why you're out here in the dark, waiting for the bear or creature or goblin that killed your brother? Is that where your grief comes from, and your sense of loss? Just chemical reactions?"

He found it hard to say. "Well, ultimately, I suppose so."

"Baloney."

"Listen—"

"You're just trying to deal with pain by sticking it in a test tube. That way, it isn't really yours."

He had no answer for that.

AFTER YEARS of living in Hyde River, Levi could have several of the town dogs barking and scrapping right outside his window and he'd sleep right through it. But tonight he awoke, and not just from the howling of the dogs. Something else was stirring outside his window. It was something unseen, yet he could feel it with his spirit, settling thick and black over the streets and rusting metal roofs like factory smoke, creeping through the cracks, seeping through the old framed walls and brittle window panes and invading every heart, every mind, every soul, even as people slept. Years ago, when he'd felt it for the first time, it came for only a moment, and then it was gone. In these recent days, when it came, it lingered like an endless haunting.

Tonight, it was back, stronger and darker than ever. He knew there would be trouble.

ONE THIRTY-FIVE in the morning. Steve looked toward Tracy and could tell she was awake. "So what about Bly's story of an Indian massacre? Any truth to that?"

Tracy sounded sleepy as she answered, "I've never heard that story before. But if there ever was a fight with the Indians, it was probably the Indians who got killed. The founders of this town were a rough bunch. They didn't let anybody get in their way."

"You never heard about the Indians' snake god, or this being sacred ground and all that?"

"If you want my opinion, I think Bly made it all up."

"So what really happened in Hyde Hall to make people so afraid of it?"

"I don't know."

Steve was skeptical. "You grew up here and you don't know?"

"Hey, that's how it works around here," she said defensively. "Some of this stuff goes without explanation." A moment passed, and then she blurted, "But Bly's full of phony stories, you know? Like that garbage about me leaving a trail of broken hearts."

Steve was amused. "Are you still stewing about that?"

"Well, he was making insinuations about my private life, something he knows nothing about and has no right to say anything about."

"Maybe he just meant there were a lot of guys who—"

"I know what he meant!"

Oooh, she's getting feisty. "Okay, okay," Steve said. "Brother. He sure upset you."

"You're darn right he did. Telling stuff like that to a total stranger. What nerve!"

"So how many hearts have you broken?" he asked teasingly.

She hesitated, and then conceded, "Not that many."

"So now the truth comes out."

"Well, I wouldn't call them broken hearts. More like, false starts. But we were young. What did we know? I was—"

Steve's hand was up. A signal.

She froze, half-reclining on the old boards. Steve sat on the rock, motionless, his eyes toward the river.

They listened. They could hear the sigh of the river, the sleepy whisper of the cottonwood leaves, the crickets. Nothing more.

Tracy rose slowly to a sitting position, a firm grip on her rifle, straining to see. Suddenly her heart was in her throat; the darkness around her felt heavy and threatening.

Steve raised his nose slightly and took a deep breath. He couldn't detect anything, not yet.

"What is it?" Tracy asked in the quietest of whispers.

He took a moment before replying in a hushed voice, "I might have something."

She listened. Nothing. An eternity passed.

Steve kept his eyes across the river, scanning slowly back and forth, up and down the distant mountain slope, looking for an image, any image. Sometimes he could sense something out there, and sometimes doubt would set in, but the instinctive chill in his bones, the inkling of danger, was steady enough. Sure, he was scared, but right now the hunter in him was in charge.

"Can I move?" Tracy asked.

He beckoned to her, and she stole over to the rock and sat there, her eyes following his.

Steve kept searching the black expanse of mountains. He'd heard a sound that stood apart from the quiet sigh of the river, the whisper of the breeze, the gentle applause of the leaves overhead. On many a hunting trip, he'd learned to recognize the sound an animal makes as it steals through the forest. Just now, he thought he'd heard that sound: a rustling, a breaking twig, the hiss of fur through grass. He wanted to hear it again.

LEVI SAT on his bed, phone receiver in hand, listening to the phone on the other end ring and ring. Then a machine answered, "Hi, this is Tracy. Leave a message after the beep." He left no message but replaced the receiver, then sat there, troubled by a flurry of feelings, impressions, and stark fears. He prayed for certainty. Was he right? Were his impressions true?

He got up and started pulling on his clothes. If something was brewing out in those mountains, he wanted to be there.

ACROSS THE RIVER, so far away the exact direction was hard to determine, a large limb snapped. It was the first sound Tracy had heard in all the silence they'd maintained for the last—how many minutes had it been? Long enough. She didn't dare look down at her watch.

"Halfway up the mountain, see it?" said Steve.

Tracy scanned the area, trying to see an image. Part of her didn't want to see anything, but—

There. Then not there. Where now? There they were again, two yellow pinpoints that could have been retinal reflections. Not a vehicle. No, they moved up and down, to and fro, like eyes on a creature's head. Then they were gone again, winking out behind trees.

"What is it?" she asked.

"Might be a bear. Can't tell," Steve whispered.

It didn't matter. Her hands were shaking no matter what it was, and her stomach felt so tight she thought she would double over.

The "eyes" appeared again.

"How do they glow like that?" she wondered.

Steve shook his head. He had no answer. Then he spoke just above a whisper, his lips barely moving, "I think it's following my trail. I drove the long way around and hiked down that way, from across the river." He watched a moment longer, and then he was sure. "Yeah. It's tracking me."

CHARLIE MACK awoke and rolled out of bed in anguish, his body soaked in sweat. He felt as if the point of a spear was digging into the area over his heart. He lay on the floor, his face the picture of torment, his breath coming in desperate gasps, trying to clear his mind of bloody images.

"WE'D BETTER SEPARATE, spread out," said Steve. "Can you get across the street?"

Tracy rose silently and put on her backpack.

"Keep your light handy. Don't shoot until you're sure of your target."

"Same to you."

She touched his back long enough to say good luck, then let her hand slip away. Keeping low and moving carefully, she made her way out of Hyde Hall and through the grass and brush toward the old Masonic Lodge.

Steve chambered a round, his eyes across the river. Now there was nothing but the black mountainside again. A breeze was picking up, and the trees were sighing. The extra noise would not help.

SOMETHING WAS visiting Phil Garrett that night as well. Half drunk, he sat in the corner of his weather-beaten shack on the cold linoleum floor, staring around the dark room, his fist clenched tightly around the neck of a flask of whiskey. To his blurry eyes, the old table, the chair, even his jacket hanging from a sixteenpenny nail, were all alive and sinister. He cowered there, in a stupor of fear, his other hand grasping his chest.

STEVE HAD an intense desire to get off that rock and hide somewhere, but he knew that would defeat his purpose. He would have to be the bait, at least until he could get a good shot. He looked toward the Masonic Lodge, but Tracy was out of sight.

"You still there?" he called as loudly as he dared.

He could see the palm of her hand pop up out of the grass and wave to him. All right. Now they would have two lines of fire and better chances of getting a clear shot.

Steve stayed right there on that rock, plainly visible as the breeze kept the cottonwoods steadily sighing. He took some deep breaths to steady himself.

He thought of Vic and of Maggie. He had heard Vic yelling,

and Levi had said Maggie was singing. If that was what the creature wanted, he would give it to him. In quavering, pitifully inaccurate tones he began to sing. "Hand me down my walkin' cane . . ."

He heard a click from the Masonic Lodge. Tracy had chambered a round.

Steve kept on singing . . . "Hand me down my walkin' cane—oh!" A bat fluttered close, totally silent, visible for only an instant before changing course and disappearing in the dark.

"Steve!" Tracy hissed from somewhere in the dark.

"It was a bat," he answered, then began singing again. "Hand me down my walkin' cane, I'm a-gonna leave on the mornin' train . . ."

"How's that thing going to get across the river?"

"What?"

"How's it going to get across the river, I mean, without giving itself away?"

Suddenly, there was a whooshing sound from across the river. Then, only the gentle sound of the breeze overhead. Steve had the icy sense that they'd just been given the answer to Tracy's question.

It was all he could do to sing again. "My sins they have overtaken me . . ."

There was that sound again. Whoosh! . . . whoosh!

This time it didn't come from across the river. It was above the river.

In one quick, fluid movement, Steve set the 30.06 aside and grabbed the shotgun. He didn't want to miss. Forget preserving a trophy, he only wanted to live.

Now there was a steady wind approaching across the river, a rushing with a high-pitched edge. Steve searched the sky but could see nothing but stars.

Whoosh!

A curtain fell across the sky. The stars vanished. Steve blinked. Had he gone blind?

BOOM!!!

Tracy fired a round, and the sound went right through him. He bolted from the rock and just about fell backward. In the light of the blast he saw a metallic glimmer high overhead, and he heard Tracy scream.

BOOM!!! She fired again.

Around him, the remains of Hyde Hall seemed to be caving in. The one wall wrenched, the nails shrieked, and the boards splintered. He pointed the shotgun skyward, where he had seen the metallic glimmer, and squeezed the trigger. Only a few feet above him, he saw something flashing like heat lightning.

Then something huge and dark swept in from his left and struck him. He tumbled through space, totally unable to see, and came down with a rib-cracking crash on some fallen lumber, the shotgun still in his hand.

Somewhere, Tracy was firing round after round and screaming like an incensed commando.

Suddenly Tracy's shots lit up a shimmering, metallic canopy above him in eerie stop-motion. He aimed the shotgun skyward and fired again. And again. And again. He knew the blasts had hit something, because he could hear the impact. But all he could see were sparks and flashes in a myriad of colors. This couldn't be real.

Something hit the top of Hyde Hall's stone chimney, and some stones clattered on the brittle boards below, filling the air with mortar dust.

Steve guessed an aim and fired. The mass above him lurched backward and collided with the wall nearest the river. Boards cracked and splintered, and the ground trembled under his feet.

He could hear Tracy coming across the road, still screaming. "Get out of there!"

Hyde Hall took another blow, and a splintered board whistled by Steve's head. He ducked down, then ran in frantic leaps, bounding over the foundation and rolling into the dirt.

Tracy was nearby, groping, muttering a mile a minute, trying to reload in the dark. She was frantic, out of her mind.

A cloud, a shroud, a formless mass of black went skyward,

hiding the stars, kicking up rapid, chugging volleys of wind. The sound moved out over the river, then weakened, slowed, and dropped earthward.

From the size and duration of the splash, a mountain had fallen into the river.

Steve was into Hyde Hall and out again with his 30.06 and his backpack before he knew it. He found Tracy in the middle of the road, still fussing with her rifle. "Come on!"

"Where'd it go?"

Tracy's question was answered a moment later. The creature was aloft again, pounding at the air, kicking up wind. They fell to the earth out of instinct, out of terror. Tracy gave an anguished cry. Steve covered his head. They could hear and feel cold water and spray from the river falling around them.

The sound moved up river, then came down again with another thunderous splash.

"We got it!" Steve yelled, scrambling to his feet. "It's hobbling, we hit it!"

Tracy curled up on the ground and took a few moments to breathe, just breathe.

He scrambled through the brush to her. "You okay?"

Her voice, like her nerves, was in tatters. "I have no idea!"

"Good shooting!"

She flopped in the grass on her back, unable to move. "What—what now?"

"We'll go back and get our gear. We need the lights, and we'll have to reload."

She struggled up on one elbow, looked toward the river, then up at him, then toward the river again, discerning what he was thinking and not liking it.

He offered her his hand. "Come on. We're going after it!"

Sam wasn't all that big or tough, but the guys in the platoon were still afraid of him. He could stare down anybody, and there was something spooky about him, like maybe he could sic some demons on you if he wanted. We got along okay 'cause any time Sam felt like bragging I'd just listen.

From a memoir written by Dennis Mason,
an old army buddy of Samuel Harrison Bly, sent to the Bly
family after Sam, fifty-three, disappeared in 1981
———

TEN

Perfect

THEY WERE cursing the darkness, longing for daylight, for steady hands, cramming ammunition into the rifles and shotgun in the quivering beams of their flashlights, their bodies trembling with stark terror and adrenaline.

"Two more, two more," Tracy said, and Steve dug the cartridges out of the box and slapped them into her hand. She jammed the first into the magazine; the second flipped out of her shaking fingers and disappeared into the tall grass.

Steve shined his light on the ground while she groped for the fallen cartridge. He was looking toward the river and the mountain slope just beyond it, pained by the passing of each precious second. That thing was still alive out there and getting away. If it managed to hide itself somewhere, perhaps crawl into a cave and die, they might never find it at all.

Tracy found the cartridge and slammed it in. She got to her feet and slung the rifle over her shoulder.

"Let's go," said Steve.

They headed for the river, stumbling in the dark, thrashing through the brush.

"What was it? Did you see it?" Tracy gasped as they ran.

"I saw a lot of sparks, and that was about it," Steve said.

"Where'd it go?"

"Upstream. Watch your step."

They reached the embankment just above the rolling current, then moved upstream. The riverbed widened, and they stepped onto a shore of dry river rocks.

"Okay, here we go," Steve said quickly, his light sweeping over the expansive riverbed ahead of them. The rocks, normally above the river's level and sunbaked this time of year, were wet, as if a wave had just washed over them.

"That first big splash we heard," said Steve. "There was another one farther upstream."

They ran, chasing the circles of light from their flashlights over river rocks, clumps of grass, boulders, and high-water debris.

Then Steve noticed that the bushes around them were dripping, the rocks darkened and glistening. This was the second point of impact.

They stopped and searched every direction with their lights.

The river slid quietly but quickly over the rocks. Here and there, water rippled and splashed around a boulder. They waited. They listened.

A limb snapped somewhere across the river. There was a thrashing in the brush.

They shined their lights on the river, probing its depths. The river ran wide and shallow here, maybe shallow enough to ford, Steve thought. He slung his rifle and shotgun over his shoulders and went in first, wading several yards into the moving water until it was up to his knees. He waved with his light and Tracy followed. Inch by inch, they waded through the painfully cold water. The moment either of them lifted a foot off the slippery rocks, the water carried it sideways. They slipped, stumbled, and helped each other regain their balance. Finally, they made it to the middle of the river, where the water was well over their knees.

They pressed on. The water began to drop away. She felt a surge of hope. Then relief. They were going to make it.

Finally they splashed through water only ankle deep and made it to the opposite shore, their legs numb with cold, their hearts racing. They hurried through tall river grass, away from the sound of the river, then stopped to listen. They felt vulnerable, exposed. Whatever they were after, there was no longer a river between them, only darkness, which had to be to the creature's advantage, not theirs.

They heard it again, moving slowly through thickets and dry twigs far up the mountain.

Steve looked at his watch. "Two-fifteen," he whispered. "Two more hours and we'll start getting some light."

Silence. They listened. Nothing.

"But what is it?" Tracy asked. "We don't even know what we're chasing."

"We know its approximate position," Steve replied. "If we can keep tabs on it until daylight, we might get a look at it."

Tracy's light swept across Steve's face. "Did you know you're bleeding?"

"Where?"

Tracy brushed the hair from his brow to expose a wound. He winced a little, touched it saw blood on his fingers.

"How bad is it?"

"Not too bad. You banged your head on something—or something banged you."

"It didn't hurt until now."

He pulled out a bandanna and tied it around his head. That would do it.

"No lights unless absolutely necessary. Let's go."

They started up the slope, sometimes on all fours, pushing through thickets and deadwood, grabbing at bushes and limbs, groping for footholds. It was impossible to be silent. They had to pause frequently to listen. Sometimes they could hear a sound above them, sometimes not.

They pushed up the steep grade through thick, low growth for several hundred feet and finally broke through to a more gradual, grassy slope peppered with outcroppings of rock. They were in the open again. They crouched low and listened.

Above them, there was a slow, dragging sound. Dry leaves, twigs, and gravel grated against the rocks. Some pebbles tinkled and pattered down the mountain. The sound was closer now. They were closing the distance.

Steve paused. "We'd better pace this a bit. I don't want to catch up with it, not in the dark."

"This is crazy," Tracy whispered. "We don't even know what that thing is. And what if—what if you're right? What if that thing killed your brother, and Maggie, and Vic?"

"I'm sure it did. And I want it."

Tracy could only repeat, with genuine fear in her voice, "This is crazy."

He touched her shoulder gently. She took it as comfort. Then he pushed her a bit. "Let's spread out. Stay about fifty yards over that way. We'll whistle to locate each other."

She wasn't happy about it, but she moved away from him, carefully making her way across the rocky meadow while he began working his way toward a tree line above him.

They advanced up the mountain, pushing into thick pine and fir forest, taking it slow, closed in by branches, foliage, and blackness. Slowly. Slowly. There were no trails here, no easy hiking. Sometimes they could hear movement higher up the mountain; mostly they only heard each other.

Steve halted. He had been pushing branches out of the way, snapping some of them off. Suddenly he felt no branches. They seemed to have been broken off already. He clicked on his flashlight for a better look. The space ahead of him was clear. Yes. The branches were freshly broken.

At last. He'd actually found the creature's trail. He whistled to Tracy, then softly called her, and she rejoined him. They followed the trail of matted-down grass, broken limbs, overturned stones, fresh, clawed dirt. Measured against the trail usually left by big game, this creature was leaving a superhighway.

They climbed, and they climbed some more, and always, the unseen creature stayed just ahead of them, as if matching them step for step. It would push through branches and kick over rocks, and they would follow the sound. It would fall silent, and they would wait. Then it would move again, and they would follow again, and on it went.

FRIDAY NIGHT had become Saturday morning, and the darkness was showing a hint of gray when Charlie Mack finally fell asleep, his body thrown fitfully across his bed now stripped of sheets and blankets by the night's ravings and terrors.

Phil Garrett had long since passed out on the floor, his fears momentarily forgotten somewhere in his liquor-scrambled brain, the pain over his heart quelled by the booze, at least for now.

Harold Bly slept rather well through the night, except for one brief moment when he was awakened by what sounded like distant gunfire. He gave it a good listen, some careful thought, and then smiled to himself and lay his head down again, unruffled. The rest of his night was uneventful.

FOUR O'CLOCK rolled around, and the stars began to fade behind a sky of dark blue velvet. Across the valley, the ridgeline of the far mountains was emerging from the night, sharp and distinct. It would be a clear, crisp morning.

With the light of dawn, Steve quickly made a new discovery: blood on the ground, some more on a low limb.

"It's wounded, all right."

They quickened their pace, still following the trail, now seeing spots of fresh blood every few yards.

The forest gave way to acres of broken, tumbled rocks, a vast rock slide. They followed the blood trail across it, the rocks teetering and tilting under their feet, their ankles stressed and aching. Then came more forest, mostly thin, wind-ravaged pines, the roots groping for any available crack in the rocky ground.

They were close to the ridgeline, the jagged, rocky spine of the mountain. The air was cold and thin, and now, especially after a night of hard climbing and no sleep, both Tracy and Steve could feel the altitude.

Tracy sank to an inviting rock to rest a moment. Steve, after some consideration, joined her. She was breathing hard now, but so was he, and he had a pounding headache.

"Oxygen debt," he muttered. "Hypoxia."

"Try exhaustion," she complained. "That thing's wearing us out, and we aren't even wounded. I'm cold, I'm still wet, and my feet are killing me."

Steve couldn't blame her for griping. He was pretty miserable himself. But he wasn't about to give up. "Have you noticed this creature's behavior?" he asked. He looked ahead and could still see some drops of blood for them to follow.

"What do you mean?" Tracy asked, wincing as she rubbed one of her sore ankles.

"He keeps giving himself away, unlike any other animal. If he just would have hidden quietly we would have lost him, but every time we stop to listen, he makes more noise." He paused to breathe, to survey the vast mountain stretching below them. "From one perspective, you could say we're chasing him and making him retreat. From another perspective, you'd think he was leading us, almost daring us to follow him. It's strange."

"Strange is right," Tracy agreed. "When do you think he's going to run out of blood?"

"I don't know, but that has to be a factor by now. He can't go on forever."

"Neither can we."

Steve rose to his feet. "So come on, let's end this."

"Tell him that."

Steve started out again, following the drops of blood, and Tracy stayed with him, listening intently and warily eyeing the ridge above.

The trail followed just below the ridge for another mile and then disappeared around a towering formation of rock. A blind corner. They stopped.

"Great spot for an ambush," Steve whispered.

Steve brought the 30.06 down from his shoulder, and Tracy did the same. They each chambered a round.

Then, necks craning, backs close to the rock, they inched their way around the corner, watching ahead, above, behind.

On the other side, the blood trail led upward over fallen, broken rocks and into a towering gap in a sheer rock cliff. They looked at each other.

"I think he's come home," Steve whispered. "You take that side."

They separated again, Steve on the right, Tracy on the left, and carefully approached the opening, rifles ready.

The breach in the cliff was about ten feet wide and appeared to be the entrance to a larger cavity in the rock, a vast room, open to the sky. They couldn't see how far back it went, but the walls reached at least sixty feet above their heads. They hurried to positions tight against the rock walls on either side of the entrance, rifles ready. It reminded Tracy of a police bust.

What now?

Steve motioned for Tracy to remain where she was, then stole carefully into the breach, his rifle level at his waist, the barrel aimed ahead. He advanced a few paces, stopped to look and listen, then advanced a few more.

Tracy leaned into the entrance, craning her neck to keep an eye on him, her rifle barrel aimed skyward. Elk fever was setting in, and she didn't trust her trigger finger. The narrow passage took a slight turn, and Steve disappeared around a corner. Out of sight. Not good, she thought.

A moment passed.

"Steve?" she called quietly. "Talk to me, Steve."

There was silence, and then he let out a tired, "Oh . . ." Tracy thought he sounded disappointed.

"Steve?"

"Come on in," he answered. "Take a look."

She slipped hurriedly through the opening, went up over a mound of rubble, then turned the corner to find Steve standing just inside, his rifle at rest in his hand.

On the floor at his feet, there lay a large mound of brown fur. A grizzly. It was dead.

Tracy rested against the stone wall and sighed, feeling deflated. It was only a grizzly? Only a huge bear? She knew she was supposed to be relieved, be glad it was all over, be glad they'd succeeded in the kill, but—all this for a grizzly?

She engaged the safety on her rifle and let the rifle rest at her side. "You were right," she said at last. "It was a grizzly."

Steve set down his rifle and shotgun. His disappointment was evident, as was his perplexity as he circled the bear, examining it. He checked the front claws, spread the jaws open to check the teeth, tried to estimate the length and shoulder height. He ran his fingers over the neck, the back, the belly, looking for wounds.

"Fairly young boar," he reported, and then found a small metal tag on the ear. "Number 201. Marcus DuFresne would know all about him."

"I don't understand this," she said, as events of the previous night started coming back to her. "How could this bear—I mean— were we imagining things?"

Steve withdrew his hand from the bear's neck. Blood covered his fingers. He'd found the wound.

"Gotcha!" came a third voice. Tracy jumped. Steve grabbed his rifle. They both swung around, and then . . .

Recognition. Relief. They saw a familiar face in the narrow entrance. A beard. Wire-rim glasses. A cowboy hat.

Levi Cobb.

Tracy did not appreciate being scared like that, much less seeing this man in this place at this time. "What are you doing here?"

Levi remained in the entrance, one hand leaning against the towering wall. He looked up at the narrow strip of sky visible through the rift, then surveyed the tight pocket in which they all stood. "Saving your lives, I expect."

Steve was angry. "By endangering your own? Don't you realize we were on a hunt, that our nerves were on edge? We could have shot you."

Levi was unruffled. "Oh, it was a hunt, all right. If I was the dragon, you'd be breakfast."

Tracy only sighed and shook her bowed head. Here we go again.

"Go ahead," said Levi. "Look around. Just say I'm the dragon. How would you get out of here?"

Tracy turned to walk away. "I am not in the mood for one of your lectures, Levi!" In this tight space she couldn't walk far, but just to make a statement, she walked as far as she could.

Steve didn't know what to think. True to form, Levi was mixing his weird superstitions and folksy ways with practical truths, which made it hard to dismiss him out-of-hand. Call him a fanatic or a nut, be enraged at his theatrics, but he was right about this cavity in the rocks: there was no way out. If there was a dragon and Levi was it, then . . . Steve couldn't help being a bit embarrassed.

Levi insisted, "G'won, Professor, take a good look at that bear. He wasn't shot. Not a mark on him except for the throat, am I right?"

Steve had already discovered the throat was slit. "How did you know that?"

"A guess, mostly. If I was the dragon and wanted a quick source of blood, that's what I'd do."

"Levi, we've been chasing this bear all night, and I'm a little tired. Please, just make your point."

"You weren't chasing the bear, Professor. The dragon caught that bear and cut it to leave a blood trail for you to follow. And you did."

Tracy was insulted. "Do you honestly expect us to believe that? You probably killed this bear!"

"Yeah, with my bare hands," Levi said, "and I cut out that whole trail through the woods too, broke off all the limbs, dug up the ground, led you along—" He looked at the dead bear. "—and lugged that carcass all the way up the mountain on my back, just to fool you, just to have a good time."

"All right, all right," said Steve. "Levi, just get to the point!" He gave a snort of disgust.

Levi looked straight and level into Steve's eyes. "If you don't buy what I have to say, well, I'm used to it. But I'll have you know, Professor, the dragon can fly. He don't have to smash and claw his way through the woods, leaving a trail the size of a freeway—unless he wanted you to follow him." He looked around the cavity in the rocks one more time, then locked eyes with Steve again. "He was hunting you, Benson. Take a look. Haven't you used this method yourself? Set out some bait, find a good blind, a good vantage point, wait for the game to come after the bait, and when he does, you take him." He motioned toward the bear. "You were so intent on that old bear you didn't even hear me coming."

Steve looked down at the bear. Levi was right. The grizzly had drawn his full attention. He had dropped his guard.

Tracy stormed toward the entrance. "I want no part of this!"

"He would have trapped you! Can't you see that?" Levi asked.

She only pushed her way past him and got out of there.

For a long moment, Levi and Steve just gazed at each other, Levi hoping to convince, Steve reluctant to believe.

"Maybe you should explain something first," Steve said. "I'd like to know how you got here and how you found us."

"Followed you. That was easy enough."

"How did you even know what we were doing?"

"God told me—and besides that, I could hear you shooting up Old Town. It wasn't hard to figure out."

"So you just sneaked behind us all that time? Why?"

Levi looked the direction Tracy had gone. "What I say don't carry a lot of weight around here. I had to let you walk into it so I could make my point."

Tracy's voice echoed through the narrow entrance, "Steve, don't even listen to him! He's totally out of touch with reality!"

Was he? That was one thing about Levi, you could never be sure one way or the other.

But Levi responded to Tracy's remark by beckoning to Steve. "C'mon, Professor. If you must see to believe, c'mon."

They went out through the rift. Tracy was back down the mountain a short distance, sitting on a rock, looking out over the valley, waiting. When she heard them come out over the rocks, she looked in their direction long enough to shout, "Steve, don't waste your time! Let's go!"

"Your choice, Professor," Levi said.

Steve sighed. "All right. Five minutes, Levi, and that's all."

"Fair enough. Just follow me."

Steve followed Levi several yards along the rock face until they came to an outcropping. Steve followed Levi up the steep formation, finding plenty of foot- and handholds on the way. Before long, they stood above the deep well in the rocks and could see the bear's carcass on the narrow floor far below.

"I guess you could call this a bear stand," Levi said. "That ol' lizard was up here watching you, just waiting for his chance."

There was every reason to doubt what Levi was saying, and yet, as Steve looked down into that rocky pit with one narrow entrance, he had to admit it made an ideal trap.

"How do you know he was up here?"

"Made a little side trip up here on a hunch. Come see what I found."

Steve followed him to a flat area about fifteen feet back from the edge.

"Soil's a bit scarce up here," Levi said, "but that old snake put his foot in some of it. Don't know if he meant to, but here it is."

Levi pointed to a patch of dry, sandy soil. "See here? These are the toes. There's three of 'em, see? And up here, see, here's where the tips of the claws poked in."

Steve thought that the scratchmarks and indentations in the soil were difficult to interpret, but someone with a vivid imagination might see them as an immense footprint, about thirty inches from heel to tip of toe.

Steve played along, figuring he could sort fact from fiction later. "And I suppose this down here is some kind of opposing thumb?"

"Yeah, he has those on all four feet."

Steve was almost amused. "You seem to know a lot about this creature, right down to how many toes it has."

"I've tracked it before."

"And how do I know you didn't create this footprint yourself?"

"How do you know you were just shooting at a bear?"

Steve had no answer. He could not deny that the dead bear hadn't died from one of his or Tracy's bullets, and Levi seemed to know that. The big mechanic was getting the upper hand in this discussion, Steve thought. Actually, he may have had it since the word "gotcha."

Okay, so he would listen, Steve told himself, and sort it all out later. "So where did it go?"

"Well—" Levi looked a little sheepish. "It flew off."

"Why would it fly off when it had two perfectly good meals walking into its trap?"

Levi scuffed the ground with the toe of one boot before answering quietly, "It just doesn't like being around me."

"Oohh." Of course, Levi. Of course. "Anything else?"

Levi seemed to know he hadn't made a sale. "I've taken your five minutes. I guess that'll have to do."

Tracy called from below, "Steve! Come on!"

Steve started back down. "Thanks for the input," he said over his shoulder.

"She's married," Levi said.

Steve stopped. Now that bit of information he had not asked for! He gave Levi a glaring look to shut him up.

The big bearded man just gazed back at Steve, his eyes steady.

Well. Now Steve could see why Levi Cobb had so many enemies. It seemed to be his peculiar gift.

"Steve!" came Tracy's voice. "Are you through up there?"

"Quite through!" he hollered back, and headed down over the rocks.

"SO—" TRACY THOUGHT out loud as they hiked down a mountain trail. They were heading back by an easier route, a popular hiking trail that followed the ridge and connected some alpine lakes known for their hungry trout populations. "Levi saw us tracking the bear and thought he'd make a big dragon story out of it. It's that simple."

"Tracy, you do recall what we went through in Old Town, don't you? You emptied your rifle at something, I got this bump on my head, and we were both scared senseless."

"It was a windstorm, that's all. The wind knocked over parts of Hyde Hall, and in the dark we made it out to be more than it was."

"Is that why we were both firing into the air? If I'm not mistaken, there was something up there. It could even have been flying."

"It was just the wind knocking Hyde Hall around. I shot in the direction of the sound."

"What about the splashes in the river?"

"The bear, running from the noise. We hit it, and it was trying to get away from us."

Steve realized that he hadn't told Tracy how the bear had died. "Tracy, we didn't kill the bear, we didn't even hit it once!"

"What are you talking about?" she asked crossly. "We followed a trail of blood, didn't we?"

"Yes," Steve agreed, "we did. But that bear wasn't hit with a bullet. Someone managed to cut its throat—a five-hundred-pound bear!"

Tracy was determined to put the event into a rational context. "Well, wait now. The bear came back to Old Town, and that's when the windstorm blew up. Then when the boards fell from Hyde Hall, maybe one of them hit the bear, cutting its throat open, and it ran and splashed across the river, and that's what we heard. Of course we were going nuts, shooting at falling boards, treetops, who knows what else. In the dark we could have been shooting at anything."

"Tracy, don't you think that's pretty far-fetched?"

"Steve, come on, it's the only scenario that fits!"

Steve came to another halt and faced her. "The only scenario that really fits is Levi's."

Levi. It was like a magic word that could change a beautiful woman to stone. "Steve, no. I can't accept that!"

He was amazed. "What is it about that guy that eats at you so much?"

It was a tough question for her to answer. "He's a fanatic! He's a—he's a nosy, mouthy, always-poking-around religious fanatic!"

"Well, he certainly holds a powerful grip on you."

"I beg your pardon?"

"The way you let him affect you. All he has to do is enter the situation and suddenly, poof, your objectivity is gone, and you're concocting untenable theories—"

"*I'm* concocting untenable theories?"

"Yes. Just to keep him from being right."

Now she was angry. "That is not true! I simply do not regard Levi Cobb as a reliable source of any information!"

"Are you still married?"

Bull's-eye. Her mouth dropped open with horror and indignation. "Did he tell you that?"

"Yeah."

She put her hands on her hips and said angrily, "How dare he tell you that!"

Steve was content to stand right there in her path and get this settled. "Are you?"

She was too concerned with what Levi had done to hear Steve's question. "You see what I mean? My private life is none of his business!"

"So he's lying."

"It's none of his business!"

"He's not lying?"

"He's invading my privacy, that's what he's doing!"

"Well, are you married or aren't you?"

"No." Then, "Well . . ." She was silent for a moment, then said, "I'm married on paper." Then she quickly added, "But I'm not married in my heart, and I think there's a big difference!"

His expression was puzzled. "You're married, but not really?"

She thought that over and then nodded.

He stood there on the narrow trail just musing over this new development, then finally answered, "Well, I'm divorced. Really. And when you asked me, I didn't equivocate."

That hit a bull's-eye of another kind. She looked ashamed. "Steve, I'm sorry. I should have been up front about it."

"So who's the lucky guy?"

"Doug. Doug Ellis. You met him in the tavern."

Steve's eyes widened in surprise. "You married Doug?"

She cocked her head to one side, her eyes saying, Need I say more?

Steve replayed the memory of the tavern scuffle and the big roughneck looking for trouble. "I would say we more than met. Why in the world did you marry him—if I may ask?"

"It was a mistake, okay? He made a lot of promises, and I was in love, and I believed him. He was going to go into computers, and we were going to move away from here."

Steve tried not to look incredulous, but it wasn't easy. "Doug? In computers?"

"Well, if he didn't have such a thick head he could have done it. Besides that, he likes the valley, and all his buddies are here, and his buddies come before me, so . . . what can I say? All the dreams died."

"So how long have you not really been married to him?"

"We've been separated about two months."

Steve slowly turned down the trail again. "I see." Well, he thought, that can't be all bad news, now can it?

"Steve . . ."

He stopped and looked back.

"I'm . . . well, I'm tired. I know a cabin near here. What do you say we take a break, have some breakfast or something?"

Or something? He scolded himself. All right, Steve, now cut it out. He finally said, "I guess I'd be agreeable to that."

HOMER WESTON's log cabin on Lake Pauline was a welcome sight. Homer, a retired timber worker and longtime friend of Tracy's parents, had built the place as a vacation getaway forty years ago and shared it with Tracy's family for many a lazy summer. Homer and his wife were back East visiting relatives, but Tracy knew where the key was kept and was sure Homer wouldn't mind their using it.

Lake Pauline was one of those small and serene alpine pools hidden in a forested hollow, a placid home for trout and crappie, a mirror to perfectly reflect the grandeur of the mountain peaks that towered above it. As they descended the winding trail toward the cabin, Steve could sense the quiet of this place enfolding his soul like a comforting hand, and for the first time anywhere in this valley, he felt welcome. Tracy began to relax as well, as if each step she took was a step back in time.

"You wouldn't believe the trout in this lake," she said. "My folks and my sister and I would catch our limit every time we came up here."

"Too bad we didn't bring fishing rods."

"I'm sure there are some at the cabin, but I don't think we'll have time." She smiled wistfully. "It sure would be nice, though."

The trail came to a flight of stairs made from flat stones. They descended the stairs quickly, the green metal roof of the cabin and the jewel-blue lake visible through the trees.

"I'm ready for this," said Tracy. "A good rest, something to eat . . ."

"I hear you," said Steve, genuinely tired and wanting nothing more than a soft bed and a long nap.

"From here it's about a two-hour walk back to Hyde River, so I suppose we could get back to where you parked your camper in less time than that. We could stick around here until this afternoon if we want."

They made it to the bottom of the stairs and onto a veranda of crude planks that wrapped around the cabin from the back to the front. Tracy found the key in its same old hiding place, atop a rafter just over the front door. She opened the squeaky screen door, unlocked the old paneled door, and they were in.

"Wow," she said, making several turns to take it all in, "it hasn't changed a bit."

Steve looked around and smiled. "My kind of place, no question."

The cabin consisted of one big room, separated by the furnishings into kitchen, dining, and sleeping areas. The rough-hewn table and chairs, the old wood-burning cookstove, and the two double bunks were all holdovers from an earlier time. The cabin had a particular smell that reminded Steve of family vacations, summer camp, roughing it, and childhood in the woods. At either end of the cabin were sleeping lofts accessible only by ladders, the kind of thing every kid loved to turn into a fort, a hideout, an adventure.

Tracy sat at the table and delicately removed her shoes and socks, moaning with relief. Steve did the same. Then they opened their backpacks and pulled out the food provisions they'd brought: some instant soup, a few sandwiches, some instant coffee. The sandwiches would do for now. Neither had the patience or energy to build a fire for hot water.

Tracy munched on a tuna sandwich, downed a long drink of water from her canteen, and then asked, "Steve, what are we going to do next?"

Steve had a large bite of his salami sandwich in his mouth. He swallowed quickly so he could answer, "You tell me. You're the one who knows Hyde River."

"That's what has me over a barrel right now. I'm supposed to be the cop, protecting Hyde Valley from the likes of you, and now I've helped you shoot up Old Town and meddle with Hyde River's best-kept secret."

Steve raised his eyebrows. "What happened to the windstorm you were trying to sell me?"

She had to admit it. "It was more than that."

"More than a bear?"

She hesitated, then managed to say, "Yeah. A lot more."

Steve kept one eyebrow up and narrowed the other eye. "Careful now. You might be affirming Levi's claims."

She laughed. "Oh, hardly. It's still up to me to determine exactly what it was I saw last night." Saying that freed her to say the rest of it, but it still wasn't easy. "Steve, a thing like this takes time to sink in, you know? As long as I've lived here, it was nothing but superstition and folk tales; it wasn't real. Now—well, we ran into something last night that scared the daylights out of me."

Steve nodded. "And it scared Evelyn too—scared her out of her mind."

Tracy rested her forehead on her fingers. "Her condition makes sense now, doesn't it?" She looked up. "But why should anyone believe it, Steve? I mean, consider how long this tradition has gone on and how long that thing's managed to hide in these mountains. How could it go undetected for so long? You've got hunters, anglers, campers, hikers, Fish and Game, the Forest Service—and nobody's seen anything? What's the trick here?"

Steve rested his chin on his knuckles and thought that one over. "This may sound far-fetched, but perhaps the creature used to be smaller, so it could hide more easily. If it's still growing, if it's as big now as it appeared to be last night, then I don't think it can hide much longer. It's going to be detected. It has to be."

Now it was her turn to raise an eyebrow at him. "I would say that's already happened."

He laughed. "Oh yeah, it sure has. But I wish I knew what the creature is, and what its habits are."

"It's going to be tricky finding out. Don't forget, we're still up against a whole town that's trying to hide that thing and protect it. They worship that thing. They've made a religion out of it."

"With Harold Bly at the center of that religion, am I right?"

Tracy nodded. "And taking full advantage. I can see now it's more than just talk." Then she added grimly, "And Doug's involved somehow, I know it. There were things he just wouldn't discuss with me and I always had a hunch about it."

"So," Steve ventured, "I guess it's safe to say my brother wasn't killed by Harold Bly."

"Not directly, anyway." When he looked at her strangely, she tried to qualify herself. "Well, maybe he has that creature trained, you never know."

"That's just too weird to think about."

Tracy reminded him, "I don't think Harold was above killing Maggie, though. That was still in his interests, however it happened."

Steve took another bite of his sandwich. Finally, he said, "We might take another look at the legends and traditions. In all the fiction, we might find some clues as to the facts.

"You're talking about a lot of fiction, Steve."

"Well, how about Levi? What can we glean from his version?" Steve did want to know, but he also figured he'd test her reaction again.

She reacted calmly, but she was still resolute. "There are other sources we can turn to." She took another bite of her sandwich, considered while she chewed, and then revealed, "I have a new informant in Hyde River who calls me every once in a while. I think things are heating up, people are getting nervous, so he's daring to break the Oath and leak information. He's scared, so he's talking. I'm thinking if he's scared, maybe somebody else is too."

Steve cocked his head to one side and asked, "He wouldn't be a Frenchman, by any chance?"

She stared at him. "He's called you too?"

"Twice now. He was the first one to tell me about Old Town, and he tipped me off that Vic Moore was heading for Hyde Hall—and you know the rest of that story."

"Why didn't you tell me?"

"You weren't exactly in my camp at the time." He was pleased to see that she looked a little sheepish. "Anyway, do you know who he is?"

"No, but we're going to find out. We have to be careful, though. The folks of Hyde Valley aren't going to appreciate us getting this close to their—whatever-it-is."

Steve allowed himself a slight sneer. "Well, that's too bad, isn't it?"

"Steve—"

"It makes no sense to me that anyone would want to hide and protect something that's killing people."

"Steve, this is Hyde Valley. Things don't have to make sense." She could see he was bothered. "What?"

"Why in the world do you stay here?"

She didn't mind the question. Actually, she welcomed it. "I'm running out of good reasons. My father passed away two years ago, and my mom moved to Idaho to live with my aunt. I've told you what it's like trying to be a cop around here, and as far as love is concerned, you know how that's going. I'm married, but—"

"But not really."

"No. Not really."

She looked up at the large, rough-hewn center post that held up the ceiling. "Just look at that."

He followed her gaze and saw names carved in the wood. He rose and went closer.

"Agnes, Jerry, Cindy," he read.

"My mom and dad and my little sister."

"And Tracy."

"I carved that when I was twelve years old." She searched his eyes as she asked, "Remember being twelve?"

He did. Go-carts, skateboards, swimming in the lake, building a fort in the woods, and definitely, camping out with his mom, dad, and Cliff. He smiled and nodded. "Did you enjoy it?"

"I did. Back then, everything was—oh, the way it should be. Seems like that was the last time it was ever that way."

Feeling weary, Steve went over to a bunk. "You've got time, Tracy. Don't waste it; that's all I can say."

She smiled at him. "You're right."

"Talk to you later," he said, flopping down to get some sleep.

"Have a good nap," she replied, taking the bunk across the room.

He was asleep within moments, and she lay on her side gazing at him, as she had wanted to do since she first met him. Now, she took all the time she wanted to study his strong, square chin, his ruddy complexion, his jet-black hair with just the right touch of gray. She heaved a deep sigh. Wish you'd been around a lot sooner, Steve Benson.

Finally, she too fell asleep, her eyelids closing on his image.

STEVE WOKE UP slowly, savoring that sweet state between dreaming and reality. A breeze carried the scent of pine into the cabin, and Steve could hear the clear song of the birds, feel the warmth of a summer day. They reminded him of every great vacation of his life. He was a kid again, with no trouble, no pain, no worries.

But slowly, steadily, the real world returned, nudging him when he didn't want to be nudged. He sat up, regrouping and thinking about his situation. The angle of the sun had changed. It must be almost noon, he thought. He looked at his watch. Yep. That meant he'd slept about two hours. He felt he could sleep the rest of the day, but necessity got him to his feet. They had to get back to Hyde River, back to business.

Tracy's backpack was still leaning against the center post that bore her carved name, but she wasn't in the cabin. He went out the front door, across the veranda, and down the short trail to the lake's edge. He expected he would find her down there, and it gave him a good excuse to see the lake. He couldn't be in a place this beautiful without taking a moment to enjoy it.

Old Homer had worked hard getting a beach established, Steve thought. The coarse sand under his feet was not typical for a mountain lake; it had to have been put there, probably over many backbreaking days. More labor had gone into a rough-hewn dock that reached out into the lake. To one side of the beach, Steve saw a small rowboat lying with its hull to the sun.

Steve never tired of a beautiful sight, and he took plenty of time relishing this one. The lake was a mirror today, and the mountains on the other side seemed to reach into infinity, their height doubled by the lake reflection. He wished he had a camera, and yet a camera couldn't do it justice. The deep green of the trees against the blue of that water . . .

The trees. Steve blinked and looked again. He was still a little sleepy, and he'd been up all night. It was probably a third of a mile across the lake, so distance could have been a factor. He may have imagined it.

He stood very still and kept watching. Now the trees along the distant lakeshore were clear and distinct and every trunk, every vertical line, solid. Nothing unusual. So . . . maybe it was a flashback of sorts; maybe it was wishful thinking; maybe he hadn't seen the same, weird mirage he'd see from Old Town.

But his instinct was nagging him again, the same as before Danger, it said. Pay attention! He looked away to clear his eyes and hopefully his mind. He was too tired to trust his senses.

Then he saw Tracy, and all thoughts of the mirage disappeared. If his instinct was still speaking, he was no longer listening.

She was swimming in the lake, just now coming out from behind a fallen, sun-bleached snag that dipped into the water. Around her, the water sparkled like diamonds in the sun, and as her strong arms propelled her along, the morning light made her fair skin shimmer. Maybe I shouldn't be watching, he thought, but she hadn't seen him yet, and like everything else around here, she was a breathtaking sight.

He quickly scanned the shore and spotted her clothes, hung on the dead branches of the fallen snag. Was he dreaming? Was she a mirage? No. He was awake, and she was there, all right, with a considerable stretch of open space between herself and her clothing.

For an instant, he thought she looked his way, that their eyes met as she paused to push back the wet hair from her face. But her behavior didn't indicate she was aware of his presence, especially as she swam to the shore, climbed up on the rocks, and crossed the open space to where her clothes were hanging.

In the fleeting moment it took for Tracy to gather her clothing and disappear into the trees, Steve's curiosity was fully satisfied. He was pleased to find that his initial guess had been less than correct: He'd figured she would be nearly perfect. Now he knew she was quite perfect.

We have talked in the past about Harold's scare tactics as he tries to intimidate the other children, and I'm afraid he still lapses into such behavior from time to time. Today during recess he found a garter snake, cut off its head, and told two girls the same thing would happen to them if they didn't let him copy their homework. The tale about the pet monster who eats children came up again as well. I think another parent-teacher conference would be in order.

From a letter by Marian Clayburg, Harold Bly's
fourth grade teacher, to Sam and Lois Bly,
circa 1960

ELEVEN

Charlie

WHEN HAROLD BLY came knocking at Dottie Moore's door, she was almost expecting it. The town, in its peculiar, hush-hush way, had been buzzing about Vic's disappearance since Thursday night, and the news was bound to reach Bly's ears sooner or later.

Now it was Saturday afternoon, and he stood at her door, dressed up, cleaned up, the perfect gentleman, his hat in his hand, and asked if she'd heard anything.

She was sick with dread and worry but knew she was obliged to talk to him. She told him what he had to know already. "I haven't heard a thing, Mr. Bly, not a thing. Some of the guys went looking for him up the draw, and I think they've checked the river downstream."

"No calls?" he asked.

"No, no calls. I've been on the phone with Phil and Carl, and I talked to Pastor Woods, too. Everybody's looking and calling around."

"Have you called the sheriff?"

In Hyde River there was only one correct answer to that question. "No. You know how Vic feels about that."

Bly nodded with understanding. "Listen, Dottie, if there's anything I can do, please let me know. I'm here to help, you know that."

Again, her response was correct. "I know. I appreciate it."

"And that goes for the financial side of things, too. I know you and Vic were struggling, and—"

"We were doing all right."

It was as if he didn't hear her. "If it comes down to it, and you feel you need to move on to a better life somewhere else, just remember, I'm ready and willing to unburden you."

She was offended, but guarded her answer. "If you want to buy the business, you'll have to talk to Vic."

Unruffled, he only smiled at her. "I'm sure you and I will talk again."

Meaning, Dottie knew, that she had no option.

THAT NIGHT, in the ruins, another prayer was said at the stone and another scrap of paper was burned. This one bore the name of Dottie Moore.

SUNDAY MORNING, Carl Ingfeldt went into Charlie's, sat on a barstool between Phil Garrett and Andy Schuller, who were already eating, and ordered the Number Two breakfast, ham and two eggs with toast.

Bernie was the only one there to take his order. After he went into the kitchen to fry it up, Carl asked quietly, "Where's Charlie?"

Phil and Andy looked at him with a secret in their eyes.

"Says he's sick," said Phil.

Andy added, "He's been sick since Friday morning; you know that?"

Carl was getting the picture. "Since we found out Vic disappeared."

"He's hiding, that's what," Phil said.

"And I'll thank you to keep your mouth shut," Andy said.

"Well he thinks he's next; that's what I think."

Andy stiffened. There was fire in his eyes as he said, "You keep talking about it and we're all dead. Now shut up!"

Phil surrendered. "Hey, sorry."

"We've got more trouble," Carl said. "I just got a call from Sara down at the RV park. That professor is back."

Andy and Phil said nothing, but their stunned faces said everything.

Carl continued, "Pulled in with his camper last night, all set to stay awhile."

"I thought you said he was gone!" Phil protested.

"He was. Sara said he looked like he'd been out hunting. Didn't look like he got anything, though."

They looked at one another. Then Phil ventured, "Could be Harold's right. He thinks—" He lowered his voice. "—that Tracy and the professor have taken a shine to each other."

"That professor's what started the trouble in the first place!" Carl said, pounding his fist on the counter. "It's too bad about his brother, but if he'd just left things alone . . ."

"Harold says it's gonna be just like Maggie and that guy's brother, all over again."

"Does Doug know about it?" Andy asked.

"Ain't nothing to know yet. But I'm betting Harold's right." Carl took a swallow of coffee. "Well, if she's gone soft on that guy, there's gonna be a change in the rules around here."

"You got that right," Andy said.

"I don't care if she wants to play sheriff, but if she's gonna—"

The front door opened.

It was Deputy Tracy Ellis, in uniform, apparently there on business. "Good morning."

"Good morning," said Bernie the fry cook. He was just setting Carl's plate in front of him.

"Morning," the three conferees muttered into their breakfast plates.

She approached the bar in a casual mood. "Is Charlie here?"

"No," said Bernie. "He's been pretty sick the last few days."

"Oh, I'm sorry to hear that."

She looked at the three men who looked back at her with the familiar Hyde River expression reserved for strangers. She smiled and laughed a little, hoping that would loosen things up. "Hey guys, nobody's in trouble. I just wanted to say hi."

"Well," said Phil, "hi."

"Hi," said Carl.

"Hi," said Andy, going back to his eggs.

"So, is Charlie at home?" she asked.

Phil said nothing, Andy shrugged, Carl started to say "I don't know," and Bernie answered directly, "Yeah, he's stuck at home. I don't think he's going anywhere."

Phil dropped his fork and grabbed it again before it went off the bar.

Tracy said thanks and went out.

The moment the door closed, Bernie received a concert of rebukes. "Are you nuts?" "What'd you tell her for?" "She's snooping around again, can't you tell?"

Bernie just threw up his hands, "Hey, she asked me, I told her. What's the big deal?"

"Aw, forget it," said Andy.

Phil started to say, "We think maybe she's—"

"Forget it!" Andy insisted, so Phil did.

Bernie went back to work in the kitchen. The three ate in silence for a moment.

"She looked pretty nice," Carl observed.

"Smelled nice too," said Phil. "Little bit of perfume, little bit of makeup, eh?"

"Doug's gonna kill that guy," muttered Andy.

AN HOUR LATER, Tracy eased her Ford Ranger to a halt near the gutted shell of an old filling station. Steve appeared from behind a rusting truck chassis and climbed in.

"Charlie's at home," she told him. "I called him, and he's expecting us."

"How can you be sure he's the Frenchman?"

"Oh, I think I heard him using that accent in the tavern one night. He never was very good at it."

Steve crouched down below the windows while Tracy drove up the hill past the church and then doubled back the next road over, easing down behind Charlie's little two-bedroom house with the white lap siding and green metal roof. They were trying to avoid being seen, but in this town, secrecy was nearly an impossible dream, and they knew it.

They went to the back door, and Tracy knocked. There was no answer.

"Charlie?" Tracy called, not too loudly.

He was just inside the door. "Who is it?"

"It's Tracy Ellis."

"Did you bring the professor?"

"Yes. He's right here with me."

They heard a chair slide away from the door, and then the rattling of the lock, and finally the door opened a crack. Charlie took a look first, then opened the door so they could come in.

Without a word between them, Tracy and Steve knew they were seeing a repeat of Maggie Bly's condition, the same nightmare revisited. The kitchen was a case study in neglect, with cupboard doors left open, all the counters cluttered with food, dishes, jars, and containers from the refrigerator. The living room was a mess as well, and dark. The draperies were all pulled; it was hot and stuffy, and the air was permeated with a horrible smell, as if something had died. Some boards had been nailed across the front door, and a large stuffed chair had been pushed against it. A crude cross made of sticks lashed together with duct tape hung on the door, and to one side, a hunting rifle leaned against the wall, apparently loaded and ready.

Charlie was a dirty, pitiful, sweat-soaked mess, wearing only pajama bottoms and a T-shirt stretched tightly over his round belly. His hair was disheveled, and his crooked glasses had slid down his slick face so they were even more crooked. He was crouching a little, as if expecting gunfire through the windows any moment, and fingering an oversized bronze crucifix hanging around his neck.

"Sorry for the mess," he said in a trembling voice.

"Why don't you sit down, Charlie," Tracy suggested in a gentle voice.

The man hesitated as if unsure what she meant, then sank onto the couch, clutching the crucifix in a shaking hand, his face contorted and his eyes filled with fear. Tracy also sat down on the couch, and Steve pulled a chair over. Charlie just sat there, looking from Steve to Tracy and back again.

"Charlie," Tracy began, "do you know why we're here?"

Charlie looked at Steve. "You're back. You came back."

Steve nodded. "I thought we should talk face to face."

Charlie looked at Tracy. "Vic Moore is gone; did you know that?" Before she could answer, Charlie turned to Steve. "Did you see anything down in Old Town?"

"So you're the Frenchman?" Steve asked.

Charlie sat there dumbfounded, caught and speechless.

Tracy touched his arm. "Charlie, it's okay, we're here to help."

Charlie swallowed, his throat dry. "It—it wants me next. Please—you can't let it take me!"

"Can't let what take you?" Steve asked.

It was as if Charlie's brain had malfunctioned. He looked at Steve and tried to answer, but his mouth refused to form the words.

Steve took over. "Charlie, listen. We both went back to Old Town Friday night, the night after Vic disappeared. We staked the place out, and we saw something."

"Aaaaawww . . ." Charlie let out a weak little wail of terror and put his finger in his mouth.

Steve quickly recapped the previous night's events, saying only as much as he thought the trembling man could take. Charlie drew no comfort from the tale, that was obvious.

"Did you kill it?" Charlie cried. "Did you kill it?"

Steve was sorry to answer. "No. It got away."

Charlie wailed louder as he clutched his heart. "Now we're all dead! You didn't kill it. Now it's only madder!"

Tracy insisted, "Charlie, do you know what it is?"

The very question terrified him, and his brain seemed to go on the fritz again.

Steve pressed the question. "We saw something, Charlie. We heard it, we tracked it all night. So there's more to this thing than just—" Steve didn't want to say superstition, not to Charlie.

"You've got to kill it! You've got to kill it before it takes us all!"

"We need your help, Charlie. You need to tell us anything you know about the creature."

"The cops never do anything. They just stand around and do what Harold tells them."

That annoyed Tracy a bit, but she wasn't about to argue with someone half out of his mind.

Charlie leaned toward Steve in earnest. "I thought you could do it! You're an outsider, you don't owe anybody anything, you're not afraid, you could do it! You've got to do it, do it before the dragon finds out—" Having let that dreadful word slip, he cried out in pain, and looked about the room as if the thing would come through the walls at him. "Aawww, I can't tell you!"

"Why not?" Tracy demanded.

He looked at her dumbly.

"Why not?" she demanded again.

"You—you talk about it, it gets mad, and you get killed."

Tracy looked around the room. "So, if you don't talk about it you're going to get killed anyway, right?" He couldn't answer. "Did Vic ever tell anybody about the dragon?"

"No."

"So what happened to him?"

At the thought of Vic, Charlie just stuttered.

"So what difference does it make?"

"I—I can't."

Tracy stood up. "Okay, Charlie. Tell you what. You help us; we'll help you. You keep stonewalling, and we're out of here. It'll be just you and the dragon; he can have you anytime he wants."

It was as if she'd dropped a stick of dynamite at his feet. "No— NO!!" he cried.

She stood in her place and looked down at him, waiting. He just sat there, his brain numbed by fear, by generations of tradition.

Steve grabbed Charlie's arm and leaned in close. "Charlie. We shot it, and I think we hit it, so it's not a ghost or a spirit or a god. It's an animal, and that's all. There doesn't have to be anything mysterious about it." It was a tiny germ of hope, at least. It seemed to calm him.

Charlie looked from Steve to Tracy and back again. "Can you kill it? I'll—I'll pay you to kill it."

"Charlie," Steve said, "listen to me. I don't need money. I need information. I need to know what I'm up against, what its habits are, its strengths, its weaknesses. I have to be able to anticipate its behavior."

Charlie shook his head. "But if I talk about the dragon, the dragon'll know."

"Who says?" said Tracy.

No answer.

"Did Harold tell you that?"

He shook his head in fear. "I'm not talking about Harold." Then he looked up at the ceiling and shouted as if to God, "I'm not talking about Harold! I'm not saying anything about him!"

"Okay, okay. Calm down, Charlie." Tracy shot a glance at Steve. "Harold Bly again."

"I'm not talking about him!" Charlie repeated.

"Are you afraid of Harold Bly?"

"I'm not talking about him."

"And you won't tell us anything about the dragon either?"

Charlie just sat there, staring into space. Tracy sighed and looked at Steve, about to give it up.

Then Charlie muttered, "I don't know why the dragon's gotta

pick on us. We didn't do anything. It's the Hydes; they're the ones who did it."

Tracy was almost afraid to ask a question for fear Charlie would clam up again. "The Hyde family, you mean?"

"They're the ones who brought us all the trouble, and that was a hundred years ago. I'm not a Hyde. I didn't ask for any trouble. Why's the dragon have to come after me?"

Steve ventured, "What did the Hyde family do a hundred years ago?"

"Made a deal with the dragon, that's what. They gave him the town. But I didn't give him the town. Nobody asked me."

Calmly, carefully, Steve asked, "So, are there particular people in this town who—who have contact with the dragon? Does the dragon work for them?"

Charlie nodded. "Oh, yeah. You bet. Make a wrong move, or say too much, and—" He made a slashing sound and ran his finger across his throat. Then he added loudly, "But I'm not talking about Harold!"

"No, of course not."

"The dragon knows where you are. He can come after you, tear you apart, and eat you while you're sleeping."

"I doubt he could get in here," Steve said, looking at all the precautions Charlie was taking.

"I don't know. Maybe he can. Harold says—I mean, I've heard—the dragon can go anywhere. He's like a ghost. He's not really alive; he just floats around, and he can disappear. You can't stop him."

"He's not a ghost," Steve insisted. "He's a big, dumb animal, and somebody's been lying to you."

That kind of talk scared the man. "No! Don't talk that way! The dragon'll know!"

Tracy rolled her eyes. "Now you're starting to sound like Levi Cobb."

The magic word again. Tracy may have used it on purpose, Steve thought. Charlie was offended, which snapped him out of his stupor. "Hey! No, no, no, that isn't fair, and it isn't true! I'm not crazy! Levi's crazy; I'm not!"

"I think you're giving the dragon way too much credit, just like Levi does," Tracy said.

Those were fighting words for Charlie. "I'm not like Levi! I'm not a bigot and a crackpot and a religious nut! He is! I'm a fair and honest businessman, and I've got a right to do what I'm doing!"

Tracy was fishing. "Is that so?"

"Yeah, that's so! Ebo Denning was never gonna go anyplace with that mercantile! I'm gonna make it go places! I'm gonna bring some life back to this town! It was the right thing to do, and I gave Ebo a fair price!"

"So what are you afraid of?"

He fell silent, still fuming. Then he finally blurted, "Just kill that thing, that's all! You kill that thing and everything else will be fine."

Steve sighed heavily. He was beginning to lose his patience. "So what can you tell us about it?" he asked again.

"I don't know anything."

Tracy tried another approach. "So tell us somebody who does know something."

"What about Jules Cryor?" Charlie asked.

"Sorry," said Tracy, not recalling the name.

"He's working a claim up on Saddlehorse, been there for years. He's got a perfect view of the whole valley from up there, and he lives as he pleases, does what he wants."

"How do we get there?"

"He's a hermit, though, and I hear he's kind of strange. He might shoot you just for coming close to his claim, I don't know."

"It's a start," said Steve, taking out his pen and pad. "Give us some directions."

While Charlie dictated how to get to Jules Cryor's cabin, Tracy recalled another name. "There's also Clayton Gentry. He's a young fellow, a logger, down toward Backup. The guys at Charlie's can't say anything nice about him. It never occurred to me until now, but maybe he's seen something and talked about it, and that's why the guys don't like him."

Steve finished writing the directions. "Anybody else?"

Charlie shrugged. "I don't know anything. And I'm not really talking about anything."

"No," Steve agreed, "you sure aren't."

"We'll check these people out," Tracy said. "In the meantime—Charlie?"

He looked at her.

"Whatever you do, stay away from Old Town, you hear me?"

Sam learned the rituals from his mother Charlotte, who learned them from her father James Hyde, who learned them from his father, Benjamin Hyde. So it's run in the family ever since Sam's great-grandfather started up the town in the 1800s. The rituals always required some blood, which Sam usually got from a sheep or a goat, and they almost always took place in or near Hyde Hall in the old part of town, where it all started.

I don't know if Sam really had control of an invisible demon beast, but he sincerely believed he did, and to see the fear he could invoke in people, they believed it too.

From the diary of Abby Bly, Sam Bly's estranged wife and Harold Bly's mother, dated November 14, 1973, three days before she disappeared without a trace. Her disappearance was attributed to a bear attack.

———

TWELVE

Stirrings

Harold Bly, grim-faced and impatient, went into Charlie's Tavern and Mercantile on Sunday afternoon to check the books, do a quick inventory of the stock, observe the flow of business, inspect for neatness and cleanliness—in short, to check everything.

"Where's Charlie?" he asked, carrying the accounting books to a table near the video games.

"Uh—he's home," Bernie said. "He's been sick."

Harold's eyebrows went up. "Oh, has he now?"

"Yeah."

Harold took a seat and then glared up at Bernie. "Have a seat, Bernie."

Bernie obeyed, sitting across from Bly. Talking to Bly always made him nervous. The man had a short fuse.

"Do you understand the partnership I have with Charlie?"

"Well—you bought into the business, right?"

"I bought most of it." Harold jerked his thumb toward the mercantile. "I bought the tavern so Charlie could buy the mercantile.

The tavern's worth seventy percent of the whole shebang, so that makes me seventy percent owner, which makes me boss."

"Yes sir."

"So Charlie's sick. Who's taking his place?"

Bernie shrugged. He wished he were anyplace but sitting across from Harold Bly, having to answer his questions. "There's me, Melinda the waitress—you know, whoever."

"I want somebody running this place, not whoever. You got it? I want this place adequately staffed at all times. We're here to make money."

Bernie cringed. "Okay, yeah, right."

"How long you worked here?"

"Five, six years."

"You always leave that much grease on the grill?"

"Uh—" Bernie looked toward the kitchen as if an answer would come floating out the door at him.

"Times are changing, Bernie. People are paranoid about fat and cholesterol, right?"

"Right."

"No more grease. And we're going to go over the menu. We need good meals cooked correctly, something to fit the times. You got it?"

"Yeah, yeah, Harold. I got it."

Bly opened one of the accounting books and scanned the columns. "You move a lot of beer in this place."

Bernie smiled sheepishly. "Well, yeah. It's a tavern. It's a restaurant, but it's a tavern too. The guys like to come over and—you know—"

"We need a happy hour right after quitting time at the mine. But only an hour, you got it? Let's give the men some incentive to drink more. And put out some pretzels. Keep the guys thirsty."

"Okay."

"Bernie, I think you'd better write this stuff down; I've got more."

"Oh." Just my luck, Bernie thought. He ran to get a pencil and paper. By the time he got back, Carl, Phil, Andy, Paul, and Doug had gathered around Bly's table to have a word with him. Bly was listening intently.

"It's about Charlie," Phil murmured

"Well, is he sick or isn't he?" Bly asked.

"He's been acting weird," Andy said.

"I saw Tracy and that professor guy over at Charlie's house," said Carl, with an aside to Doug. "Sorry, Doug."

Doug only listened grimly.

"But if Charlie's talking to that outsider, we could all be in real trouble," Phil said, his head tilted a little. His ear was still bothering him.

"Somebody needs to shut him up," Carl said.

The others agreed.

Harold raised a hand to quiet them down. "You guys worry too much."

They started to protest, "Well, what about Vic and Maggie?"

"We've got things to worry about, don't you think?"

"Hey, I want to be around next week, you know?"

He had to quiet them down again. "Get yourselves under control. That's Charlie's problem right now. He isn't in control. He's feeling guilty about this Ebo Denning thing, so he's hiding out, afraid he's going to be next." He glared at them. "Somebody gets killed in a car accident, you don't stop driving; am I right? Or somebody dies of lung cancer, you don't stop smoking, right? Or somebody gets in an accident because they were drunk, you don't stop drinking, do you? Life goes on, guys, and you live it as you please and let the chips fall where they may. If something happened to Vic and Maggie, that doesn't mean anything's going to happen to you. Charlie just needs time to figure that out." There were more protests, and Harold had to shout over them. "Hey, he's no different than you are, and you're no different than him! I'll tell you what's going to happen: He'll hide out at home for a week or so, and then he'll get over it—and hopefully, so will all of you." Then he added, meeting every eye, "And Charlie doesn't need any help getting himself together, you follow me? No rough stuff. Let him be."

"But what about the professor?" Phil demanded. "Ain't he the cause of all the trouble?"

Bly glared at Phil. "I think we were talking about his sister-in-law, weren't we?"

Chastised, Phil looked down at the floor and said nothing.

"Besides—" Harold paused for effect. "I think I've made it clear enough that there isn't any trouble. Maggie's with her mother, and Vic is off somewhere on a drunk. Forget about both of them."

Nobody said anything, but it was easy to see nobody believed that for a second.

"And that's the way it is!" Harold emphasized.

"Oh, yeah, that's the way it is," said Paul sarcastically, scratching his chest. All heads turned in his direction, and he just looked back at them derisively. "I think I've finally figured this whole mess out. The problem is, there isn't any you-know-what, but you think there is one, so you act and talk like there isn't one because for some reason, if anybody thought there was one, there really would be one. Why don't you guys just believe there isn't one? You do that and bingo, the whole problem's gone."

There were angry mutterings. Andy took a step forward, ready to punch Paul. Doug was right behind him, ready to assist.

But Bly shot his arms out to restore order. "Hey!" They listened. He relaxed in his chair again, his eyes ablaze, and reminded them all, "Paul's right. Think about it."

They all looked at Bly, then at one another questioningly.

Harold spoke soothingly and firmly. "We all agree, right, that there isn't any—we won't mention it by name? If that's the case, then Maggie's all right, and there's nothing to worry about. Vic is okay, so we don't need to worry about him. As for Charlie, he's got nothing to say to anybody because there's nothing to talk about. As for this professor, he'll never find anything, and as for his brother, you heard what the cops said: it was a grizzly." He looked at Doug. "As for Tracy's little fling with the professor—Doug, it's a tough break, but you'll live. It's your problem, and it has nothing to do with the rest of this town." He scanned the group, looking each of them in the eye. "If there really is anything to worry about, we'll know when the time comes, and we'll know what to do. Other than that, I don't see why we need to be having this meeting and getting each other all stirred up."

"What about Cobb?" asked Doug.

Bly repeated, "We'll know what to do when the time comes." He looked again at the balance sheets before him. "Now get out of here. I'm busy."

They moved away, unsatisfied, murmuring a bit, troubled, and Bly noticed.

But he was troubled too. Charlie? Why Charlie? He never had had a bad thought about Charlie. Or had he? Maybe he dreamed it without knowing it.

Then he brightened. What if Charlie? Hmm. It wouldn't hurt Bly's situation, now would it?

He acted casual and unruffled, but scribbled a little reminder in his notepad, "Contact Metzger regarding full acquisition." Metzger was his lawyer, and Bly wanted to be sure he could take full ownership of the tavern and mercantile in the event of Charlie's—well, in the event Charlie decided to leave town for an indefinite period.

He also made a note to call Sheriff Collins. One of Collins's deputies was stepping out of line.

In the corner, enjoying some quiet time with his wife and children after a Sunday church service, Reverend Ron Woods couldn't help overhearing most of the heated conversation. Things were getting stirred up, all right, and would soon be out of control. It was time to get involved.

CLAYTON GENTRY was a man in his early thirties with a young wife and two small children. He and his brother ran a small logging company, and he lived in a homestead he'd built on some river frontage not far from Backup. His place wasn't hard to find, just a turn off the Hyde River Road and a short trip up his driveway. When Tracy called him, he seemed a little hesitant, but finally he agreed to meet with her and Steve if they could keep it low-profile.

Now Tracy and Steve sat on the Gentry front porch with Clayton and his wife Jessie while the two little girls played in and around a plastic swimming pool in the front yard.

"Some people are really crazy around here," he said. "Here you are talking to me, you oughta be talking to them."

"But they don't talk," Tracy said.

He laughed. "And they don't like people who do. I found that out the hard way."

"What happened?"

"I saw something and I talked about it, and they didn't like it."

"Tell us about what you saw," Steve said.

Clayton looked north, up the valley toward Hyde River and Saddlehorse Mountain. "My brother and I were doing some logging on private land up past Saddlehorse—"

Jessie interrupted. "Clay, don't talk too loud. I don't want the girls to hear this."

Clayton shot a glance at his two little girls, still totally involved in playing around the little pool, and lowered his voice. Steve and Tracy had to lean close to hear him. "Anyway, one afternoon I was up there by myself, just cleaning up some slash and drawing in the cable. We were finished, you know." He was silent a moment, then said, "Listen, I've done a lot of hunting; I go out every year, so I'm not new to the woods. I know how to spot game; I know what it looks like. Anyway I was standing by the rig, pulling in cable, when I heard a noise and I froze. You know, when you're used to hunting you do that 'cause it might be game." His expression grew troubled, and he looked upward, as if trying to find the exact words he needed. "I looked up the mountain some hundred yards or so," he continued, "and I saw something up there, something moving, but it wasn't a deer or an elk—you know, I expected I'd see a brown or black or tan color—and it wasn't a bear or a moose. But it was big, whatever it was. I mean—" He sighed heavily. "It's hard to describe it." He turned to his wife. "Jessie, you got your little mirror around, the one you use in the bathroom?"

Tracy and Steve looked at each other, puzzled.

While Jessie went inside, Clayton rubbed his chin, thinking. Finally he said, "It was kind of like looking at a mirage or something. It didn't seem real, you know?"

Steve nodded. He knew.

"You see it, but then you wonder if you're really seeing it."

"You say it was big," Steve said. "How big?"

He thought it over. "Well, what I saw was at least thirty feet long, maybe longer. I mean, I was trying to see where the ends of it were, and it never seemed to quit."

Jessie brought the mirror, just a small rectangle.

"Okay, look at this."

Clayton put the edge of the mirror against the side of the house and tilted it back and forth. "You see here, how if you put the mirror at the right angle, it kind of looks like the siding on the house just goes right on through, like the mirror isn't there? Then you move the mirror just a little and then you know it's a reflection 'cause the siding on the house bends, it breaks in the middle."

Steve recognized the effect and tried not to show the chill it gave him. He'd seen it himself, across the river from Old Town, and maybe on the other side of Lake Pauline. Gentry's description was quite accurate.

Gentry continued, "Pretend the thing was like a mirror. You couldn't really see it—it was more like you were seeing where it was, like you were seeing the reflection of other stuff on it."

Only a few days earlier, Steve and Tracy would have scoffed. Now they were spellbound—especially Steve.

"How long did this go on?" Steve asked.

"Not long. Maybe ten seconds or so. I was thinking of getting my gun out of the truck, but the thing was gone before I could move."

Steve nodded. Gentry's experience nearly matched his own.

"It didn't scare me too much," Clayton continued. "I guess it was so weird I didn't know what to think." He smiled grimly. "If I'd known what it was, maybe I would've been a little more nervous about it." He laughed. "The scarier part was when I stopped in Hyde River for a beer and told somebody about it. Now that's when things got scary!"

"You said the wrong thing," Tracy volunteered.

He nodded emphatically. "That was quite an experience, being surrounded by all those tough miners and being told, number one, I didn't really see anything, and number two, I'd better not talk about it, and number three, they didn't want me around there anymore. Like I said, some people can really be crazy around here."

"How long ago was this?"

"Two summers ago."

Steve prompted, "But there was one other time you saw it?"

"Yeah. I was doing some dozer work just a little south of Hyde River, and believe it or not I saw it flying. It was still kind of like that mirror thing I showed you, but—" He wiggled his hands, trying to come up with a description. "—it's kind of like the light was hitting it wrong 'cause I could see the outline pretty good."

"What time of day was that?"

"Right about sunset. I was getting ready to quit for the day."

So it's not strictly nocturnal, Steve thought. Then he asked, "What were the sky conditions?"

He thought for a moment, then said, "High clouds. They were turning pink from the sunset and, yeah, when I saw it, it was passing in front of a pink cloud, but it was still blue like the sky. That's how I saw it."

"What did it look like?" Steve was finding it hard to contain his excitement. Finally they were getting somewhere!

"At first I thought it was the biggest goose I'd ever seen," Clayton said. "Well here, you want me to try and draw it for you? I'm no artist, but it's easier than trying to describe the thing." Steve handed Clayton his pen and writing pad. Clayton drew it as he described it. "It had a long, slender neck, slender body, big wings, kind of like a heron—wide wingspan." He looked up from his drawing. "I thought at first maybe it was one of those home-built airplanes that look kind of funny, like they're built backward? But it was flying like a bird, you know, the wings were moving like an eagle does, but in slow motion." He moved his arms slowly up and down to recreate the effect, the pen in one hand, the writing pad in the other. Then he went back to the drawing. "Oh, and it had a long tail too, as long as the neck." He finished the drawing and handed it to Steve. "You know how those flying dinosaurs looked? It looked kind of like that."

Clayton had drawn what looked like a long-necked lizard with wings.

"Like a reptile, then?"

"Right," Clayton said. He turned and pointed north, toward Saddlehorse Mountain. It came out from behind Saddlehorse and then moved south across the valley and then went down behind those hills over there to the east. I watched it the whole time."

Steve and Tracy peered toward the mountains as if the thing might appear again. Right now, the sky looked slightly cloudy and quite uneventful.

"When was this?" Steve asked.

"Just a couple months ago." Then he gave Steve a direct look. "And you're the first person I've told other than Jessie."

Tracy asked Jessie, "Have you ever seen it?"

Jessie only gave a little shiver. "No, and I don't want to. It scares me just hearing about it."

"You've no guess as to what it is?" Steve asked Clayton.

"No idea," Clayton said. "And I've learned better than to ask." Then he added, "And I'm sure some other people have seen it too; don't let them kid you. They've seen it. They just don't talk about it."

Steve kept looking toward Saddlehorse. That beast had to have a lair, a nest, somewhere. Up on that craggy peak, perhaps?

"Some rumors have gotten around, though," Clayton volunteered. "I've heard it's a dragon—you know, like it breathes fire and everything. And then there's the legend that it's the devil, like a hundred years ago the early settlers made a pact with the devil and the devil became the patron saint of Hyde River. You hear wild stuff like that."

"So how could a thing that size hide itself for so long?" Tracy asked.

"Maybe it wasn't always that size," Clayton responded. "And anyway," he continued, "I don't think it would have any problem hiding. First of all, nobody'll talk about it. Second, you can hardly see it anyway, even when it's right in front of you. And third, those mountains up there are full of caves and old mines, and some of them go really deep. It could find a place to hide, all right, and if it never came out except at night, it could go for years without being seen."

"I never thought about the caves," Tracy said. "But you're right. That's where Benjamin Hyde first found gold and silver. Some of the mines were started in the caves. They've been dug out and scoured so deeply—some of them go for miles."

"So have you ever heard of it killing anyone?" Steve asked Clayton.

"Well, you must know about that guy who got killed up on Wells Peak a week or so ago. The rumors going around are that the creature did it."

"Clay—" Jessie cautioned.

Clayton lowered his voice again, but countered, "Jessie, don't worry so much." He turned to Tracy and Steve. "There's another legend that it only eats wicked people." He chuckled and put his feet up on the porch railing. "Guess that gets me off the hook. I'm a pretty good person. I'll probably do all right."

Tracy and Steve stood and thanked Clayton for talking to them. As he walked to Tracy's Ranger, Steve found himself hoping that Clayton was right—that he was off the hook. But Steve was convinced there were no guarantees.

"DEPUTY ELLIS, I'll see you in my office."

Collins was sharp, abrupt, and didn't even look at her as he marched into his office. Tracy, just returned from her Sunday shift, followed him, knowing her rear end was about to get fried.

"Close the door."

Yep. Fried.

She closed the door and stood silently before him while he gathered his thoughts and his papers and arranged his desk. Finally he said, "So how was your day and how did you spend it?"

"Largely uneventful, sir. I spent a lot of time with Professor Benson, helping him to resolve some issues so he could be on his way."

Collins looked up. Perhaps he wasn't expecting such a direct answer. "On the department's time?"

"It was my regular shift, yes. I did my rounds, and he basically tagged along. I covered Hyde River, the upper Hatchet Creek draw, I stopped in to check a complaint regarding Charlie Mack—"

"What complaint?"

"Maybe I shouldn't say complaint. It was more of a concern, actually. He hadn't shown up at the tavern for a few days, so I stopped in at Charlie's home to make sure he was okay "

"And you had the professor with you?"

"Yes."

"And why were you not driving your patrol car?"

"Sir?"

"Is something wrong with it?"

"No sir."

"Then why were you driving your own private vehicle when you visited Charlie Mack?"

She thought for a moment, but didn't lie. "Quite frankly, sir, I didn't think it would look good for people to see a sheriff's deputy with a man sharing her patrol car."

Collins leapt to his feet. "But that was exactly the case, wasn't it, Deputy? You were seen, in uniform, on duty, in the company of a man—a man, I might add, who is not popular out there in Hyde River, am I right?"

"You're right, sir."

"That was foolish, Deputy! Foolish and stupid!" He came around his desk and approached closely enough to yell directly into her face like a drill sergeant. It was an intimidation tactic, and it worked. She tried not to cringe, but couldn't help it. "When you are in this uniform you shall conduct yourself like a deputy sheriff's officer, and any personal interests you may have will be put aside, is that clear?"

"Sir—I was not acting out of personal interests."

He smiled cruelly. "That's perfume you're wearing, isn't it?"

"Why do you ask, sir?"

"You know good and well why I'm asking."

"You wear aftershave; I wear perfume. Are you discriminating between the two, sir?"

He backed off. "Deputy—Tracy—let's play it straight with each other. Your personal life is your business, and I won't tell you what to do. But you've been spending time with this guy from Colorado while in uniform, and the folks in Hyde River are whining about it."

She thought before responding. "I understand, sir."

He locked eyes with her. "Meaning?"

"Meaning, I'll be careful about appearances from now on."

Her answer didn't quite satisfy him. "Keep going."

"I won't let it interfere with my police work, sir."

"So I won't hear anything further about this, will I?"

"No sir."

"All right. I'll hold you to that."

"Sir?"

"Yes."

"Who told you about all this?"

He scowled at her, his hands on his hips, his head cocked sideways. "I don't think that's any of your concern."

"And yet these people feel it's their place to spy on me and question my actions right down to which vehicle I'm driving, as if I'm not allowed one inch of discretion? I'm not comfortable with that."

"I don't care a whole lot about your comfort level, Deputy. It's my job to make sure you effectively do yours; that's what it really comes down to."

"Was it Harold Bly?"

He was about to snap at her, but let it go. "Good guess."

She made no effort to hide her disgust. "I guess there's nothing I can say to that."

"No, there isn't. We work for him. We work for all the people of this county. When they call, we answer."

"Will that be all?" she asked, hoping her anger wasn't evident in her voice.

"One more thing."

"Yes sir?"

"How's Evelyn Benson doing? Has Benson said anything about her condition?"

"I understand she's doing well, sir."

"Has she remembered anything she may have seen up on Wells Peak?"

"I haven't heard. Who's asking?"

"Oh—I was just wondering."

Oh, I bet, she thought.

SUNDAY EVENING Harold Bly arrived home with the pretty red-head Rosie Carson on his arm, not at all ready to find Phil Garrett waiting on his front steps.

"What do you want?"

"Boss, can I talk to you a minute?"

Harold said to Rosie, "Go on inside."

She hurried past Phil and went into the house.

"All right, Phil, what is it?"

"What you said back at the tavern, I mean—"

"What?"

"Boss, you can't just sit back and do nothing. You know we've got a problem here!"

Harold smiled a cunning smile. "Phil, you're the one who has a problem, not me."

Phil didn't argue.

"What's wrong with your chest, Phil?"

Phil jerked his hand away from his heart. He hadn't even realized he was rubbing it. "Huh?"

"What've you got there, a mosquito bite or something?"

"Uh, yeah. Bad bite, Harold, that's all."

Harold bent close and spoke softly into Phil's good ear. "You afraid of the dragon, Phil? Is that it?"

Phil struggled to get an answer out, then finally nodded.

"Phil, you're the only one who can do anything about that."

"But, boss, can't you—"

"If you think the dragon's after you, then, hey, if I were you, I'd be thinking of a way to appease the dragon, you follow me?"

"Appease him?"

"Sure. Make him happy, show him you're on his side, do him a favor, you follow me?"

"But what can I do?"

Harold straightened up. "We've already talked about it, Phil. There's somebody out there who's seen the dragon. She could tell people about it—unless somebody does something to stop her." He crossed the porch to his front door, then turned. "Let me know when you get it done. Once you get it done . . . I'll see what I can do."

And with that, he disappeared inside his house.

CLAYTON AND JESSIE GENTRY were sitting in their living room watching television, and their two girls were in bed asleep. Clayton was in sweats, Jessie in pajamas and a robe. There was a bowl of popcorn between them on the couch, half-eaten. It was a very typical evening, and they weren't expecting company, so when they heard a firm knock on the door, they looked at each other in surprise. Jessie, being closest, rose to answer it.

She opened the door and saw six men in black hoods standing on the porch. She gasped, then screamed. Clayton came on the run, and they both tried to slam the door shut, but a huge arm and a foot blocked the door, holding it open.

Jessie's scream had awakened their daughters, who began to cry.

"Clayton," came a rough-sounding voice, "this has got nothing to do with your wife and kids. Figure it out."

"All right, all right!" Clayton hollered back.

Jessie looked at her husband, too frightened to speak

"Go on, take care of the girls," Clayton said.

She hesitated.

"Go on!" he repeated, then called out the door, "Ease up! I'm coming out!"

"NO!" Jessie cried. At that moment, the two little girls ran into the living room. She put her arms around them, and they clung to her.

Clayton took a last look at his family and then stepped outside, closing the door behind him.

"Now what do you want!" He was immediately seized by two men and pulled off the porch.

"Don't worry," said a third. "This won't take long."

The first blow landed in his stomach. He doubled over. Another hooded man grabbed a fistful of Clayton's hair and straightened him up again.

"Didn't we warn you about talking?" the man said, right before delivering a stunning blow to his jaw.

He tried to answer, but someone else hit him first, and then someone else, and then someone else . . .

STEVE HAD settled in for the night in his camper, and now he sat at the table, poring over Forest Service maps again, trying to compare Clayton Gentry's sighting of the creature with the location of Saddlehorse Mountain. If the creature had a nest or den anywhere near Saddlehorse, then Gentry's sighting made sense. The real clincher would be talking with Jules Cryor, the miner working a claim right on the mountain. Steve was double-checking the directions Charlie had given him. The map showed several old mines in that area, so he figured the old man's mine shouldn't be too hard to locate. If Cryor could report any sightings, the search would be narrowed down indeed.

The next trick would be to gain some tangible evidence to establish that an undiscovered species really existed. He might be able to find droppings somewhere—droppings from a creature of this size should be unmistakable—or footprints from which to make plaster casts. The greatest prize would be a good photograph. With strong evidence, he could request help from the university, from the paleontologists he knew, from the entire academic and scientific community. Without such evidence, however, he was still chasing after a myth, and such professional people had no time for any more Sasquatches, Yetis, or Loch Ness monsters.

At any rate, having taken the leap and having accepted the existence of the creature and its basic description—he marveled at that development alone—he was willing to postulate that the creature was a nonextinct flying dinosaur. The famed Loch Ness monster, if it existed, was thought by many to be a prehistoric species that had managed to survive the millennia in the great depths of Loch Ness. Steve could theorize that the "Hyde River dragon" had managed to survive in these mountains because of its nocturnal habits, its below-ground habitat, and its unique and uncanny ability to conceal itself—an ability yet to be explained.

Steve tried to remain objective, but he was getting excited despite himself. The possibilities were absolutely staggering!

There had to be more than one if the species had survived from prehistoric times; perhaps there was a whole colony of them nesting under the mountain somewhere. Perhaps the creature really was carnivorous, a cunning hunter. Perhaps, in addition to wild game, it had also acquired a taste for human flesh, which would not be unusual. If so, the Coincidence Theory could make sense after all. A bear didn't fit the theory too well, but a carnivorous dinosaur could fit nicely, coming back regularly to Old Town knowing it might find lone, distracted humans there, ready for the eating.

From these premises it was easy to see where all the myths and legends of Hyde River came from, and how those myths and legends served to conceal the creature's existence from the outside world. A quirk of evolution, an anomaly, had fallen into the hands of simple people, and they'd attached moral, even spiritual significance to it. Like ancient pagans who worshiped the sun, they were worshiping and fearing something they didn't understand.

Disturbing. Awesome. Incredible. Steve had to get back into those mountains. He had to learn more, and quickly! He—

The knock on the camper door was gentle, but it still made him jump. He was irritated at the interruption, then curious. These days, he never knew who might be outside this door. Or what their motive might be. He double-checked the accessibility of his .357 and then asked, "Who is it?"

"It's Sara, Dr. Benson. I've got someone here to see you."

Sara, the lady who ran the RV park. He opened the door.

She was standing next to a tall, lanky, Lincolnesque character dressed in work clothes. "Dr. Benson, this is Reverend Woods from Hyde River. He'd like to have a word with you, if you don't mind."

"I hope I'm not disturbing you," said the minister.

"No. Come on in."

"Thank you."

"Good luck, Reverend," Sara said, walking away. Steve wondered what she meant by that.

Steve put away his maps and cleared a seat for Woods to sit down. "To what do I owe this visit?" Steve asked, pulling two cans of soda from the small refrigerator and offering one to the minister.

"Thanks." Woods seemed uncomfortable. "I'm really sorry to barge in on you like this."

"You've obviously got something on your mind."

Ron Woods was looking around the camper as if unable to meet Steve's eyes. "Well, yes, I do."

Steve was still wondering about Sara's "good luck" comment. "Did Sara ask you to come over?"

"Oh, no, no," he said quickly. "I called her to find out where I might locate you. Then when I got here she showed me where you were parked, that's all. But she's a longtime resident of Hyde Valley," he added, "and she picks up on things. She's concerned."

"Concerned about what?"

His words were measured, cautious. "Well, Dr. Benson, let me lay some groundwork first, would that be all right?"

"Sure."

"First of all, I'm here to speak for myself and no one else. Second, I'm sure you've had a chance to feel out this valley, and you've gotten a sense of how the people respond to strangers, to outsiders—"

"Oh, in many ways, yes," Steve said, hoping he didn't sound too sarcastic.

"All right, so maybe this will make sense to you: Dr. Benson, I would be less than honest if I didn't tell you that—" He wasn't quite sure how to say it. "I think you might be putting yourself in danger."

For Steve this was no big surprise. "I'm listening."

Woods continued, "I've—I've been around the town, talked to some folks, heard things. People confide in me, you know. Anyway, I've gotten a clear picture that the town right now is far from tranquil. These people have a lot of deep-seated traditions and fears, and they seem to regard you as a threat to those traditions."

Let's get to it, Steve thought. "Are you talking about the dragon, perchance?"

Woods actually chuckled with relief. Now he wouldn't have to cover all that ground. "Yes, that is part of it, bizarre as it may sound."

"Oh, it's bizarre, all right. But listen: You need to realize, and maybe you can help them realize, I'm not here to violate any of their traditions. I'm only trying to find whatever animal is responsible for killing my brother." Steve knew that was no longer the only reason, but it was reason enough for now. He knew too little about Woods to trust him with any more than that.

Woods stared at Steve, puzzled. "But—I understand you shot a grizzly."

"It's a long story, but the evidence we gathered virtually eliminates a grizzly as the culprit."

"So, you're not hunting for a particular bear?"

"No."

Woods studied him for a moment, and then his face began to show a rising incredulity. "You don't think—are you thinking there really is a dragon?"

Steve admitted, "Well, I wouldn't call it a dragon. But I am exploring the possibility of a creature that could be construed to be a dragon."

"Ohhh. No wonder people are upset." He shook his head, visibly dismayed. "Oh, Dr. Benson, I am sorry. You've been led astray." He smiled, partly from amusement, partly from embarrassment. "You've been talking to Levi Cobb, am I correct?"

"Among others, yes."

"Oooo-kay."

"Just what is it about Levi Cobb that elicits such reactions from people?" Steve asked.

"That's a difficult question," Woods said. "Levi is—well, first of all, he's a part of the town. I mean, he is a child of Hyde River, with all its beliefs and fears and superstitions. He had a rough life before he embraced religion—lots of fights, drinking—we won't get into that. He goes to my church, and we love him; we put up with him, but, I'm sure you've noticed, he is one dogmatic character. He tends to see everything in black and white, right and wrong, true and false, and—well, if I were to define him, I would say he's a Hyde River religionist. He holds to a dogmatic theology with all the Hyde River mythology mixed in. So he sees the mythological dragon in religious terms, and he'll preach about it to anyone who will listen—which at this point is no one in the town, except you.

"And if you listen to him long enough, he'll eventually try to make a convert out of you. This is why so many people dislike him, and I hate to say this, but guilt by association does work around here. People see you with Levi, and they equate you, they put you in the same camp."

Steve laughed.

"It really is serious," Woods insisted.

Steve couldn't stop himself from laughing again. "Levi Cobb and I in the same camp!" Then he said, "All right, sure, it's serious. But can you see it from my perspective? Here I am, a wildlife biologist, alone in this area, and my brother's been killed by some sort of creature, and I want to find out what it is. Now I find I'm offending people because they've made a religion out of whatever this creature is and because I'm associating with someone they don't like. I have a hard time understanding that."

Woods took a sip of his soft drink, then asked. "Have you heard of the Hyde River massacre?"

"Something to do with Indians?"

"No. There were no Native Americans involved."

"Hmm. Well, tell me about it."

"Like everything else in Hyde River, it's a closely kept secret. Some of the older folks know about it but won't discuss it, not even with their children, so the memory is fading with the generations. As I've been able to piece it together, there was a major disturbance, a fight, a riot, something like that, back in 1882. Two different factions were fighting for control of the town and all the mineral wealth. One of the factions was led by Benjamin Hyde and his family. The other faction was . . . well, we may never know who they were because they were all wiped out, murdered. But that all took place on July 19, 1882. That's when the Hyde faction gained full control of the town and wrote up a new charter, which they all signed."

Steve raised an eyebrow. "Ah, now that's the part Harold Bly didn't mention."

Woods's eyebrows went up. "Oh, you know about this?"

"Only about the town's charter being signed. I saw the portrait of Benjamin Hyde in Harold Bly's house, and I saw the table with the date carved in it."

"Ah, yes, that's right. I suppose Harold Bly told you he's a direct descendant of the town's founder?"

"Oh, yes. He seemed pretty proud of that."

Woods's expression went a little sour. "It's nothing to be proud of. It was a terrible day. A lot of people died, and while their bodies were still warm, Hyde and his cronies gathered in Hyde Hall and signed that charter with the blood of the people they'd killed. Now that's a pretty gruesome way to start a town, and I believe it's that heritage, that bloody beginning, that has given rise to the fears and superstitions."

"What about the Oath, the whole secrecy thing?"

Woods nodded with recollection. "That goes back to the charter. The signers of the charter took an oath of secrecy that they would never betray the town's dark secrets to outsiders, and that tradition has stuck. That's why so little is known about the massacre to this day and why people still conceal things and won't involve the authorities. The town settles things its own way."

"Tracy Ellis told me a little about that," Steve said. "But I'm curious now about that charter. Is there a copy around?"

"Levi claims to have a copy. I don't know if it's genuine, but he swears it is. He's collected a lot of old documents over the years. It's part of his obsession with all this."

"So does the charter explain any of this?"

Woods shook his head. "I read it—that is, I've read the copy Levi has—but it said nothing about the specific acts that were shrouded behind the Oath. As I recall, it was basically a declaration of the settlers' aspirations and dreams, the common goals that held them together. The signers asserted their inherent goodness and wisdom—"

"Inherent goodness?"

Woods smiled. "Well, of course. There were statements to the effect that they could build the town and run it by themselves, falling back on their own wisdom and resources, and that's not an unusual attitude; it's the typical pioneer spirit. But as for any details on what happened or any confession of wrongdoing—it's all buried with that generation, and it's been kept under wraps ever since.

"Anyway, this is why people are so sensitive about strangers asking questions, and so afraid of Old Town, and have superstitions about Hyde Hall, and are afraid of Harold Bly—"

"I certainly got the impression that people are afraid of Harold Bly," Steve said. "I know he's a powerful man in the town and all, but people's fears seem to go beyond that. Why are they so afraid?"

"He's a descendant of the original Hyde clan, and so all the curses and superstitions and secrets are still associated with him. You wouldn't believe the rumors that go around: that he once danced with the devil, or that the devil lives in Hyde Hall and Harold Bly has lunch with him on occasion, or that the dragon is the devil's pet and it knows Harold and obeys him. It's all rubbish, of course. But in that town, it works, and I think he enjoys it."

"When I spoke to him, he made it sound like it was a real hassle for him."

Woods smirked. "Don't believe Bly. He enjoys it. People cower around him, and that gives him power. As far as I'm concerned, the dragon is Harold Bly's way of ruling the town through fear." Woods stopped to draw a deep breath. "And that's why I'm here, to—enlighten you, I suppose, to let you know that you've been drawn into the middle of something that is not going to be worth the trouble—and I mean a lot of trouble. Now, I know Levi can make the dragon sound like it's just as real as you and I sitting here. To hear some people tell it, that dragon lives right up in the mountains, and all you have to do is go up there and take a look and you'll see it. But trust me, the dragon is a myth, a tale that grew out of Hyde River's sordid past."

"How?"

"How? How what?"

"Well, okay, you've got murder and greed and grabbing for land

and power. I can understand that those things lead to superstitions, fears, and a code of silence. But a dragon? How do you get a dragon to pop up in the middle of all this?"

Woods shook his head. "The Hydes again. I think it's a scare tactic they concocted a century ago, and it's worked ever since. As for why it works so well, I have my theories."

"Let's hear them."

"I think there may be a lingering guilt, a sense of participation in what happened a hundred years ago. The tradition of silence won't let people talk about it, so they can't deal with it. In a way, I think they're punishing themselves with this imaginary beast. The dragon is retribution for what happened over a hundred years ago, and, I suppose, anything else that's happened since then."

Steve digested that a moment. "So you're saying there's no such thing?"

"It's real in people's hearts and minds, and that's one of the reasons people are so upset right now. The way I see it, the dragon is an embodiment of guilt feelings. That's why, if an outsider like you comes into town and starts asking about the dragon or hunting it, they feel as if someone is prying into their inner secrets, their hidden faults. Let's face it. Nobody likes that."

Steve thought that over and then asked, "Well, what if there really was a dragon? Wouldn't those people be glad to be rid of it?"

"There isn't one."

"But I'm saying, if there was, wouldn't they want to be rid of it?"

"I know this may sound strange," Woods said, "but I don't think so."

"Why not? Why would they want to keep a creature around that eats them up?"

"It goes back to guilt again," Woods answered. "It's a psychological thing."

My brother must have felt awfully guilty, Steve thought.

Reverend Woods stood. "I think I've taken up enough of your time," he said. "I hope you'll think over what I've told you."

Steve stood and extended his hand. "I will," he said. "You've given me a lot to think about."

At the door of the camper, Reverend Woods turned and said, "I also hope you'll keep the town's traditions in mind. And," he added, "be careful."

"I will," Steve said. "To both." He watched the minister walk away, then closed the door and grabbed another soda out of the refrigerator. He put it back. Reverend Woods was gone now. He grabbed a beer. Then he sat down to think things over.

So Bly must have concocted that tale about the Indians being responsible for the massacre. Tracy'd never heard the tale, and Woods had contradicted it. Steve could understand a descendant of Benjamin Hyde wanting to hide his ancestors' hideous sins. Besides that, Steve didn't like Bly anyway, so Bly could be a liar without damaging Steve's impression of him.

As for Reverend Woods's insistence that the dragon was a myth, that raised another nagging question. Was he protesting too loudly? Considering the weight of Steve's own recent experiences and observations, Woods's denials rang a little hollow. If nothing else, the minister seemed to be right in sync with the rest of the town. If there was a dragon, he was helping the town protect and hide it.

But Steve was intrigued by one new bit of information: Levi Cobb had documents. What they could mean, he had no idea, but one of the biggest challenges in this whole hunt was sorting truth from fantasy, actual events from rumor. No matter what anybody said about Levi, he'd been right on many points, wrong on—Steve couldn't think of an instance when Levi had been clearly, obviously wrong. Whacky, maybe, but not wrong. Levi had been doing his homework, Steve figured, and those documents, whatever they were, had to be a part of his body of knowledge.

But that would come later. For now, there was one more witness who needed to be interviewed. Steve laid out the Forest Service map again and tried to locate the mine of Jules Cryor. So far, no luck.

He checked his watch. It was a little after seven. He had Charlie's home phone number and the number of the tavern. After Woods's warnings he felt just a little hesitant about calling the tavern owner, but, as he'd promised, he intended to be careful.

He picked up his mobile phone and punched in Charlie's number at home.

No answer.

Nuts. What did that mean? He was home but afraid to answer? He was out wandering around? He was dead?

Steve would have to call the tavern. He punched in the number.

"Charlie's," a voice answered. Steve could hear voices, music, the clatter of dishes in the background.

The voice was unmistakable. "Uh—Charlie?"

"Yeah. Who's this?"

"Charlie, this is Steve Benson."

The voice brightened. "Oh, yeah, how you doin'?"

"Well I'm all right. How are you?"

"Just dandy."

Just dandy. Since when? Why? "I tried calling you at home. I thought you'd be there."

"Heck no. I got a business to run. So what's up?"

"I wanted to double-check the directions you gave me—"

"You mean Jules Cryor's mine?"

Yeah. It was Charlie, all right. "Yeah, that's right." Steve looked at the map. "I'm not sure which service road I'm supposed to take after I get to the end of forty-seven. Do I go up fifty-one or take . . . sixty-three?"

"Take sixty-three. Fifty-one'll just take you around the other side. You got your map there?"

"Right in front of me."

"You'll see that it looks like sixty-three and fifty-one connect on the map, but they don't, there's a big cliff between 'em. So you take sixty-three, and sixty-three'll wind up the east side 'til you get up to Potter's mine. You see that?"

"Potter's mine, Potter's mine . . . ah! Got it."

"Okay, stay on sixty-three and follow it 'til it runs out. Cryor's place is right up the slope from there, you can't miss it."

"Great, thanks."

"I just hope he misses you; you get what I mean?" He laughed. "Why do you even want to go up there?"

Steve sensed that he should be careful about what he said. "I just thought I'd like to talk to him, see how the hunting is up there."

Charlie chuckled. "You're wasting your time."

"What?"

Charlie lowered his voice. "Listen, you really don't have to take all this dragon stuff seriously. It's a mind game people play around here. That doesn't mean it's real."

Something had happened; something was going on. "So you're saying there is no dragon?"

"Well—no. Listen, I was out of my head. I know I said a lot of crazy things."

"Charlie, you sounded pretty convinced—"

"Look, it happens sometimes. You get under some pressure, you start feeling kinda down, and all that stuff gets to you. But, hey, you can't let things get you down forever. You gotta get on with life."

Steve was knocked off balance by what Charlie was saying. "Charlie . . ."

"Gotta run. Be careful up there."

Click. He was gone.

Steve sat there, the phone in his hand, dumbfounded, suspicious, puzzled.

The phone rang in his hand, and he just about dropped it.

"Hello?"

"Steve, it's Tracy." Her voice sounded urgent. "I just got a call. Evelyn's been attacked."

Steve felt as if someone had punched him in the stomach. "What do you mean? What's happened?"

"Somebody broke into the house and attacked her."

"Is she all right?"

"I think she's okay, but I don't know the details yet. The Oak Springs police are there now, and I'm in touch with them. Can you meet me in West Fork and lead the way?"

"I'm already moving," he replied, keeping the mobile phone to his ear as he hopped out of the camper and started unhooking the water and power. "Where do you want to meet?"

"I'll be in my patrol car at Snyder's Restaurant, right where the Hyde River Road comes into town."

"Have you called the house?"

"I don't have her number."

"I'll call her as soon as I hang up with you."

"See you at Snyder's."

He ended the call with Tracy and banged out Evelyn's number. The line was busy. He quickly unhooked the camper and was ready to roll.

He turned the engine over, cursing under his breath—cursing the town, the valley, the stupid, backward people and their warped, deranged ways. If Evelyn was hurt, if as much as a finger was laid on her—

He roared out of the RV park, the tires squealing as he accelerated down the Hyde River Road toward West Fork.

In the years that followed, a hellish and capricious contagion beset my brother-in-law. As with almost everything else that touched his life, Benjamin remained secretive and hid it from us until it reached such an advanced stage that concealing it was impossible. Among our close family and personal physicians we tested many theories as to its cause and origin: Some thought it came from the mines and first took hold in Ben's lungs; some thought Ben had drunk water contaminated by the mine tailings. One theory, which I believe was shared by all though spoken by none, reflected back to his secret practices and the Oath we all took in Hyde Hall. In timid silence, we all feared that he had brought this plague upon himself, and not only that, but that we would soon see it brought upon our own heads because of what we had done.

From the diary of Abigail Homestead,
Benjamin Hyde's sister-in-law,
dated March 9, 1915

———

THIRTEEN

The Memory

THE OAK SPRINGS police had arrived at Evelyn's house to find the front screen door hanging crookedly to the side on its hinges. Inside the two-story white colonial, a trail of strewn clothing, dirt from houseplants, broken picture frames, overturned furniture, and a broken lamp showed a path of struggle from the bedroom, through the hall, and into the living room. After determining that Evelyn had not been seriously injured, the police moved carefully through the house, documenting the evidence and reconstructing what had happened. A photographer was en route to get shots of everything.

Evelyn sat on the couch in the living room, her son Travis by her side, as one officer, a mild-mannered and polite veteran on the force, sat in the stuffed chair opposite her, pen and pad in hand, getting her statement.

She was shaken, her blouse was torn, and some bruises were starting to show on her arms and face, but she was coherent and strong, and her eyes were steady.

The officer was carefully retracing the events. "And you came home about seven—"

"About seven," she confirmed.

She had come home with a load of groceries, driven into the garage, turned off the engine, closed the automatic garage door . . . it was all routine, totally ordinary. It was only afterward that Travis went out and discovered that the back door to the garage had been left open, something the family never did because they didn't want the cat getting into the garage. The conclusion was that the attacker had entered that way.

"Where was Travis when you arrived home?" the officer asked.

"Upstairs in my room," he replied. "I had some music going, so I didn't hear anything at first." He looked a little sheepish.

"Then what happened?"

Evelyn recounted what had happened, and the officer took it down. "I brought all the groceries in and set them in the kitchen, and then I went into the bedroom to put my purse on the dresser . . ."

She saw the whole terrifying scene passing before her eyes and began to describe it: The closet door bursting open like an explosion. A figure pouncing on her like a panther, knocking her to the floor. All the while he was trying to subdue her, she was delivering blows to his body, fighting like an animal . . .

Dark. So dark. A massive weight, a monstrous presence. No voice, no sound but the crashing of tree limbs, the digging and scraping of stones and earth. The smell of blood . . .

Evelyn stopped in her recounting and closed her eyes, her hand on her forehead.

"Mrs. Benson?" the officer asked. "Are you all right?"

"Give me a second," was all she said. Frantic, scrambled, mixed-up images were swirling through her mind, the memories of two attacks now edited together. The horrible events of this night were bringing back in crystal clarity the events of that night, and it was all she could do to distinguish between them. With great resolve, she continued to describe what had happened tonight. "I pushed him off me and ran out into the hallway," she continued as the officer wrote it down. "He pulled out a knife and kept trying to stab me."

"Stab you?" the officer repeated.

She could recall the knife in his hand and her own hand around that wrist in an iron grip that now amazed her. They wrestled down the hallway, spinning, crashing into the family photographs hanging on the wall. He slammed her against the wall, the knife gouging the wallboard inches from her face. She delivered a kick to his groin, and he doubled over. Then she had him against the opposite wall and planted a haymaker to his jaw . . .

She was knocked backward into grass and stones, and the beast continued to grapple with something on the ground. On her feet again, crazed with anger and instinct, she pounced on the creature, her arms about its neck. It lurched backward, and her feet left the ground. She was being whipped about, the limbs of trees slapping and lashing at her. For some reason her arms would not let go.

"Um." She had to pause. What happened next—not on that night, but here in the house? "The next thing I remember, we were in the living room here." She gave the officer an awkward smile— "I guess I jumped on his back. I had my left arm around his throat, and I just kept hitting him with my other hand . . .

She was high above the ground, up in the limbs of trees, whipping about, hanging on, her grip relentless, the creature's neck like cold armor. Now her legs were locked around the neck, and she rode it like a bucking horse, stabbing at it with her knife. The blade only glanced off the scales. The creature's neck dropped down, slamming her into the ground, then whipped upward again, breaking off tree limbs in the process. She felt no pain.

"Mrs. Benson?" the officer asked. "Do you need to take a break?" He was looking at her with grave concern.

"No," she said. "I'm—I'm all right." She considered the sudden return of her memory, the uncovering of all that had been buried. She was beaten and shaken, but she felt whole again. "I'm quite all right."

The officer smiled. "Sounds to me like your attacker got a lot more than he bargained for."

She only looked at Travis. "I don't know how it would have turned out if Travis hadn't been here."

Travis was still shaken from the experience. His voice quavered slightly as he said, "I heard noise down in the living room and Mom hollering and the guy hollering, and I ran downstairs. The guy had just knocked Mom off his back and I saw that he had a knife."

The knife found an opening, a gap between the scales. It plunged in, and the scales closed on it like a vise. Suddenly she was encased in iron fingers and glistening claws that wrenched her loose. The knife broke off. She fell.

Evelyn reached over and gently touched Travis's hand. "Travis hit him so hard his nose almost came off. He looked like his whole face was bleeding."

The officer looked toward the front door. A clear trail of blood led from the front entry, through the door, and down the front walk. Another officer was just now taking samples.

The officer shook his head. "It's a good thing you were here, son."

Travis looked down. "But he got away."

The officer regarded the front door flung open and the screen broken from a violent collision. "Travis, what matters is, he was leaving, as fast as he could go."

The officer and Travis were talking, but Evelyn's mind went for one final moment to the top of Wells Peak in the dark of night.

The thing was gone as if it had never been there. She found Cliff on the ground, his upper body and head obscured by shadow. She reached to touch his face. She felt only the grass, wet and sticky with his blood.

Back in the living room of her home, she broke down and wept.

"NOW YOU GOT me and I got you," the jukebox twanged, "gonna turn in my ace for the life of a deuce . . ."

Sunday night at Charlie's. Great times, great drinks, great food, lots of chatter, and the cash register busy. Seemed like everybody was there tonight, racking up for pool, plugging quarters into the video games, and enjoying the ribs and fries.

Charlie was behind the bar, feeling on top of the world. "Course now, when I get that mercantile going, it's gonna be one huge tourist attraction, just you wait," he was saying to Paul Myers, who was sitting at the bar in his usual spot under the television, nursing a shot glass of whiskey.

Paul was not so giddy. "Yeah, live it up, Charlie. Things are going your way. I'm happy for you."

Charlie leaned over the bar, the compassionate bartender. "Hey, it can't be all that bad, Paul."

Paul only smirked. "Jimmy took off with half the business, Charlie!" He wanted to spit, but Charlie didn't allow spitting in his place, so he only made the motion with his mouth.

"How much?" Charlie asked.

"Not how much, what! The truck, the hoses, the whole thing! I can't pump septic tanks without the pump truck, now can I? What am I supposed to do, bail them out with a bucket?" He looked into space—actually, he was seeing the face of his no-good partner, Jimmy Yates—and his expression turned vicious. "I just want to kill that guy!"

Charlie grinned. "Wouldn't be that hard around here."

"What do you mean?"

"You can take care of him and just—" Charlie lowered his voice but didn't lose his grin. "Blame it on the dragon. End of story." Then he winked.

Paul was sick of that stuff. "The dragon—hah!"

"Might work," Charlie said, wiping down the bar. "Around here, people are just dumb enough to buy it, and you know the sheriff isn't going to do anything. You mention the dragon, and he just looks the other way."

Paul was disgusted. "You're talking stupid, Charlie, you know that?"

Charlie leaned on both elbows and looked at Paul, nose to nose. "Think so? Well, let me tell you something. You'd be surprised how much you can get away with."

Paul leaned away. Up close, Charlie had a bad smell.

A few others at the bar were noticing it too and were exchanging glances, as if to say, Do you smell that?

"Like that old black boy, Ebo Denning. Hey, a little while ago I was standing in your shoes, you know? Had big dreams for my business and then had 'em shot down in one day. Ebo didn't have any right to buy that mercantile. Sam Calley was my neighbor, you know, did business right next door to me. People'd come to the mercantile; he'd send them over here if they wanted a drink and some lunch. If people came in here and needed to get something, I'd send them over to Sam's. It was like neighbors, you know?"

Charlie was getting a little loud. Andy could hear him clear over by the pool table, and that was over the usual tavern clatter and the jukebox.

"I coulda bought that mercantile straight out if I'd only known Sam was selling it. I coulda got a loan or something. Ebo had cash 'cause he never had to buy anything, you know what I mean? Same old car, same old clothes—the guy's house was a junkyard." Charlie frowned. "Probably got all his money from the government, out of our pockets!"

Doug Ellis and his perpetual second-in-command, Kyle Figgin, were only a few barstools farther down the bar, trying to get down some beer and ribs but having their appetites curbed by the foul odor coming from Charlie's direction.

"You smell that?" Doug asked.

Kyle wrinkled his nose. "What is it? Smells like something died."

Elmer McCoy and Joe Staggart were there as well, smelling it just fine, thank you, but not saying anything. Instead, they were watching and listening to Charlie.

"But I got him!" Charlie proclaimed, looking about and including everyone else in what used to be a conversation between him and Paul. "Remember when the water pipe broke under the mercantile? Cost Ebo a lot of money to clean up that mess, now didn't it?" Charlie lowered his voice and moved over to Doug and Kyle to share the secret. "Did it with my little hacksaw! Didn't take much, but it worked!"

Doug and Kyle looked at each other. Yeah, the smell was Charlie, all right. It must be that black stuff he'd spilled on the front of his shirt. Didn't he know about it?

"Course," said Charlie, standing back from the bar and addressing the whole group seated on the barstools, "you folks had a lot to do with it. There's nobody here who wanted to have to do business with an old blackie. A black man owning a business—whoever heard of that? Ebo should have kept on sweeping the place and been happy with that and not got so uppity, ain't that right?"

Some seated at the bar may have agreed with him privately, but right now they were all gawking at him and growing more uncomfortable by the moment.

Carl Ingfeldt had been sitting at a table eating dinner with his wife. Now he ventured closer to hear and see what all the commotion was. The moment he got a clear look at Charlie, his eyes locked on the growing, black stain over Charlie's heart.

"Too bad we aren't down in the Old South," Charlie complained. "Back then, people down there knew how to handle things like this, and they knew how to get away with it." He laughed. "Well, that's okay, I guess. We got old Ebo to move out, and we got away with it!"

Now Andy stopped shooting pool and stared at Charlie. Some of the other patrons were beginning to notice the bartender getting noisy, too, as if he'd had too much to drink himself.

"We did a nice job of it. Yes sir. Now we've got ourselves a white-owned business the way it ought to be, and I wanna tell you something, we're going up from here!"

By now the stain on the front of Charlie's shirt was no secret to anyone but Charlie. As for his loud boasting, Elmer and Joe had heard enough. They made a quick path to the cash register at the end of the bar to pay up and get out of there. Melinda took their money.

"So, Paul," Charlie said, "what're you so worried about? Kill the guy! That'll show him! Do what you feel like doing."

Paul slid off his barstool and headed for the cash register. Charlie watched him go by. "Do what you want, Paul!" He looked at Doug. "And you too, Doug! Some scum comes along and starts messing with your wife, you oughta just go out there and shoot him!"

Doug and Kyle didn't want any more ribs. They headed for the cash register. Now a line was forming.

Charlie was pouring himself a beer. "Quit worrying; that's what I say. I got it all figured out. Do what you want and get what you got coming." He turned to the people standing in line to pay up and leave. Andy was there now, along with Carl and his wife. "You know, you people really make me sick! Look at you, all tied up and scared and worried. You got nothing to worry about!"

They didn't respond. They just stared at him. "Come on, hurry it up!" one said to Melinda, who was trying to hurry just so she could get out of there.

"Well, look at me!" Charlie yelled, some foam from his beer on his lip. "I did what I had to do, and now I'm on top! God ain't stopping me, and there sure ain't no dragon either! The sooner you figure that out, the better for all of you!"

"I'll pay you later," Andy said, ducking out the door.

Carl and his wife did the same.

The place was emptying out.

THE OAK SPRINGS police had been advised that an officer with the county sheriff would be arriving, so when Steve pulled up in his camper, followed by Tracy in her patrol car, they were expected. Tracy immediately conferred with the police, but Steve hurried past the broken screen door, the trail of blood, and the broken lamp and went straight into the kitchen where Evelyn was preparing some dinner for her boys.

"A paramedic checked her over," the officer told Tracy. "She came through it with some bruises, but that is one feisty gal. She beat the tar out of him, and he couldn't wait to get out of here." He told her the details, including a description of the suspect, then added, "We'll have her come downtown tomorrow to look through some mug shots, but I don't think he'll be hard to find, considering—"

"I know who it is," Tracy responded, her voice betraying a seething anger. "He's from Hyde River."

Evelyn, Samuel, and Travis were at the kitchen table, eating some warmed-over pizza. It was not a full-scale meal by any means, but no one was complaining. Right now they were glad just to be alive and together. Steve needed to be told several times that everyone was all right before he could settle down, accept a cup of coffee, and hear the story.

Samuel was sorry he'd missed it. He'd been playing at a friend's house.

"Just be glad you weren't here," his mother chided him.

"Did you get a good look at him?" Steve asked, looking from Evelyn to Travis. "Was there anything special about him?"

"His ear," Evelyn said, touching her own. "It was all scarred like he'd been in an accident or something."

"It was stitched on," said Travis. "I may have knocked it loose again. There was a lot of blood!"

Just then Tracy walked into the kitchen. She'd heard the description from the police officer and now caught the tail end of the conversation in the kitchen.

"Phil Garrett," she said.

"Absolutely," Steve said.

"Was he about—" Tracy held her hand out to a height just above her own. "—this tall?"

"Yes," Evelyn said.

"Black hair and big ears—one with stitches—and kind of a round head?"

"Yes."

Tracy was satisfied. "Phil Garrett."

"Who is he?" Evelyn asked, perplexed. "Why would he—"

"He's a roughneck who lives out in Hyde River. He gets into a lot of fights, and the last time he got into one the other guy nearly bit his ear off."

Samuel thought that was funny but put his hands over his mouth to try and hide his laughter. Travis and Evelyn could see both the humor and the horror of it. But Samuel's boyish laughter relieved the tension.

"But what does he want with me?" Evelyn asked.

Tracy sighed and looked at Steve. They both hesitated, but finally Steve said aloud what they were thinking. "I guess things are heating up."

"You bet they are," Tracy said, taking the chair Evelyn offered her. "But it's more than that." She said to Steve, "It's a conspiracy. Phil Garrett works for Harold Bly as kind of a miner and an odd-job man. And now those questions Bly was asking you about Evelyn make sense. I talked to Collins today, and he was asking me the same thing, whether Evelyn remembered anything or not."

Steve found that disturbing, though not shocking. "Collins? You think he's in on this?"

Evelyn finally cut in. "Sounds like an exciting story. I'd love to hear it," she said dryly. "Especially since it concerns me."

Steve apologized for talking in front of her. "Sorry. We're kind of beside ourselves."

She smiled. "I can identify with that!"

Steve started to explain. "Evie, it's a long story, but—brother, where do I start?"

Tracy took over. "There are people in Hyde River who have some strong beliefs about—well, about some things that go on in that town, and they're afraid—they think that you might know something about all that."

Evelyn raised an eyebrow. "Can you be more specific?"

But Tracy was being pulled in several directions. "Listen. I know Steve can explain it all to you. I've got to get coordinated with the Oak Springs police and get on the trail of this guy."

"What if he comes back?" asked Travis.

"The police are going to be watching the house to make sure it doesn't happen again." She rose. "They gave me your statement and your description, and now I can't sit around anymore. I have to get going while the trail's hot."

Evelyn smiled. "Please be careful."

"Don't worry. I've been wanting a suspect to question for a long time, and now I've got one!" She looked at Steve. "And believe me, he's going to talk!"

CHARLIE'S TAVERN was empty now except for Bernie, Melinda, and Charlie. They would be closing early. Bernie totally absorbed himself in cleaning up in the kitchen, and Melinda was standing by the cash register, hurriedly counting up the evening's receipts. Neither of them said a word to Charlie or went near him.

Charlie remained behind the bar, leaning on it with his elbows and finishing up one last beer, still chuckling and laughing at whatever amusing thoughts came to him, as if he were listening to a comedy tape through headphones.

Finally, he tossed back the beer, finishing it in several swallows. Then he wiped his mouth with his arm, slammed down the beer glass, and started toward the cash register.

Melinda shied away, grabbed a cloth, and hurried across the room to wipe the tables. Most of the tables had not even been cleared.

Charlie looked at the cash register and the money still lying on the bar where Melinda had stacked it in piles by denomination. "So how'd we do?"

Melinda answered from a safe distance, halfway across the tavern, "We did good, Charlie. It was a good Sunday night."

"Fine, fine." He grabbed his coat. "Well, lock up, will you? I'm going for a drive."

Melinda looked directly at him, concerned. "Where are you going?"

"Oh, I don't know." He looked at her, and she looked back at him, and then it hit him. "I'm not going to Old Town, don't worry."

Her voice trembled. "Then—then where are you going?"

He laughed. "Oh, come on, what are you so worried about? I'm fine, gonna be just fine. I think I'll head on down the valley, park someplace, and enjoy the moonlight."

"Well, you be careful."

He put on his jacket. "You don't have to worry about me." As he zipped it up, black ooze from his shirt soiled his fingers. He didn't seem to notice. Then he went out the door, the bell above it clanging.

At that sound, Bernie poked his head in from the kitchen, his eyes darting about the room. He looked at Melinda. "Is he gone?"

She was heading for the front door to lock it. "Yeah."

"Then I'm out of here." Bernie spun and made a mad dash for his coat hanging in the back of the kitchen, passing by the dirty pots and pans that he had decided would just have to stay that way.

Melinda's hands were shaking so much she had trouble throwing the lock on the door. Finally the bolt slid into place, and she, too, made a desperate beeline for her coat and the back door.

They parted outside without another word, each headed for home. He drove off in his truck, the tires squealing. She ran for all she was worth.

All either of them wanted to do was get home and hide.

TRAVIS AND SAMUEL had finished their dinner.

"Boys," said Evelyn, "why don't you go upstairs and watch TV or something? I'd like to talk to your uncle in private."

They left the kitchen, which was okay with them; they wouldn't have to do the dishes.

Steve was glad she'd made that move. After what had happened tonight, he knew he had to tell Evelyn the truth about Cliff's death. And he couldn't tell her in front of the boys.

But Evelyn started the conversation herself with a blunt question. "Steve, do you really believe a grizzly killed Cliff?"

He hesitated, then said, "Evelyn, I'm going to answer your question, and I'm not stalling. But I need to ask you a few questions first."

She considered that. "As long as we get back to my question."

"We will, I promise." He leaned forward, his hands clasped on the table. "Evelyn, how familiar are you with the town of Hyde River?"

"Not very familiar. Cliff and I drove through it a couple times, but we never stopped there."

"Do you know anyone who lives there?"

"No."

"Have you ever heard any of the stories, legends, folk tales that have come out of there?"

"No."

He looked at her carefully. "One last question. How are you? Are you—?"

"I'm all here, Steve. I'm back together again." She paused to study him for a moment. "And I'm ready to hear the truth. Do you believe a grizzly killed my husband?"

He thought a moment and decided it was time to be honest. "No. I don't think it was a grizzly."

Her eyes were steady and resolute. "Steve, I remember what happened. I remember what I saw."

THE HYDE RIVER ROAD was a long, winding ribbon of unlit asphalt, visible only in Charlie's headlights. He had no idea where he was going and didn't care. He just wanted to drive, to control a vehicle, to choose his own direction. The car radio was tuned to a country station, the volume turned up. He was feeling good.

The road curved to the right, and he followed the white line.

He'd been up and down this road a thousand times; he knew what was coming. The curve straightened, and now the road stretched out ahead of him as straight as a rail, cutting through flat pastureland for the next mile. He pressed the accelerator, and the car surged forward, the speedometer topping sixty.

One of his favorite songs was playing on the radio, and he started singing along, finding notes the song's creator never thought of. It was over now—all the worry, all the pain, all the fear. He was free. Like the road, the future was laid out straight and true ahead of him, with no surprises—

He yanked his foot from the accelerator. In the far, fading reach of his headlights, he could see something crossing the road. He couldn't make out what it was, perhaps a deer or an elk. He'd collided with a deer once, and he didn't want that kind of damage done to his car again, so he applied the brake and slowed to forty. As he drew closer and his headlights illuminated more of the area, something didn't look right. He couldn't see an animal—it was more like a huge shadow falling across the road. The center line seemed to waver. He slowed some more.

Suddenly the road was clear again, just like that, stretching out straight in front of him as if a cloud of fog had just rolled past.

He wondered what it was he had seen. Maybe—

THUD! The front of the car crumpled, and the car swayed and fishtailed. Charlie felt his shoulder belt cutting across his chest like a knife edge, and his head lurched forward.

I've hit a moose, he thought.

The car slowed to a stop within seconds, pushing something ahead of it. When Charlie's body slammed back against the seat he saw flashes of silver, gold, emerald, and ruby, a shimmering display just outside the windshield, a moving, shifting wall of neon metallic scales, flickering and flashing like sunlight off lake water.

I've hit a trout!

He blinked, rubbed his head and eyes, looked again.

The shimmering wall lifted like a curtain. He could see the road again in the headlights.

What a relief, he thought. He must have had more to drink than he thought. He put his foot on the accelerator—

CRASH! The roof of the car caved in as if a tree had landed on it. The windows shattered. Charlie watched in horror as huge steel hooks—no, metal claws!—curled in through the passenger window.

"AAWWW!" Charlie screamed as the claws barely missed his head then clamped around the car's roof. The car teetered, rocked, and slid sideways.

Then something hit the hood of the car, mangling the metal. Glass from the windshield showered into Charlie's lap. He recoiled in horror at what he saw through the glittering, broken opening.

An immense, leathery, clawed hand rested on the hood, the gnarled, sinewy fingers stretching from one side of the hood to the other.

Then the claws that were inside the car pulled upward. The metal groaned, rivets popped, glass went flying. The roof was peeled back like the lid of a sardine can.

Dazed and panicked, Charlie groped for the door handle, and the door flew open. But he couldn't move—and he realized his seat belt still held him in. He groped for the buckle.

Above him, where the roof had been, he caught sight of something metallic, something glittering.

A huge hand was reaching for him. The fingers curled around him, and his ribs snapped and cracked with a sound like burning cedar; his lungs filled with blood, and he choked it up.

The seat belt broke away from his body, and the car dropped away below him.

He could see eyes—huge, golden eyes—the instant before he died.

"SO TELL ME, Steve, do you think I'm crazy?"

He looked back at Evelyn and could hardly speak. Her recounting of what had happened that night on the mountain had become the core around which all the other data he'd gathered, all the hunches, all the eyewitness testimony, and all his own experiences, were finally bonding into one cohesive whole. He was overwhelmed.

Evelyn misread his silence. "Well I'm sorry, but I gave you everything, just the way I saw it."

He was quick to reassure her. "I believe you, Evelyn."

She found it hard to believe that. "It's hard to swallow, I know."

He touched her hand. "Listen to me. Tracy and I—well, we set out some bait and encountered the same thing a few nights ago. We didn't see it clearly, but we tracked it all through the night and into the next morning. We know it's out there. We just don't know what it is."

She thought it over, then said, "I think 'dragon' will do."

He nodded. "Okay. But there's something I need to tell you. The people in the valley know about the dragon. But it's some kind of religious thing with them, and they don't want anyone else to know about it. And now we know they'll even kill to keep the secret from getting out. That's what I was trying to tell you on the phone—to keep quiet about it, to not tell anybody."

Steve could see the fear in Evelyn's eyes.

"But why?" she asked him. "Why are they trying to hide it?"

"I wish I knew. I'm as perplexed as you are."

"It kills people, Steve! This doesn't make any sense at all."

"I know."

She was visibly flustered, even angry. "So what about the police? What about the Forest Service? The army! I mean—" She came to a halt, realizing the answer even as he said it.

"That creature knows how to hide," he said. "And no one outside the valley would ever believe there was a dragon hiding in the mountains."

Evelyn took a deep breath to calm down then rested her chin on her hand. "Okay. So what can we do?"

Steve grappled with that; there was no easy answer. "Well, the problem isn't going to just go away..."

"It certainly isn't!"

"When the dragon killed Cliff—someone from outside the valley—and left part of the body behind, that opened things up to the outside world. It sucked you and me into it. Now all we can do is take it one step at a time. Tracy's going to arrest Phil Garrett, if he hasn't fled to Mexico or something, and then maybe the authorities will have a reason to start unraveling what's going on up there. But I don't think I can wait for that. I have to find that creature and contain it before it kills anybody else."

"Steve . . ."

"Yeah."

"How much do you know about Tracy?" Evelyn asked with caution.

Had the question come from anyone else, he wouldn't have liked it. "Oh, quite a bit for the short amount of time I've known her. Why?"

Evelyn shook her head. "I don't feel right about her. Even before Cliff died, I had a feeling, a sense that something was wrong, that something was creeping into our marriage and into him. Whatever it was, it came out of Hyde River. But I think it's affecting Tracy, too. I think she's part of whatever it is."

Steve didn't know what to say. How could he argue with such an intangible thing as a woman's intuition? "Well, you don't know Tracy."

"And you do?"

"Of course."

"How can you be sure she's not one of them?"

He rolled his eyes at that. "Evelyn, come on. They want her hide as much as they want mine. She could lose her job over this."

She gave a slight nod. "I know." By her tone, he could tell she was not convinced.

"Listen, I'll watch myself. Don't worry."

"It's something spiritual, Steve."

He raised one eyebrow.

"Hey, listen, I know that doesn't get very far with you, but just for the record, I'm sure that something's behind all of this: the dragon, the valley, Tracy, Phil Garrett—even what happened to Cliff. It's all part of the same thing, and it's not—" She groped for the words. "—it's not of this world, okay? I'm afraid for you."

"Don't be."

"Promise me you'll be careful."

"I promise." He got up. "I have got to get back. You have my mobile phone number. Call if you have any trouble, and don't be afraid to tell me what you're thinking and feeling. Any information you can give me is welcome."

"I'm going to be praying; I'll tell you that."

He smiled. "That's fine with me."

IT TOOK Steve forty minutes to drive back over Johnson's Pass and through West Fork. From there, he turned north on the Hyde River Road and made his way through the valley, his hands just a little tighter on the steering wheel and his adrenaline pumping. He was returning to the trouble, and he knew it.

Halfway to the town of Hyde River, as he came around a curve in the road and then onto a long straight stretch, he saw the flashing lights of emergency vehicles, and not just a few. This had to be a major pileup, Steve thought—if it wasn't something else. He was on edge, expecting anything.

A county sheriff's patrol car was parked across the road to block traffic, its blue lights flashing. Already, two vehicles ahead of Steve had been turned back by the deputy holding a flare.

Steve had no intention of being turned back. When he reached the patrol car and the deputy approached his window, he had his bluff ready.

"I'm sorry, sir, you can't go through here," said the deputy.

"I'm Dr. Steve Benson. I got a call."

The deputy bought it. "Go right ahead, Doctor."

Steve inched his camper around the patrol car and kept going.

Well, he did have his doctorate in biology, and he had gotten a few calls lately.

The accident scene was another quarter-mile ahead. He pulled onto the shoulder only a hundred feet away, extinguished his lights, and got out of the camper, wanting a good look before anyone approached him. He could see Sheriff Collins standing by his patrol car, hands on hips, surveying the scene, supervising. Two fire trucks were parked alongside the road, lights flashing, radios squawking, fire hoses snaked all over the pavement. An aid car waited, its rear door open.

In the center of it all were the remains of a car, the roof peeled completely back, the tires flattened, the windows shattered. The whole vehicle was charred black. The pavement was still wet from fire hoses.

Steve saw flashlight beams sweeping in the pastures on either side of the road. The police and firefighters must be searching for something, perhaps the victim or victims.

He reached into the cab of his camper and got his flashlight, then ducked through the barbed-wire fence to join the others in the pasture. He swept his light to and fro, becoming one of the searchers. Somehow he had to find out what had happened and what they were looking for.

He drew close to a volunteer firefighter walking along the fence line near the shoulder of the road. "You got anything?"

"No," the fireman answered. "We've swept the area within a hundred feet of the road. Either he's on the other side of the road or he took off."

"Is there any kind of a description?"

"Well, we think the car belongs to Charlie Mack. You know, the guy who owns the tavern in Hyde River?"

Steve didn't have to fake his surprise. "Charlie?" He looked back toward the road and the charred, mutilated car. "Does anybody know what happened?"

"He hit something, but we don't know what. As near as we can tell, it was another vehicle that fled the scene."

"How'd the roof get torn off?"

"Beats me. It was that way when we got here. The whole car was on fire, the roof was torn off, and there was nobody inside."

"So what started the fire? Did the gas tank explode?"

"No, and that's the oddest thing of all. The gas tank's intact." The man shook his head. "This whole thing is weird." He called to another firefighter out in the pasture. "Joan, I'm going to the other side!"

"Okay," came the answer. "I'll work here a little longer."

The man ducked through the barbed-wire fence and started to the other side of the road.

Steve followed him as far as the road shoulder, then lowered his light to cast a shallower angle on the soft ground, making the shadows more pronounced. He walked along the shoulder slowly, up past the wreck, then past the aid vehicle still standing empty, then back again, examining the patterns in the gravel. Plenty of human footprints, tire marks, even some hoofprints left by local equestrians. Nothing unusual.

He followed the road shoulder almost to his camper, then crossed the road and started up the other side. He was getting close to Collins's patrol car, so he kept his head down, his face turned away, glad that it was dark.

He'd just passed the patrol car and was abreast of the wreck when he stopped. The furrows and scratches in the gravel could be what he was looking for, but he wasn't sure. He looked closely, shining his light at the pattern from different angles. Then he shined his light off the shoulder and into the soft grass below. Now he was almost positive. The scratch patterns and impressions in the ground resembled those he'd found on Wells Peak as well as the supposed "footprint" Levi had shown him above the dragon's "trap."

He didn't want to jump to conclusions, but already he was fearing the worst.

He crossed over the road to the wreck for a close look, searching inside and out with his light. The inside of the car was burned, melted, obliterated. The damage to the front end did not indicate a high-speed crash, although the hood was crushed in as if something had smashed it from above. The roof—now that was a mystery. It had not been cut through, as rescuers would do if a victim had to be extracted. It had been torn away in one piece, crumpled, and was just lying on the rear of the car. It was punctured in several places as if with huge spikes.

Claws, perhaps? No. Maybe. He couldn't be sure . . .

Steve was filled with fear and foreboding. If this was the work of the dragon, then that thing was getting bolder by the minute, and no place was safe, day or night. Had the beast torn this roof off? And had the fire come from—

"Benson!" It was Collins's voice.

Steve turned to face the sheriff marching toward him with his powerful light right in Steve's eyes. Steve blocked the beam with his hand.

"How did you get in here?" Collins demanded.

"I volunteered."

"We don't want your help. Now get out of here!"

"Was it Charlie Mack?"

"We don't know who it was."

"How'd the roof get torn off the car?"

"We had to pull it off to get the victims out."

Steve looked at the empty aid vehicle. "If the victims were in the car, why are men searching the fields?"

Collins grabbed Steve by the arm. "You've got one minute to clear the area before I place you under arrest, you got it?"

Steve returned his glare and responded, "Good night, then."

He headed for his camper, his light still sweeping the shoulder of the road in case there was anything else to see.

There was. One of the searchers in the other field was just coming back, and he was also shining his light along the road shoulder. He was wearing a dark jacket and a drooping hat to hide his face, but Steve recognized the gray beard and wire-rim glasses.

Levi Cobb.

Their eyes locked. Levi gave Steve a challenging look, almost as if asking, Seen enough?

Steve turned and went to his camper. He knew Collins would be watching, and he didn't want to be seen talking to Levi Cobb.

But the answer was yes. He'd seen enough.

WHEN MONDAY morning dawned, the brooding, foreboding spirit of the night remained like a heavy overcast, and fear like a sooty residue; Hyde Valley had changed, and even those who hadn't heard of the past night's dark events could sense it, and wondered.

People driving along the Hyde River Road in the early light of morning found no indication that any accident had ever happened, though. Sheriff Lester Collins had ordered the site swept and hosed clean and the wrecked car hauled to a scrapyard, where it was lost amid an acre of rusting hulks.

The men and women of the valley volunteer fire department returned to their jobs and routines and said little about the accident because there was so little to say. They all had to wonder whatever became of the victim; they knew no one could have survived such a terrible accident. There would always be questions, but none of the questions would ever be asked.

Before the town of Hyde River had awakened, and without a word to anyone, Steve Benson drove his camper north through town, over several miles of rough roads, and turned off on Service Road 63, the road that would take him up Saddlehorse to Potter's Mine, and beyond that, the diggings of Jules Cryor. His firearms were loaded and with him in the cab, and he'd prepared his backpack for several days in the back country.

BEFORE OPENING his garage for business on Monday morning, Levi Cobb went out into the small yard behind his shop to sort through parts, old farm implements, axles, springs, and sheet metal, looking for just the right materials. "C'mon, don't be so stubborn, just move . . . Well there you are. I've been looking all over for you . . . Have any of you seen that old drill steel I had laying around here?"

He finally found the object of his search, an old drill steel from a pneumatic drill, once used to drill through solid rock in the mines. It was one tough piece of steel, about eight feet long. He set it aside. Next he uncovered a tooth broken from the back claw of a county bulldozer. He knew it would take some work to shape and hone it, but it was a good start.

He paused to peer over his scrap-iron fence. The mountains were slightly obscured in morning mist but would be clear enough to touch in a few hours. A cool breeze was blowing, and he could hear birds singing.

He felt no joy. He could sense an atmosphere that was hot, close, and heavy, the trouble-laden stuff that storms are made of.

The disturbance had already begun. Evil had been set loose and was on its way.

He ducked inside, his materials in hand, switched on an overhead worklight, and cleared some parts from his work area. His welding torch ignited with a pop, and he put the flame to steel. He had work to do, and not a moment to lose.

A man with power is not
at the mercy of a man with ideals.

. . . . .

He who has the money signs the cheques.
He who signs the cheques makes the rules.
He who makes the rules has the Power.
He who has the Power has the money.

. . . . .

Power Prevails.

. . . .

If this be sin, let sin be served.

*Plaques of Benjamin Hyde's favorite slogans,
created and placed in Hyde's office by his son Samuel after
Benjamin Hyde's mysterious disappearance—declared a hunting
accident—in 1898. The plaques remain there to this day.*

FOURTEEN

Saddlehorse

IN CHARLIE'S TAVERN, the dollar bills still lay stacked by denomination on the bar next to the cash register. Two glasses of beer, one full, one half empty, both warm, remained on the bar exactly where Elmer and Joe had left them. At the pool table, the cue ball remained in perfect line to sink the three ball in the corner, the shot Andy Schuller never took. On the screen of a video game, a jerky-motioned martial artist made high kicks at thugs while the machine begged, Insert a Quarter, Insert a Quarter, Insert a Quarter. All around the tavern dinner had been served, but the steaks, ribs, and barbecued chicken lay cold.

Across the room, opposite the bar, the new doorway to the mercantile was open, and beyond it, neat shelves of dry goods, wool shirts, rods and lures could be seen. The mercantile was clean, painted, polished, rearranged, and ready to open.

In the bathroom past the storeroom, a man was whimpering, cursing, agonizing.

Harold Bly, the new lord of it all, the unrivaled ruler of one more piece of real estate, held the key to the front door in a desperate, iron grip as he pounded the edge of the sink in torment.

His shirt was open. In the mirror over the sink he could see a red, burning welt snaking down his chest. He pulled a wad of paper towels from the dispenser, soaked them under the faucet, and dabbed at the sore. There was no relief. "No!" he cried, and rubbed at the mark. It would not go away.

"No!" he said again, shaking his head, refusing to believe it. He struck the sink. "NO! Not me! I'm not the one you want!" He cursed in rage, in pain, in the agony of betrayal. "I'm on your side! What's the matter with you?"

He held the wad of paper towels to his chest to cool the burning. I'm not like Maggie, he thought. Not like Vic, or Charlie. I'm Harold Bly. I'm a Hyde. I've never been marked, never been touched. I'm good for this town!

I don't deserve this!

He heard the distant clanging of the bell over the tavern door. He cursed again. He'd left the door unlocked!

He removed the wet towels from his chest. The mark was still there, but no stain had come off on the towels. As far as he could tell, there was no stench. Maybe it wasn't going to be serious. Maybe it wasn't permanent.

Maybe it was a warning.

"Hello?" came a voice from the tavern. "Anybody here?"

He recognized the voice of Tracy Ellis. Clark County Sheriff's Deputy Tracy Ellis. This early? Oh no, he thought. Something had gone wrong.

He buttoned up his shirt, straightened his hair, and hurried through the mercantile to the tavern. "Hello! We're not open yet."

He found Tracy Ellis standing by the bar, looking at the unfinished drinks, the uneaten dinners, the bizarre, frozen-in-time state of the place. Her eyes were cold and probing. She wasn't here to say hello—she was here as a cop.

No matter. He was still Harold Bly, and this was his place. "Hi, Tracy. What can I do for you?"

She was still looking around the room when she asked, "You know about Charlie?"

His voice was already tense. All he had to do was add a little sorrow. "Yes. I heard about it last night. Did you see what happened?"

"I was in Oak Springs on another case."

"Have they found him yet?"

"No. They haven't found him," she said angrily. "And there's been no sign of Vic Moore either, and Maggie isn't visiting her mother."

Of course. Bly was offended. "What are you saying, deputy? I suppose you called Maggie's mother?"

Very good, Harold. You get a gold star. "Yes. That's exactly what I did."

Bly had no comment, and she wasn't expecting one. She looked around the room again. "What happened here last night? It looks like there was a fire drill and nobody came back."

"I don't know. I wasn't here." His temperature was rising. "So why are you here?"

"I'm looking for an employee of yours, Phil Garrett. Any idea where he is?"

"No. No idea," Bly said quickly.

"He does work for you, doesn't he?"

"Yes, but I don't know where he is."

It was Monday morning, and Bly had no idea where one of his employees was? She didn't force the issue. "He broke into Evelyn Benson's home yesterday and tried to kill her." She paused to let that sink in, checking his reaction. "Now why do you suppose he'd do a thing like that?"

Bly's face remained like stone. "When you find him, ask him. Phil Garrett can answer for his own actions."

"Oh, he will."

"So where's your friend the professor?" he asked, to put her on the defensive.

She didn't flinch. "My guess would be he's hunting."

"Hunting? For what?"

"For whatever he finally kills. Listen, I have a warrant for Phil's arrest. That makes him a fugitive, which could make it rough for anyone who tries to aid and abet him. I just want you to understand that."

Time to push some weight. "Have you talked to Sheriff Collins about this?"

She cocked her head and gave him a knowing look. "I'm sure I'll hear from him soon enough. When I do, he'll get a full report." She turned to go. "Let me know if you see Phil."

She closed the door behind her, the bell clanging.

Bly remained where he was, brooding, seething. His hand went to his chest. The pain was still there. But now he knew why.

Phil had botched the job, and Evelyn Benson was still alive, alive to remember, to talk, to reveal everything. Charlie was dead, but he'd talked. Levi Cobb was still alive, preaching and meddling. Tracy Ellis was tearing away secrets like scabs off wounds.

And Benson the outsider was "hunting."

No wonder there was trouble. Things had slipped out of his control.

But he was Harold Bly; he could fix it. He'd taken too long, that was all; he'd been too soft, too easy. He could change that.

New hope refreshed him and soothed the pain in his chest. He had a chance. Of course he had a chance. He was finally able to smile as he stood alone in the deserted tavern, formulating his plan.

Then, abruptly, he dashed behind the bar and into the kitchen, then grabbed the telephone off the wall. It was time to contain this mess and take back control, and he would start by climbing all over Sheriff Collins.

CHARLIE MACK was right. Once Steve had pressed on past Potter's Mine and challenged the rutted, potholed dirt road that wound further around Saddlehorse, he finally did come to another mining effort, this one the least impressive of any he'd seen thus far. The road emptied onto a precarious shelf of rock, a man-made—probably one-man-made—shoulder of broken, blasted rubble, the "muck" and waste from Jules Cryor's little mine. It was just wide enough to accommodate Steve's truck and the old Dodge four-wheel-drive already parked there, brown with rust wherever the green paint had worn off. Just beyond the Dodge, steel rails for an ore car curved toward the mountain and disappeared down the entrance to the mine.

Directly above, perched on another precarious shoulder of hewn rock, was the log cabin of Jules Cryor, a rather haphazard structure with little thought given to such petty details as level, plumb, and square. Steve surmised that the logs had been cut from the immediate area, hauled to this spot, and dropped into a roughly rectangular shape until the pile was high enough to live in.

Jules Cryor must have heard him coming, Steve thought, for he appeared from behind the Dodge, the very image of an old prospector with a gray beard reaching to his belly and a weathered hat with the brim low over his eyes. The only thing missing was a cantankerous mule loaded down with picks, shovels, and jangling canteens.

He was also cradling a shotgun in his arms, sending Steve a clear message.

Steve shut off the engine, trying to think of ways to look harmless and well-meaning. Being armed to the teeth didn't help. He unbuckled his sidearm and put it on the seat, then tried smiling through the windshield and giving Cryor a little wave of greeting. Cryor waved back without a smile, then sat on the front bumper of the Dodge, as if waiting for this visitor to explain himself. He seemed in no particular hurry to use the gun, so Steve figured it would be safe to climb out.

"Jules Cryor?" he asked.

"Yes," the man replied. "And who might you be?" His resonant voice and clear diction were a surprise to anyone expecting the raspy voice of a stereotypical prospector.

"My name is Steve Benson. I'm a professor of biology at Colorado State University. I'm here—" This part was always difficult to explain.

Cryor's eyes narrowed as he studied Steve's camouflage clothing and inventoried the rifles in the cab of the truck. "Looks to me like you're here to hunt. May I remind you, the season is some months away."

Steve smiled. "I'm not here to hunt—well, not in the usual sense. I'm involved in an investigation. A little over a week ago, a man was killed, half eaten, by an animal up on Wells Peak. We're trying to locate the animal."

"Who's 'we'?"

"Well—myself."

Cryor seemed to accept that, for he nodded. "A rogue grizzly, I suppose?"

"No, not a grizzly. We're looking for something—bigger." Steve was dropping a hint to see if Cryor would pick up on it.

Cryor said nothing for the longest time but sat there on the bumper of the old truck, eyeing his visitor. Finally, he said, "Mr. Benson, considering your conventional and very obvious means of getting here—the size of your truck, the clouds of dust you've kicked up, the sound of your engine—I would say you've lost some advantage already. Your quarry knows you're here. Have you ever seen him?"

"Yes. I believe so."

"Then he's seen you." Cryor rose to his feet. "Come on, you'd better get inside."

Steve followed his host up a steep, rocky path to the cabin. Cryor opened the door and showed him in.

The cabin was furnished with the barest essentials: a wooden table and chairs, an old desk, a bed in one corner, an old overstuffed chair. Along one wall was a shelf of books—some manuals on mining and minerals, some law books, and some novels. The rest of the space was filled with tools: shovels, picks, drills, augers, cable, and chain.

And dynamite. Cases of it. It made Steve nervous.

Cryor could tell. "Don't be alarmed by the explosives. I go through a lot of it, so it's all fresh and well packaged—no leaking nitroglycerine or instability. You can see my bed there in the corner. I sleep with it every night." Then he added, laughing, "But of course, I don't smoke."

"Well and good," Steve replied, still staring.

"Please, have a seat."

Steve sat at the rough-hewn plank table, and Cryor brought him a beer from a small refrigerator that didn't seem to be working at the moment.

"I have a generator to chill things down twice a day," the miner explained, removing his dusty, droopy hat, revealing a full mane of graying hair. He tossed the hat on the table as he said, "No plumbing to speak of, but plenty of water available from the spring out back, a safe distance from the outhouse, of course."

"How long have you been here?"

"Twenty-three years. I've not struck it rich, but I've done well enough. My broker tells me I'll be able to retire comfortably."

Steve's eyes were drawn to the cabin's back door, now open, which led not to the outdoors but to a narrow tunnel carved deep into the mountain.

"My brainchild, like most everything else," Cryor explained. "I built the cabin over my original access tunnel. That way I don't have to commute to work. I'm already there."

Steve ventured to say, "You're not at all what I expected."

Cryor smiled. "An eccentric old hermit, wielding a shotgun to keep people away?" He laughed. "Mr. Benson, if that's what you expected, that's exactly what you found. I'm not a trusting sort." He took a swallow of his own beer. "My degree is in law." His eyes narrowed but kept a certain twinkle. "Hence my disillusionment, and the shotgun." He glanced out the window. "I'd like to know your intentions regarding our mutual friend, and depending on those intentions, I may try to dissuade you."

"So you are familiar with this creature?"

He considered that, but shook his head. "Not familiar. No one can ever get that close. No one should try. The danger, Mr. Benson, is in tampering with the beast, encroaching on its turf. It doesn't like to be hunted; it doesn't like to be known. My wisdom has been to respect and live by that policy, and that's why I've been able to live here for twenty-three years and never be bothered. As long as I leave it alone, it leaves me alone."

"But of course, you've seen it."

He looked off in the distance. "Yes," he said slowly, "now and again, at various times. Living up here in the wilds, in the midst of its habitat, I suppose I have more opportunity."

"Would you say it's nocturnal? I've heard reports of its going out at night and returning to its lair at dawn."

"Don't count on that. I think he prefers to operate at night, but what times he goes out could also depend on the business at hand. I've seen him in broad daylight."

So have I, Steve thought. "Where? Doing what?"

Cryor pointed out the window. "Up there, on Saddlehorse, up against that rock face. He was camouflaged, you know, blending with the surroundings, but the light was right this time, and he was casting a shadow. I think he was watching me." He smiled playfully. "So I waved at him. I don't think he waved back." He leaned over the table, his expression now serious. "And I'll give you a hint about spotting him. If you can keep moving, keep changing perspectives on him, you'll see his outline. He'll emerge from his background."

"But that would mean exposing my own position."

Cryor considered that. "That would be a drawback only if you've made yourself an adversary. Which I have never done," he added, "and so you see, I'm still here, not encroaching, and therefore, not encroached upon."

"Actually," Steve said, "this thing isn't living and letting live anymore. Besides the death of the man on Wells Peak, who posed absolutely no threat to the creature, several other people are missing."

"Missing?"

"So far there have been three disappearances since the Wells Peak attack. The victims are gone without a trace."

"With no other explanation?"

"Are you familiar with the customs in Hyde River?"

He nodded and motioned with his hand for Steve to continue.

"The most recent disappearance was last night. A car was wrecked on the Hyde River Road. The roof was torn off, the inside was burned out, and the driver, Charlie Mack, is missing."

That stunned the miner. "Charlie Mack?"

"You knew him?"

"Knew of him. Who else?"

"Vic Moore, a contractor."

Cryor shook his head.

"Maggie Bly, wife of Harold Bly."

Cryor was visibly shocked at that. "You can't be serious!"

"She wandered into Old Town and was never seen again. The same with Vic Moore."

The miner stroked his beard, obviously troubled by this news. "If it's the creature, there must be a reason. I've never known him to be malicious or predacious."

"From what other people have told me, he's always been a predator. It's the frequency of his kills that's changed. I understand there haven't been killings of this kind at this rate before."

Cryor raised an eyebrow. "Have the killings taken place during the same stretch of time you've been hunting him?"

That gave Steve pause.

Cryor repeated his argument. "Hunt him, and he'll hunt you."

"Ignore him and he'll just go away?"

Steve's slightly sarcastic response gave the miner pause. "There's no guarantee of that, is there? Once a dog starts killing chickens it's hard to change his behavior. He looked out the window again, but his casual, playful mood was gone. "He does seem to be appearing more often. I was wondering about it."

"Has he grown any?"

Cryor gave Steve a curious look and took a moment to think. "Perhaps . . ."

"So you might have an increase in activity combined with an increase in size, which could explain why you're seeing him more frequently."

Cryor rose from his chair and stood by the window, scanning the mountains and sky. "You say Charlie Mack's car was burned?"

"Yes, and it's weird, because the gas tank was still intact."

"He's a fire-breather, you know."

That stopped Steve cold. "Uh—what did you say?"

"The creature breathes fire."

Oh no, thought Steve. Just when I thought we might get somewhere, here's one more myth to cloud things up. "Breathes fire?"

"It's some kind of process I don't fully understand. Could be he processes methane from his digestive tract and injects it with pure oxygen to produce a flame. I'm only theorizing, mind you."

Steve leaned forward. "You've seen this?"

Cryor nodded. "An incredible sight. Beyond belief. He uses it for defense, I imagine." He looked at the cases of explosives stacked up against the walls. "That's why I sleep with my dynamite. He never bothers me, so he never bothers my explosives."

Steve had to say, "Until now."

"Maybe." Cryor was obviously reluctant to change his views. "How can you be sure the creature is responsible for these deaths . . . well, this death and these three disappearances?"

"I have a witness to the known death. The man's wife was there and saw the dragon kill her husband." He felt obligated to add, "I call it the dragon for lack of a better term."

"No no, that's fine. The label is quite appropriate. But is this woman reliable? How well do you know her?"

"She's my sister-in-law. Her husband was my brother Cliff."

Cryor's eyes widened in surprise. "Well," he said, "the plot does thicken. I won't be able to dissuade you at all, will I?"

"No sir."

He looked away and muttered, "It's understandable."

"Is there anything else you can tell me?"

Cryor sat down again and remained motionless for a long time, staring into his beer. Finally he spoke haltingly, quietly. "The dragon—lives on Saddlehorse, I don't know where exactly. There are old mines up here. Some of them were formerly caverns in the mountain, dug out and enlarged by mining. The tunnels go for miles." He looked directly at Steve. "I don't recommend you try cornering him in a cavern. He'll be on his own ground, and he could and would withstand you indefinitely—if not kill you."

"Then how do I—"

"I don't know that you can kill him. It's never been done, so there is no precedent, no best way."

"Can you help me find him?"

Cryor only shook his head pessimistically. "To find him, you'd have to see him, and that can be next to impossible. But I have something to show you." He reached over and took a small cloth bundle from the drawer of his old desk. "It will give you a better idea of what you're up against." He unwrapped the cloth and then held up a flat, platelike object, shaped roughly like a teardrop and slightly curled along its length. At first, Steve thought it was a silver pendant. Cryor set the object down on the woven tablecloth. "Watch closely, but don't touch it." Steve looked at it closely. Now he could see it wasn't metal, but some kind of bone, perhaps a piece of tortoise shell or a crosscut of an antler, but—

What was this? Steve backed away, changed his angle of view, then came closer, unsure of what he was seeing.

The pendant was slowly changing color, the change barely discernible. The silver color was giving way to red! Then along with the red came a deep green. Then purple. All the colors found in the tablecloth.

The pendant was mimicking the pattern of the tablecloth beneath it!

"It's getting old," said Cryor. "When it was new it could change as fast as you moved it. Now it takes about a minute."

After a minute had passed, the object, from any angle, looked like a piece of the tablecloth. It not only mimicked the various colors, it also recreated the individual threads in the fabric, a few bread crumbs, and one small brown stain.

Steve was not just fascinated. He was aghast.

Cryor explained, "It's one of the dragon's scales. A lucky find, to be sure. It caught the glint of the sun just enough for me to find it on the ridge above the cabin."

It was all Steve could do to remain calm. After an overabundance of superstition, fantasy, myth, and legend, some empirical evidence had finally presented itself. The scale was real, its implications mind-boggling.

"I'd love to take it back to the university."

Cryor was pleasant, but shook his head. "Kill the dragon, Mr. Benson, and you can help yourself to all the scales you want." Cryor rewrapped the scale and placed it back in his drawer. "My intent here is to emphasize the dragon can match its surroundings, not only by color, but by texture, down to the smallest blade of grass, the minutest pebble. You should go on the assumption that the dragon will always see you first. But having said that . . ."

Cryor reached over to a nearby shelf for a map. "I can show you where the mines and caverns are and advise you as to the best routes to get there. From there, the hunt is all yours." He spread the map out on the table. "There are two mines that were first dug out in the 1800s. The dragon legends go back that far, so we might assume he's taken up his abode in one of them. But there's also a cavern made into a mine that would be worth investigating . . ."

HAROLD BLY sat alone in his big, echoing office on the top floor of the old Hyde Mining Building. From his window he could see the mining complex immediately below him, the once-majestic kingdom of Benjamin Hyde and his progeny now a dismal, decaying clutter of half-used concrete buildings and rusting metal roofs arranged helter-skelter on the side of the mountain. These days, after paying the soaring costs of mining, there wasn't much money left for repairs and upkeep.

Most of the miners were about a mile under the earth right now, blasting and hauling out the ore, but still the complex seemed very quiet compared to how busy it used to be. Once in a while Bly could see a member of the surface crew in a yellow hard hat walking along a ramp or a gravel road or one of the narrow alleyways between the buildings, but apart from that, it was hard to notice whether any work was going on down there.

Bly's desk, two filing cabinets, and his chair were the only furniture left in the huge room, and his office the only room still being used on the entire floor. The clerks, engineers, brokers, and secretaries were all gone except for a small crew of five working downstairs. All but one room's worth of desks, typewriters, phones, drawing boards, and adding machines had been liquidated.

So the company was not booming, just getting by. Nevertheless, Bly ruled. Bly would always rule, even if harsh measures had to be taken.

"Now, take it easy, Phil," he was saying into the phone. "Don't lose control here."

"The cops are after me, I just know it!" Phil's voice was whining and frantic. "I blew it, Harold, I'm sorry."

"But you tried," said Bly, comforting Phil as a father would comfort his struck-out Little Leaguer. "That has to count for something."

"Oh, man, you shoulda been there."

"She must have been quite a fighter."

"She was a maniac; she was like an animal. And my ear . . ."

Bly sounded intensely concerned. "How is your ear, Phil? Is it still on?"

"Yeah. But I've got to see the doctor."

"Then come back and we'll get it taken care of."

"But the cops are looking for me."

"Phil, don't worry about the police. I'll take care of that. We'll work something out. I know Sheriff Collins, and he's a reasonable man."

"Are you sure?"

Bly smiled as he thought of the poor fool on the other end.

"The sheriff listens to me. If I tell him you were right here, working for me last night, he'll buy that."

"You think so?"

"I know so."

"Well—okay."

"Come on back to Hyde River. I'll get you in to see the doctor, and we'll work it all out. Trust me."

"Okay."

"That's a good man."

"Hey, Harold, thanks."

"No problem."

Harold hung up and looked at his watch. Then he punched in the number of Tracy Ellis's mobile phone.

"Deputy Ellis."

"Tracy, this is Harold Bly. I've heard from Phil Garrett."

"I'm listening."

"Phil called me from a pay phone up in Wyler County somewhere. I convinced him to come back and face the music."

"He's coming back to Hyde River?"

"Mm-hm."

"When?"

"I'll let you know."

Tracy seemed a little dubious as she signed off. "Okay, Harold. I'll wait to hear from you."

"Good-bye."

He hung up, satisfied. Now he had the ingredients to get folks stirred up, and once folks around here got stirred up, all they needed was a nudge in the right direction. His hand went to his chest. The mark was still there. No problem. Within a few days he'd be rid of it.

SADDLEHORSE MOUNTAIN was a towering crag of rock, heavily forested on its lower flanks but scarred and bare along its ridges and summit. Here and there, like wounds that could never heal, the tailings and muck from the century-old mines formed gray, gravelly aprons down the mountainside through which only the hardiest trees now attempted a slow-growing comeback. There were still old roads snaking and coiling around the mountain, rutted, overgrown, and rarely traveled. Steve backtracked on Service Road 63 past Potter's mine, then, following Jules Cryor's directions, found an unnamed, unmarked road that circled the mountain in the other direction. He followed that road as far as his truck could negotiate it, pushing over the tops of low brush and sickly young trees that had established themselves on the road, and carefully dipping into and then back out of deep washouts. It was slow going.

After an hour of driving, virtually carving a new road on top of the old one, he finally came up against a massive fir that had toppled across the road, blocking any further progress.

End of the line. He climbed out, got his backpack and firearms, and continued on foot, ducking under the huge fallen tree and making his way up the road.

The trees began to thin out. He was breaking free of the heavier forestland and moving into the higher reaches of Saddlehorse, where rocky crags and bare fields of gravel were the rule and trees were the exception. He moved slowly, scanning the environment all around, mindful of Cliff, Maggie, Vic, and Charlie, and his own encounter with this so-called dragon. If the dragon wanted to pounce, it certainly wouldn't advertise. There would be no warning.

Up ahead, through the thinning forest, he could see the old road cutting through a field of mine tailings, and at the top of this expanse of lifeless, sun-baked gravel, he could discern some old pilings, now collapsed upon each other like jackstraws. He'd found the first of the two original mines.

He concealed himself behind the toppled, bug-eaten corpse of an old fir to appraise his situation. There was no cover between him and the mine entrance; he would have to run across wide open space. He slung the shotgun over one shoulder where he could grab it easily. His .357 was ready on his hip, the 30.06 was in his hands. In the event he might have to explore some of those tunnels, he took a small flashlight from his backpack and clipped it to his belt. He was wearing camouflage trousers and shirt, which would have helped had there been any greenery around, but would be of marginal effectiveness against bare, gray rock. Of course Steve had no idea whether or not the dragon could see color; he just had to assume it could.

That led to the question: What else could it do? Sense body heat? See infrared? It had to have excellent night vision. Perhaps it even employed sonar, as bats did. Being reptilian, it might be able to sense low-frequency vibrations through the ground—footsteps, crawling, any movement. For all Steve knew, it might have such a sophisticated array of sensory inputs as to make detection unpreventable.

As far as the dragon having an excellent sense of smell, Steve counted on it. But with that, he could already see he was at a disadvantage. The day was warm, the rocks were hot, and the air was moving uphill. If he tried to approach the mine from below, the air would carry his scent ahead of him. If the dragon was up there, he'd know Steve was coming.

Steve studied the mountain face. There was one chance of avoiding detection, at least by smell. If he climbed directly to the top of the ridge, he could get out of the airstream moving toward the mine entrance. Then, if all went well, he could descend from the ridge to the mine, opposite the wind. There was also a little more cover directly above him; he might be able to stay out of sight a little longer. He chose that route and after slinging the rifle over his other shoulder, he set out, leaving his backpack stowed beneath the fallen fir.

The climb was not difficult, but Steve stopped frequently, standing motionless, a plant-green speck on the vast mountainside, scanning the mountain and the sky above for anything out of place, any clue to the dragon's whereabouts.

He had to remind himself that his own imagination could

deceive him. As he scanned the rock formations above him, or the fields of gravel and mine tailings across the mountain face, or even the forests below, he realized that it was remarkably, maddeningly easy to see a dragon concealed in them. He continually had to weigh his perceptions against the real sightings he'd had and the descriptions he'd heard from Clayton Gentry and Jules Cryor. He looked for mirrorlike images, for any unusual shadows, for lines breaking with any movement. As he moved, he looked for any shape that might emerge from the background.

No dragon. At least, he didn't see one.

Steve pressed on and made it to the top of the ridge. From here, he could see the mountains in every direction, stretching to the horizon, green and rolling like a vast stormy ocean frozen in time, their edges and detail softened in the distance by a thin blue haze.

Maybe that thing really could hide up here for years and years, he thought. There's plenty of room.

Now he could see the tailings from the old mine below him. He would approach slowly, continually scanning for signs and also sniffing for scents; the wind was in his favor now.

He started down, taking one careful step at a time over the bare, jagged rocks. Occasionally a rock would teeter. Some pebbles would roll and plink down the slope. Low frequency vibrations! he thought.

He could make out the scattered timbers and then a nearly buried set of ore-car tracks emerging from the mountain. How in the world had those early miners gotten all that stuff up here?

He froze again, scanning the area. He could imagine all kinds of things, but he saw nothing.

He reached the level shelf of hewn rock outside the mine entrance. He was feeling a little more at ease now—a dangerous condition if it caused him to drop his guard, he knew. But the mine entrance was small, not much bigger than a standard door, and now partially hidden by fallen rocks and timbers. No creature the size of the dragon could pass through that. Scattered around that small, black hole were old timbers in a precarious pile, pieces of steel, a virtual carpet of broken core samples, and two rusted ore cars still sitting on the half-buried tracks.

Steve pressed his body tightly against the side of the mountain and scanned the area carefully. The rocks, the scattered debris, the dusty rails, the ore cars—all seemed to have been undisturbed for a century of seasons.

He sighed with some relief, and took a moment to rest and consult the map Jules Cryor had given him. Mine number one had turned up nothing so far. He could come back to investigate it further if the situation warranted it. For now, he decided it might be best to locate mine number two and the cavern Jules Cryor had indicated, and in the process become more generally familiar with the mountain.

According to the map, mine number two was farther around the mountain and could be reached by following the same old road— what was left of it—that brought Steve here. As for the cavern, Jules Cryor was strangely vague as to its exact location. He'd marked a few possible locations, but couldn't be sure about any one of them.

Steve walked down a fairly easy slope of hewn rock and found the road again, dusty and barren in the sun. He consulted the map as he walked along, his feet raising little clouds of dust and leaving tracks behind him. Cryor seemed to think the road would dead-end at mine number two, meaning Steve would have to find his own trail in search of the cavern. Steve figured he might make a circle around the crown of the mountain, cross over the ridge from the backside, and eventually come back to his starting point, where he could regather his backpack and call it a day. Judging from the distance and terrain, he should have enough daylight to do that.

He continued on, constantly scanning until it became wearisome. Even his imagination became tired of the game, which he regarded as a blessing: now he was seeing less imaginary, magical dragons in the rock formations.

He walked for the better part of an hour, following the road as it curved around the mountain toward the south, catching some breathtaking views of Hyde Valley and the opposite mountain range. Finally, just about when Steve's boredom threshold was being challenged, he caught sight of another mound of mine tailings high above the road.

Okay, same procedure, he told himself. Ascend to the ridge, sneak up on the mine from above, keep an eye out.

He did, and it took him another hour. When he reached the mine entrance, it didn't look much different from the first one. Again, the entrance itself was not much bigger than a standard doorway, certainly too small to accommodate a forty-foot reptilian something-or-other. There was debris around this mine as well: some steel scrap, a few old timbers soaked in black creosote, a rusted pickhead without a handle. Steve studied the ground carefully, looking for tracks, droppings, those familiar claw scratchings.

There was nothing here.

He circled the mountain, finding the backside not much different than the front except that mining operations had not come this far, so there was no scarring. He did catch sight of a black bear galloping across a draw far below, and a squirrel perched on a limb gave him a sound scolding. The bear was no problem; the noisy squirrel was only a nuisance.

As for any cavern, he found zilch.

By now his camouflage shirt was streaked with sweat. He rolled up his shirt sleeves then turned and climbed to the top of the ridge, where a cool breeze stroked his face. Again, he scanned all around, and again he detected nothing. He was starting to feel a little foolish.

Now he could see the tailings from mine number one and the old road below that. He chose a route that would bring him back down to the road just past the mine. From there, he could double back to his starting point. He was careful as he descended, but he could feel fatigue catching up with him and knew he'd had enough for one day.

The shadows on the west side were growing long as he reached the dusty road and absently noted his footprints, heading for mine number two. Suddenly he started to shake. Instinctively, he dropped to a crouch and with unsteady hands reached for the rifle slung over his shoulder.

Ahead of him there were new prints in that dust, some of them directly on top of his own, obliterating them. They were the tracks of the creature, at once marvelous and terrifying. Because of the soft dust and the fact they had been made recently, these were the clearest tracks he'd seen. The vague scratchings Levi Cobb had shown him were merely a sketch—these were the completed painting. Steve could recognize the prints of front paws, feet, or hands, and those of hind feet. Each print clearly showed three elongated toes, with a sharp puncture out in front of each one indicating a long, curved claw. Extending from the heel was an opposing toe, much like a thumb, its clawmark less definite. The hind feet were longer than the front, with a pronounced heel and the opposing toe extended rearward. Steve shuddered as he realized the implication of these prints: They were headed in the same direction as his own.

That thing was following him.

Carefully scanning all around, rifle ready, he half-stood and approached the footprints for a closer study. He estimated the front print to be at least four feet from the heel to the tip of the center toe. The hind prints were even larger.

He had no idea how much of a lead he had on the beast, how far it might be behind him. But if it was still following him . . .

He had to make some decisions—and quickly. Did he really want to take this thing on? Alone? And, if so, where did he set his ambush?

He might never have a chance like this again; he had to conquer his terror; he had to take the beast on.

The decision made, he looked around for a place to wait in ambush. The top of the ridge would probably be the best spot, he thought. He might be able to see it coming from there, but if he couldn't, the creature might reveal its position in other ways—sounds, moving brush, teetering rocks, anything.

He chose a different path back up to the ridge, staying low, constantly scanning the area. Once over the top, he found a niche in the rocks where he could conceal himself and maintain a wide perspective of the mountain below. He could see the way he'd come, just along the edge of some small pines and scattered shrub. He began a careful scan of his route, focusing on small segments at a time, studying each segment for movement. He listened. He sniffed for scents. So far, nothing.

That squirrel wasn't chattering anymore, not that that meant anything. But at least it wouldn't be covering up other sounds.

The air was still moving uphill; Steve could feel it brushing over his face. It carried no odd smells.

He looked at his watch. There were just a few hours of daylight left. When it turned dark, he would have virtually no advantage and the dragon would have it all.

Suddenly he tensed. A rustling.

His eyes darted to the spot, apparently on the route he had taken, about a hundred yards down the slope and far to the left. There was no movement.

Wait—he had been wrong. A small pine stirred as something scraped past it. The rocks behind the pine shimmered and wavered as if distorted by heat waves.

Farther along, another small tree bent . . . and then it broke in the middle, the top half lagging behind.

"That's it," Steve whispered.

He concentrated on that area and just ahead of it, waiting for another indication of the creature's presence. All his senses were on alert.

Then on the ground he saw something. A shadow, just a shadow, with nothing there to cast it. It slithered eerily along the rocks like a thin black film, up, down, rippling with the terrain, sometimes disappearing behind obstructions.

Steve had the 30.06 ready. But what could he shoot at? He could see only the shadow. From that, he could estimate where the creature was, but where would the vital organs be? Without a clear shot at the heart and lungs or the head, he couldn't be sure of a kill. He might nick the creature, or wound it, and he might rile it. If he didn't kill it when he shot he would be giving away his position and risking his own life.

He could feel panic starting to well up, but he forced himself to overcome it. He remained where he was, just sitting, waiting, watching.

The shadow was gone now, invisible beyond a rise in the terrain. But Steve saw the tops of some small trees wiggling. The forest just beyond them seemed distorted.

For only an instant, he could see a distinct area of distortion pass in front of a stand of trees like a bubble bending the light, like a long, elliptical lens. He was using his imagination, he knew, but he could almost make out a long, slithery shape, a lizardlike creature with a gracefully arching spine.

Then he saw nothing. He'd lost contact.

He sat and waited. He listened, he watched.

Then some treetops quivered almost directly below him, but farther down in the forest, nowhere near his original route. The creature had diverted downhill. It may have lost his trail, he didn't know, but now some rustlings and cracklings from dry branches came wafting up the slope, and he had another fix on the dragon's position. It was definitely moving away.

"Huh-uh, Mr. Dragon. You won't get away that easily."

Steve left his hiding place and set off down the mountain as quietly as he could, trying to keep the creature's movements and sounds within sight and earshot. It was moving quickly; he'd have to hurry.

He quickstepped down over a rockslide until he reached the edge of the forest. The trees and brush were sparse here, which meant he still had a chance of seeing the dragon before it evaded him entirely. He could still hear it moving farther down the mountain. Trees and undergrowth hissed and cracked as the creature brushed by them, but as heavy as that beast had to be, Steve could neither hear footfalls nor feel any vibration of the ground. Steve followed the rustling sounds, moving quickly while trying to gauge how much cover remained between the dragon and himself.

His eye caught a familiar distortion against some trees and brush downhill and to the right. He dropped to a crouch, hoping some brambles would hide his own outline.

He could see an old, sun-bleached snag leaning toward the valley below. He watched in stunned amazement as it seemed to break into two sections, the upper part clear and motionless, the lower part rippling and warping, as if the dragon's slender tail was passing by it. Then the apparition was gone, and the snag was one complete trunk again.

Steve moved again, vaulting over logs and hurrying through the trees. He reached the snag and checked the ground for signs. Amazingly, he found none of the things he expected. There were no footprints in the soil here, no broken branches, nothing to indicate that a massive creature had walked through this area only minutes before. He stared through the forest, looking in the direction the thing had gone. How could any creature that size move so delicately?

Then he heard a strange sound up ahead, and he stood, his whole body rigid, as he listened. It was a long, steady sound, like something sliding.

Then it hit him. That thing wasn't walking, it was slithering, moving almost silently, leaving no footprints, disbursing its weight throughout the length of its body!

Steve felt he had to be absolutely nuts to be following this monster, but he could not help himself. He was terrified, but he was also fascinated. He moved stealthily from tree to log to tree to thicket, eyes wide open, heart pounding, a viselike grip on his rifle, his instincts screaming danger.

He continued along the mountain's flank until he saw dark gray and rust through the trees. He stopped. It must be a rock formation, perhaps a cliff.

Perhaps it was the dragon. He took a few steps, studying that surface carefully. Careful, he told himself.

He could see no distortions. Nothing changed as he approached in a zigzag formation, trying to get something to emerge, aware as he did so, that by trying to get the creature to move, he might be risking his own life.

He came closer, rifle aimed, his finger on the trigger. His palms were greasy with sweat, and a drop trickled down his forehead and burned one eye.

He got through the trees that blocked his view and found himself at the base of a towering cliff. Sharp-edged boulders lay scattered on the mountain slope below. Off to his left and around the curve of the cliff, he could just spot a sizable apron of loose gravel and fine shards of rock, very much like the mine tailings he'd seen.

Possibly, just possibly, there'd been some digging under the cliff and he was seeing the waste. It could be just another mine, and yet . . .

Possibly, just possibly, he'd found the creature's den.

He listened for a sound, looked for a movement, but found nothing. By now it wouldn't take much to persuade him to return with a good-size army. But even he didn't believe what he was stalking. How would anyone else believe it?

What he needed to do, whether or not anyone believed him, was to establish if he'd actually found the creature's den.

He wiped the sweat from his brow and palms. He knew he was broadcasting human scent like an alarm. If one little breeze passed over his body and into that den there would be no more secrets.

He edged along the base of the cliff, craning his neck to see what was around the other side.

He could see the mound of waste clearly now. It didn't look like a natural rockslide; it had to have been put there.

A few more steps. The face of the cliff was curling inward. It could be the mouth of a cave.

He edged closer.

He'd come to the mouth of a cave. It was about ten feet wide, and about his height, not a vast opening. But it was big enough to accommodate the local dragon. Scratchings, tracks, and a furrow, perhaps cut by a long, slender tail, marked the loose soil and gravel on the floor of the entrance.

The dragon had come home.

He rested against the rough stone. What now? His mind was almost coming apart with conflict. Part of him wanted nothing more than to flee from that place in a blind panic, satisfied just to be alive. But another part of him couldn't give up. He'd come so far, he'd come so close, he wanted that dragon.

He had to know more, see more.

His heart was pounding almost audibly, and it was only by blocking certain thoughts and images from his mind—the size of those footprints, Charlie's scorched and mangled car, the reported size of this beast—that he could keep his hands steady. With his left hand he carefully, quietly took the flashlight from his belt then edged around the corner and started down that seemingly bottomless pit. His back to the wall, he advanced slowly, peering in every direction. He didn't want to use the flashlight unless absolutely necessary.

The dragon has the advantage, his logical mind insisted. The dragon has the advantage.

I want him, his soul answered.

He can see in here, you can't; he knows these tunnels, you don't; he could corner you so easily!

I'll be careful, he argued. The fact that he was terrified was beside the point.

The cave entrance immediately opened into a room that at first seemed limitless. From the light coming from outside, Steve could make out a domed ceiling, arcing down to the sandy floor.

There seemed to be an object on the floor in the center of the room. Steve stayed by the wall and didn't move. His eyes still needed to adjust to the darkness. He'd give them time.

The object looked like a piece of clothing, but in the semidarkness Steve couldn't tell. He listened, smelled, watched. Nothing. The dragon must have continued deep into the heart of the mountain. Like Jules Cryor said, these tunnels went for miles.

Without stirring from his position, he shifted the rifle to his left hand and the flashlight to his right. He aimed the light low, clicked it on, then slowly moved the beam outward across the room until it found the object.

It was cloth, perhaps a shirt.

He dared to move the light farther across the room, then around the walls, exploring the room's limits. Except for the one object in the center of the floor, the room was empty. Directly across the room from where he stood Steve saw a tunnel. He kept his eye on that tunnel as he crossed the cave floor to take a look at the shirt or whatever it was.

Yes. Half a flannel shirt, dark with blood, torn and perforated.

He could feel queasiness setting in and his throat tightening with nausea. This shirt could have been Cliff's, or maybe Vic Moore's, or Charlie's. It could have belonged to another victim no one even knew about. He dropped it and turned away. This was not the time to think about that.

He looked ahead. The tracks clearly led to the tunnel beyond. He shouldered the rifle and took the shotgun in hand. He didn't know how far he would venture in there, maybe only far enough to gain some knowledge of the cave's layout. He kept the flashlight beam low and made his way across the room.

The tunnel was slightly smaller than the cave entrance. The dragon's ability to wriggle through such tight places was impressive, Steve thought. It had to be part snake, all right. It had walked across the large room, but here it appeared to have slithered. The floor of the tunnel was scraped smooth.

He looked over his shoulder, double-checking his escape route. Then he gathered his courage and ventured, step by step, down the tunnel.

It sloped downhill. He kept close to the wall and proceeded slowly, carefully.

What was that? He stopped abruptly, his heart hammering. He had heard some faint, rustling noises.

Everything was silent, and he started forward again—then

almost laughed as he realized what the sound had been. It was his jacket, brushing against the wall.

Cautiously he moved deeper into the cave. The sand was still smooth as if a grader had run over it, although in several places it had been pushed aside and was piled in small berms against the cave walls. He had never been bothered by claustrophobia, but he was beginning to feel the weight of the mountain above him. Still, he pressed on.

He saw a corner up ahead. He clicked off his flashlight so that if the creature was on the other side, it wouldn't see light flickering on the cave walls.

As Steve waited for his eyes to adjust to the darkness, he realized that there was light coming from around the corner. Was it possible? He approached the corner slowly, feeling his way along the wall. Yeah. There was a hint of daylight coming from around the corner. Another entrance?

He pressed tightly against the wall and moved in slow, slow motion until he could peer around the corner with one eye. Now he could see light coming down through a sizable shaft. Yes, there was an opening high above, but it was a nearly impossible climb.

He looked behind him, then ahead, then moved carefully around the corner.

Surprise. The cave ended here. There was just that one shaft, which must have been cut through the rock years before, and nothing else.

No dragon.

No other way out, either, he realized. Just the main entrance. The thought slowly entered his mind; I've been in this situation before—

A rock fell down the shaft, rattling against the sides and then thudding into the sandy floor. Steve leapt aside, startled out of his wits, an involuntary cry escaping his throat.

Another rock, this one bigger! Then another, rattling down the shaft, clacking and thudding against the first stones that fell, kicking up a choking dust.

The shaft was breaking up! Caving in!

Or being broken up?

Now huge stones, dust, gravel, and debris were pouring through the hole above. The light was vanishing in chunks, the air filling with dust.

A trap, Steve thought. I've been caught in a trap.

Steve clicked on his flashlight and dashed back up the tunnel as gray, choking dust billowed like a wave behind him. He ducked to avoid a low-hanging formation, smashed his shoulder into another, but kept going, retracing his tracks.

Levi, he thought. Bait. Trap. No way out. Gotcha.

How long was this tunnel? he wondered, beginning to panic. He should be back to that room by now, back to the entrance—

Then he saw a faint glimmer of daylight! He clipped the flashlight back on his belt, then lunged out of the tunnel and into the room.

But the room was no longer empty. It was nearly filled with a curled, serpentine shape—and the stench of death.

He gasped, stopped, and turned to dive back into the tunnel. Three monstrous, elongated fingers, claws glistening in the dim light, swatted him. He tumbled in the sand, then righted himself, his eyes darting about the room, his mind screaming for options. A long, tapered tail of silver armor now lay across the cave entrance. He turned toward the tunnel. A large scaly, clawed hand guarded it. He was cornered.

Stretched between the tunnel and the entrance, its scales glistening like highway reflectors in the dim light, its huge golden eyes narrow with malice, crouched a beast the size of a whale, the shape of a lizard, its neck and tail like a serpent. No camouflage now; Steve could see it clearly, every inch of it.

The dragon.

I, my wife Abigail, her sister Lois who had married Benjamin Hyde, and Ben's young son James, all stood in grim and dreadful silence there on the bank of the Hyde River under a stark, full moon. Ben was never one to tolerate dissension in the ranks, much less in the family, and so we were assembled there at his behest, or rather, his order, to be forever convinced of his power.

With only a few muttered incantations Ben was able to produce from the river a spirit the likes of which I had never seen, nor wish ever to see again. It was a drooling, slithering thing, much like an alligator but more like a lizard of that size, displaying an uncanny level of awareness and intelligence. We were terrified, of course, and would have fled for our very lives, save for Ben's intervention. He commanded the beast to remain crouched by the river's edge, and it obeyed even though its yellow eyes glowered at us like lamps and its bared teeth continued to gnash, ready, I suppose, to dismember its first victim if Ben would but say the word.

From an account written in 1892 by Carson Homestead
and inserted as a supplement in the diary of his wife
Abigail, Benjamin Hyde's sister-in-law,
on March 9, 1915

FIFTEEN

The Diary

STEVE TURNED animal. He had no thoughts, no feelings, only the raging instinct for survival. He aimed the shotgun without a plan, and the blast exploded into the dragon's chest at the base of the neck with fiery sparks, the shock rippling through the scales the length of its body with flashes of emerald and ruby. The creature lurched, its face wrinkling, as if in pain. Steve fired again. The blast ignited a violent splash of color on the flank just behind the foreleg. The clawed hand came up, palm out, and blocked the third shot, then the fourth as lead shot pelted the cave walls. Steve let out a cry of terror as the giant hand filled his vision and pummeled him into the rock wall. He struck his head against the stone and dropped to his knees, dazed.

Somehow, even as his head was spinning and his body teetering, he got off another shot that hit the dragon midway down its neck.

Suddenly the shotgun was gone. Steve was just realizing there was nothing in his hands when he saw the dragon, razor teeth bared in anger, hurl the gun across the cave where it clattered against the stone wall near the entrance and landed in the sand.

Steve slipped the 30.06 from his shoulder.

The dragon snatched it away and hurled it against the wall of the cave on the other side.

Now Steve was eye to eye with the monster and had only his sidearm. He chose not to move but remained as stone, on his knees in the sand. The dragon was looking down at him . . .

Steve could see anger, hatred in the glowing, golden eyes. This creature could think! And it seemed to be pondering what to do with him.

Steve shot a glance toward the entrance. The tail was still stationed there, ready to crush him if he tried it.

His eyes returned along the length of the dragon, from the tail to the face, recording for this last instant of his life the creature that would chew, dismember, kill, and eat him, in that order. The scales still shimmered, like light reflected off water, each one a living thing; silken wings, tightly folded, clung to the contour of the creature's back like a second skin; the elongated neck, tightly curled in this small space, supported the head with rock-steady strength; above the golden eyes, two silvery horns swept backward from the crown of the head.

And now the dragon seemed to be smiling—no, leering—at him in mockery and derision.

In his mind he could see that half-eaten mouse back at the motel, its upper half gone. Now I'm the mouse, he thought. This is how it feels.

Still Steve did not move. Perhaps that was the only thing buying him the time, he thought.

Suddenly the dragon drew back its head, its horns scraping against the ceiling as it drew a long, hissing breath through its nostrils, expanding its rib cage. It swallowed. The neck and chest began to heave as if it might vomit.

Oh, God, no . .

The creature looked toward the entrance and gave a quick, short puff out the side of its mouth. The fumes ignited into blue flame, a brief flash.

No . . . no! He cringed in terror.

The beast looked down at him, as if to see his reaction. Steve had tried not to react, but that was impossible. He was eye to eye with a most hideous death, an unimaginable horror.

The beast gave another puff, this one longer in duration, the flame larger. Then it took a deep breath, and a blast of blue-and-yellow-flame came straight out through its fangs and incisors, flashing and licking across the ceiling of the cave with the roar of a furnace. The creature drew another deep breath, and this time the golden eyes centered on Steve.

"No . . . NOOOOO!"

Instinctively Steve leapt, then rolled in the sand as the burning gases struck the cave wall and flared out sideways. He scrambled toward the tunnel. Another blast drove him back.

I'm being played with. I'm dead.

Now there was only darkness. The dragon was a vague shape, the glowing eyes suspended in the smoke, studying him. Then the powerful neck curled slightly to the side, and with a concentrated, prolonged flame, the dragon incinerated Steve's rifle, blackening the barrel, charring the stock, exploding the rounds in the magazine like a string of cherry bombs while Steve dug into the sand, covering his head with his arms.

Black smoke billowed around him. Steve couldn't breathe. He began to gag.

A blast of flame rolled at him from the right, lighting up the cave walls. He dodged it, leaping to the left. The dragon followed with a steady rotation of its head, keeping the flame inches behind him as he ran.

Then more flames, this time in front. Steve dug in, reversed direction, leapt and rolled in the sand trying to dodge the flames, but they caught his arm and set his sleeve on fire. He beat his arm against the sand to put out the flames, a searing pain flowing over his skin like molten lava. Screams were bursting from deep inside him and echoing off the cave walls like ghostly taunts, adding to his terror.

Flames roared right over his head. He hit the sand flat out. The heat was so intense he thought his body had ignited.

Then another wave of flame came from his right, flashing and rolling along the floor. Out of pure reflex, he rolled to his left and scrambled to his feet. He was blinded by the smoke. His lungs were burning.

The tunnel! It was open, not blocked! Like a frightened animal he tumbled inside, scrambling on hands and knees down the sandy floor, gasping for breath. The air was dusty and filthy, but there was no smoke, no burning vapors.

A hunted animal, Steve crawled and groped his way along the rock wall, hoping against hope for some crevice in which to hide, some place out of that thing's reach. He kept crawling until he came to the end of the tunnel where rubble now almost filled the shaft above. Then he collapsed in pain and terror on the dusty stones. It was all over. The dragon had him.

But nothing happened.

Suddenly a faint beam of light cut through the haze and smoke. Steve looked up and saw light coming in through the partially blocked shaft. He tried to be still and think.

There was no sound other than that of his own wheezing. So far he was still alone at the bottom of the tunnel. He looked back in the direction of the main room. There was silence and cool air and dust. Was the thing gone?

He dared not believe it. Yet he could not hear it slithering down the tunnel toward him. Well, he couldn't stay here, he thought. The only way out was back up the tunnel. If the dragon was going to kill him, it would kill him whether he stayed here or not.

Calling on his last reserves of strength, Steve crawled around the corner toward the tunnel, then sat leaning against the wall, breathing heavily and listening. There was silence and total darkness in the tunnel. Suddenly Steve realized he still had his flashlight on his belt. With shaking fingers he unclipped it and shined it up the tunnel. It was clear. Slowly, painfully, he began to crawl up it, too exhausted to walk.

The trip back up the tunnel seemed interminable, but at last he reached the main room. He flashed the light around. It was empty. The smoke was clearing, and he could see light filtering in to the entrance of the tunnel.

The dragon was gone!

Over against the cave wall, he saw his rifle, black and smoldering, the magazine blown open and the spent shells scattered about on the sand. He crawled over to the wall, then pulled himself to his feet, his legs rubbery, and stole quietly to the entrance. Nothing but fading, reddening daylight out there.

And air. Clear, crisp, breathable air.

He emerged from the cave filthy, scorched, stinking of smoke, and trembling like a leaf. Below him, the thin, struggling trees remained undisturbed. Saddlehorse Peak was awash in the warm light of the late-afternoon sun.

He sank to his knees on the sandy shelf in front of the cave entrance then flopped onto his back to breathe for a while, to recover, to think. He had to get going before it got dark, he knew. But right now he couldn't move.

Oh God, just let me rest and be alive for a while. Just let me feel the cool earth under my back and see the sky overhead . . .

His hand fell on something small and metallic. He glanced over at it, then picked it up.

It was one of the dragon's scales. All he had to do was hold it, and it mimicked the color and texture of his hand. Maybe one of his shots had broken it loose. It showed no damage, though, no dents or abrasions.

He rested his head in the sand and looked up at the sky, clear except for a few cirrus clouds.

Levi tried to warn me, he thought. This was a repeat of the last time, only Levi wasn't here and I walked right into it. Stupid, stupid, stupid!

As hard as it was for him to accept, Steve realized that the creature could think. It knew what he was thinking; it knew him. He didn't—he couldn't—understand it, but he knew that the creature was aware of his own motivations.

But then, why did it let me go? he wondered. Why didn't it eat me? What was all that flame-throwing for? Was it just showing off?

Steve's rational mind began to kick in. He was weak, but he forced himself to get up and to walk away from the cave toward some bushes, where he collapsed again and began to rethink what had happened.

He realized now that he should have gotten a clue from the tracks in the sand. There was only one set and only one furrow left by the tail. The thing didn't come here all the time. In fact, it had only been there once recently—once, just to trap him.

He should have known that. He should have seen it.

He sat there for several minutes replaying the whole scene, mentally kicking himself for being so stupid. I should have known . . . I should have anticipated . . . I should have . . . I should have . . . I should have . . .

CHARLIE WAS gone, and everyone knew it. A story went around town about Charlie being the victim of a hit-and-run truck—Lester Collins came up with that one—and another one about Charlie hitting a moose but such stories were destined for an early death in Hyde River. No one said a word, at least not very loud, about what really had happened to Charlie Mack, but everyone knew.

They knew about Maggie too, and Vic, and by now they knew Cliff Benson by name and knew whose brother he was and what Steve the professor was after. Those from the old school, like Elmer McCoy and Joe Staggart, knew better than to talk openly about it, but they were still ready to give hushed, two- or three-word answers to the younger folks who dared to ask questions. The community was closing in tightly.

Crucifixes began to appear around town. Carl Ingfeldt's wife never went anywhere without the old silver cross her mother had given her. Doug Ellis welded one together out of bits of sheet metal and copper wire and kept it around his neck even when he showered.

Carlotta and Rosie nailed a wooden cross to their front door but went one step further by tacking garlic cloves to it. Kyle Figgin had a brainstorm and fetched a bottle of holy water from West Fork, asking only a dollar a portion to cover his trouble and expense.

Those of purely secular minds invested in more firearms and ammunition. Even Paul the skeptic could feel something brewing and oiled up the locks on his doors and windows, something he hadn't done as long as he'd lived in the town.

The people of Hyde River were afraid. Reverend Ron Woods could sense it clearly as they greeted him on the street or in the hardware store or even came by to help him nail shingles onto the church roof. They all wanted to talk, to see how he was, to talk about—well, about any old thing having nothing to do with what was really bothering them. He was happy enough to visit with them and reassure them, but since they had no questions, he couldn't venture any answers, and of course, they could not talk about The Problem. Anything but that.

Levi knew the talk going around; he could feel the fear spreading through the town. He knew the closeness of the evil and the shortness of the time.

So he continued working, grinding and honing the edge of the old bulldozer backclaw tooth, heating it, hammering it, forming it into a broad-tipped, razor-sharp spearhead. "Out of the fire, a tool fit for the master's hand. Ha! Just you watch. Any time now, might even be tonight, that cocky professor's gonna come through my door, and this time he's gonna be ready to listen. We gotta be ready by then, am I right?"

THE COWBELL over the door to Charlie's tavern jangled.

The moment Tracy Ellis stepped inside, she could tell the town's center of socializing had become like a bunker under siege. There was some kind of meeting going on in the far corner, she'd walked into the middle of it, and now she was drawing icy stares from all the attendees. Andy Schuller and his pool-shooting buddies were part of that meeting, leaning against the far wall, the pool table and cues totally ignored. There was no clatter from the kitchen, for Bernie was out of his apron and seated with the others. Carl Ingfeldt was there, along with Paul Myers, and across the table from them sat the town's two girlfriends-at-large, Carlotta and Rosie, smoking cigarettes and looking nervous. Tracy's estranged husband, Doug, was there, along with his loyal sidekick Kyle Figgin, and right next to them were the old-timers Elmer McCoy and Joe Staggart. Seeing McCoy and Staggart, Tracy realized that this gathering had to be important. Those two usually stayed in a clique of their own.

"Hi," she said casually. "Hope I'm not interrupting anything." She knew she was.

Not a soul answered. Some looked away. Some fidgeted. Others stared daggers at her.

She crossed the room at an easy pace, passing between the empty tables, feeling as safe as a piece of raw meat in a kennel of mad dogs.

They were eyeing her, checking her out. She was definitely in the role of cop tonight, carrying her sidearm, her nightstick, even her handcuffs.

She was feeling like a pretty lonely cop right now. Deputy Jerry Fisk didn't want to make waves in Hyde River, Deputy Matson wouldn't sneeze without Collins's permission, and Johanson was on the other side of the county. Oh well, so be it. Phil Garrett was here now, by arrangement, and Tracy would not be turned away.

"Hi, Tracy," Doug finally said. "What brings you here tonight?"

Tracy looked past several people to the center of the crowd, the empty chair right by the door to the mercantile. Harold Bly's chair. Mr. Bly was nowhere to be seen. Seated right next to that empty chair, however, was the real object of Tracy's visit: Phil Garrett. He was slouching a little but looking cocky, drumming his fingers on his knees in time to some tune going through his head as he looked up at her. A new bandage totally covered the side of his head but did not hide some fresh welts and bruises on his face.

"Anybody seen Harold?" she asked offhandedly.

"He should be here any minute," Doug answered. "We're having a meeting."

How handy, she thought. First he snitches, then he hides.

It was Harold Bly who had called her, telling her she could find Phil at the tavern, and when. Now Bly was conveniently late, distancing himself from the whole situation, sidestepping all the fireworks so he wouldn't have to be involved. He had to be playing one of his little games.

No matter. Tracy wanted her man.

She was scared, but she couldn't let anyone know that, so she put on her cop demeanor and stepped forward, slowly working her way through the outer edges of the crowd. When she came up against Doug, he stood in her way. "Excuse me."

Phil snickered a bit.

Doug was not angry or defiant. His tone of voice was concerned as he asked, "Tracy, are you sure you want to do this?"

"It's my job," she said.

He gently put his hands on her shoulders and spoke in a near whisper, "I know you're mad at me, and I know we have our problems. But I couldn't bear to see anything happen to you. Please—don't do this."

She glared up at him, her hand on her nightstick, and said coldly, "Same old sweet words, huh, Doug? If you care so much for me, then what are you doing here with these people?"

He had no answer.

She looked down at his hands on her shoulders. "I think you'd better get your hands off me."

He took his hands away and stepped aside.

"Hey—" Phil started to object.

Tracy looked down at him. "Phil, I have to place you under arrest."

He looked at the others, then at her, chuckling with disbelief. "Hey, haven't you talked to Sheriff Collins?"

"Every day, Phil."

"Then what's this all about?"

"Breaking and entering, assault with a deadly weapon—"

"But Sheriff Collins was gonna take care of it!"

"I'm taking care of it! Now get up and face the wall!"

"No! Sheriff Collins was gonna fix it! Harold said—"

She grabbed his arm to get him to his feet. "Come on."

He leapt to his feet and shoved her away. "Forget you, little girl!"

She came off some bodies standing behind her like a wrestler off the ropes, her nightstick in her hand. Phil was mocking her with his eyes. They both knew he was surrounded by friends.

She addressed the crowd. "He broke into a lady's house and waited for her to come home, and then he attacked her and tried to stab her. The only reason she's still alive is because she was able to fight him off."

"She didn't fight me off!" Phil objected.

Carlotta gasped.

Tracy kept going. "Oh, yes, she did, Phil! She and her son. He hit you so hard he about knocked your ear off; isn't that right?"

But now Phil could see the shocked expressions on some, the disdain in the eyes of others, and clammed up.

Tracy spoke to the crowd again. "Phil has to answer for what he's done. I'd appreciate your help."

Elmer McCoy muttered, "I think she asked for it."

Andy saw it that way. "Yeah, I don't blame Phil. She was poking her nose into our business."

Carlotta couldn't believe what she was hearing. "What?"

Elmer explained, "You know that professor who's been snooping and hunting around here? She was his sister-in-law."

Carlotta fell silent. She knew the Bensons were trouble.

Well, Tracy thought, I won't come out of this popular if I come out of it alive, but I'm not going to be the coward! "Phil," she said, "you're coming with me and that's that." She prodded him with the stick. "Turn around, hands behind your back."

He grabbed the arm holding the nightstick, his grip like a vise, his eyes full of malice.

For an instant, she saw him as Evelyn had seen him. Cold, desperate, deadly.

When she kicked him in the groin it was an act of desperation. He bent over in pain, and his grip weakened enough for her to break loose. When she beaned him with her nightstick she was scared enough to make it count, and when he fell to the floor she leapt on top of him just to keep him from getting up again. She was crazed with fear and anger, but she managed to stick to procedure and hold him down with her knee in his spine while she grabbed her handcuffs.

"Get her off me!" Phil squalled into the floor.

"Hey!" Andy Schuller stepped forward.

"Stay out of this!" she warned him, cuffing one of Phil's wrists.

"Stay out of it," Doug advised, his tone emphatic.

Andy looked at Doug and then at Tracy, and backed off.

"Give me that hand!" Tracy shouted, grabbing for Phil's one free, flailing hand. She got it and cuffed it. "You have the right to remain silent—"

"Get her off me!"

She yanked him to his knees, then to his feet, nightstick ready to pop him again if she had to. "Anything you say can and will be used against you in a court of law—get out of the way!"

The crowd cleared a path, and she pushed Phil through it. "You have the right to an attorney—"

"Help me, will you?" Phil screamed. "Don't just stand there!"

They just stood there.

She pushed him along, keeping him off balance, heading for the door. She called to the others, "Thank you for your cooperation. Have a good evening," and got him outside.

JUST DOWN THE STREET, Harold Bly was hiding behind a tenton dump truck, smoking a cigarette and waiting. He saw Tracy burst through the door of the tavern with Phil in hand, still bawling and squalling and even calling his name, "Harold! Harold!"

"Get in the car!" she ordered, stuffing him inside while dodging his kicking feet.

Harold didn't answer Phil's cries. He just waited until Tracy had strong-armed Phil into the car, slammed the door shut, and driven off. Then he dropped the cigarette, crushed it out with his toe, and walked to the tavern with the relaxed, casual manner of someone oblivious to what had just happened.

When Bly came in the front door, those who had witnessed the arrest surrounded him. "You missed it!" "Where've you been? Tracy came in here—" "She hit him right on the head!" "She's a dirty traitor!" "She arrested him!" "We didn't know what to do!" "Do something!"

He asked a few questions and got a volley of answers. He listened while they expressed their outrage. He could see the anger, the frustration, the desperation growing, reaching a fever pitch. Something had to be done! they were all saying.

Very good.

When it was his turn to speak, he asked a calculated question. "So what are you willing to do?"

LEVI OPENED the back door of his shop to find a soot-blackened, sand-soiled, and weary man leaning against the doorpost.

"Hi, Levi."

Levi studied Professor Steve Benson up and down, taking special note of the beleaguered man's charred rifle. "Looks like you came pretty close."

Steve nodded. "I need to talk to you."

WHILE LEVI attended to him with soap and towels, Steve put his whole head under the faucet of the big shop sink and let the cool water pour over him, then washed his upper body as best he could.

Levi brought some ointment for the burns on Steve's left arm and shoulder. Steve winced as Levi smeared it on.

"It breathes fire," Steve reported. "It just about fried me."

"Uh-huh," said Levi, like he'd known it all along.

"I was up on Saddlehorse. I think that's where it lives."

"Yeah," Levi acknowledged, "that would be my guess." Then he added, "I suppose he trapped you?"

Steve took a towel from Levi and vigorously rubbed his hair dry, taking a long time to finally answer, "I suppose he did." Then he came out from under the towel and asked, "So why didn't he kill me? He had the chance."

"He chooses his own time for that. He might take you tomorrow; he might wait twenty years. You can't tell when he'll catch up and collect."

"So why'd he trap me?"

Levi had to laugh. "Aw, he just wanted to play with you a bit just to keep you interested."

Steve dried his body gingerly, lightly dabbing at the burns. "What do you mean, keep me interested?"

"He can't kill you, not yet. He doesn't own you. But if he can keep you around until he gets you hooked, then he can do whatever he wants." Levi handed Steve a fresh shirt. "Here, borrow this for now."

"Thanks." Steve took the shirt and slipped into it. Levi was shorter than he was, but his shirt was plenty big enough. "You're talking in riddles again."

"Yeah, I know. I keep forgetting how far behind you are."

Steve was on edge. "Then get me caught up! Listen, from all the people I've talked to, there's no one else in this valley as universally hated and discredited as you, which means you're probably the only one with guts enough to tell the truth. So okay. You've got your audience. Speak up."

Levi smiled. "You up to doing some reading tonight?"

"To be honest, I'm ready for bed, and that's about it."

"Come on upstairs. It won't take long."

Steve followed Levi up the back stairs to Levi's apartment over the garage.

Levi went to his desk and pulled open a bottom drawer. "I'm gonna start you at the beginning." He pulled out a thick three-ring binder and opened it up, flipping through pages of photocopied text. "Do you know about the big massacre of 1882?"

"I've heard conflicting accounts about it."

"Right. That it was the Indians—"

"Yeah."

"Or that two factions were fighting over the town and the gold."

"I heard that, too."

Levi shook his head. "It's all a person can do to find out what really happened, this town gets so hush-hush about its past. Anyway, now you get to hear it from people who were there." He set the binder on the desk. "Some years back, I had a nice lady in my Bible study, one of the older folks who'd lived here all her life, you know? She came out to church for quite awhile, and finally she accepted Christ and got free of a lot of old sins in her life—and that's a whole other story—but she was part of the old school, the old Hyde River Oath, you understand? She had secrets she could never talk about until she got saved, and then she was free of all that stuff."

"Okay." Steve was ready to listen even if he had to listen to a sermon in the process.

"So one day she pulls me aside, and she says, 'You know that old plastering on the back wall of the church basement? I've heard that a lady hid a strongbox back there when they put that plaster up,' and I said, 'What're you talking about,' and she told me a secret she got from her folks about a lady who used to run the local whorehouse back in Hyde River in the 1880s. The story goes that this madam kept a diary of everything that happened back then and left it to her daughter when she died. Then the daughter found some more things—you know, letters, notes, newspaper articles—and hid them all away in the wall of the church not long before she died.

"Well, I didn't do anything about it then because I didn't want to start tearing the church up, but just a few years ago, we had to redo some plumbing back there, which meant we had to strip the wall down to the old studs. Well, what do you think? I remembered Maybelle—her name was Maybelle Crowder—telling me about the old strongbox, so I did a little extra tearing off and digging in, and lo and behold, there it was. The diary was inside, and some letters and old newspaper clippings, and I want to tell you, what that lady had was dangerous to have, all right. You'll see what I mean when you read it." He started thumbing through the binder, pointing out the photocopied documents as he explained, "This here is that madam's diary . . . and this here is a letter some gal wrote back in 1880 to her sister after her son got beat up. Here's a letter a man included with his will, and here's a newspaper article about a gal getting killed because she was talking too much . . . All this stuff was in that strongbox.

"Anyway, Maybelle went to be with the Lord that same year, but she said I could keep all this stuff, so I did. But it got me thinking, so I started looking around, writing a few letters, tracking people down, and guess what? It turns out Harold Bly had an aunt who wasn't regarded as part of the family anymore." He flipped to a section. "Clarice Stevens was Harold Bly's mother's half-sister, and it took me about two years to finally track her down in Oregon. When Harold's mother disappeared, Clarice Stevens felt sure the Blys had everything to do with it, so she had nothing good to say about the Blys or the Hydes ever since. But look here: Abigail Homestead, Benjamin Hyde's sister-in-law, and Abby Bly, Harold's mother, both passed their diaries down to Clarice, and before Clarice died, she passed along copies to me.

"The rest of this stuff . . . this here's from the West Fork Historical Society . . . Oh, and you remember Harold Bly talking about the town charter of 1882? Here's a copy of that right here . . . This here's from a book I found in the library . . . this Dennis Mason is an old army buddy of Sam Bly. He's still alive and gave me a copy of what he wrote." Levi chuckled. "I even got some good stuff from Harold's old fourth grade teacher. She never liked him much either!"

Levi handed the binder to Steve, and Steve thumbed through it, impressed at the volume of research it represented. "With all this, you had to have made some enemies."

"That's why you're looking at copies. The originals are in a safe-deposit box." Levi sniffed a derisive laugh. "I've found that diaries and letters and documents, anything that might tell people the truth, tend to get stolen around here, so I've had to be careful. People don't like to hear the truth, and they don't like people who tell it."

Steve's tone was a little testy. "And I suppose you're a teller of the truth, is that it?"

"You can be the judge of that. But go ahead, read the madam's diary and some of the letters. Read the charter of 1882. It'll give you a good idea where the dragon came from and what it's all about." Then he added, "And then you'll have a better idea how to kill it."

"From a hundred-year-old diary?"

"Read it, and we'll talk about it."

"What about Reverend Woods? Has he seen this?"

"Well, he's seen it, but he hasn't read it. I got him to read the town charter, but . . . eh, he doesn't want to get into this stuff. We differ a lot in our theology."

"Theology?" Did that have to come into everything Levi did?

"He believes we should keep the peace, but I like to shoot my mouth off. Just read it. Here, let me show you . . ." Levi marked the pages. If you read from here to . . . here . . . that'll be enough of the diary. The lady's name was Holly Ann Mayfield, and I think she told the truth. Maybe she's the only one who ever did. The other diaries and letters and clippings'll make a lot more sense once you read what she had to say."

IT WAS past the end of Tracy's shift when she finally grappled and shoved the kicking and cursing Phil Garrett through the door of the station in West Fork. By now she'd reached her limit with this scumbag, and it was difficult to be nice. Phil was a difficult prisoner to contain as it was, but now he was getting worse, and he smelled bad besides, like he hadn't had a bath in years, like he had a dead rat in his pocket. The patrol car reeked of it, and the jail would probably reek of it. It was nauseating.

Since it was after-hours, the station was deserted. The on-duty deputy was out on his rounds, and all incoming calls had been forwarded to a central dispatcher. She'd have to process the prisoner herself. Great. Just great.

With one hand on his arm just to keep track of him, she reached over the counter for the keys to the cell block.

"I've got to see a doctor!" Phil whined. "I think you busted my ear loose again!"

"In the morning," she answered, unlocking the big iron door.

"But—you—you can't leave me here!" Tracy couldn't believe it—the cocky little buzzard was actually scared. "You can't leave me here alone!"

She pushed him through the door. "It's just for one night. I'm going to get you processed, and then the Oak Springs cops can come and get you."

He resisted. "No—listen, I can't stay here!"

They moved somewhat haltingly down a narrow hall and around a corner to a row of three jail cells. She gave him another shove to keep him moving. "Phil, come on; we can't afford a nice hotel, all right?"

"You just don't get it."

"I saved the best room in the house for you, right on the end. There's a nice view of Sunset Avenue—"

That only made him more upset. "There's a window?"

"Well, it has bars on it, but you can still see out."

"Don't put me in there! I—"

"You what?"

The man was pale and shaking with fear, but could say nothing more.

Just like Charlie, she thought. Just like Maggie.

The front door to the station burst open. Somebody was coming their way in a big hurry. Tracy quickly got the cell door open and pushed Phil inside, locking the door behind him. One handful of trouble was enough.

She'd only taken one step toward the front when Sheriff Lester Collins, in his street clothes and red as a beet, came storming around the corner into the cell block.

"Sheriff!" Phil cried. "Sheriff, you gotta get me out of this!"

This was going to be tough. Collins was furious. "What in blue blazes is going on here?"

She started to answer, "I'm—"

"What are you doing with this man?"

"He's under arrest."

"Oh no, he isn't!"

"Oh yes, he is. Now if you'll excuse me—" She slipped around him, heading for the front office.

Collins was stomping right at her heels. "On what charges?"

"He's a suspect in the attack on Evelyn Benson."

Collins was still behind her, but she could just about hear him rolling his eyes. "Deputy, that is ridiculous!"

"She described her attacker as a wiry little round-headed coward with one ear sewed on. Now you know who that is, and I know who that is, and we both know what the law says and what our job is, so I'm throwing him in the can!"

They got to the front office. Tracy slammed the cell-block door shut and locked it.

"But you can't be sure!" Collins protested. "Deputy, you're talking about an attack that happened miles away! How do you know Phil was there and not out in the valley?"

She hurried around the counter and sat at a desk. "Sheriff, if I may say so, you're not being objective."

"What do you mean I'm not being objective?"

"You know what I mean. You're the sheriff around here. Given the same evidence and complaint you would have done the same— if you weren't so afraid of Harold Bly."

He couldn't answer. Instead, he slammed the counter and headed for the cell block. "I'm releasing him."

"No, you're not."

He got to the iron door. It was locked. He looked at the key rack behind the counter. "All right, where are the keys?"

She was jamming an arrest report form into a typewriter. "I have the keys on my person."

"Then hand them over, Deputy! That's an order!"

She started banging on the typewriter. "By law the prisoner can be held for seventy-two hours pending formal charges."

"Hand over those keys!"

She turned on him and used a tone of voice that more than matched his own. "You know the law, Sheriff Collins! Are you ordering me to violate my duty?"

He fell silent, fuming, hissing air through his nose, and drumming the counter. He was looking bad, and he knew it.

"The prisoner hasn't had a phone call yet. If you want to provide that for him . . ."

Collins went for that. "So let's have the keys."

Tracy grabbed the station's cordless phone and handed it over the counter. "He can use this. I'm not letting him out of there."

Collins took the phone grudgingly. "So how about the key to the door here?"

She peeled it off the key ring and handed it to him.

He snatched it out of her hand and rattled the lock open.

"UH-UH, NO, not here, not tonight!"

Sara, the little old lady who ran the White Tail RV Park, was running alongside Steve's camper, waving at him, shouting.

He stopped and rolled the window down. "What's the matter?"

She was puffing a bit and shaking her head. "No! You're not staying here tonight! We're full up!"

Steve could see his slot. There was a motor home on one side and a camper on the other, but his space was still empty. "Sara, I paid for that space tonight. Is there a problem?"

"No problem. We're full, that's all."

"But my space is empty. It's mine. I paid for it."

"It's full. Somebody else is going to take it."

He stopped. He knew what was happening here, and there'd be no fixing it.

Sara was pointing toward the highway, and her tone was emphatic. "I want you to get out of here, and right now!"

He sighed. No use fighting it. "What about my ten dollars for the space?"

She dug her wallet from her jeans hip pocket and poked a ten-dollar bill in his face. "There. Now leave!"

He took his money and left.

HAROLD BLY was relaxing in his home when the phone rang. He was expecting the call. "Hello?"

"Harold—Harold, this is Phil."

He took on the tone of a concerned father again. "Yes, Phil. How are you?"

"I'm scared, man, real scared. They've got me locked up in a cell. I can't get out of here!"

"Mm-hm."

"Well . . . aren't you going to do something?"

"Well, Phil—" Bly sounded surprised at such a question. "What do you expect me to do? You attacked someone, you almost killed them. You deserve to be in jail."

"But—but you said—"

"I don't remember telling you to kill anyone."

"Harold, you've gotta get me out of here! I might—I can't run anywhere, I can't—I can't hide! I can't get away."

Bly's voice was cool and even. "You blew it, Phil. Whatever you were trying to do, you botched it. Now you're in jail, and you'll just have to take whatever comes. I can't help you."

"But—"

"Good-bye, Phil."

Bly hung up with a satisfied smile. He would wait a few minutes, and then he would call Sheriff Collins. He'd have to sound angry, but that was never difficult for him.

COLLINS HAD just returned from the cell block, Phil's screams and cursings echoing behind him, when the cordless phone warbled in his hand.

"I'm sure it's for you," Tracy said, finishing up her arrest report.

Collins clicked the switch over to TALK and said, "Clark County Sheriff."

"Lester, it's Harold Bly."

Collins stole a quick look in Tracy's direction. She was watching and seemed to know who was on the other end. He ducked into his office and closed the door.

"What is it?" he asked, not too patiently.

"We've got a real problem developing," said Bly. "Have you talked to your deputy tonight?"

"Yes. She's here right now. She has Phil Garrett in custody."

"And what are you doing about it?"

"Looking into it."

Bly's tone was chilling but controlled. "Collins, don't even try to bluff me. I've got a whole town that's ready to string you and your deputy up, and if they don't get you, we know who will. I can't stop that now."

"Harold—"

"Excuses won't buy you time, Lester! If I were you I'd be thinking of ways to make everyone a little happier with your performance. I'd be working on that right now."

Collins was over a barrel. "But what can I do? She's within the law!"

"The law!" Bly only snickered at that argument. "We're not talking about the law, Lester. We're talking about control. You've lost it, and you need to get it back."

"I can't—"

"You will. If you value your life."

"What do you want me to do?"

"We'll talk more about this tonight. But here's what you do first . . ."

WHEN COLLINS emerged from his office, he looked very tired. "All right," he said. "We'll let everything stand for now."

"What did Bly say?"

"For your information, that was Bob Suski with the Oak Springs police," Collins said. "He was wondering if I had any updates on the Evelyn Benson case. I was happy to tell him we have the suspect in custody."

You're lying, Tracy thought, but she said, "Well, good enough. They can come get him in the morning, and we'll be finished with the whole thing, no sweat."

"Except for one thing."

"Yes?"

"I want a positive ID before we go any further with this. I want you to give Evelyn Benson a call and get her down here to positively identify him."

"Why? She can do that in Oak Springs when the cops take him there."

Collins was ready to admit, "Politics, okay? I've got some very angry people I'd like to make a little happier, and it would help if they knew I did my best to give Phil every chance. Now, can you do that for me?"

Well, she thought, at least he's offering me a compromise instead of firing me. "All right. I'll give Evelyn a call and see if she can come in tomorrow morning."

"Yeah, the sooner the better. I want this thing off our hands as soon as we can get rid of it."

"Oh, I agree." But, she thought, Phil owes me some answers first.

STEVE HEADED down the Hyde River Road away from the town of Hyde River, hoping that the growing hostility might diminish a bit with distance. At least it was worth a try to camp somewhere away from the trouble. When he found a wide turnoff with a few other campers parked there for the night, he pulled off and joined them.

He didn't take the time to level the camper; it was level enough. He just wanted to peruse Levi's materials, get out of his dirty clothes, and get some sleep.

He sat in the dinette, clicked on the battery-operated light, and opened up the binder to the pages Levi had selected.

Okay, Holly Ann Mayfield, who in the world were you, and what do you have to say?

> We are pioneers in a new land and ours is a new day, a new future.
> With gold and glory in our grasp, we will not turn back, for ours
> is a growing, living town.

With candor and a fascination for detail, Miss Mayfield had used words to paint strong, vivid images of an earlier time. As he deciphered the fading, fluid handwriting, he could imagine the scenes like an old, flickering movie in sepia tones. He could see the Hyde River of that day—Old Town when it was new, booming and growing on the banks of the river as hundreds of gold seekers arrived on flatbottomed steamers to work the mines or stake their own claims. He could imagine the overgrown and desolate streets of Old Town busy and bustling, all ice and snow in the winter, deep mud in the spring, and powdery dust in the hot summer.

He could see the mining crews, mustached, bearded, posing stern-faced and rigid for an old photograph, standing against a line of ore cars with shovels and picks in their burly hands. He could see the women too, always in short supply, wearing the finest dresses and enormous hats, all that gold could buy. He could hear the sound of hammers and saws over the constant rumbling of wagon wheels and foot traffic as new buildings went up—Carlson's Livery, the Gold Nugget Saloon, the Masonic Lodge, and the Ames Hotel—

He could imagine the wild nights in the saloons, the raucous parties thrown by the Hyde Mining Company in Hyde Hall, the constant flow of customers through the portals of Holly Ann Mayfield's establishment on Cottonwood Lane, a short walk down the riverfront, just one of many quaint residences.

I will have two more ladies joining us next week. They hail from San Francisco and are a proper sort, accustomed to fine company and the discerning tastes of the elite. So we are growing with the town, and I've wondered if our good fortune might never end.

Miss Mayfield did feel optimistic about her enterprise and recorded some examples of recent receipts. All was going well until . . Enter the villain.

I have always striven to be a person of good will and neighborliness, as have those with whom I associate, but I must admit that any good will remaining to me is quickly exhausted in the presence of that man. He is altogether harsh and condemning, and finds no greater joy than to consign all persons save himself to the fires of hell. My ladies are afraid of him, I find him disgusting, and I fear Ben's hatred of the man has reached murderous proportions.

To hear Holly Ann Mayfield tell it, the Rev. Charles DuBois, a black-garbed, wizened little preacher of unknown origins, had only one mission in life: to clean up and convert the town of Hyde River, whether it wanted to be converted or not.

His leaflets are everywhere, tacked to every post, every building, with or without permission, advertising the evils of Hyde River and the meetings he is conducting in Hyde Hall to turn souls away from their deadly course. Three of my ladies have attended recently, and I daresay their performance has dropped, as has the number of their clientele. The discord in the house is growing with the number of DuBois's converts.

From her descriptions of Reverend DuBois—a weasel, an encroaching, uninvited vermin who chews on people as a rat would chew cheese . . . the only trouble this town has ever had—it was easy to see that Holly Ann Mayfield had a very low opinion of the man. Given that, Steve couldn't be sure how sinister and disgusting DuBois was in reality, but the madam's accounts were entertaining nevertheless.

Thanks to DuBois's thundering orations, which I have no trouble hearing even from my own drawing room, there are those in town who are beginning to concern themselves with the hereafter and their eternal reward, and so they have become overly burdened with questions of morality. They not only speak against me and the conducting of my affairs, they also question the number of saloons in town and rail against the "moral climate" of Hyde River out of concern, they say, for their children.

Ben is the most distraught. With these new concerns about morality, some have questioned his control of their houses and lands and the rents he levies upon them. I can sympathize with their low wages, but I would still argue that they had a choice whether or not to come here and work for Hyde Mining. This is, after all, Ben's town. If they find that disagreeable, there are other places to go.

Steve chuckled. So things weren't all roses for Benjamin Hyde. Too bad. It seemed you just couldn't be a despot in a company town without somebody complaining about it.

At long last, Ben has closed Hyde Hall to any more of DuBois's meetings. I'm glad, but still disappointed. It seems the damage

done to my business and to the saloons and the gaming establish-
ments was not sufficient cause for such action. Only when a
sizable group began drafting a new town charter and calling for
an elected town council did Ben feel a pinch. Oh, well. At least a
firm stand has been taken and a statement made. What DuBois
will do now remains to be seen, although he seems to have gained
a substantial momentum behind his cause.

Then the story grew intriguing.

JULY 17, 1882

Ben cannot come to dinner tonight, but must preside over a special meeting he would tell me nothing about. He has been in a
deeply preoccupied mood lately, and so have the other businessmen, and I venture to guess they are meeting to discuss whatever
it is they have been so broody about. I can guess it has to do with
our present troubles, the bothersome shift of mood brought here
by DuBois.

JULY 18, 1882

Reverend DuBois did not surprise me, not in the slightest. Others were horrified and dismayed. Two of my ladies, once his converts, returned to me. I knew his devious side must come to light
sooner or later. What disturbs me so terribly is how it finally came
to light, and what followed.

Poor Karlyn! So it was she he'd taken a shine to! No wonder
she never told us about it. We've all tried to be understanding, but
of course I had to chide her for her surreptitious business arrangement while under my roof, and she has promised to recompense
me with my agreed percentage.

She had been the most holy reverend's consort for the better
part of a month, she says, and he paid her well. She does admit
being afraid of him, however, and relates how he was given to

unprovoked fits of rage and visions of demons. Last night, he flew into one such fit of rage, began to beat her, and, she says, would have killed her had she not escaped and fled to Ben for help.

The town went into an uproar. The Reverend was confined under guard in Hyde Hall while Ben and his associates decided what to do with him, but there were plenty who wanted the man hanged, including myself.

As for Karlyn, she is still in seclusion in Ben's home, not talking to anyone. It makes me wonder, now that the trouble is over, why she will not come back to this, her home. When DuBois abused her, why did she not come to me first, since we share the same roof, but instead ran to Ben? Karlyn did not seem seriously injured when I did see her, but she would answer none of my questions as to her condition.

So the Reverend got caught with his pants down, so to speak, which turned out to be just the occasion Benjamin Hyde and his cronies were looking for. All hell broke loose after that.

I could not go out for fear. Reverend DuBois was hanged in Hyde Hall with Ben and his friends in attendance and a mob in the street cheering. I had hoped it would have ended there, but from there it only spread like a fire. Men from the mining company began scouring the town for any of DuBois's sympathizers, anyone at all who attended his meetings, spoke well of him, became his converts, or raised moral objections to Ben's leadership. All night long, the town was overrun with madness. I have seen mobs running by my house, dragging my neighbors out of their homes, dashing their belongings out in the street. Three of Ben's assistants came to our door demanding the women who converted in one of the meetings, but since Ben had no quarrel with me I was able to speak on my ladies' behalf and they were spared.

Early this morning, Suzanne brought further word from Hyde Hall: DuBois was given no trial. With no witnesses called and no opportunity to defend himself, he was quickly and summarily put to death. I should not be bothered by that, since I so despised the man, and yet, and I write this knowing Ben will never read it, I am beginning to have questions about Karlyn's account, DuBois's guilt, and Ben's response.

In the past, we have winked at Karlyn's penchant for elaborate tales and excuses, but now, having seen people die around me, I am haunted, no, terrified, by the possibility that her tale of DuBois's violence against her could be just that: a tale. I have questioned the other ladies thoroughly, and not one of them has ever seen DuBois anywhere near this house or near Karlyn, for that matter. Indeed, her sudden account of DuBois abusing her came as a shock to all of us.

As for Ben, there is no question in my mind that today's violence and carnage will, in the end, be all to his advantage. After what has happened today, who will dare to question his power?

I think I've heard this story before, Steve thought.

For the next several pages, Mayfield chronicled the events of that night and the following day in a hurried, cursory account.

The Abner Smyths were driven from their home. Abner fought against the mob and was shot. I don't know what happened to his wife and children.

Cecil Ames, owner of the Ames Hotel, was untouched, but Timothy Stanley, the desk clerk, was dragged into the street and shot.

The Norwegian family three doors down had no connection with DuBois that I know of, but were deeply religious to begin with. John Sanders and his brothers wanted to torch the house, but Ben was able to prevent it, fearing the fire would spread. The family left on today's steamer.

The Larsons, newlyweds, were converted at one of DuBois's meetings. They were shot.

Hiram Walters, one of the drafters of the failed town charter, was shot along with his wife and two sons.

Amos Tyler, friend of Walters, was shot.

Jeremiah Carson, editor of the Hyde River Post, was shot. He was sympathetic to the shifting moral climate and ready to sign the Walters charter.

Joseph Gustafson, a miner, was shot
Matthew Farwell, a miner, was shot.
William DeWalt, a miner, was shot.
Clarence Miles, a miner, was shot, and so was his wife Clarice Their two children were sent away on the steamer.

A fire broke out in the livery. The livery burned down, but the fire didn't spread.

Someone pushed Kenneth Chatney's wagon into the river. It floated downstream and then overturned on the rocks. Then Kenneth Chatney was shot. He owned the mercantile. The property will revert to the Hyde Mining Company.

Horace Davis, chief assayer for the company, shot and killed three men who had come to kill him before he himself was shot.

And so it went, for page after page. Then came something familiar, something that brought back the memory of that special table in the home of Harold Bly.

Having done away with the trouble, Ben produced a new town charter and invited me to be one of the signatories in Hyde Hall. I thought it strange that he could prepare a fresh document so quickly on the tail of such an upheaval—to be honest, I have no doubt that the charter was prepared before the great purging—but I agreed to attend and to sign. It would be the first time I dared to venture from my home.

The names of the signatories are on the document. With the signing, a new future was to unfold, a clearer vision for the town of Hyde River. The past, especially this day and the preceding night, are to be forever buried and forgotten.

But I will never forget.

Twenty-seven people died that I know of, and I can only guess the others fled with whatever they could carry away. I could hear the screams and the shooting all night long, and I dared not venture out.

The Reverend DuBois was left hanging in Hyde Hall until this afternoon. I informed Ben and the others that I would not attend the signing of the charter until the body was removed, so Ben ordered it cut down, taken out, and buried with the others.

By late afternoon, the people who remained in Hyde River were back in the mines as if nothing had happened, and I also attended to my business. After nightfall, we gathered in Hyde Hall under cover of darkness and signed the charter. With the signing of our names we took an oath of silence, so I cannot speak of these things but only write them secretly.

The trouble is over, but I am no happier. I am afraid of what we have done. I am afraid of tomorrow.

The eyes were like pure gold, and as it returned my gaze I could sense a remarkable intelligence but also a hatred so intense I feared for my life. I guessed it to be the size of a large horse, though it slunk like a lizard, and it was only visible for a moment before vanishing into the forest on the other side of the river. Totally beside myself, I ran back into town and immediately met Harrison Bly coming the other way. I tried to tell him what I had seen, but he only laughed in my face, delighted to see me in such a state.

"So how do you like our little pet?" he asked, and acted as if he knew all about it.

"You were right, Clarice, and your warnings well-founded after all. Harrison Bly, having married into the Hyde family, has followed them in contracting with the devil himself."

From a confidential letter written by Mrs. Sarah Alice Thompson, a resident of Hyde River, to Mrs. Clarice Stevens, half-sister of Abby Bly, Harold Bly's mother

SIXTEEN

The Mark

Tᴿᴬᶜʏ ᵂᴬˢ ᴴᴼᴾᴵᴺᴳ Phil's fear would encourage him to open up, but it seemed the opposite was true. She stood outside his cell, trying to be casual and conversational, even telling a few little jokes to loosen things up. But all he did was sit on his little bunk, staring at the concrete floor and wringing his hands.

"Phil, come on. If somebody put you up to this, they're going to walk if you don't say anything."

He said not a word.

"I don't think you'd assault a total stranger for no reason. Come on, Phil, what's going on here?"

Nothing.

She leaned against the wall, arms crossed, trying to come up with something else to get him talking. "Of course, you don't have to say anything, I know. But you could make things easier on your-self. Have you thought of that? You could turn state's witness, cut a bargain. I don't think you're all alone in this thing. Am I right?"

He trembled a little but did not respond.

"What about Harold Bly? Did he put you up to this?"

"No!" he said emphatically.

Well. A response. "Phil—what are you afraid of?"

"I'm not afraid."

"Well you could've fooled me. Just look at yourself. You're shaking, you're nervous—"

"I'm not afraid!" he insisted.

"What about the Oath, Phil? You know, the old Hyde River Oath? Is that why you can't say anything?"

He seemed almost apologetic. "I can't tell you anything, Tracy. I just can't."

She went close to the bars and sank down so she was at his eye level. "Phil, I talked to Charlie not long before he had that car crash. He was scared too, just like you are. And you know what else? I talked to Maggie just before she disappeared, and she was acting just like you are, really scared. And I kept wondering just what they were so afraid of. Phil, what are you afraid of?"

"I'm not afraid."

It was time to bring up the forbidden subject. "Did I tell you about my hunting trip the other day? Professor Benson and I tracked something all night long, something huge."

For the first time, he looked at her, his eyes widening with a new horror.

"We never saw it clearly, but apparently, it could fly. It dropped right out of the sky and just about killed both of us. We shot at it, but it got away." Then she added, "Oh. Did I tell you we were in Hyde Hall at the time?"

His eyes got wider, and his whole body started to quiver.

"Yeah. We started by staking out Hyde Hall because that was where Maggie and Vic both disappeared. Well, we just about found out what happened to them, but like I said, it got away."

He began shaking his head back and forth, his eyes wide, his voice weak and trembling. "Oh, you shouldn't have done that. You . . . oh, why did you—"

"Is that what you're afraid of, Phil? Is there really something out there that might—come and get you?" He reacted as if the question had stabbed him like a knife. She tried another one. "Is that why you tried to kill Evelyn Benson, because she saw it, because she knows what it is?"

"No . . ."

"Why are you protecting it, Phil? Why are you protecting something that kills people?"

"No!" he screamed. "I'm not saying anything! I'm not gonna talk about anything!"

Like Charlie, she thought.

She rose and looked down at the pitiful wreck of a man. He was bent over, his head almost between his knees, rocking gently, muttering in fear, "I didn't talk . . . I didn't do anything . . . I'm not saying anything . . ."

Well. At least he was in a jail cell. This would be the first victim who couldn't wander or drive off.

"Try to get some sleep," she said finally. "I'll see you again in the morning."

She clicked off the hall light and left him there.

FLIPPING THROUGH the pages of the binder, Steve came to a photocopy of a finely lettered document with a large, bold title:

OFFICIAL CHARTER OF THE CITY OF HYDE RIVER

Not a bad piece of work for something so hastily thrown together, he thought. Holly Ann Mayfield could have been right: Benjamin Hyde already had this thing drawn up before the massacre, meaning he could have planned the massacre all along, including the trumped-up charge against Charles DuBois that triggered it.

One giveaway was the date, July 19, 1882, which had all the appearance of being filled in after the fact. Steve had to chuckle at the recollection of how proud Harold Bly was of his great, great granddaddy.

"Whereas," the document began, like so many documents did. Okay, we'll read what these killers have to say for themselves.

Whereas the undersigned, having founded and established the city of Hyde River through their own resources, wisdom, and resolve, and. . . .

Whereas, no appeal has been made to, nor any strength or assistance received from, the so-called Almighty or any deity of any kind, and. . . .

Whereas, the undersigned, confident of their own capacity for good, do wish to pursue happiness, peace, and contentment by whatever avenue they may choose. . . .

We the undersigned do declare and affirm that. .

We are the masters and makers of our own destiny.

There is no God but Reason.

Only by Reason can Truth be established.

Only by living according to the Truth we have Established, shall we secure for ourselves and our posterity enduring Wealth and Happiness, our supreme goal.

These precepts shall be the Creed and Guiding Light of the City of Hyde River, for ourselves and for our posterity.

If This Be Sin, Let Sin Be Served.

It seemed a rather flimsy set of precepts on which to found a town, Steve thought, more of a reaction against the influence of the Reverend DuBois than a workable charter. But such a vague document gave Benjamin Hyde all the room he needed to run things his way, so in that sense, it must have satisfied the signatories.

Steve looked over the signatures and counted thirty-two. Holly Ann Mayfield's signature was near the bottom, written in the same fluid hand as her diary.

Benjamin Hyde had signed his name in large, bold letters as if mimicking John Hancock, and then reiterated just above his name; "If this be Sin, let Sin be served."

So take that, DuBois!

Now Steve turned the page. There were still many docu ments—old letters, news clippings, diary entries—to go through Steve had been cynical when he started reading, but now he was downright intrigued. He started skimming, then he went back to double-check what he'd read, then he began to read every docu ment with steadily growing interest. What in the world—?

The knock on the camper door jolted him back from the 1880s to the present so quickly he felt he'd dropped his heart somewhere along the way.

"Steve?" It was Tracy!

He didn't need her finding out he'd been talking to Levi. He scrambled to hide the binder, throwing it into a cupboard before he opened the door.

At the sight of her face, a smile came easily. "Well, hello, stranger."

"Hello," she said, smiling up at him. "I was on my way home and I thought I recognized this camper. What happened to the RV Park?"

"I got kicked out."

She immediately understood everything that meant. "So it's all hitting the fan."

He offered his hand. "Please, come in." With a strong but gentle tug, he helped her inside. She sat down at the table.

"I arrested Phil Garrett," she announced. "I'm sure that's one reason for the trouble."

"Yeah, I'll bet it is," he agreed. "Did he say anything?"

"Not a thing. He's under the same Oath. I tried to talk to him for about an hour, but all he did was blubber and sweat and stink the same way Charlie and Maggie did. He was scared silly."

Steve was immediately concerned. "But you do have him locked up?"

"Oh, yeah. He can't wander off."

"Okay." Steve shifted gears so he could share the biggest news of the day. "Listen. I saw the dragon."

She froze. "You—What do you mean, you saw it?"

"I went after it, up on Saddlehorse, and—"

She held up her hand. "Wait." He stopped. "Why don't we get out of here? I've had a rough day, and I want to get out of this uniform. And you look like you need a shower."

He looked apologetically at his dirt-covered pants.

Her eyes sparkled. "You've never been to my place, have you?"

"What about my camper?"

"Bring it with you! Just follow me!"

"Well . . ."

"Going once," she teased, "going twice—"

"Sold," he blurted. "Sold!"

IT WAS not at the night's darkest hour, not midway between dusk and dawn. The shadows were not their deepest, the setting was not at its macabre, gloomy best.

But Harold Bly was desperate as he knelt before the stone that had become an altar, muttering to his god, trying to find an explanation other than the one that kept recurring in his mind despite his best efforts to ignore it: I'm not controlling it. I didn't call for some people to die and they're dead; I called for others to die and they're still alive. The dragon's doing what it pleases, marking and killing whoever it wants, including me. It's not doing my will at all.

No, no, he argued back, that couldn't be it. Things are just getting out of hand, that's all. I haven't acted quickly and decisively enough. But no problem. I'll just get it straightened out. The dragon's upset, and I can't blame him, but he's still my dragon. The dragon and my family, we go way back, and now I'm the very last of the Hydes, the only soulmate that creature will ever have.

"So hey," he said to the stone, the ruins, the withered trees, "I'm taking care of it. I've already started squaring it all up. You're going to like it."

He felt alone in this place. He could remember being here with his father and grandfather, his mother and family, all one powerful group. Maybe, as a group, they had had more power than he had now, kneeling here by himself.

Then again, he no longer shared the power with anyone; it was all his. That thought reassured him and even made him smile.

His was the one and only will, the only voice. He could strike a bargain, cut a deal. The dragon would know a good offer when he saw it. He'd buy, Harold was sure of it.

Bly felt better as he considered the cleverness of his plan and the sly steps he'd already taken. I'm Harold Bly. I can fix it. I can fix anything.

STEVE SANK into the soft couch with a deep sigh of relief. It was one of those sensations he'd gone a long time without. He hadn't realized how much he missed the sheer warmth of being in a real home instead of a motel or a camper.

Tracy was renting a quaint, one-bedroom cottage on ten acres about two miles up the Nelson Creek drainage, a quiet valley east of the river. The cottage was nothing fancy, but Tracy had lived there long enough to instill it with her own personality. All around the house and along the stone walkways, she'd brought the old flowerbeds back to life, and now the roses, petunias, and marigolds were flourishing. Inside, she'd tastefully surrounded herself with the things that brought her joy: dried flowers, pottery, handwoven tablecloths and pillows, sculptures and woodcarvings of eagles, Indians, and wolves.

Steve, fresh and clean from a shower, was dressed in the last set of clean clothes he had, a pair of dress slacks—he had brought them in case he had to attend a meeting—and a University of Colorado T-shirt. The rest of his wardrobe, down to the last dirty sock, was presently in the washing machine churning away in the enclosed back porch. He could feel the machine's progress reports rumbling through the floor.

He could also hear the shower running in the corner of the house adjacent to the bedroom. Tracy was taking her turn. He hoped he hadn't used all the hot water.

He smiled. He could imagine her in that shower right now; he knew what she looked like.

He ran his fingers over the burns on his arms. Not too bad. Kind of like a bad sunburn in places. He'd come through the encounter very well, considering how it could have turned out.

He leaned his head back on the couch and thought about the diary. A fascinating story. No, more than that. Devastating. Disturbing. No wonder it had lain buried for so long. No wonder the town had become so self-contained, so secretive. Fear of discovery had become a heritage, passed from generation to generation. One could even call it an inherited sense of guilt. Reverend Woods had said something about that.

In terms of guilt—forget about guilt.

Tracy had just come into the room, looking fresh, clean, and very cute in leggings and an oversized pullover. She paused to look him over, and perhaps to let him look her over.

"My, don't you look comfortable!" she said.

"I'm very comfortable," he replied, sitting up a little, "thanks to your hospitality."

"How do I look?" she asked.

He grinned. "Like a woman instead of a law enforcement officer."

She settled gracefully into a love seat to his right, looking relaxed and at ease. "Hmm. Do I detect a note of sexism?"

"Sex has everything to do with it."

She was in a teasing mood. "Go ahead, Professor. Explain."

In fun, he caricatured himself and waxed professorial. "When you are Clark County Deputy Tracy Ellis, in uniform, the whole question of sex—that is, gender—is a nonquestion: it's disallowed. Given that, any observations regarding your appearance would have to be confined to such adjectives as 'well-groomed,' 'neat and clean'—you know the drill. But I don't think you'd hear such observations as 'pretty,' or 'good-looking,' and you would most certainly never hear such adjectives as 'sexy,' or 'alluring,' seeing as such comments might be deemed inappropriate in the workplace. Anyway, all that is to say, I think it's safe and appropriate in our present context to acknowledge your gender and tell you—" He became himself. "You look beautiful."

She smiled. "Well thank you, Professor. I'm flattered."

They looked at each other for so long it became awkward. Finally she broke the silence. "Would you like a glass of wine?"

"Oh. Yes, please."

She was already up from the love seat and heading for the kitchen. The living room and kitchen were actually the same room, divided by a counter, apartment-style. As Tracy went to the cupboard for glasses, Steve was able to keep her constantly in sight.

It was remarkable how long ago, how remote, his encounter with the dragon now seemed. Right now, all he really wanted to think about was Tracy. But he had come here to tell her what had happened that day. "I, uh, I went up Saddlehorse and had a chance to talk to Jules Cryor."

She was about to pour the wine when she stopped, the bottle in mid-tip. "Of course, that shouldn't matter—"

That muddled his train of thought. "Huh?"

"Whether or not I . . . well, you know, how I look."

"Oh." So they were still on that subject. Well, that was okay with him. "In regards to your—your person, your professional skills, everything that makes up your potential as a human being . . . no, I suppose it doesn't really matter."

"But it's fun to think about—I guess." She couldn't think of any more words, so she filled one glass.

"I like to think about it. You make it easy to think about—if you don't mind my saying so."

She caught the subtle compliment and smiled. "I don't mind."

He hid behind the professor role again. "But could I venture the proposition that being a woman is a part of everything you are?"

"Well, of course."

"And perhaps, just maybe, for practical, workaday reasons, that part of you has been pushed aside, usurped by your career?"

She stopped to mull that over, then answered his question with one of her own. "So how about you?"

"What about me?"

She filled the second glass, then walked toward him. "You're a professor of biology, a strict professional, a man with a scientific explanation for everything—and a man without a meaningful relationship. How much room does that give you to be a total person?" She handed him his glass, then sank into the soft couch next to him.

"I believe I'm a total person."

"A person who cares about love?"

Now that was a big question to throw at him. "Whoa!"

"Is there such a thing?"

He got defensive. "What kind of a question is that?"

"Remember that night in Hyde Hall? You were trying to tell me love was nothing but chemical reactions in the brain or something like that."

"Well, that's true."

"And I think I said 'baloney.'"

"I do recall that."

"So? How can you be a total person while denying the existence of one of life's most important ingredients? I mean, love is what being a total person is all about, in my book."

"I'm not denying the existence of love. I'm just trying to be realistic."

"I think you're hiding."

"Hiding?" He laughed at that.

"You're hiding from who you are. You're a wildlife biologist, sure, a Ph.D. But you're also a man, a human being, and I think you're hiding from that."

He took a sip of wine. It was easier than replying.

"Remember the lake?" she asked.

He remembered it, but he played dumb. "Huh?"

"You were watching me."

Steve managed to look her in the eye. "I—I don't think you were on duty."

She placed her hand on his shoulder. Then her fingers touched the back of his neck. "And I don't think you were being scientific."

As he looked into her eyes, as he saw her perfect skin in the warm glow of the lamplight, he began to concede that some forces of nature were beyond empirical study and explanation. He cleared his throat. "I—uh—I don't suppose you want to hear about my encounter with the dragon?"

Her eyes sparkled playfully. "What dragon?"

He set his wine glass on the coffee table. "I guess it can wait."

It waited. As a matter of fact, the subject never crossed their minds the rest of the night.

WHEN TRACY opened her eyes, the bedroom was already waking up with sunlight. The alarm clock would ring in another five minutes; she reached over and clicked it off. Then she lay quietly, her head on her pillow, looking at the man sharing her bed. He was still asleep, and he was magnificent, like a Greek god in repose, powerful yet serene, his arms like finely sculptured bronze, his face darkening with manly stubble.

And he didn't even snore! Was the world suddenly perfect or what? she asked herself.

"You're mine now," she whispered softly, longing to touch him. "I have you, and I'll never let you go."

Quietly so as not to wake him, she slipped out from between the sheets and stole into the kitchen to get the coffeemaker—and her day—started. Then she showered, selected a freshly pressed uniform, and became a cop again, her mind shifting into police mode, laying out the day's agenda over a cup of coffee and an English muffin. Evelyn Benson was due at the station at nine to ID her attacker, thus completing that little political favor for Sheriff Collins. After that . . .

Hmm. After that, she could call the Oak Springs police and have them take custody of the suspect. Take over. Handle the whole case. She could get out of it.

It occurred to her that only yesterday, the case was important to her and she had felt reluctant to bow out. This morning, well, things were different. Now she could envision herself turning in her uniform and moving far away from Hyde River, from Doug, from everything. She could envision herself having a good life in Colorado.

An hour later, as she drove her Ranger toward West Fork, she checked her appearance in the rearview mirror, making sure her collar was straight, her hair in place. She looked sharp, and that was always important to her. But having checked her professional appearance, she lingered.

Was she really beautiful? She thought she'd like her auburn hair a little longer so she could do more with it, but then again, the shorter length was easier to take care of. She was glad she looked younger than thirty—but maybe she looked too young, perhaps immature. She could try a little more makeup, perhaps.

Brother. Enough of this! She turned her attention back to her driving, smiling at herself and her thoughts. Yes, things were different this morning.

STEVE AWOKE, read a cute little note from Tracy on her pillow—she'd gone to work, would call later, hoped he had a nice day—another note on the coffeemaker, telling him to help himself to muffins and cereal, and a third note on the bathroom mirror in which she informed him what she would be doing that day: meeting Evelyn at the station and having her ID Phil Garrett so the Oak Springs police could take over. She closed this last note by saying she'd be thinking of him today and signed it "Love, Tracy."

Steve removed the note from the mirror so he could see to shave and opened up the shave kit he'd brought in from his camper.

Well. Evelyn's coming to West Fork. All right. That should get the case cleared up neatly enough.

Love, Tracy. Love? What were they starting here? What he was feeling this morning wasn't what love was supposed to feel like. He couldn't stop thinking about Doug—yeah, Steve, remember Doug? Her husband? To whom she's married?—and what that big guy would have thought or done had he found them in bed together. Not that it mattered from a moral point of view. Tracy was separated from Doug, and this was something both he and Tracy had decided together to do. Besides, where was Doug's halo? But Steve still had some practical concerns, such as getting through the day—or the next several days, for that matter—with his life and body intact.

He lathered his face and started shaving.

I hope this doesn't turn out to be some big deal, he thought. I mean, it was just one night. Tracy wanted it, I wanted it, and we both needed it, we've been through so much together. Now she's gone to work like she always does and here I am, a wildlife biologist and college professor like I've always been, and she'll go on being a deputy and I'll be teaching again fall quarter, so nothing's really different. We can both walk away like it never happened.

He rinsed his razor under the hot tap water and continued.

Like it never happened? Why would I want to pretend that? Was there something wrong with what happened last night? Man oh man! Here we go with that guilt question again! Aw, give it a rest!

He finished shaving and rinsed his razor under the tap again.

Then he stopped. Now what had he done to himself? The burns on his arms were still there, and the bruises, well, they came with the territory. But what was this discoloration over his heart? It looked kind of like varicose veins, squiggly and branchlike. Hmm. Had to be from his encounter with the dragon. He'd bashed and bruised himself so many times in that incident he'd lost track. This could be a broken blood vessel from all the exertion.

It was no big deal. A guy in his line of work wouldn't get much done if he worried about every little mark he got. It kind of hurt, though.

He put away his razor and shaving cream. He had to get going. Tracy was meeting Evelyn, Evelyn was going to ID Phil Garrett, the whole case was going to be handed off to the Oak Springs police, and then . . .

Legally speaking, the case against Phil Garrett seemed tight enough, so he would most likely do some time. But unless some hard evidence materialized, it was doubtful anyone else would be charged with anything. As far as Steve knew, the dragon really was responsible for all the deaths that had been blamed on it.

It was the political/cultural climate that now presented the biggest problem, aggravated, of course, by the arrest of Phil Garrett. Steve had confirmed that Hyde Valley and its surrounding environs were inhabited by a large, reptilian creature, most likely a carry-over from prehistoric times. But what complicated any further research—indeed, what had already cost human lives and was sure to cost more—was the local culture, the belief system, that had grown up around this creature. Steve would have to deal directly with that belief system. The people of Hyde River had to realize that the creature could not be hidden any longer but would have to be studied. They also had to realize that the beast could not be allowed to kill again.

Steve's course of action was bold and simple: He'd go right to the top, to Harold Bly, and just tell him that the secret was out, the whole scientific world would soon be waiting at Hyde River's doorstep, and the people of Hyde River needed to adjust their thinking. Simple enough. Good grief. If Harold Bly was smart, he'd start figuring out ways to capitalize on it.

He finished dressing and gathered up the gear he'd brought in from the camper: his backpack, his shaving kit, and of course, all the laundry Tracy had washed last night. Tracy might expect him to stay another night, another week, however long she could keep him, but he couldn't let that get started, especially if he wanted to make peace with the town.

Ouch! His hand went to his chest. What had he done to him-self? This broken blood vessel, or whatever it was, was burning. He dug through his first-aid kit and found some ointment for insect bites. It might work. He opened his shirt and smeared some on. The pain didn't subside, but perhaps it would, given time.

But now he had to make that phone call. He found the number of the Hyde Mining Company in the local phone book and dialed it.

The old mining company had shrunk a bit. Steve recognized Harold Bly's voice as Bly answered the phone himself. "Hyde Mining."

"Mr. Bly?"

"Yeah, who's this?"

Bly was sounding a bit gruff this morning. Steve did not ex-pect a kind response when he answered, "Mr. Bly, this is Steve Benson."

Suddenly Bly's tone changed, as if he were hearing from an old friend. "Ohhh, Dr. Benson! How are you?"

"Fine, sir, and how are you?"

"Oh, getting by, I guess. What can I do for you?"

"Well . . ." He had to think a moment. How should he phrase this? "If you're agreeable, I'd like to meet with you and talk about a few matters." Boy, that was vague enough.

Bly sounded agreeable as he said, "I think that could be arranged."

"Would you be free this morning?"

"Sure. How about meeting me at the tavern for a beer, say, ten o'clock or so?"

"That'll be fine. I'll see you there, ten o'clock at the tavern."

Steve hung up feeling relieved. Maybe this wouldn't be as dif-ficult as he first thought.

WELL, thought Harold Bly. How handy could things get?

He started punching numbers on his phone. He had to gather his people and get things set up. By tonight the trouble would be all over.

TIME TO get moving, Steve thought. He slung his pack over his shoulder, picked up his laundry bag of clean clothes, made sure the coffeemaker was off as he passed by the kitchen, then went out to his camper.

As he headed down the gulch toward the Hyde River Road, his imagination was working overtime. Perhaps the weird superstitions of Hyde River would be displaced by more practical considerations, like money. Hyde River could become a real center for scientific investigation as well as tourism. Visitors would need rooms, meals, guides, rides. The mercantile could stock cheap binoculars and little stuffed dragons, and the tavern could serve dragon burgers. Yeah, flame-broiled! He started to laugh. He was getting carried away.

Nevertheless, Harold Bly just might go for ideas like that. Why not?

As for the binder containing the diary of Holly Ann Mayfield, Steve wanted to stop first at Levi's to give it back to him, hopefully before anyone found out he'd been consulting with the big mechanic. It was going to be tough enough getting back into Harold Bly's good graces without the bad blood between Bly and Cobb coming into it.

Even so, the whole story of the massacre and the legends that sprang from it were another thing that could benefit the town if handled in the right way. That kind of stuff always sold well. The legend of Hyde River. The Hyde River dragon. He could see it now. Too bad old Levi took everything so seriously.

TRACY ARRIVED at the station in West Fork a few minutes before eight, parking her Ranger in its usual slot alongside the old stone building. Sheriff Collins's patrol car was already in its slot. Since it was for his exclusive use, he drove it to and from work each day. He was the boss, so he was always early, if only to chew out anybody who came in late.

The side door, her usual entry, was unlocked. Inside, she found the station quiet, with no one in sight, not even a deputy on duty behind the counter. She checked the clock on the wall. Still a minute or two before eight. Either the deputy had stepped away from the counter, was working in the Motor Vehicles section, or was going to catch a good share of flak for being late.

She went directly to the station logbook at the end of the counter near the key rack and quickly signed herself in, noting that she and Sheriff Collins were the only ones there so far.

Deputy Matson was supposed to be manning the office today, but Tracy noted that Collins had signed him off for a leave of absence. All the more work for me, she complained to herself. Anyway, she was here, and on time. Just for good measure, she went to the sheriff's door and tapped on it. "Morning, Sheriff."

"Good morning," came his voice from inside.

She poked her head in. "How's the prisoner?"

He looked up from his desk only momentarily. "He's your prisoner. I'll leave that to you."

He was still miffed at her. "Yes sir."

She returned his door to its former, slightly ajar position and went to the cell-block door, still locked from the previous night. The key, however, was back on the key rack where she'd left it, apparently unused since last night's confrontation. She unlocked the big steel door and swung it open.

An all-too-familiar stench met her like a wall, and she recoiled. The smell of rotting flesh. The air was thick and heavy with it, worse than ever. She turned her head away in horror, in disgust. She drew a breath and steadied herself.

Trouble had found its way in here, Tracy thought. She could sense it in the place, like a loathsome creature concealing itself in some dark corner. She couldn't see Phil's cell from where she stood. "Phil?" she called, not too loudly.

There was no answer.

Half from procedure, half from instinct, she closed the cell-block door behind her and locked it, then pocketed the key. Now the problem would be contained, whatever it was, though she found no comfort in the fact that she was locked in with it.

"Phil?" she called again, moving forward toward the corner of the passage.

No answer. She reached for her nightstick, then chose her revolver instead, resting her hand on it, ready. She peeked around the corner, down the narrow, dismal cell block with the three cells. The door to Phil's cell was still closed. Nothing looked out of place.

She pulled the revolver anyway, aiming it at the ceiling, mindful of the concrete floor and walls.

"Phil!" she called firmly. "Hey, answer me!"

No answer.

She inched down the cell block until Phil's cell came into view. Shock and nausea hit her like a punch in the stomach.

Phil's scarred face, gray with death, the mouth limp and drooling, stared vacantly down at her through half-open, unblinking eyes. His body was suspended from the grille in the ceiling by a slime-blackened shirt knotted around his neck. His feet dangled limply above the floor.

Tracy fell back against the wall, her left hand covering her mouth, her knees weak, her gun sinking slowly downward until the handgrip came to rest against the concrete. She was trembling, and it was only by a shred of conscious thought that she kept the gun in her hand.

Drip. Drip. Drip.

Like a slow, steady leak, black, viscid ooze trickled from an open sore over Phil's heart, slid down his bare chest, crawled in a snaking rivulet down his pant leg, and then hung from the sole of his shoe like dog's drool until it stretched to breaking and plopped to a puddle on the floor.

She would vomit if she didn't get out of there. She turned away and forced one foot in front of the other, her feet like lead.

Maggie. Vic. It was coming together in her mind as her throat constricted with the sourness of the air. Charlie, and now Phil. Her insides wrenched in such pain that she nearly doubled over. The dragon. The dragon!

She broke into a run, her breakfast pushing its way up her throat. She got to the cell door and only then remembered it was locked. Somehow she found the key and got it open, bursting through the door like a drowning woman finally breaking the surface.

"Sheriff!" she cried. "Sheriff!"

No answer.

She drew some deep breaths of fresh air and her breakfast settled. "Sheriff Collins!"

She dashed to his office door, still ajar, and knocked even as she pushed it open. "Sheriff!"

He wasn't there. The chair behind the desk was empty. He wasn't at the window. He wasn't—

She saw the blow coming from the corner of her eye and ducked. The black baton struck her left shoulder, sending her reeling. She fell against the desk then tumbled sideways to the floor, losing her revolver in the process. Her shoulder and arm were numb with pain.

Sheriff Collins, nightstick in hand, stood by the door he'd hidden behind, his face contorted with malice—or was it horror.

"Lester, what—"

He changed instantly. "Tracy! My god!" He put the nightstick on his desk. "I didn't know it was you." He started toward her.

Instinctively, she scrambled away from him. She spotted her revolver on the floor by the corner of the desk, but she couldn't reach it.

He grabbed her right hand and pulled her up—forcefully. "Here, let me help. Are you hurt?"

She didn't have time to answer before he flung her face first against the wall, her arm behind her back. She could hear him going for his handcuffs.

The world had exploded into meaningless pieces. Nothing made sense. She struggled, but he pressed her against the wall, her face flat against the plaster.

The first cuff went on her right wrist. "No!" she shouted.

Collins groped for her left hand. She wriggled around and jammed the fingers of her left hand into his eye. She could feel his eyeball like a large grape rolling under her fingers. He jerked away, dropping her right hand, yelling in pain, and she planted her foot in his stomach. With her back against the wall, she kicked with all her strength, flinging him backward into his desk. Then she dove for her gun.

"Hold it, Tracy!" Collins hollered as she heard his gun slip from its holster.

She curled around, revolver in hand, to see Collins aiming right for her face.

A gunshot, like two huge, invisible hands, clapped her ears.

Time froze. Her arm was extended, the revolver aimed, the handcuff dangling. There was blue smoke in the air.

Collins was standing there, still aiming his gun at her. He didn't seem to know yet what had happened; neither of them did.

Then, looking back at her in horror and disbelief, Collins fell backward against the open door of the office. It swung aside and bumped against the doorstop. Collins came to rest against the doorjamb and then crumpled to the floor, his gun still in his hand. Tracy made no other move than to keep her gun trained on him, following him every inch of his slide downward.

He tried to speak, but no words would form. His face went blank. His head sank to his chest.

Then he died.

Only then did she notice she was still aiming her gun at him, and let her arm come down.

He was gone. She had killed him. She couldn't comprehend it.

LEVI COBB blocked the door and extended his hand. "Mr. Benson, wait, don't go."

Steve stopped. "Hey. Levi. Come on, I appreciate your input. The diary was very interesting, it was good information to keep in mind, and really, I'll do that. I'll remember what you showed me."

"But did you read it?"

"Of course I read it, every page."

"What about the other stuff? The letters and clippings and—"

"Levi, I went through them, I got the general idea."

They were standing in Levi's garage, near the ladder truck Levi had been working on. The binder containing the diary and other materials lay on the workbench among the tools where Steve had set it down with a quick and courteous thank you.

"We still have to talk about it. You don't have the whole picture."

Steve tried to be patient. "Levi, it's a fascinating story, a shocking story. I can see why the people around here are so sensitive about the past. But listen, I'm not—" Oh, where were the words? "—of your religious persuasion, okay? I don't believe the way you do."

Levi shook his head. He was insistent. "That don't change a thing. The dragon don't care what you believe."

Steve gave a deep sigh of frustration. "Levi, what you believe about the dragon doesn't change anything either. I agree, the dragon is what it is. It's there, it's real, it has to be understood. That's why I'm here—to study it, not in religious or superstitious terms, but in real, scientific terms. You and the other people in this town have to see that."

Levi stood his ground. "Okay, you're a scientist, right?"

"Of course. I'm a wildlife biologist."

"So you've got an open mind, right?"

"I try to be objective and unbiased."

"Then hear me out. Don't tag me a fanatic and then run off and get yourself killed."

"I've survived thus far."

Levi took a moment to digest that comment. Then, with a slight nod, he answered, "We've all done that, Benson." His eyes were probing, and Steve could sense it. "Last night you weren't thinking about 'studying' the dragon in scientific terms. You were glad you were still alive, and you wanted to know the truth. Now you just want to get out of here." He cocked his head to one side, studying Steve so intently it made him nervous. "What have you been up to lately?" He poked Steve's chest, a simple gesture. "You seem a little different."

Steve flinched. Levi had touched that sore spot.

And Levi noticed. "You better have a seat."

TRACY ROSE from the floor, her revolver still in her hand, and drew close enough to put her trembling fingers against the side of Collins's neck. There was no pulse. A stain had soaked through his shirt, and there was a streak of blood on the doorjamb behind him.

She unbuttoned his shirt. She'd obviously shot him in the chest, but she couldn't, didn't, want to believe it. She was in a stupor. She'd always shot at targets and cans; she'd never shot at a human being. Now she'd killed one, and a law officer at that.

She touched the entry wound, a puncture just to the left of the heart. The bullet must have passed through the left ventricle.

Then she realized that the blood on Collins's chest was streaked with black from another wound. She drew her hand away. Her fingers were soiled with black oily slime. Directly over his heart, his chest had erupted with the stuff.

Horrified, she pushed herself away, backing up across the floor, unknowingly whimpering, looking around for something, anything, to wipe her hand on. The sheriff's jacket hung from a coat rack in the corner. She reached up and frantically wiped her hand clean.

The dragon. Collins. Charlie, Vic, Maggie, then Phil. They were all connected somehow. Something terrible was happening.

She sat there on the floor, trembling uncontrollably, unable to stir, alone in this room with death. Unconsciously, she wrapped her arms around herself. She felt very cold.

IT WASN'T that Steve felt any obligation to listen to Levi. It just seemed the easiest route to take. Levi could have his say, that would hopefully end the matter, and Steve could get out of that greasy old garage. He followed Levi back to the workbench where Levi grabbed the binder and started flipping through the pages.

"Go ahead, have a seat," said Levi, still paging through the binder. "You probably won't care about anything I have to say—"

"Probably not," Steve responded, sitting down on a wooden tool chest.

Levi came over to Steve, looked him in the eye, and said, "But if you want to live, you'll care." Steve looked away. Levi bent down and forced Steve to look him in the eye. "You have to care, Benson!" Now Steve was paying attention, so Levi eased a little. "The minute you stop caring . . . it's over."

"Okay," Steve said, to satisfy him.

Levi stood up straight, found the page he wanted, and put it under Steve's nose. "Remember the Hyde River Charter? Did you read it?"

"Yes, I did."

Levi pointed at the signatures near the bottom of the document. "Look here, the last sentence of the charter and what Benjamin Hyde wrote above his name: 'If This Be Sin, Let Sin Be Served.'"

I should have known, Steve thought. "I saw that."

Levi set the binder aside then pulled over a small stool and sat on it. "Now, Mr. Benson, you can play the part of high-minded scientist, but you and I both know you've got a conscience in there somewhere. I want you to dig it out for me, okay? That's the man I want to talk to."

Levi cocked his thumb toward the binder. "What you have here is a whole town that made up its mind to kill its conscience. Somebody came along with some rules; somebody came along and said 'There's a God to be reckoned with,' and they strung him up. They thought that'd make 'em free. They thought they could do anything they wanted after that. But look what happened: They turned God out and got another master instead: 'If This Be Sin,

Let Sin Be Served.' Harold Bly's still got that for a plaque on his office wall!"

"Okay," said Steve, "so you're saying the dragon is God's judgment on a sinful town?"

Levi's answer surprised him a little. "No. God gives you a way to escape. God can show grace and mercy. The dragon never heard of the words."

"And so? Your explanation?"

Levi pointed to the mountains. "Benson, I'll tell you what you saw up there. What you saw up there—" He pointed to Steve's heart, and Steve actually raised a hand to deflect another touch. "—is what you have in here. The dragon isn't God's judgment for sin—the dragon is sin. Way back there this town, this valley, sold itself out to sin, and with the charter they made it law. After that, the people thought they were free, but they weren't. Benjamin Hyde may have thought he was boss, but he wasn't. Sin was in charge. Sin was running things. Sin owned the whole valley and every heart in it."

Levi looked through the window toward the mountains, troubled. "Benson, sooner or later, sin's gonna show. Maybe the folks a hundred years ago could hide it. Maybe our parents could hide it and hush it up. Maybe we thought we could go on acting like it wasn't there." He frowned with disgust. "You got people in this town who won't talk about it 'cause they think that'll make it go away. 'If we don't talk about it, if we just ignore it, then it won't really be there.'"

"But not anymore. You read the articles, the letters, right? The Hydes, the Blys, they worshiped and tampered and played with sin so much it became a thing with wings and scales and legs and teeth. People do that, you know, hang onto sin like it was a little pet. Problem with this pet is, it grows. It gets big and ugly and obvious, and before long it starts calling the shots. And it kills people, Benson. Used to be it was small enough and you could beat it off with a stick. Then it got big enough to scarf you down in small pieces. Now it's big enough to take you down in two, three bites. It hooks you like a fish, hooks you right through the heart, and then it reels you in. Oh, and it can wait. It can choose the time. It might wait for years, but it takes you sooner or later. Always does." Levi snickered derisively. "And the Hydes thought they were controlling it! Benson, sin never works for anybody, we work for it." He looked toward Steve, impassioned by his beliefs. "And it finally killed Benjamin Hyde. It killed Sam Bly. It'll kill Harold Bly, too, if he doesn't turn around. And that's what I've tried to tell people, only they don't want to hear it. Things can't go on the same. Used to be sin was a dirty little secret you could keep inside. Well, not anymore. It's too big now, too mean, too hungry. It's pay day. Like God told Cain, 'Sin is crouching at the door, wanting to devour you.'"

Steve nodded and remarked with no malice, only new understanding, "I can see why you're so unpopular around here."

"EVELYN!" Tracy cried from Collins's office. "Evelyn, don't come in here!"

Evelyn backed up against the nearest wall and let it hold her up as she tried to resume breathing. She couldn't see Tracy at all, only hear her voice coming from the office. "Tracy, are you all right?"

Tracy was still on the floor, still trying to recover her senses. "I'm alive."

"What's happened?"

"Stay back."

Evelyn was too wound up to keep her voice down. "I am staying back! Now tell me what happened!"

Tracy was still trying to believe it as she said it. "Sheriff Collins tried to kill me."

"What?"

Tracy's voice started to tremble. She was about to fall apart, and she couldn't help it. "He made sure the other deputy wouldn't be here. Then when I came into his office he jumped me and tried to shoot me. I think he was going to kill both of us."

"Oh, Lord . . ."

"Just like Phil tried to kill you. It's the—the Hyde Valley thing. The Oath, the—the—"

"The dragon."

"Yes," Tracy admitted with reluctance. "I think so."

"Are you sure you're all right?"

"I'm alive. He didn't hurt me." Evelyn took a few steps, and Tracy heard her. "Don't come in here!"

Evelyn stopped, but now she was closer to Collins's body. "Tracy . . ."

"You saw the dragon, didn't you?"

Every time she thought of that night, Evelyn felt a deep, wrenching pain. "Yes." She had to force herself to say it. "I saw it. I saw it . . . eat Cliff."

"Then you'd better get out of here. Get away. I don't know who we can trust anymore."

"Tracy, what's that on the sheriff's chest?"

Tracy didn't want to look at it. "I don't know. Some other people had the same thing. Phil Garrett had it, and Charlie Mack—and Maggie Bly."

Evelyn's voice choked with emotion. "Cliff had it. He was trying to hide it, but I could see it—I could smell it."

"Oh, my god." Tracy's hand started going to her heart, but she quickly withdrew it. "Evelyn—"

"Tracy, I'm coming in there!"

"Stay away!" Tracy's eyes flooded with tears. Her hand went to her heart. Her eyes focused on Collins's oozing chest. "I have it, too."

SEVENTEEN

The Tavern

EVELYN'S MIND was racing, putting pieces together. Cliff. The dead sheriff at her feet. Now Tracy.

And if Tracy, then— "Tracy, where's Steve?"

Tracy couldn't answer.

"Tracy! Do you know where Steve is?"

Tracy winced as the wound over her heart stung her. "He's—" A flash of pain stole her voice.

Evelyn decided she was going to go into that room and help Tracy whether Tracy wanted help or not. She carefully stepped over Collins's fallen body. Now she could see Tracy across the room, huddled on the floor near the coat rack, arms tightly clasped around her, pain etched in her face.

"Don't come in here!" Tracy almost screamed.

Evelyn came no closer, but she would not be turned back. "You are hurt."

"I'm not really hurt. It's just this—this thing on my chest."

Evelyn locked her eyes on Tracy and asked again, "Do you know where Steve is?"

Tracy finally got it out; it felt like a confession. "He's at my place. At least he was this morning."

Evelyn took hold of the doorjamb to steady herself. Tracy had not fired another shot, but Evelyn felt a bullet pierce her soul. Tracy had just confirmed Evelyn's deepest fear.

Tracy could see it. "Evelyn, it's okay . . ."

Evelyn tried to be stoic even as tears filled her eyes. "Tracy, was Cliff—seeing someone?"

Tracy hesitated, but the cornered look on her face gave away the answer.

"Who was she?"

Could more news do more damage? Probably. But Tracy knew she'd have to deliver it anyway. "It was Maggie Bly. She was the wife of the town boss . . ."

"Was?"

Tracy felt a wave of shame coming from somewhere as she explained, "She's dead. The dragon took her."

More confirmation. Pain and sorrow threatened to overwhelm her, but Evelyn gathered her strength. It was all she could do. "And she was marked just like you are, just like those others."

Tracy couldn't answer. The answer was too obvious and it terrified her.

Then Evelyn pushed further. "So now Steve must have it, too."

"We don't know that."

"Well, didn't you sleep with him last night?"

"I don't think that's any of your concern."

Evelyn pressed on, more sorrowful than angry. "Tracy, I'm not trying to act like your mother. But let's face it, people are dying. The dragon's killing people, and people are killing people for the dragon, and now you're on his list and my brother-in-law is too."

"You don't know that!"

"I know it and you know it!"

Tracy looked away.

"And you're saying it's none of my concern? Somebody tried to kill me too, remember?"

Tracy sighed and looked at the floor. "Phil Garrett is dead."

Another blow! "And he was marked, too, did I hear you right?" Evelyn asked, her temper flaring.

"Just get a grip, will you?"

"This is all so pointless! I can't believe it!"

Tracy had done enough talking. She gathered her strength and got up from the floor, still wincing with pain, then slipped her gun back into its holster. "You don't have to believe it."

"So, what now?"

Tracy went to the sheriff's body and searched for the key to the handcuffs. "You're going to get as far away from Hyde Valley as you can."

"We should call the police."

Tracy found the key and unlocked the cuff around her right wrist. "I am the police—the only one you can trust, anyway."

"What are you going to do?"

"I've got to find Steve. If they tried to kill me they'll try to kill him—and you, don't forget. We can call for help later. First we've got to get out of here."

JUST WHEN Steve thought Levi had finished, just when he was sure Levi couldn't get more weird and enigmatic, Levi went behind the phone company's ladder truck, clanked, clattered, and rummaged around, then came back with a long steel rod tipped with a—

"What in the world is that?"

Levi let the butt end settle to the concrete floor and held it at his side like a Roman soldier holding a lance. He looked up at the broad spear tip welded to the end and answered, "My best guess at how to kill that thing."

Steve sighed. "You are pushing my credibility. No. No, you've pushed way beyond it! I suppose this has a horse and shining armor to go with it?"

Levi actually smiled in amusement. "I suppose you'd like to take your burned-up rifle you told me about and try it again?"

"This can never work!"

"Well, just about never. You'd have to get up under the dragon to use it." He brought the tip down so Steve could see it close. "You see, bullets can't get through the scales; they're too strong—I'm sure you've noticed that. But this tip here can slide between the scales, knife up under 'em like going between shingles, you see what I mean? Once you get through those scales, you just keep shoving 'til you hit something vital."

"Okay, functionally, it makes sense," Steve agreed. "But of course you've figured out how to get under the dragon without him knowing it, and how to make him hold still while you probe around with that thing?"

Levi chuckled. "Not entirely."

"I didn't think so," Steve said, and smiled.

Levi continued. "But things might be swinging our way a bit. The old boy's getting careless; he's getting cocky. He killed your brother, somebody who didn't even live around here, and left part of him behind. He tore Charlie's car open, not something you'd do if you wanted to stay a secret. He played with you a little bit. He's getting bold now, coming out in the open."

Levi set the lance down and took his seat on the shop stool. "So, I'm thinking maybe the dragon'll get crazy sometime, get all distracted with what he's doing so he won't guess what we're up to."

"What do you mean, we?"

"It would take two people: one to be the lure and one to handle the lance. The dragon goes after one man, and the other man comes up under the dragon from behind and rams the lance under the scales. Heh. That oughta do it."

"But what if the dragon falls on the guy holding the lance?"

"That's one of the problems with this whole idea," Levi admitted.

"Yeah, and another problem is that the dragon could eat the 'lure' before the other person could even get the lance in place," Steve pointed out.

Levi nodded. "Yep, that's another problem. But maybe there's another way." He cocked his head and looked at Steve. "Maybe we could prop the lance up somewhere and get the dragon to back up and stab himself."

Steve rolled his eyes as he said, "Oh, right. It's bad enough that someone has to be dragon bait. How do you propose we get the dragon to back up?"

"You can't," Levi said. "The dragon would kill you. As far as I know, the dragon's only ever backed away from two people—your sister-in-law Evelyn and me."

"What are you talking about?"

"Evelyn's a religious woman; she knows Jesus, right? Just like I do. He lives in her heart."

Steve shrugged. "Well, yeah, I guess." Where was Levi going with this crazy line of thought?

"It's pure and simple logic," Levi continued. "The dragon is sin. So since Jesus is living in our hearts—Evelyn's and mine—we're saved from sin, which means we're saved from the dragon and it can't touch us."

"Oh, that's logical all right," Steve said sarcastically. "We set the lance up somewhere. Then we get the dragon to follow me, and then somehow you get between the dragon and me and get it to back up and kill itself. That's a ludicrous plan!"

"I don't know . . . seems the Lord gave it to me. He must know how it's going to work."

Okay. Steve had given Levi his time, he'd listened to Levi's pitch, he'd paid whatever courtesy was due, and now he was satisfied: If Levi wasn't crazy he certainly came close. It was time to end this meeting. "Well, I doubt we'll need your spear anyway, Levi. I'm going to go back to Colorado and report my findings. After that, I'm sure we'll be able to raise all the help we need to capture that creature." He looked at his watch, then rose to leave.

"Hold on," said Levi.

"I'm late for another appointment."

Levi stood in his way again and took a moment to study his face. "Benson, listen to me. You aren't going to capture the dragon. He's already captured you. It's his game now, not yours."

Steve looked around as if missing something. "Levi, the dragon hasn't captured me. I'm sitting right here talking to you—ow!" He grabbed his chest in pain. Levi had poked him.

Levi raised an eyebrow. "He's got you, all right. Right through the heart." Levi poked him again and it hurt. "Got you hooked like a fish, all set to pull you in."

He was about to poke Steve again, but Steve blocked him. "All right, that's enough!"

Levi withdrew his hand. "Be glad it still hurts. When you get close to the end, you don't feel a thing." He sighed and shook his head. "You could have escaped, Benson. You could've steered clear, but now you're in the thick of it, and it's too late, just like it's too late for this town."

Steve just kept his hand over his chest and glared at him.

The big mechanic pointed toward the mountains. "That dragon's bigger and stronger and madder and more hungry than he's ever been before, and he's gonna get what he wants. You can count on it. And he wants you, Benson. You're hooked. I tried to warn you about getting tangled up with that woman."

Steve tensed. Levi had said exactly the wrong thing. "This meeting is adjourned." His tone could have frozen a lake.

Levi still blocked his way. "She's married, Benson. That makes you a thief, Tracy a promise-breaker, and both of you liars. How clear does it have to be before you can see it?"

Steve pointed a finger in Levi's face. "Not that it's any of your business, Cobb," he said angrily, "but let me remind you that Tracy's separated from Doug—she can do whatever she pleases!"

"It ain't the first time she's 'separated' from Doug," Levi muttered. "Ain't the second time, either. It's a pattern with her. And you ain't the first person she's hooked up with, either."

"You've crossed the line, Cobb! I've had it with your gossip. If Tracy keeps leaving Doug as you say, then there must be a reason. He's a real hothead. I wouldn't be surprised if he's a wife-beater."

Levi kept his voice steady and calm as he said, "Doug has his problems, sure, but wife-beating isn't one of them. He's got a lot of changing to do, but he still loves Tracy."

"If Tracy wants to find a better man, isn't that her business?"

Levi couldn't hold back a smirk. "A better man? Benson, you're the kind of guy who sleeps around. Doug ain't much, but at least he's stayed true. As for you, how many other Tracys have there been? How many will come after her?"

Enough. Steve landed a punch on Levi's jaw. The big man absorbed the blow without taking a step, but his glasses went flying. He didn't retaliate. He just stood there, sadness in his eyes.

Steve rubbed his fist. "I'm sorry. But you brought it on yourself. I don't like anyone sticking their nose into my personal life!"

Levi responded, "Yeah, and they don't want you messing with their dragon either." With those words, he stepped aside and let Steve pass.

TRACY HAD tried to reach Steve at her home and via his mobile phone, but couldn't get an answer at either number. Now she feared the worst as she drove at breakneck speed along the Hyde River Road.

It's just you and me, Steve, she thought. I've plugged the county sheriff, and who knows what trouble you're about to get into! It's us against them.

Evelyn was already on her way back to Oak Springs, and if she took Tracy's advice, she'd be going farther than that. Tracy was hoping she and Steve could make a quick exit as well, but first she had to find him.

When she finally pulled up in front of her little house on Nelson Creek, she could see his camper was gone.

She found a note on the kitchen table:

Dear Tracy,

Gone to Hyde River to meet with Harold Bly at ten. I think we can talk the whole thing out. Will call later, or you call me. Join us if you can. We'll be at the tavern.

Steve

She grimaced. He was walking right into it!

STEVE DROVE his camper slowly down the main street through town, not wanting trouble but looking out for it. He was sure he would not be welcome, but somehow he had to change that. He would talk it out with Harold Bly, man to man, with all the cards on the table. No more sneaking around, no more us-against-them mentality. It was time for tolerance, time to negotiate, compromise, do whatever it took to make peace. Harold Bly was not a man Steve admired, but he had to have a mind for business, an eye that could see an economic advantage when it presented itself. Steve would try to approach him on that level, addressing Bly's business concerns and suggesting new ideas that would further those concerns. With the right incentives, Bly might even be willing to talk openly about the dragon and find ways for both the town and science to benefit.

As he pulled up in front of Charlie's Tavern and Mercantile, Steve actually smiled. He was seeing things in a fresh new light now. Okay, so now it was known: There was a creature up there, a predator responsible for killing Cliff and the others. Okay. That was just nature's way. No one blamed grizzlies for acting on their instincts, so no one needed to blame this creature either. The creature needed to be understood, not killed, and if people wanted to worship that thing or serve it, well, that was their business.

He opened the door and stepped out, smiling at some folks passing by. They didn't return his smile. Fine. Things would change soon enough. Steve noticed all the trucks parked in front of the tavern. That was odd for a weekday morning, he thought. Maybe Harold Bly had created a new holiday. Maybe even a holiday in honor of the dragon. Steve smiled again.

"Here he comes," said Bernie, spotting Steve through a front window.

Harold Bly sat in his usual corner, smoking a cigar and enjoying a cold beer. Sitting with him was Rosie, who seemed to be settling into a long-term relationship.

"Honey," he told her, "why don't you go on home? This could get unpleasant."

Her grip on his hand lingered as she rose from the table. "You be careful, Hal."

"Don't worry," he told her.

She left through the back door.

Harold caught the eye of his favorite retired employees, Elmer McCoy and Joe Staggart, who were seated at tables on either side of Bly. They nodded. Andy Schuller and his two buddies immediately started playing a game of pool and looking like they didn't have a .357, a .38, and a .44 hidden in the ball rack under the table.

Bernie went back to polishing glasses. His rifle was behind the bar, within easy reach.

Paul Myers was in his usual place at the end of the bar, under the television. He too was armed; he'd been assigned the back door.

Carl Ingfeldt was stationed at a table near the front door, with Kyle Figgin.

The door opened; the cowbell clanged. Steve Benson came into the tavern.

"Hey, Professor," said Bernie.

"Hello. Is Harold Bly around?"

Harold called from his table in the back, "Over here."

Andy made a shot. The balls clacked around the table. Paul sipped from his beer and reached for a pretzel. Carl said nothing; he didn't think his voice would sound steady.

Steve crossed over to Harold's table. "Thanks for seeing me."

Harold stood and extended his hand. "I'm glad you called. It's about time we talked this thing out. Would you like a beer, on the house?"

"Yes, thank you."

Bernie was already on his way with a tall, cold one. He set it in front of Steve as the two men sat down.

Steve looked around the tavern before getting too settled.

Here was Harold Bly right across the table from him; two older gentlemen were positioned strategically at tables on either side; Carl and Doug Ellis's sidekick, two guys you wouldn't expect to see together, were now sitting together, and by the door. Andy Schuller and his buddies, who once had had such a vital interest in punching Steve's lights out, were now so absorbed in their game they didn't seem to notice he'd come in. All of this didn't feel right, and on top of that, Steve was very aware that his back was to the room.

Oh, well. There was fear and mistrust on both sides, he was sure. Now was the time to defuse it all.

"I'm not sure exactly where to begin," Steve said.

"Perhaps I can help." Bly said. "I understand you finally found the dragon."

Maybe Bly was trying to shock him, Steve thought. But no matter; they'd gone directly to the key topic. Steve smiled and proceeded carefully. "Word does get around in this town."

Harold chuckled disarmingly. "Just a hunch, really. We saw you looking a bit singed when you went to Levi's."

Amazing. Bly seemed to have eyes everywhere. Steve saw no advantage in denying it. "Mr. Bly, I meant no harm in coming here. I only wanted to find out what happened to my brother, and now I have. So that's what we need to talk about. I want you to know—" He looked around the room and spoke to anyone who might be listening. "I want all of you to know that I respect your beliefs and traditions. I don't want to violate them." Then his gaze centered on Bly. "The dragon's there, it's real, and I'm a wildlife biologist. It's my job to study nature, to attempt to understand it, to discover things we've never known about before—"

Bly held up his hand. "Mr. Benson, here's the first thing you need to understand: This is our valley. The dragon is our dragon. It's nobody else's business."

But that was the primary thing Steve could not understand. "Well, correct me if I'm wrong, but isn't the dragon killing people? It's eating them, am I right?"

Bly exchanged glances with some others in the room. "That's all a matter of opinion, like anything else."

"No," Steve said firmly. "Listen, I'm sorry, but it's not a matter of opinion. My brother, Cliff, was half eaten, and his wife was there and saw it happen. There's no question in my mind that the dragon is a predator. It needs to be studied before it kills more people. Maybe it can even be contained."

Bly raised an eyebrow. "What gives you a right to come in here and 'study' something that doesn't belong to you?"

Steve could only reiterate, "It's killing people!"

Harold leaned back in his chair, looking relaxed. "We prefer not to think about that."

"Mr. Bly, I'm sorry, but this isn't making any sense!"

Bly leaned over the table, his palms flat on its surface, his eyes intense and the cigar clenched in his teeth. "Mr. Benson, who are you to tell me what makes sense?" He called out, "Doug!"

Doug Ellis came through the passage from the mercantile and took a chair directly to Steve's left. He didn't look altogether vicious, but he didn't look warm and friendly either.

"You remember Doug Ellis?" said Bly. "Tracy's husband, right?"

Steve didn't comment.

Bly continued, relishing the moment. "Word has it you and Doug's wife got a little frisky last night. Is that true?"

Then Bly and Doug Ellis sat there waiting for an answer. Steve could only stare back at them, frantically searching his mind for any answer they might find acceptable. Such an answer did not exist.

Bly knew that. This was a great moment for him. "Doug and Tracy are married. Man and wife. Now does shacking up with another man's wife make a lot of sense?"

Steve attempted an answer. "She's separated from him. She moved out. She's free to make her own choices."

"We're not talking about her!" Bly snapped. "We're talking about you, and what you did, and why. Bly shot a glance at Doug, who now, to Steve, looked bigger and meaner than ever before.

"You know, if I was Doug, I'd have a good mind to tear you apart, maybe even kill you if it came to that."

Doug eyed Steve up and down, as if deciding what he was going to do with him. "Let me tell you something, mister," Doug said slowly. "Tracy's a good woman, but she's got a wild side, sure. Everybody around here knows it. This isn't the first time she's moved out and taken up with someone. But I made up my mind she was the only woman I was ever gonna love, and as far as I'm concerned, she still is. There's nothing I wouldn't do to get her back again." He leaned forward and spoke directly into Steve's face. "And you don't know what pain is until you lose the only good thing you ever had to some—some—" Doug hit the table with his fist, and Steve jumped. Then Doug sat back in his chair and looked away.

Steve remained silent, knowing that anything he might say now would only make the situation worse.

"Let's get back to the point," Bly said to Steve. "Here you are, just back from Levi Cobb's Sunday school class, all convinced the dragon's our fault and how you've got to save us from our own dragon, isn't that right?"

"Hey," Steve tried to protest, "that's where you're wrong. I don't give a rip about what Levi Cobb says—"

"Then try listening to me!" said Bly, catching Carl's eye.

Carl and Kyle rose and guarded the front door while Paul went to the back door and did the same.

I'm dead, Steve thought.

TRACY KEPT the patrol car rolling at well over eighty, slowing only for the treacherous curves in the road as it followed the meandering Hyde River. She was mapping out the town in her mind, rehearsing what she would do, where she would go, trying to anticipate Bly's strategy, where his cronies might be lurking, what armaments they might use.

She was armed herself, not only with her weapons, but also with the shotgun from Sheriff Collins's car and the sheriff's sidearm. This whole thing was going to be crazy. If Collins was one of Bly's pawns, her uniform wasn't going to count for much. They were going to be ready, spring-loaded, desperate . . .

This wasn't going to be crazy; it was going to be suicide.

Call for help, a voice inside told her. Get some backup.

I've shot the sheriff of Clark County, she replied, and kept driving.

HAROLD BLY was in no hurry, it seemed. He just kept looking at Steve, watching him worry as the trap closed around him. "How you feeling, Benson? Got some pain in your chest? Huh?"

Steve didn't answer, but his silence was answer enough.

Bly only smiled at him and proceeded to unbutton his own shirt. The reddening scar over his heart was unmistakable. The horror and recognition must have been obvious on Steve's face because Bly gave a harsh laugh. "Look familiar? Some earn this with greed, and some with hate, and some with envy. Stevie, I earned this by being the meanest, toughest boss man this valley ever saw. I own the land, I have the jobs, I call the shots. This is heaven and I'm God, and I'm about to make a bigger contribution to this town's history than old man Hyde himself."

Steve could feel cold terror crawling down his spine. The biggest contribution old man Hyde had made to the town's history was wanton murder.

"Andy!" Bly called. "Show him what you've got!"

Andy set down his pool cue and unbuttoned his shirt. There was a dark brown welt on his chest.

Bly hollered and gestured, "Come on, all of you! Let's get it right out in the open!"

All around the room, the same mark appeared. Some were faint red, others darker, some brown, others almost black.

"Clayton!" Bly hollered.

Clayton? Steve turned. There was a man at the bar just turning around.

It was Clayton Gentry, the young logger from down the valley. Steve saw that his face was black and blue and puffy as if he'd been beaten. He hadn't opened his shirt, and it was easy to see he didn't want to.

"Clayton, this man needs to see you're in the same boat with the rest of us!"

Clayton's voice was quiet but defiant. "No, he doesn't."

Bly stared him down for a moment, but then let it go with a laugh. "Pardon him. He's still a little timid about it. We all try to hide it at first. Maggie tried to hide it, Charlie tried to hide it, we all did, even I did, but who were we kidding?" He drew a deep breath and sighed. "Why hide anything when we all have it? We are what we are, so we do what we do and nobody needs to apologize. You get used to it—real used to it."

Bly shook his head at the memory. "You should have seen Maggie the night she died—oh, excuse me, left town. She was standing outside my door, happy as a clam, just proud as a fool about what she'd done and how she'd gotten away with it for so long—and she was dripping and stinking like rotten meat, and everybody knew it but her.

"Charlie was the same. He had a doozy. You could smell it across the room. But he thought he could hide it!" Bly laughed at that, the laugh hissing through his nose. "Aw, but in the end, he didn't care either. Nobody does. We don't, and neither will you."

Steve was incredulous, staring at one man, then another, his eyes traveling about the room.

Bly banged the table to get his full attention again. "So listen, Stevie, I don't think you're in any position to help us out, you know? You're no better than we are, no smarter. You're just like us, and you're marked just like us, and you're going to end up just like us. Shacking up with another man's wife wasn't all that original, but hey, it got you in, so it'll do."

TRACY SLOWED as she entered town, wishing that she and her patrol car were invisible. In Hyde River, someone was always watching.

She rounded a turn and could see the wider part of town—the four-way stop, the hardware store, the two-pump Chevron station, and Charlie's Tavern and Mercantile—a few blocks ahead. She immediately spotted Steve's camper parked in front of the tavern, along with a number of familiar-looking trucks.

And she knew there was trouble.

All the tires were slashed, and the camper was sitting on the rims. The people in the street—she knew many of them—were not in their usual, stop-to-talk clusters, and there were no casual conversations going on. Every person looked stationed where he or she stood. Two men stood close to the camper as if guarding it. Three more stood across the street, their eyes toward the tavern, watching.

Up and down the street, men and women stood in their little yards as if waiting for a parade, their eyes toward the tavern. Obviously, no one was working today, Tracy thought. That meant big trouble.

Two blocks before the main part of town, Tracy wrenched the steering wheel to the left, went down a narrow street, turned into an alley, and tucked the car into a narrow gap between an empty concrete-block house and a long-defunct machine shop. She hoped she hadn't been seen but knew it was a slim hope, at best.

Now, how could she carry two shotguns while using one of them? Where could she carry the extra sidearm? Which was the safest and quickest route to the tavern? How could she keep from getting stopped—or shot?

HAROLD BLY buttoned up his shirt, as did the others. They'd made their point in devastating fashion.

"Messing around with another man's wife did it for your brother, too," said Bly. "Kind of funny you didn't learn anything from that." Bly reflected on it and shook his head. "But what's to learn anyway? Do what you want, I say, and when your time comes, you cash in."

Steve didn't understand everything Bly was saying, but he did get the impression he'd contracted a fatal disease that was killing him this very moment.

Bly leaned back in his chair and gloated. "How about it, Stevie? Feeling proud yet? Feeling immortal? I'll bet your brother Cliff did. Just ask Evelyn. They all did: Cliff did, Maggie did, so did Vic and Charlie. And now they're dragon manure."

"So you *are* saying the dragon ate them?"

Bly smirked. "What do you think?"

Steve touched his chest. "And this is the dragon's doing?"

Bly raised his eyebrows as though impressed. "Hey, you're learning. A little late, though. You should have gotten out of here while you had the chance."

Steve looked around the room. "Why do you let this happen to you? Why don't you just leave?"

"Why should we?"

"Doesn't this mark mean—? Well, I think I hear you saying the dragon is going to eat you."

"Could be."

"Then don't you want to leave? Escape?"

Bly exchanged glances with the others. "We like it here, Benson. Don't you?"

Steve didn't like it here at all, but he knew better than to say so.

Bly answered for him, "Sure you do. We all do You just haven't figured that out yet." Bly picked up his beer mug and raised it high. "But you've been selected, buddy, so drink up. You're one of us now."

Bly took a long drink from his beer. The others in the room did the same, as if it were a toast. It was eerie. Suddenly everyone seemed so jovial, but Steve could clearly sense they were dancing on his grave.

He went with the flow and drank. Maybe they were all crazy. Maybe he was dreaming. In any event, maybe, just maybe, he'd get out of there alive if he went along.

Bly set his mug down and eyed Steve slyly. "But listen, it's not a done deal; I wouldn't want you to think that. The way I look at it, you can get out of just about anything if you know the right strings to pull. We've got ourselves a little problem, but all we've got to do is get rid of what's causing it. Get rid of the troublemaker, and you're rid of the trouble."

Benjamin Hyde, Steve thought. I'm drinking beer with Benjamin Hyde. "Mr. Bly, I don't want to cause trouble. That's why I'm here, to talk this thing through."

Bly picked up his beer mug again. "So, drink up, and we'll talk it through."

Steve picked up his beer again and put it to his lips just as the back door swung open.

"Don't drink that!" a voice ordered.

Tracy! Steve twisted in his chair to see her standing just inside the back door, awkwardly grasping a shotgun in her right hand while carrying another in her left, and wearing a sidearm on each hip. She was just aiming a shotgun at Bernie behind the bar. "Hands, Bernie! Let's see those hands!"

Bernie, who had been reaching for something, raised his hands.

Tracy panned the room with the muzzle of the shotgun, and hands went up like weeds growing. "No one move! Steve, come on!"

Steve protested, "Tracy, I'm trying to make friends here."

"Get away from that door!" she ordered Carl, who sat back down. "Hands, Andy! Hands!" Andy withdrew his hands from behind the pool table and held them high.

"Does your boss know where you are?" Harold Bly asked in a condescending tone.

"I shot him, Harold."

She said that so quickly and simply that it took a moment for the others in the room to grasp it. There was a shocked silence, and everyone in the room, except Steve, looked at Bly.

Bly didn't believe her, and sneered. "Oh, come on, Tracy."

"I'm here, aren't I?" she fired back. "If he was still alive then I'd be dead, and I think you know it. I think you put him up to it. And I'll bet you've got a nasty wound over your heart just like he did."

Bly gave a derisive chuckle as he exchanged a quick glance with the others. "And how is yours?" he asked.

She looked at him with seething hatred. "Like fire, Harold. Like fire. So I'm very upset right now, like I want to shoot somebody. Steve, get over here. They're out to kill you, too."

Looking warily all directions, Steve got up from the table.

"Come on!" Tracy urged.

He hurried across the room. She handed him the extra shotgun, then addressed the room. "Okay. You want to be rid of the trouble. Well the trouble's leaving right now. We're through with you; we're through with the valley. You can have the dragon, all right? He's all yours. We're out of here."

She reached behind her, yanked the back door open, and they made their escape, Tracy leading, Steve covering the rear.

The door closed, and every man went for his gun.

"Easy now," Bly shouted, jumping up from his place. "Go with the plan! Go with the plan! Elmer! Joe! Take the south end! Carl, take the north! Move!"

STEVE'S FIRST thought was to head for his camper. Tracy grabbed his arm and pulled him down the alley. "Forget it, the tires are slashed!"

Adrenaline pumping, Steve followed Tracy, his senses alert, the shotgun ready.

They ran full speed behind the old businesses, past garbage cans and loading doors, along cracked retaining walls and over deep potholes, fearing a sniper in every window, an assailant around every corner. They could hear shouting from the streets out front and the growling of engines starting.

They came out of the alley and onto a gravel street. There was a shout from the main road. A woman had spotted them and was alerting someone farther down.

"Hurry!" Tracy urged. "If they find the patrol car we're in deep soup."

They got across that street and ducked down another alley, racing past small homes and cluttered yards, along a cyclone fence with two yapping dogs chasing them on the other side, through a small flock of free-ranging chickens that squawked and long-stepped for cover.

They came to what looked like an old machine shop, now deserted, and Tracy pressed close against the building as Steve came up silently behind her. They inched toward the corner, and Tracy peeked around into the alley beyond.

"Okay," she whispered, and they rounded the corner.

The patrol car looked okay. They jumped in. Tracy started the engine and drove down the alley to the next cross street. From there, the only route available was the main highway.

"Hang on."

With a burst of power and rocks flying from under the spinning tires, the car surged for the highway, skidded around the corner, and roared south on the Hyde River Road toward the edge of town.

They rounded the corner and Tracy braked.

Elmer McCoy's flatbed truck and Joe Staggart's old school-bus-turned-into-a-camper had just arrived and were parked across the road, blocking their way. Andy Schuller and his buddies were already there, looking grimly from under their billed caps, armed with hunting rifles, waiting, backed up by some more crew from the mine and Bly's small logging company, at least ten men.

Tracy veered onto the right shoulder, cranked the wheel all the way left, and shrieked out a tight circle that barely missed the old bus and the men standing by it. Steve, slouching down in his seat, shotgun in hand, could see their bellies and belt buckles blurring right by his window. He turned and saw them running after the car, trying to line up a shot. The car bounded and bounced off the narrow road, over the shoulder, and into the widow Dorning's little yard, where it took out Mrs. Dorning's birdbath, half a row of marigolds, three painted concrete squirrels, and a plastic Bambi before fishtailing onto the highway again and turning north, back through town.

"They're going to have the other end cut off, too!" Steve shouted.

"So what do you suggest?" she shouted back. "There are only two ways out of town."

"We may have to hoof it if we can't get out by car."

"Hoof it where? Over those mountains?"

It was not a promising alternative.

The car raced by Cobb's Garage. Both the big doors were open, but Steve saw no sign of Levi.

"Levi!"

Tracy kept driving without a response.

Steve shouted to her, "What about Levi?"

"What about him?"

"If they're after us, they have to be after him!"

"He'll have to take care of himself."

"We can't leave him here!"

Tracy only hit the gas harder and accelerated through the four-way stop. "We don't have a choice."

At the north end of town, where the little train of ore cars sat alongside the road, one of Harold Bly's big logging trucks now spanned the highway, blocking their path. Carl Ingfeldt was manning the roadblock, along with some of the mine crew.

"Hold on again!" Tracy cranked the wheel for another skidding, squealing, gravel-throwing one-eighty-degree turn. Once again, Steve could see huge wheels, iron, chrome, and human bodies blurring by the window as the car skidded around.

Then he caught a glimpse of a face: Doug Ellis. Ellis started running after the car. "I'll kill you, Benson!"

Carl Ingfeldt raised a shotgun.

"Duck!" Steve hollered just as the rear window exploded in a shower of glass.

FROM THE PORCH of his little parsonage next to the church, Reverend Ron Woods could hear the gunshot, the shouting, the roar of vehicles racing through the town below.

It's finally happening, he thought.

It was something he'd long feared, long expected. He'd heard the murmuring around town, the rumors, the bitter talk about the professor and the turncoat sheriff's deputy. He'd heard the hatred being spat in Levi's direction. He knew Harold Bly's ways.

And now it was finally happening. The hatred, the fear, the superstitions of the town had erupted. Now people might even be killed.

But he remained where he was, above it all, safe—and helpless. What could he do? How could he stop it? How could this kind of madness even listen to reason? How long had he tried to quell it, soothe it, make it go away by continuous words of peace and goodwill? This thing simply would not die, only hide for a while to crop up again later. Woods's theology could not account for it. What wisdom he thought he had was exhausted.

But one thing had become clear to him, even as he listened to the trouble below: He could stay there on his front porch and pretend he was different, but he was not. He was like them. He was them.

Like the people below, his own heart harbored bitter secrets. Like his neighbors, he had come face to face with what he was.

He had discovered the red mark over his heart that morning when he awoke. He'd heard enough of the folk tales to know what it was. By now it had grown to several inches long, was a deep red, and burned with the slightest touch.

JUST AS the patrol car neared the four-way stop, a dump truck and a pickup approached from the opposite direction, side by side, taking up both lanes. The net was closing.

Not yet, Tracy thought. She roared into the four-way stop and cut a hard left turn, slamming Steve into the side of the car. Instead of straightening up, he remained leaning against the door. His whole body felt heavy, and he was having trouble focusing. Snap out of it! he ordered himself and forced his body upright. He recovered just in time to see the massive, concrete Hyde Mining

Company building ahead. The car rumbled and bounced over a timber bridge, then Tracy veered to the right, up a narrow ramp that paralleled the river. There was a tunnel coming up, a yawning black cave that ran under the building.

"The railroad used to come through here," she explained. "They've torn the tracks up, so maybe—"

Maybe, Steve heard, as if from a distance.

Tracy drove into the black tunnel, the roar of the engine rumbling back at them off the water-streaked concrete walls. They burst through into sunlight again, into a wide expanse, once a loading area. On one side, built into the mountain, was the loading complex with huge ore chutes that had once been used to fill trains. On the other side was a thick concrete wall and beyond that, a deadly vertical drop to the river. Straight ahead, another tunnel went through the foot of the mountain.

It could have led them into the clear, hopefully beyond the roadblock, but the tunnel was blocked, barricaded with many years' worth of old timbers, metal scrap, and empty diesel drums.

Tracy braked to a growling, skidding stop, then gave the steering wheel an angry pound and slumped back against the seat. "Now what?" she said to herself, looking around.

"Why'd we stop?" Steve asked groggily.

She flung her door open and jumped out. Then she looked back. He was still sitting there, bewildered. "Steve, come on! We've got to find a way out of here!"

Steve groped for the door handle, finally found it, and pushed the door open. He staggered out of the car just as the rumble of vehicles echoed out of the tunnel behind them.

There were doors along the wall beneath the ore chutes. Tracy ran along, trying each one. They had been locked years ago and wouldn't budge. Then she saw an iron stairway leading up to a catwalk. "The stairs! Let's go!"

She ran past Steve toward the stairway. He turned to follow her but crumpled to the ground.

"Steve!"

He tried to stand up but flopped to the ground again. The earth was reeling and rocking beneath him and wouldn't stop.

Tracy grabbed his hand. "I knew it! They put something in your beer. Come on. Try to get up!"

"I'm coming . . ." he said, not moving at all.

A pickup shot out of the tunnel and screeched to a halt, then another, then an old van, and then a station wagon. Doors flew open, men leapt out, guns appeared.

Harold Bly stood at the head of the crowd, a revolver in his hand. Beside him stood Doug Ellis; behind him, Elmer and Joe; over on the left, Andy Schuller and friends; on the right, Carl Ingfeldt and Kyle Figgin.

Tracy looked toward the stairway.

Carl and Kyle moved quickly, guns aimed, and cut her off. "Don't try it," Kyle said. "We'll only have to shoot you."

She hesitated, still holding Steve's hand. Steve was getting weaker by the moment.

Bly ordered, "Drop that rifle or I'll drop you right now!"

Steve had already dropped his shotgun simply because he couldn't hold it any longer. He knew he was slipping away. Still, he could hear the roar of some kind of machine, but he didn't know where it was coming from.

"Harold," Tracy said, still holding her shotgun, "this won't accomplish anything."

"Sure, it will," he replied. "You're the ones who brought the dragon down on us. If you would have left things alone—"

"We're trying to save you from the dragon! You can't stop the dragon by killing us!"

"Oh, you're going to save us, all right. By going first."

Steve was slipping from consciousness. Now the ground was not only swaying under his feet, it was also quivering and shaking.

"Harold, what's that?" Andy asked.

Steve heard the question but couldn't make out the answer. He could barely raise his head, but he saw people moving around. Something was upsetting everybody.

"Drop that gun, Tracy!" Harold ordered again.

"Why should I?" she countered. "If you're going to kill me anyway, then go ahead!"

"What the—" Carl yelled.

"Who's that?" Andy wondered.

Another vehicle was approaching, the roar of its engine rumbling and echoing out of the barricaded tunnel behind Tracy and Steve. Whatever it was, it was making the ground shake.

Harold Bly was the first to catch a view of it over the barricade. "Why, that old fool!"

Wisps of black smoke curled out of the tunnel. Then the barricade broke open like a bursting dam, hitting the timbers, the scrap, and the diesel drums and pushing the debris right along in front of it. As Tracy dragged Steve out of the way and the mob scattered backward, the pile of debris and waste rolled over the patrol car like an ocean breaker and then carried it along, moving into the center of the loading yard.

Above that tumbling, clattering, dust-raising pile appeared the yellow driver's cab of the county's monstrous articulated loader, and at the wheel, cowboy hat squarely in place, sat Levi Cobb. He pushed that iron monster onward, the timbers cracking and dragging, the immense tires rumbling like an avalanche, the patrol car skidding sideways before the big front bucket, until he'd come between the crowd and the two people they were chasing. Then he halted, idled the throttle, and let the bucket down with a crunch. He stood in the cab, looked at the astounded group, and hollered, "All right now, you people know better than this!"

The ground seemed to pull Steve down. He collapsed, one ear in the dirt. With the other ear he could make out Levi hollering something and Harold Bly hollering something back. He could feel Tracy's hand on his shoulder.

Levi was saying something . . . sounded like he was trying to talk the crowd out of all this . . .

A gunshot. Steve winced. Levi wasn't talking anymore. Some people were cheering.

With all his remaining strength, Steve raised his head to see Levi slumped over the wheel of the loader and Harold Bly just lowering his revolver, a cold hatred in his eyes.

More cheers.

Tracy let go of his shoulder. He heard her running.

Then everything went black.

EIGHTEEN

Pursued

EVERYTHING HURT. Somebody must have beat him up. Maybe he'd fallen from a building or tumbled down a rocky cliff. If he could just wake up a little more, Steve thought, maybe he could locate the arms, fingers, legs, and toes that seemed to be reporting all this pain.

Now more reports came in. His head reported a hangover. His shoulders and then his arms started reporting aches and cramps from immobility. And there was his chest again, still aching, still burning. He began to remember the tavern, the beer he drank, the chase through town—and gunfire. Levi. Tracy.

So the nightmare wasn't over. He'd been drugged. While drugged and delirious he'd had dreams about being far from Hyde Valley, at work in his normal, everyday, safe little world: the university, his classes, his research. He even dreamed about safer activities like chasing and tagging sweet, innocent grizzly bears.

He forced his eyes open and saw the ground only inches beyond his nose. Tall grass. A few weeds. Everything was blurry, but he concentrated on getting his eyes to focus.

Ouch! Now his wrists were protesting.

He realized they were behind him. Then he realized they were going to stay there. They were bound. He curled his fingers around to feel what it was that held them.

It was a chain. A cold, hard, circulation-stopping chain.

He was half-sitting, half-lying on the ground. When he tried to move, his muscles punished him for the idea. He must have been like this for quite some time, he thought.

He pushed with his feet—at least they were free—so he could get his posterior directly beneath the rest of him, and then, inch by inch, his back against some huge object, he managed to sit upright.

The world continued to come into focus, and the ground grew steady as his mind cleared.

He saw that he was sitting in tall grass, surrounded by weathered, teetering ruins. His heart sank as he realized where he was. I've come full circle, he thought. I'm back at ground zero.

He was sitting chained in the center of Hyde Hall. This big object at his back had to be the rock he'd sat on that other night. Well, now he was chained to it, and it didn't take him long to guess why.

I'm going to be a peace offering to the dragon. Harold Bly was acting in the grand tradition of Benjamin Hyde: Give the people a scapegoat; destroy the messenger, bury the memory, and the trouble will go away.

Yeah, I'll go away, all right. Without a trace. No shots fired, no witnesses, no body, no evidence. The outside world will think a bear ate me.

How handy.

There had to be a way out of here, he thought. After scanning the area to make sure his captors weren't around, Steve pulled against the chains, then eased back to see how much slack he could give himself. There was virtually no slack. He moved sideways, then tried lifting himself and his bonds up over the rock. It didn't work.

Where was Tracy? he wondered. And Levi? Were they dead?

Were they chained somewhere? He strained and searched all around one more time, but didn't see or hear anything.

Quietly he called, "Tracy!" No answer. "Tracy!"

There was no answer but a breeze through the towering cottonwoods and the lazy rush of the river.

So when should he expect the dragon? He tried to recall any incident when the dragon attacked in daylight. Cliff was killed at night, so was Maggie, and it was the same with Vic and Charlie. Steve noted the position of the sun. If the dragon preferred hunting at night, there could be several hours yet to go before any action.

Then again, the dragon hadn't minded playing hide-and-seek with him during the afternoon up on Saddlehorse.

The final conclusion was, the dragon would do whatever it wanted, whenever it wanted.

How comforting.

A MILE SOUTH of Hyde River, just above a wide heap of mine tailings near the river's edge, some rotting planks were suddenly kicked out and away from a tight opening in the rock.

Tracy, her face and uniform muddied from a long crawl, wriggled through the opening she'd made and tumbled into the brush now obscuring the old tunnel. She righted herself, staying concealed in the bushes, and then looked up and down the Hyde River Road just across the river. No one in sight.

Well. She had made out like a bandit. This old tunnel had gotten a bit tighter since she was a kid and the entrance had all but disappeared behind new growth, but it was still there, just as she remembered it.

Now to get down the river to the Stewarts' ranch before some of her childhood playmates, now her pursuers, also remembered it.

STEVE HAD been sitting there forever and wasn't sure he could trust his perceptions. Was that just the breeze he heard behind him, or was someone—or something—coming through the tall grass?

He stilled his breathing and listened carefully for the kind of slinking, slithering sounds he'd come to know up on Saddlehorse. There it was again! It could have been footsteps, but he couldn't be sure. Whatever it was, it was getting closer.

Then, from a different direction, he heard another sound. This sound rose and fell, stopped and started, like something moving as light as mist over the ground. The hairs on the back of his neck stood on end.

He knew the sound—it was the slow, steady, incredibly light touch of the dragon's belly slithering over the terrain. Frantically, he scanned the trees, the brush, the tall grass. That thing would try to hide itself, but by now he knew what to look for.

He thought of praying. He resisted the idea. Who was there to pray to?

"God help me," crossed his lips anyway.

He relentlessly scanned the terrain in front of him, the old ruins, the scraggly trees—

The eyes appeared first. There they were, just like that, suspended in space in a small tree at the opposite end of Hyde Hall. It was as if nature itself had sprouted eyes and was looking down at him.

Their eyes met and then Steve winced, even cried out as the wound over his heart began to burn. Psychosomatic reaction, he thought. Power of suggestion . . .

We're linked! He recoiled in horror at that realization. We're linked.

That thing was digging into his heart, his soul, and he was totally helpless. Steve broke out in a cold sweat.

The eyes moved slightly as the head turned. Steve could discern the shape of the head, horns, and neck emerging from the forested background.

A red tongue, long, forked, and wet, whipped about like a snake in midair and then vanished again.

"Oh, God . . ." This time the words came easily, though his voice was shaking. "Oh, God, if you're there, help me."

A low bush just inside Hyde Hall's foundation flattened. The foundation wall rippled as the shape of an elongated, lizardlike foot passed in front of it.

Then another foot.

Steve could smell the thing now, an all too familiar smell of death, of rotting meat. Just like Maggie. And Charlie.

This time the dragon wasn't going to let him go.

"God, help me!" Steve cried.

Then he heard a sound behind him. A stumbling, a staggering, then a body falling in the grass.

The dragon's scales fell out of sync with the background. They flashed, they scrambled, the colors raced and flickered like a Las Vegas display gone mad. Then the camouflage broke down, and Steve could clearly see the dragon was right there, right in front of him, the golden eyes locked on whatever was making the noise behind him.

Then, loud enough to spike Steve's terror, a familiar, gruff voice hollered, "GO ON! GIT! GET OUT OF HERE!"

Suddenly all Steve could see from one side to the other were wings, flashing silver at first, then fading quickly to the sky's blue. A blast of wind hit him like a wall, and he turned his face away, his eyes shut.

He could hear the dragon's wings pounding the air with power-ful strokes. When he opened his eyes, the tops of the cottonwoods were still swaying and fluttering from turbulence.

But the beast was gone.

It was gone! Steve thought. I'm alive. What a feeling! Right now even the pain in his wrists, his arms, his shoulders, and yes, his chest, was welcome.

There is a God, he thought as he released a held breath.

"Levi!" Steve called over his shoulder to the man who had just saved his life.

"Yeah!" Levi hollered back.

He could hear the big man struggling as he made his way across Hyde Hall. His breathing was labored, and Steve heard him groan, as if in pain. It didn't sound good.

"Levi, are you all right?"

"No, I'm not all right," came the impatient reply.

Steve heard Levi take a few more steps and finally caught sight of him over his left shoulder.

A few more steps, and Levi collapsed to the ground right in front of him.

Levi's shirt was soaked in blood. He lay there a moment just breathing, almost weeping from the pain. In one hand he carried a gigantic pair of bolt cutters.

Now the scene at the mining company came back to Steve. Levi had been shot.

Despite the pain, the big mechanic hadn't given up on getting his message across. "Is any of this sinking in yet?"

"It—it was afraid of you," Steve stammered.

"And Evelyn." Levi stopped to breathe and gain some strength. Then he started crawling toward Steve with the bolt cutters. "And so the townfolk don't care much for us." He fell to the ground again, weak and gasping. "They thought I was dead, and so did I. But I guess God tricked 'em. They all ran off and just left me there."

"How did you know I'd be here?"

"They were gonna sacrifice somebody. The dragon won't take me, and Tracy got away, so—"

"She got away?"

Levi pulled himself over to the rock and started groping about with the bolt cutters. He was in agony just moving his arms. "Ran. Just ran for all she was worth. Ran out through the hole I busted through with the loader."

He got the cutters' jaws around one of the links and bore down on the long handles. There was a snap.

Steve tugged.

"Hold still now," Levi instructed, "I only got half of it."

Steve held still. "How badly are you wounded?"

"Bad enough. It was Bly's doing. The dragon couldn't do it for him, so he finally did it himself. I thought it might happen this way." He bore down on the handles again, and the link finally broke.

Steve felt an immediate slackening of the chain.

"Don't pull now," Levi said. "Give me some slack to pull through here."

Levi worked at the chain, pulling it from around the rock. "This was really stupid," he said as he worked. "The dragon's after everybody. What does he care if they send somebody on ahead for him to eat?"

"You're right," Steve said. "But Bly wanted to make sure I was at the head of the list."

Levi was silent for a moment. Then, "Okay, I think we've got her."

Steve leaned forward and pulled gently. The chain slid from around the rock, loosened from around his wrists, and then fell away. He brought his arms around in front, numb and aching, and began rubbing his wrists with relief. "Levi, I owe you my life."

"You owe Jesus your life. I'll just settle for a doctor."

Steve reached over. "Let me have a look."

Levi lay down as Steve pulled his shirt open. "Do you care?"

"Of course I care."

"Not about me! About you! About the dragon! You have to care, Steve. When you stop caring, that's when the dragon'll take you."

Steve looked into those piercing eyes. "Okay. I care."

He examined Levi's wound. The bullet had ripped through the abdomen and probably damaged the liver. Blood was pouring out of the wound.

"You have to resist him," Levi urged, his voice getting weak. "The Bible says, 'Submit to God; Resist the devil and he will flee from you.' You submit to God and get clean of your sin, that ol' dragon'll be a pussycat. You'll put him down real easy."

"Try not to talk. I've got to get you out of here."

Steve was about to get to his feet, but Levi grabbed his hand. "I gotta get this said! You gotta get right with God, Steve."

"Okay, Levi. Okay."

Levi looked up at him, apparently relieved by Steve's answer. "You got yourself marked, so he's your dragon now, Steve. You're part of him; he's part of you. But you get right with God, you can kill him; just you wait and see."

"And just how is that supposed to happen?"

Levi gave a weak smile. "When the dragon sees Jesus in you, he'll back up. He will. You can fool him into backing up. You'll scare him, just like I did, just like Evelyn." His eyes closed as if to sleep. "Go to that tunnel . . . use the tunnel . . . Jesus'll take care of the rest."

Steve didn't understand, but he said, "Okay, Levi."

With intense effort, Levi took a small, brass key from his shirt pocket. "Northwest Bank," he gasped. "Oak Springs. My sister'll help you out."

Steve took the key. "Your safety deposit box."

"Yeah."

"Okay, we'll talk about that as soon as—"

Levi fell asleep, his head resting peacefully on the ground. "Levi!"

There was no answer. Steve knew there would never be one.

"HELLO, Clark County Sheriff's Office, this is Deputy Matson."

The lieutenant with the Oak Springs police took just a moment to look through the glass enclosing his office and observe the distraught woman seated just outside. The attack she'd suffered in her home just the other night could have pushed her over the edge; he didn't know.

"Hello," he said. "This is Lieutenant Jarvis with the Oak Springs Police." He framed his question carefully. "We just got a report that you were having some trouble over there. I'm trying to follow it up."

Matson didn't sound like he expected such a question. "Gee, I don't think we've had any trouble. It's been a dull morning, actually."

"Is Sheriff Collins there?"

"Yeah, hold on."

Now Lieutenant Jarvis took a long, second look at Evelyn Benson.

A voice came on the line. "Sheriff Collins."

Jarvis drew a deep breath and proceeded, "Hi, Sheriff. This is Lieutenant Jarvis with the Oak Springs police, just following up on a call we got. Any trouble over there?"

"Why? What have you heard?"

"Well . . . someone has you dead."

"Dead?"

"Yeah, shot by one of your deputies, and there's supposed to be some real trouble brewing out in Hyde River too."

"Oh, boy. Who told you all this?"

"I've got a lady sitting out in the station right now who's beside herself—"

"Is it Evelyn Benson?"

"Yeah, it sure is."

The sheriff laughed. "Oookay. I'm sorry about that. Listen, Evelyn Benson is—well, she's not a psycho, but she's under a ton of stress right now. She was attacked in her home the other night."

"Yeah, I was on that case."

"And did you know her husband was mauled and killed by a grizzly just a little over a week ago?"

"Yeah, I was aware of that. So I was kind of wondering—"

"It's been tough on her. She might need professional help; I don't know. But she's really got it in for Hyde River right now. She came to me saying there were killers all conspiring together up there, and—has she said anything to you about a dragon?"

"A what?"

"A dragon You know, big, fire-breathing lizard."

"A dragon? No. She hasn't said anything about that."

"Well, ask her about it. You'll get quite a story. She thinks a dragon ate her husband."

EVELYN STOOD up when Jarvis came out of his office. "*Now* do you believe me?"

"Mrs. Benson, why don't you sit down a minute?"

She was beyond being soothed by kind formalities. "Didn't you call them?"

"I called them."

"Who did you talk to?"

"Sheriff Collins."

She was stunned. "That's—that's impossible."

"He's all right. Everything's fine over there."

"Sheriff Collins is dead!" she said. "I saw him myself!"

"I just talked to him."

"How do you know it was him?"

Jarvis held his hand up to settle her down. "Please, just calm down."

"I'll calm down when you get excited, you follow me? You've got to do something! You've got to go out there!"

"Mrs. Benson, that's not our jurisdiction."

"Well, somebody has to do something!"

"What about the dragon, Mrs. Benson?"

That stopped her cold.

"Haven't you told people a dragon ate your husband?"

At that moment, Evelyn knew Jarvis would never believe her.

At that moment, Jarvis decided he shouldn't.

AT THE Clark County Sheriff's Office, Doug Ellis hung up the phone and rejoined the crew Bly had sent to clean out the place. Kyle Figgin got a pat on the back—he'd done a splendid job as Deputy Matson. The door was locked, a "Closed for Mainte-nance" sign was hung on the door, the shades were drawn, and the calls were forwarded to the dispatcher. Collins's body had already been wrapped and taken out the back to a waiting truck; Phil Garrett's body had gone out to the truck not long before that. In a few more minutes, the floors would be mopped and everything returned to normal, and none too soon. The second-shift deputy was due to arrive in half an hour.

Doug did wonder what explanation would be given for Collins's disappearance, but then again, why explain it at all? As always, there was no evidence, there were no witnesses, and no one would say a word, especially now.

AS THE SUN settled behind the mountains and their shadow crept across the decaying ruins of Old Town, Steve remained beside Levi's limp body, alive, free, and devastated to realize, only now, that Levi Cobb had truly been his friend. Steve was overcome with remorse. The pains he felt in his body, even the pain from the wound over his chest, were insignificant by comparison.

It should've been me, Levi, not you.

He wept, unashamedly, for Levi, for Cliff, for this whole miserable valley where death was a cherished pet, where a despised mechanic had died for a stranger.

Why? Why?

His cries of pain and remorse in that empty, decaying shell of a building kept him from hearing the approaching hoofbeats. Finally they were so close they startled him, and he looked up.

Tracy! She was free, alive! Here she came on horseback, trotting down the main street through the ruined town, leading an extra horse behind her. "Steve! Are you all right?"

His legs were weak as he tried to stand. He quickly wiped his eyes and his face, trying to compose himself. "You're alive!"

"Just barely."

She rode up alongside Hyde Hall and reined in her horse. From her worn, muddy, and torn appearance you'd think she'd been dragged behind it, Steve thought.

"How did you know where I was?" he asked.

"I can put two and two together." Tracy's expression was quizzical as she noted the chains. "How on earth did you get loose?"

"Levi came and cut me loose."

"Then quit standing there! Let's go!"

Hadn't she heard what he said? "He's—he's dead. He was shot."

She craned her neck and could see Levi's body lying in the grass. "Then let's go. I didn't *rent* these horses!"

Steve stood there. "Tracy! He saved my life! The dragon was here—"

"Leave him! If we don't get over those mountains right now we're as dead as he is!"

Steve looked down at his friend, pale with death, soaked in blood, like a fallen, forgotten soldier on a deserted battlefield. "I can't. I can't just leave him here."

"Yes, you can. You'd better. Bly and the others are going to be hot on our trail once they figure out what's happened."

Steve looked at Levi one more time. Levi was dead, and yet something he said still echoed in Steve's mind. "He told me how to kill the dragon—I think."

"Are you going to get on your horse or not?"

"What about the dragon?"

"To heck with the dragon! To heck with the whole town! They can have it!"

Steve looked at Tracy, then at Levi's body. Finally it seemed right to trust her, to run for that horse and jump into the saddle. It was reassuring to find the horse fully bridled and saddled, and the sheriff's shotgun stowed in a saddle scabbard. Tracy had to have a plan, all right.

"Just follow me," Tracy instructed over her shoulder. "I know a trail out of the valley."

He rode behind her as they headed through the ruins and then north along the river.

"Where'd you get the horses?"

"The Stewart ranch, down the valley a few miles. They weren't home, so I helped myself."

The picture was bizarre. "A deputy sheriff stealing horses?"

"Impounding horses. There's a difference."

HAROLD BLY was back in the tavern, and this time he'd opted for a shot of whiskey. Things were not going well.

Carl Ingfeldt burst in the front door, almost knocking the cowbell off its hook. Then he stood there, afraid to speak.

"Well?" Bly demanded.

Carl shook his head. "We lost her, boss. That old Skyler mine tunnel was left open. We figure she must've ducked down through there and come out below the roadblock."

"You should've thought of that!"

Carl could only shrug helplessly. "Nobody's gone in there for years. We didn't think she'd think of it."

Bly let it go. He looked over at Bernie. "Well, we figured as much. Bernie just heard from the Stewarts. They've got two horses missing."

"Two horses?"

"She's going to try and go over the mountains and take Benson with her, if she can spring him. We'd better get somebody down there to make sure it doesn't happen."

Andy Schuller burst through the door with another sorry report. "No sign of Cobb."

Bly cursed. "I should have finished him right then and there. Where'd you look?"

"We followed a trail of blood back to his garage, but he isn't there. He's hiding, or he's gone, or—"

"He's not gone. If he's alive he'll try to save Benson."

Carl looked doubtful. "So how's he gonna know where to find him?"

Stupid question, Bly's face said. "Where else would Benson be? Andy, get down there. Take some men with you. If Cobb isn't there, Tracy will be."

Andy hesitated. "You mean . . . Hyde Hall?"

"Go on! You're working for me, remember? You'll be all right."

"But it's getting dark."

"Go on!"

Andy turned toward the door just as it burst open again, and Joe and Elmer entered. "We've found Cobb."

That got everyone's attention.

"He was down in Hyde Hall," said Joe. "We figured he'd try to save Benson."

Bly was impressed. "There! You see?"

"He's dead," Elmer reported. "You killed him after all, Harold. It just took a while."

"But before he died," Joe continued, "he cut Benson loose. Benson's gone."

"And you found fresh hoofprints, am I right?" asked Bly.

Joe and Elmer looked at each other, then at Bly. "Yeah, that's right," Joe said. "How did you know?"

Bly waved his hand dismissively, then said, "So Tracy and Benson are going over the mountains."

Elmer was the first to say it. "We'll never find 'em now."

"They're gone," said Joe.

"They're marked," Bly countered. "They're marked, and the cause of all the trouble in the first place. How about it? You think they'll make it out of the valley?"

Elmer and Joe looked at each other. The others looked at Elmer and Joe.

Elmer finally said, "I think you've got a point there, Harold."

Bly finished his whiskey. "So they'll be keeping the dragon busy for a while. That'll give us time to clean out the town."

Elmer and Joe looked at each other questioningly.

"Who were Cobb's friends?" Bly asked.

Carl spoke up. "He's got that Bible study group that meets at his house."

"Don't the Carlsons go to that?"

"Yeah, them and the Malones," Andy added.

Bly nodded. "The Carlsons rent their house from me. That'll be easy. The Malones . . . well, we'll think of something."

Andy finally asked, "What are you gonna do, Harold?"

Bly's eyes narrowed. "This is the dragon's town, Andy. He doesn't like having these people in his town and he's been trying to get that point across. It's them or us." Bly brought a finger perilously close to the raw area over Andy's heart and said, "It's them or you."

TRACY AND STEVE followed the river about a half-mile above Old Town and found an obscure but navigable trail that crossed the old Hyde River Road and climbed into the hills on the west side. Elk and deer used the trail regularly; that was easy to see. As for other humans on horseback, as far as Steve could tell, no one had come through in quite a while.

"The trail will follow the river for another mile or so," Tracy said in a near whisper, "and then head up Hatchet Creek."

"I hope you realize we're going to be sitting ducks out here in these mountains in the dark."

"Don't worry about it."

Don't worry about it. Right. "We may want to find someplace to conceal ourselves until daylight."

"Steve, don't worry."

Her casual attitude bothered him. "Tracy! All of the dragon attacks we know of took place under cover of darkness. It's very likely the dragon will be out hunting after dark, which means he could very well spot us."

"Maybe he won't be able to distinguish us from the horses."

"We're marked, Tracy! The dragon will know where to find us!"

She only shot a disdainful look back at him and kept riding.

"We're linked to that thing!"

"Quit talking!" she hissed. "You want to give us away?"

She rode on, he followed. She was right. They were too close to the river, to the highway, to other roads and small homesteads to be talking. Tracy seemed to know an effective route to make an escape, and so far it was working. He would have to trust her.

Just as the shadow of evening moved across the narrow valley, the trail came to Hatchet Creek and turned west, winding up the draw into the mountains. They pressed on, often emerging from the cover of the forest into clear meadows and pasturelands, which made Steve nervous. He kept his eyes on the clear sky above them—as if that would be of any use, he thought. The dragon could be disguised as that next clump of trees just ahead, or hiding in that meadow, his iron flanks mimicking the grass and wildflowers so perfectly you'd never know he was right there, watching and waiting.

A low tree limb stretched across the trail, and Steve ducked low in the saddle, lifting the limb over and behind him with his hand.

He thought he smelled something.

Maybe I'm thinking about the dragon too much, he thought. Now I'm starting to smell it. He grabbed the front of his own shirt and pulled it toward his nose, sniffing for the familiar odor of rot and death. No, nothing there. He was relieved. The pain in his chest had even faded a little. Either that or he'd just become used to it.

He sniffed the air carefully. No, he couldn't be sure he really smelled it. He remained on the alert, however, and continually sampled the cool breeze moving down the draw. Somewhere in his mind, an insistent voice kept reminding him to care, to pay attention, to stay on top of it.

They rode up the draw. The sun was still shining on the top of the mountain, but not down here.

The top of what mountain? Steve looked long and carefully at the high, rocky ridge now illuminated by the sun.

Saddlehorse. The Hatchet Creek drainage ran just to the south of it. That thought gave him no comfort at all.

NINETEEN

The Purge

J ACK CARLSON was a young miner, the son of a miner, and he had worked for the Hyde Mining Company until being laid off just six months ago. Now his wife, Amy, had found a job in West Fork and commuted, and he was looking for work in that area. Housing had become a question, though. The rent they were paying for their company-owned, one-bedroom shanty in Hyde River had been raised several times, but it was still cheaper than what they'd have to pay in West Fork, so they stayed. Jack had heard of some stipulation regarding company housing being for employees only, but he'd never heard anything further after his layoff, and the company had been only too happy to receive his rent checks each month.

Even so, when he heard the knock on the door, he had an inkling something was up.

Amy was the one who opened the door to find Doug Ellis and four other grim-faced men standing outside with rifles in their hands and pistols on their hips.

She turned from the door. "Jack, you'd better come over here."

Jack went to the door, and she stood behind him.

Doug spoke for the group. "Jack, the company needs this house vacated. You have to leave. Now!"

"Doug . . . what's going on?" Jack asked, bewildered. "Why all the guns?"

"We want you out of town tonight."

Amy gasped.

Jack couldn't believe it. "Tonight?"

"Load up your stuff, take everything, and get out."

"What's happened? What's wrong?"

"We've always paid our rent," Amy said. "Ask Harold!"

Doug pointed his rifle in Jack's face. "We'll be back in an hour. We'd better see some progress, you got it?"

Jack was incredulous, horrified. "An hour? It's night, it's getting dark . . ."

"An hour!" said Doug as they all turned away.

SAM AND KATHY MALONE and their three children heard a pounding on their door as well. Sam opened the door and saw Andy Schuller and his pool buddies, also armed.

"What is this?" Sam asked.

"The house has been rezoned, and you're in violation," Andy said.

"What, is this some kind of joke?"

Andy gestured with his rifle. "No joke, Sam. You've been using this house for public gatherings, and that's in violation of the zoning ordinance."

"What zoning ordinance?"

Andy didn't have a good answer but tried to sound like he did. "The company's switching the town around. No more Bible studies in the homes, Sam."

"Since when?"

"Since you've been doing 'em."

"Harold Bly thinks he can tell me what I can and cannot do in my own house?" Sam said, irate.

"It might be your house, but this is his town."

"I'll just talk to a lawyer about that!"

"You have to get out tonight, Sam. Right now!"

Sam, like Jack Carlson, couldn't believe this. "What do you mean, get out?"

Having never been good with words, Andy demonstrated instead. He grabbed Sam by the collar, yanked him out the door, and sent him sprawling in the front yard. Before Sam could recover, the men had stormed into the house.

Kathy started screaming.

SOMBER AND SILENT, Steve and Tracy crossed over Hatchet Creek then followed the trail as it began to wind and switch back up the steep slope of the draw. Soon the sound of the creek faded, and all they heard were the steady plodding of the horses' hooves over the narrow, rocky trail, the quiet groaning of the leather saddles, and the song of distant crickets, unseen in the deepening dark.

We're getting close to Saddlehorse, Steve kept thinking. The light was fading fast, and soon they would have no visual advantage. The dragon would have it all. They were still hidden under the forest canopy, but Steve knew that couldn't last. Soon they would break out above the treeline, and their cover would be gone.

He'd been listening and watching, and so far there had been no sign of pursuers. What if they were not being followed? What if some kind of hiding place could be found, someplace where they could conceal themselves until daylight?

"Tracy," he called softly.

He could barely see her in the dark maze of tree trunks and overhanging limbs ahead.

"Tracy," he called again.

Finally she responded, "You know, Steve, when we get out of here we ought to go to Tanner's Lodge on Cold Creek, just the other side of this pass. You wouldn't believe the rooms they have there, all dark-stained woodwork and plush rugs and soft comforters on the beds . . ."

Well. For someone who'd just reminded him to keep quiet she was talking rather loudly. Steve kept his voice low, hoping she'd get the hint. "How much longer do you suppose we'll have the overhead cover?"

"We'll break out of it pretty soon."

He looked up and saw the black silhouettes of the treetops almost touching, obscuring all but a tiny patch of starry sky. The dragon would be unable to penetrate that thick shield without causing a warning commotion. It would be nice to keep that advantage.

"We might want to think twice before we ride out in the open," he said.

No answer. Only the quiet plodding of the horses and the rustling of low branches and brush gently sweeping the horses.

"Tracy?"

"I'm going to take a long shower when we get there," she said dreamily. "I'm going to take a shower and then jump into that big soft bed, and it's going to be sheer heaven. You're going to love it."

Now Steve's voice had some edge on it. "Tracy, did you hear what I said?"

"What did you say?"

"I said we might want to think twice before we ride out in the open."

She sounded truly puzzled. "Why? What are you so worried about?"

Brother, she really was somewhere else. "The dragon, remember? If we break out into the open we'll be perfect targets."

He couldn't see her face clearly, but he heard her sniff a derisive little laugh. "The dragon. I think we're far enough away by now."

"Tracy!" How could she be so flippant? "We're riding directly under Saddlehorse Peak. From all the sightings, it could be the dragon's headquarters. I'd say we're plenty close!"

"He's not going to look for us down here."

"You can't be sure of that."

"Bly and the others haven't come after us. Why should the dragon?"

He regretted having to remind her. "We're marked, Tracy. Remember?"

"Steve!" Her voice was playfully scolding. "Come on, the mark's nothing. Once we're out of here it'll go away."

"So just where does this trail go? How soon before we get over the pass?"

"Steve, you're making a big deal out of this."

Big deal? He thought of Vic Moore, Charlie, and Maggie, not to mention his half-eaten brother.

"I never told you about Doug's little escapades, did I?"

He didn't want to know about them, but he didn't need a spat right now either, so he went along. "No."

"I think he went out with Carlotta several times. I heard they were seen together at Tanner's Lodge."

Steve didn't think he would ever come to Doug's defense, but after that meeting in the tavern . . . "What do you mean, you heard they were seen together?"

"Someone told me."

"I have a feeling that's just gossip, Tracy."

She didn't hear a word he said. "So it's kind of poetic, you know? Kind of fair. He had her at Tanner's Lodge, but now I have you. Maybe we'll even get the room they had."

Under normal circumstances, he would have been disgusted to hear that kind of talk. He would have felt used. Instead, he felt scared.

She kept talking, "I knew there was something special about you—you know what I mean? Doug's plenty of wind and muscle on the outside, but inside he's a wimp; he's as thin as paper. What I needed was a man with a real heart, some real character. Well, I got him. I got him."

He sniffed the air. There it was. That smell. So he hadn't imagined it. "Tracy—"

"Did I ever tell you about Andy Schuller and me? Boy, was that wild! I'll tell you what ruined it: when I told him I was going to be a cop." She laughed, really enjoying the memory. "He thought I was going to say I was pregnant! I don't know which would have been worse, he took it so hard. It was like 'Wow, Tracy's got brains after all!'"

Oh God, no! Don't let it happen to her! "Tracy, are you feeling all right?"

"The whole thing was stupid, though. It never would have worked out with Andy and me. Look at him, still loafing around and shooting pool at Charlie's."

He'd heard enough. "Tracy, hold up a second."

She kept riding, even as he nudged his horse on a little faster to catch up.

"The thing with Jimmy never went anywhere either. Oh. You never met Jimmy. He was hurt in the mines and lost his leg. That was too bad. I really liked him."

The thick overhead canopy was breaking up. The sky above was widening. They were climbing above the treeline, into the open. "Tracy, just where does this trail go?"

She just kept riding and talking, so loud he had no trouble hearing her. "I knew Doug wouldn't like you. He really feels threatened when a guy like you comes along. But you know, I think that's one reason I was attracted to you in the first place."

The trail widened a bit, and Steve saw there was open sky above. Steve nudged his horse. "Tracy! Hold up! Stop!"

She didn't stop.

He came up alongside. There was barely enough room on the precarious trail for two horses. "Tracy, hold on a second. Now stop!"

"I think you're a man like other men wish they were, you know what I mean?"

He reached over and grabbed her reins. "Whoooaaa."

That irritated her. "What are you doing?"

The horses came to a halt. "Hold still now," he said to the horse and to Tracy.

Now he could see her face to face in the light of a rising moon.

Her uniform was so dirty from her crawl through the old tunnel that any other stain would not have been noticeable—until now.

In the cold moonlight, Steve could see a slick, glistening streak of black emerging through the dried mud, crawling down her shirt from her heart to her waist. The stench was unmistakable.

"Tracy.."

She looked down at herself, then brushed the area with her fingertips. The stuff clung to her fingers and as she pulled them away, the slick, putrid substance drew out in drooping black strings. She looked at it in the moonlight, dumbly fascinated.

Shocked, Steve didn't know what to do. "Tracy... are you in pain?"

She smiled, almost playfully. Then she chuckled at him. "No, I'm not in pain. Why should I be?"

He grabbed her shoulder. "Do you see what's happening, Tracy? You're not yourself! You're talking crazy."

"Just crazy for you." She giggled.

He tightened his grip on her shoulder, shook her a little, and tried to get her to look him in the eye, but her attention was wandering everywhere else. "No! Now listen to me! Bly was telling me about it. Something happens when you get this mark. You get used to it, and you don't care anymore!" He wasn't getting through. "Do you hear me?"

When she finally looked at him, she had a silly, vacant expression. "Nothing's gonna happen to me, sweetheart! I've got you now. I win!" Then she gave a drunken laugh as a new burst of black slime crawled down her chest like tar.

"We've got to get you out of here." He tried to take her horse's reins.

"No!" she said with the tone of a pouting child, giving him a playful, scolding slap on his hand. He could feel droplets of black ooze spattering his face. "You have to come with me. I got you fair and square!"

He withdrew his hand, now soiled with slime. "Tracy." He held his hand in front of her face, forcing her to look. "Look at this! Look at yourself!"

She only gazed back at him, dark mischief in her eyes, her head cocked teasingly. "You're mine now. You're all mine. I have you, and I'll never let you go!"

He drew back. That glint in her eyes—he'd seen it before. He'd heard—no, he'd felt—those words before.

In Hyde Hall, only hours ago.

"Tracy—"

"Heyaaah!" she shouted to her horse, kicking its sides. It shot forward up the trail, pounding the ground and kicking up loose rocks. "Catch me if you can!"

She was riding into the open, across a wide meadow with nothing but clear sky overhead.

"Stop! Come back!" Steve shouted.

She was out of her mind, whooping and yipping and kicking that horse.

He kicked his own horse and took off after her. If he could subdue her, get her under cover, maybe he could help her.

But the dragon had to know. This had to be his doing.

Steve kicked his horse again. "Heyahh! Come on, come on!"

The chestnut stallion leapt over the rocks and galloped across the wide meadow. Tracy had a good lead, and Steve knew it would be hard to catch her.

Bait. That was the word Levi Cobb had used. Set up a trap, put out some bait.

Steve looked up the slope, and now he could clearly make out the sawtoothed spine of Saddlehorse Peak, a dark wedge cutting into the night sky. Saddlehorse was more than close—they were riding on its slopes right now.

A trap. He was sure of it.

Tracy's horse whinnied, and Steve looked just in time to see it balking, pawing the ground and circling, refusing to continue up the trail. Just beyond, the trail passed through a gently tapering mound of rocks and small trees.

"Heyahh!" Steve kicked the stallion in deadly desperation, and it shot forward. "Tracy! TRACY, GET AWAY FROM THERE!"

She kept struggling with her horse, trying to get it headed up the trail. He was catching up, getting closer, yelling at the top of his lungs.

Finally she heard him and stopped yanking at her horse's reins.

Steve reined in his horse. Now it too was getting nervous, skittish. "Tracy!" He gestured wildly. "Get back here!"

Her horse was still fighting against her. "No! You come with me!"

How could he get through to her? "Tracy, the dragon! It's a trap!"

She shouted back at him in anger, "There isn't any dragon! Now come on!"

No, his instincts screamed, don't go one step farther.

He stayed where he was and tried coaxing her more gently. "Tracy, come on now. I love you. Just come back with me."

"I don't want to go back! I want out of this valley, with you."

He kept coaxing her. "We'll find a way. Just come this way!"

"You come with me," she begged even as her horse started toward him on its own. "If you really love me."

I can't. He knew it. His instincts, his heart, screamed it.

His horse spooked, leaping backward, bucking. He held on for all he was worth.

The meadow between him and Tracy was moving, bulging, heaving. A monstrous, tapered shaft appeared, flexing like an eel

Tracy's horse whinnied and reared up on its hind legs.

The shaft whipped violently, catching her horse under the rib cage and swatting it over on its back. Tracy disappeared in the tall meadow grass as the horse rolled, kicking and snorting, and finally righted itself. In utter panic, it ran straight downhill and disappeared into the trees.

"TRACY!" Steve grabbed the shotgun and leapt from his horse, chambering a round.

Tracy struggled to her feet, stunned and disoriented. The mound of rock was immediately behind her, and now it, too, was starting to move. "Steve . "

Steve was aiming the shotgun. "Get down!" Where could he shoot? What part of the dragon was where?

She remained standing, stunned and confused. The dragon's tail rose from the grass and swatted her backward. She fell against the rocks, and the rocks came alive with waves and ripples of red and purple light.

Suddenly Steve could see a change in her eyes, in her whole countenance. The stupor was gone. She understood, and with the awakening came the unspeakable terror of a helpless soul only inches from death. "Steve . . ." She tried to run, but as Steve watched in horror, a tree faded into three elongated, clawed fingers. The silver claws were blurred streaks as they struck her in the rib cage, spinning her, throwing her sideways to the ground.

"No!" Steve felt her pain as he saw it happen. He dashed forward, weaving from side to side, trying to see the beast's outline.

No need. The mound of rocks rippled, wavered, then faded to glimmering silver scales. Expansive wings unfurled like banners against the sky. The golden eyes, silver horns, and gnarled brow rose high above the meadow on a tree-sized neck.

Steve had his shot and took it, centering on the dragon's snout. The creature lurched as it was hit, and the shock rippled down the neck scales like bolts of electricity.

From somewhere, Tracy screamed his name, and then he saw her just below the dragon's raised neck. She was crawling toward him, her shirt hanging from her ribs in bloody shreds. "Run, Steve! Run, get out of here!"

He slammed in another round and aimed for the dragon's head, hoping for the eyes.

Oof! He didn't see the tip of the tail until it struck him across the chest, knocking him several feet backward and into the brush. He quickly got back on his feet.

Tracy was still crawling, haltingly pulling herself through the grass with one good arm, trying to get to her feet, her frightened eyes searching for Steve but not finding him.

The huge, three-fingered hand reached down, and the claws

hooked under her body and flipped her several feet into the air. She landed in the grass on her back. The clawed hands reached again.

Steve aimed the shotgun for those wicked, golden eyes.

The dragon raised its bony fingers in front of its face.

The beast held Tracy Ellis. She was limp and dying, looking down at Steve with pleading in her eyes. He felt he was seeing her across hundreds of miles.

The dragon peered around Tracy with one eye, watching for Steve's next move. Steve moved sideways, looking for a shot. The dragon kept Tracy between them, holding her up like a shield.

Tracy's mouth contorted as she tried to speak, but her punctured lungs only produced a trickle of blood from the corner of her mouth. Blood and black fluid ran down over the scaled hand that held her.

The dragon looked at Steve with both eyes, then at the woman in its grasp.

In one eternal instant, the jaws closed over Tracy Ellis's head and chest, and the teeth knifed through her body as if slicing the air, meshing together with a metallic grind.

Steve went numb. In shock, he collapsed and fell backward to the ground but didn't know it, didn't feel it. His mind could not accept the unspeakable, unfathomable horror of what he was seeing.

The dragon didn't chew. It just swallowed the first bite, then the second, then the last, and never took its eyes off him.

A sliver of sense returned to Steve only when Tracy was totally gone and the scales started shifting to the color of the night sky.

"No . . ." Steve's voice was hoarse, his throat like tight, dry leather. "No, you don't." It wasn't anger that began to fill him, but raw killing instinct. "No, you don't!"

He could still make out the shape of the torso, a bulge in the starry tapestry behind it. He fired, and the vague shape before him flashed like fireworks.

The golden eyes appeared to send a familiar message in their malicious glint: You're mine now; I'll never let you go.

Then the head, the wings, and the serpentine, scaled body all blended with the meadow, the trees, the sky. The dragon had full advantage.

Too shocked and horrified to think, Steve turned and ran for his horse.

Wind from the beating of huge wings rippled the grass; the sky overhead wrinkled and wavered. Steve hit the ground as the beast passed over, then he looked up through the grass just in time to see his horse jerk skyward like a limp puppet, shake violently from side to side, and drop to earth again, the head clipped off at the shoulders.

Steve rolled, then crawled, then scrambled for the trees farther down the hill like a small animal being chased by a hawk. He had no strategy now, no tactics, no plan; he was only running for his life. He could hear the wings beating behind him and see the meadow grass whipping in the wind as he leapt and sprinted through the brush and grass, wild with terror and adrenaline.

The trees, the trees, the trees! He ran for their shelter. He dove under their cover and tumbled to the ground among the trunks. High above, the forest canopy groaned and snapped from a sudden impact. He got to his feet and dove through the brush and brambles, slashing and fighting his way down the hill. Behind him, limbs snapped like gunshots, trees groaned and swayed, needles and branches floated and clattered to the ground.

It was coming after him, fighting its way into the trees.

JACK AND AMY CARLSON weren't able to carry out their eviction quickly enough to suit Doug Ellis. Jack had tried to stop Doug's gang but ended up on the ground in front of the house, his jaw cracked, his mouth bleeding, and Amy holding him in terror as Doug and his men ransacked the little house, throwing furniture, clothing, and every precious possession out the front door. A dresser tumbled end for end on the rocky ground, clothing from the closet flew out the bedroom window, and the bathroom mirror shattered in the yard. The big miners, loggers, and truckers took to it with wild abandon, whooping, hollering, pillaging.

Two doors up the street, the Malones were getting the same treatment. Kathy Malone was the first to notice the Carlsons fallen on their front lawn and came running.

"What is it?" Amy pleaded. "What's happening?"

"I don't know," Kathy said. "Sam's run up the street to call Pastor Woods. I think we'd better get out of here."

EVERY TIME Reverend Ron Woods put the phone down, it rang again. Another parishioner was calling, and every voice was frightened, desperate. "What's happening? They say I have to leave!" "They broke all my mother's china!" "Tim's bleeding and he can't walk!" "The kids are scared to death, and so am I!" "They're in my house right now!"

"Get out of town," he told them all. "Don't even think about what to take with you. Just get out, now!"

Some argued with him, but he never softened his message, for he saw no better or safer course of action. It had finally happened: Moral restraint had finally collapsed like a broken dam. There was no moral code to guide the town, no reasoning to give it light. There was only Harold Bly, unleashed and empowered to carry out in action all he had become in spirit. This you could not reason with; you could only flee before it.

Woods's wife Susan clutched at his arm. She was terrified. "Maybe we'd better get out of here, too."

"There's no need," he replied.

"What do you mean there's no need?" she asked, incredulous. "The town's going crazy!"

Woods didn't have time to answer. There was a pounding at the door and voices outside.

She was ready to panic and run. "Ron, what'll we do?"

He reached out and took her in his arms. "Don't worry. It'll be all right. Just wait here."

He went to the front door and swung it open. Joe Staggart, Elmer McCoy, and five other men stood outside with sidearms, rifles, and flashlights.

Elmer, billed cap still straight and level on his head and beer ponch in full bloom, was the spokesman. "Reverend Woods, you probably know why we're here."

Woods didn't say a word. He simply looked from man to man as he unbuttoned his shirt and spread it open to reveal the blackening welt over his heart.

They stared at it, then exchanged questioning looks with one another. A few rifle barrels wilted toward the ground.

Elmer finally found his voice. "Uh, we just stopped by to let you know—you'd best stay inside tonight. There's trouble in the streets."

"I'll stay out of your way," he said.

"We'd appreciate that, Reverend."

They moved on.

STEVE RAN, thrashed and beat his way down the mountain until he reached a creek. This must be Hatchet Creek, he thought, or a tributary. There was a debris jam just downstream. Sticks, dead saplings, and debris, perhaps the work of beavers, had come up against some fallen trees and created a tangled mass over the creek. By now, his presence of mind had returned enough for him to consider a hiding place. He walked into the water, slid belly-down, and headed for the debris, not splashing, only sliding, crawling, and letting the current carry him through the icy water.

Normally he would have whooped and hollered at the first shocking contact with the icy cold water. Tonight his only thought was concealment. He could hide from sight under that debris; the downslope air currents would carry his scent into the valley and away from the dragon; the cold of the creek might obscure the heat of his body in case the dragon could sense that; and the sound of the creek might cover up his breathing.

He dug his way into the tangle as the sticks poked and jabbed at him and several snapped in protest. Finally he got all the way under, hoping he could stay awhile and not be evicted by an angry beaver. He found a few sodden logs and crawled on top of them, getting at least his upper torso clear of the water. It was a compromise, a half-choice between being eaten by the dragon or risking hypothermia.

He sat very still, trying to calm himself, trying to listen. He was still alive. Maybe, just maybe, he could stay that way if he only kept his head.

So where was the dragon? What had happened? The dragon had followed him through the forest for a time, but at some moment it had stopped the pursuit, and he wasn't sure why. He doubted the forest had stopped it. True, the trees and undergrowth were thick and tangled—he'd had trouble getting through it himself—but he'd seen how the dragon's lithe, serpentine body could go just about anywhere and hardly leave any sign it had been there. Steve could think of two possibilities: either the dragon had taken to the air for some aerial reconnaissance or . . .

Or it was only a few yards away, waiting for the right moment. It could tear away this little tangle of sticks with one swipe of those claws . . .

Calm down, Steve, calm down. He had to put aside the horrible images, the stark terror, the sight of Tracy being eaten alive—

No, no, he could never forget that. He would see it before his eyes forever. "Tracy." He couldn't help whimpering there in the cold and dark. "Oh, my God—no—"

The memory of her, the horrible images of her death, now became his enemy. The more he replayed what had happened, the more he wanted to die, just crawl out in the open and get the whole thing over with.

He shook his head, then he reached into the river and splashed water in his face. Wake up, Steve! You have to live! You have to fight and prevail! He had to stop thinking of Tracy, or he would most assuredly die of despair. He couldn't let that happen. He had to think.

Any weapons? Any resources? Think! The shotgun was gone; he had no recollection of dropping it. All he remembered was running.

What if—he shuddered—the dragon had flown off to digest his meal?

Maybe I'm out of trouble for a while . . .

He caught himself. No. No cop-outs, Benson. No wishful thinking. Care! Remember what Levi said, Care! He had to assume the dragon was still hunting him, that the danger was not over. He'd seen the pattern: Right before Charlie died, Charlie didn't care anymore. Maggie had been singing and carefree; so had Vic Moore. In the tavern, Harold Bly and the others were all marked, but all they did was sit there drinking beer and laughing about it. None of them cared, either.

It was that way with Tracy, too. She hadn't cared what she said or did . . . until it was too late.

So you'd better care, Steve. You'd better care.

He felt the wound over his heart. He couldn't see it in the dark, but it felt about the same: raw to the touch, throbbing at times, burning at other times. Sometimes he didn't feel it at all.

I don't feel it when I don't care, he thought.

Tracy's had been dripping all over her, and she hadn't felt a thing.

So maybe Levi was right. Again. Maybe this mark was a matter of the heart. Levi had described this condition as being "hooked," and that concept seemed to match what Steve had observed. Somehow—okay, maybe it was a spiritual matter—the victim became linked with the dragon just as a trout became linked with the fisherman. In the case of the fish, the hook became set in the fish's mouth; in the case of the human, the hook, whatever it was, became set in the heart—the soul, the spirit, whatever—causing a festering sore. That being the case, you could fight like a fish and struggle all you wanted, but there really was no escape. You either killed the dragon, or he eventually reeled you in and you became his supper.

Unless, of course, you could get the hook out of your heart.

And according to Levi, who believed the dragon was sin, the solution was to get right with God. Find Jesus.

So—what now?

Well, whether or not the dragon's connection was spiritual or biochemical or whatever it was, this struggle was going to have some pretty weird rules. Building or finding a fortress to fend the dragon off wouldn't work, and neither would escaping the area. Either way, the hook being set, all the dragon had to do was wait until Steve didn't care anymore.

And there it was again, an incessant reminder: Care.

He struck himself in the chest, and the wound lashed back at him with a wave of fresh pain.

"Good," he said. "You just keep hurting. Don't let me forget about you."

He had to destroy the dragon; that was clear. But he would have to do it before he no longer cared to do it. Strategy. He had to build a strategy.

If he could make it back toward the mines he'd investigated yesterday—it seemed so long ago!—perhaps he could locate the cavern Jules Cryor had mentioned, the one with the tunnels and passages that went on for miles.

An ideal home for a dragon, one would think.

He had a good idea where the cavern wasn't, which would narrow his search. The last place the dragon would look for him would be in its own lair—or so he hoped. The last thing that old lizard would be expecting was a victim on the offense.

That stoked Steve's fires. Sure. Why be only the hunted? I'll do some hunting myself!

He breathed one more little prayer—boy, it could get to be a habit—and carefully wriggled out from under the debris. He looked up at the ceiling of stars stretched between the mountain ridges. The stars were clear and bright, seeming so much closer in the clean mountain air. He looked for the Big Dipper, and from there found the North Star. From that he verified the most direct route to the summit of Saddlehorse.

But . . . hey, what was this?

Now here was luck. Over on the west side of the starry canopy, the stars were jiggling to one side in sequence as if an unseen object were giving each a little nudge as it passed by. Steve kept watching, training his eyes as the phenomenon continued. He could imagine the sky as a star-patterned blanket with a small animal crawling under it, creating a hump that moved along under the stars, making them rise and then subside. Incredible!

Soon he was able to discern the dragon's flying shape, like a huge circling buzzard, high above the draw, gliding, circling, following the ridge on one side and then the ridge on the other.

Reconnaissance, no doubt. Wide sweeps.

He had to smile. That thing had lost him and didn't know his intentions.

Well! I'm one up on him! Now if I can just keep it that way.

DOUG ELLIS strode over to Elmer McCoy's big flatbed truck and yanked the driver's door open; Kyle Figgin, passionately embracing Carlotta Nelson, almost fell out. "What do you think you're doing? You're supposed to be watching this roadblock!"

Kyle grabbed the steering wheel to steady himself. "I'm watching it!"

"Get down out of there, both of you!"

Kyle clambered down from the cab under Doug's glaring eye. Carlotta followed.

Doug shook his head and pointed at Kyle's chest. "Man, look at you!"

Kyle glanced down and saw the slick, black stain on the front of his shirt. He immediately turned to Carlotta. "Look what you did to me!"

She touched the front of her blouse, now stained black, and the slime came off on her fingers. Now it was her turn to be outraged. "Look what you did to me!"

"I didn't do it!"

"You did too!"

Doug broke in and grabbed Kyle's arm. "Come on. We've got to move this roadblock. Some people are getting out of here."

Kyle jerked his arm away. "Don't you push me around!"

"Then get moving!"

"I'll move when I feel like it!"

Doug grabbed him again and helped him move whether he felt like it or not. Kyle came back swinging. Doug only had to swing once.

Now Kyle glared up at him from the ground. "You're dead meat, Ellis!"

"You smell like dead meat!" Doug retorted.

Kyle immediately glared at Carlotta, blame in his eyes

"Don't look at me!" she yelled.

Doug yanked Kyle to his feet. "Come on. You move the bus. I'll move the truck."

MRS. DORNING, the widow on the south end of town, hardly had time to mourn her broken birdbath and painted animals before Carl Ingfeldt and four other men showed up at her door.

"What is it?" she asked, standing at her door in her bathrobe.

Carl managed to sound informed. "Ma'am, the company has determined your home to be in violation of the new, retroactive setback laws. You'll have to vacate the premises so we can tear it down."

UP THE STREET, Andy Schuller and his buddies were going through Levi Cobb's garage and also his apartment upstairs, looking for anything they could salvage before somebody else did. Levi's tools vanished quickly enough. A binder left on the workbench drew little interest. It was tossed into a big waste can in the search for more useful items.

IN THE TAVERN, Harold Bly had scribbled out a list of names, then added more names as they came to mind.

"Dorning's packing," Bernie reported.

He crossed her name off. "All right, now. Who else? Who else? What about the Nelsons?"

"Andy was wondering what excuse to use."

"He doesn't need an excuse!" Bly said angrily. "I own that house, and I want them out! Simple enough!"

"Okay, okay."

"Anybody else?"

Paul offered, "I think the Hazeletts ought to go."

Bly drew a blank. "Hazeletts, Hazeletts . . . Who are they?"

"New family. They make jewelry and polish rocks, stuff like that."

Bly looked at Paul questioningly, waiting for more information.

"Uh—their business card has a little fish symbol on it," Paul said.

Bly nodded, writing down their name. "If they aren't trouble now, they will be. Take them out."

Paul went out to pass the word.

BELOW SADDLEHORSE, along a secluded stretch of the Hyde River, a breeze kicked up. It bent the tall grass along the riverbank and made the birch leaves tremble; it wrinkled the surface of the placid water with a thousand little ridges.

Then it ceased, and there was calm again.

On a gravel spit in the middle of the river, the dragon crouched, its belly, neck, and tail resting on the rocks, its weight so distributed and its touch so light it would not leave behind a discernible mark. It folded its wings, then relaxed its scales. The camouflage flickered out, and it became fully visible, a long, serpentine lizard stretched out flat on the sand and stone in the dim starlight.

It lay still, licking the air with slow, deliberate strokes of its tongue, quietly sniffing at the cool currents of air moving down the slopes and down the river valley. The golden eyes studied the surrounding mountain slopes, down one side and then up the far-reaching flanks of Saddlehorse.

Then the dragon settled into the gravel and became as gravel.

It could no longer feel the soiled spirit of its quarry, so it waited, continually listening, sampling for scents, listening for sounds, watching with eyes that now had the dull brown look of boulders.

MAYBE THERE really was a God, Steve thought. If there was, He was getting a prayer of thanks from Steve Benson right now.

All the way up the slopes of Saddlehorse, Steve had tried to move as the dragon would move, staying close to the ground and carefully sneaking through the forest. Apparently it had worked, for he reached the south crest of the mountain alive and, as far as he knew, undetected. He'd gotten his bearings from his previous exploration and, figuring the dragon would never lure him to its actual home, pushed farther in the opposite direction from that first cave, down and around the south slope, around the base of a cliff—and straight to pay dirt.

As he dropped to his belly in the meadow grass among the rocks, a peculiar sense of relief trickled through the terror. At last, something had gone right.

The opening was only a few yards above him, hidden by shadows, rock outcroppings and fallen boulders. It was small—too small to be the cavern's main entrance, but the smell drifting down the slope was as good as a signpost.

He'd found the dragon's lair.

TWENTY

The Dragon's Lair

STEVE TRIED to act like the dragon again as he moved stealthily up the slope, through the meadow grass and the scattered rock outcroppings toward the ominous little portal in the rock. He paused at the threshold to gather any information his nose and ears might bring him. There was no sound, but he could smell the distinct odor of death drifting up from the black depths. His hand went to the left breast pocket of his shirt. He unbuttoned the flap and dug out his trusty disposable lighter, his tool for lighting campfires and just about the only piece of camping gear he still had with him. Maybe this was God again; he didn't know. He had no food, no firearms, no coat, not even a compass, but he still had his lighter!

He extended his arm inside the opening before flicking the lighter and took his first look down a jagged, angular passage that dropped gradually and then turned a corner about ten feet down. This was obviously not the main entrance to the cavern, for it was too small, just a breach in the rock, or perhaps an old lava vent. It was big enough to accommodate him, however, so he slipped inside.

The lighter's fuel supply was limited, so he flicked the lighter intermittently, just enough to give him an idea of what was below, then groped his way down, feeling with hands, feet, and backside. Flick, see, crawl. Flick, see, crawl.

The tunnel steepened. He extended his feet and arms to the sides of the walls to hold himself in place and not slip downward.

He progressed a few more feet. The air was cool and dank now. His clothing, wet from the creek and most recently from sweat, was beginning to chill him. He was breathing hard, either from the exertion or from sheer anxiety. He couldn't avoid the sensation that he was going down the dragon's throat.

With both hands and his left foot anchored, he reached down with his right foot. He could not find a foothold.

Flick. He could see his foot below him in the yellow light, but nothing beyond it. He moved the lighter closer, bending almost double in the tunnel to see what was below.

The shaft was nearly vertical from this point downward, like a crooked chimney. He would have to inch his way down, foothold by foothold, spanning the shaft with his arms and legs.

He groped about in empty space with his right foot until it finally came to rest on a one-inch lip of rock. Then with his left foot he located another lip. He lowered his body down, inch by precious inch, pushing against the opposite wall with his arms to keep his back tight against the rocks.

Flick. A few more inches, a few more footholds. Sometimes he had to span the shaft with a foot on either side; sometimes he planted his behind on an available ledge, holding himself there with his feet planted against the opposite wall.

The shaft stretched into blackness above him now, curling and zigzagging out of sight. He'd descended about forty feet—not far for an elevator or a flight of stairs, but more than far enough under the circumstances, Steve thought. When he found a good combination of foothold on one side and ledge for his fanny on the other, he stopped to rest, feel, and listen.

The smell of death was stronger now; the air felt thick, heavy, and unmoving. He could sense an open expanse below him. Perhaps the shaft opened into a room.

Flick. He looked down past his feet.

Something was looking up at him.

He thought he'd been scared so often that terror had become a given, but this sight made him jump anyway, and he almost dropped the lighter. He stiffened his legs, clamping himself in the narrow passage, then sat there in total darkness again, shaking, heart racing, the lighter clenched in his fist.

What he had seen was a human skull.

After a minute or two, he calmed down enough to have another look. Flicking on the lighter, he was able to confirm it was a human skull, about ten feet below him, jaw slack so the face seemed to be laughing. It lay among other bones, scattered about on the cave floor like driftwood on a beach.

Steve continued his downward trek. The shaft was opening up, curving sideways into a larger room. Now some fallen rocks provided footing, and Steve stepped carefully from one down to the next, gaining a wider perspective of the cave floor the lower he went.

He could see that skull, still laughing . . .

Then he could see another just a few feet away, on its side with no jawbone . . .

Steve's feet finally came to rest on the sandy floor. He held the lighter above his head and kept the flame burning.

He'd landed in hell.

As far as the feeble flame could cast its light, he saw human bones and skulls. They littered the rock shelves, the ledges, the crevices. They lay among the broken stones, they clustered in the recesses and hollows, they piled layer upon layer upon the floor. Most were dry, aged, fading to the color of the sand. But some were fresh and white, picked clean but for a few blackening shreds of sinew and tendon.

Like trophies. A century of them.

Steve released the little lever, and the lighter went out. He welcomed the darkness. It veiled, at least for a moment, the horror stretched out before him. He felt he could hide in it, as a child hides under his bed covers, and for a long moment he stayed right there, regrouping, trying to comprehend the scene.

So this is where they end up, he thought. Charlie's here someplace. And Maggie. And Vic.

And Cliff.

Their final destination.

An eerie vision broke into his mind as he stood there in the dark. He could imagine Charlie's Tavern and Mercantile in Hyde River, full of townspeople. Harold Bly was there in his usual spot, Andy and his buddies were shooting pool, some teens were hammering away at the video games, Bernie was hustling the steaks, Melinda was taking orders, Paul was watching the television over the bar . . .

Then they were skeletons. Even while they ate the food, drank the beer, played the games, laughed it up, and talked about anything and everything, they were dead. Nothing but bones.

Soon they would be in this place. They would be like these people. Then again, weren't they like these people even now? Dead while they lived? What was the difference, other than time?

For the people now lying at Steve's feet, the time had run out.

For the people of Hyde River, who could say? Maybe today, maybe tomorrow . . .

But all were bound for the same end: dry bones and dragon manure.

Steve felt a particular chill. Before the night was over, Tracy would be here. In time, so would he.

He could hear the murmur of the bones: As you are, we once were; as we are, you soon will be.

His hand went to his heart. The welt had widened and was raw to the touch. It was his ticket to this place.

I'm standing in hell. I'm seeing my future, and it's not that different from my present. I'm doomed even as I live, which means there's no point to living, so why live, why struggle, why prolong my existence?

He clamped his hands around his head, afraid his mind would vaporize through his skull. Get a grip, Steve! Come on! Control!

There had to be a way out of here—in terms of destiny and in immediate terms. He had to remind himself, rather forcefully, that he was here because he was on the offense, looking for a way, any way, to turn this thing around. He had to press on.

He built up his determination, braced himself, and then flicked the lighter. "Come on, Benson, let's go," he told himself.

He set out, walking upon the bones because there was no other surface to walk upon. Each step he took was unsure. The bones twisted, rolled, and crunched under his feet. Several times he thought he would lose his balance and go down. To his right, the bones were spread evenly like bedding on a wide ledge. The dragon's bed, he figured. It made sense. That lizard was death; it loved death; therefore, it slept with death.

The light began to reach the far wall of the room, and he thought he could make out a vast, dark passage beyond that. Putting one foot carefully in front of the other, he headed that direction.

He saw a glint of metal and held the flame lower. A gold necklace. He began to spot other such relics of the past: watches, jewelry, buttons, gold coins, even an old derringer.

Information: The dragon digested any flesh, muscle, and probably some clothing. He was unable to digest bones and metallic objects, which he apparently regurgitated in this room.

That meant he'd be back to this spot before long with one more skeleton to unload. It could have been two.

Don't dwell on it! Just keep moving!

Steve tried to hurry. He had to know where the cavern went, where the entrance was. He was almost across the room now. He could see a sizable tunnel leading up and out.

Another metallic glint caught his eye.

Eyeglasses. He stooped to pick them up and recognized the same, thick lenses, the cockeyed misalignment of the temples. These glasses had belonged to Charlie Mack.

He looked around the area, hoping he would not see a skull he could recognize. He didn't, and he was glad, but he knew Charlie's bones had to be here among the others.

There were other items around: belt buckles, earrings . . .

And an old hat. It was weathered, with a wide, drooping brim. He recognized it. He picked it up and examined it closely. There was no doubt.

The hat had belonged to Jules Cryor.

Steve thought he could hold steady, but his strength failed him; he teetered, and then fell among the bones, the hat in his hand. The lighter went out, and the darkness closed in around him.

Live and let live, Cryor had said. Leave the dragon alone and he'll leave you alone. I never bother him so he never bothers me. It sounded like a nice philosophy, but now Cryor was here with the others.

If there was a rational way to process all this, he could not find it. The pragmatic mind of the university professor refused to function down here. He wasn't just close to death, he was surrounded by it, immersed in it, and as loudly as his heart cried for an answer, his mind could not provide one. He was in hell. There was no other word for it.

"Oh, Lord," he prayed, "there's got to be a way out of here." His eyes were burning with tears. "You can't let this happen!"

He flicked the lighter and saw that he wasn't far from the tunnel. It just might be his way out of there.

He tossed Jules Cryor's hat back among the bones, got his bearings, and started out again, taking one teetering step after another, from bone to bone. Finally, he stepped from bones to soft sand, the actual floor of the cavern. He was to the other side of the "trophy room" and could see into the far tunnel. The dragon's footprints and the groove left by its dragging tail were evident. He should be able to follow them to the main entrance. It would be a gradual climb, with plenty of headroom, a welcome change.

With his left hand holding the lighter high and his right hand feeling along the wall, he resumed his intermittent use of the lighter, first seeing, then feeling his way along the tunnel.

I must have some kind of advantage, he thought. After all, I'm still alive. The dragon hasn't found me yet. He was out looking for me—I saw him—but he hasn't found me.

He flicked the lighter. Another tunnel, big enough for a dragon, branched off to the right, heading down into the mountain. But Steve decided to continue following the main tunnel. He could feel air moving down through it. He might not be too far from the entrance.

Just ahead, the tunnel narrowed, and Steve noticed the century-old marks of picks and drills.

It was a typical mine tunnel, only big enough for miners and ore cars. Steve took a moment to note the tunnel's dimensions against his memory of the dragon's size. The dragon might be able to slither through, but turning around would be next to impossible.

He could feel cool fresh air moving down the tunnel from the outside, and he quickened his pace.

Another four hundred feet and he was looking at the stars again. After the darkness of the cavern, the bright, almost-full moon just rising was as good as daylight. After the cold, heavy, stench-laden air of the cavern, the crisp mountain air was nearly intoxicating. After being in the lair of death itself, he had never felt so alive.

I came through! I made it!

He looked behind him. Even from this short distance away, the cavern/mine entrance was hard to see. The cliff walls and surrounding rocks were laid out in sharp bends directly in front of it, forming an effective blind. You'd have to be right in front of it to know it was there.

But now where was he? Those mountain peaks across the valley were familiar. As a matter of fact . . .

He took off across the mountain face, leaping from rock to rock, feeling a remarkable new surge of energy. He could see, he could breathe, he could climb and jump. He was alive!

He leapt from the rocks to a field of green meadow, then dashed across the expanse, exhilarated because he could do so. He even laughed. He was back from the grave, back from hell, free to run.

I beat him! I was right there, right in his lair and he didn't know it! He's away, he's after someone else. Sure. Why not Harold Bly, or that Doug character? There are plenty of people in that town who deserve it more than I do. Maybe Tracy was right: maybe the mark will fade if I only get away from here. He looked down to check.

There was a black stain on his shirt. He touched it, and the black slime came off on his fingers. There was no pain.

The moonlight went out. A shadow passed over him like a cloud, and he dropped to the ground, rolling to a frantic stop then lying perfectly still in the grass as a gust of wind swept over the meadow. Scanning the sky, he could discern the stars wiggling in succession over the crest of Saddlehorse.

No, I'm not out of the woods. I'm still in trouble, but I let myself forget. Just like Tracy.

The wound began to ache again and strangely, he felt relieved.

A long, black shadow swept across the face of the mountain. The dragon was circling, searching. It had come so close it had to have seen him.

With a heart stained black and the memory of a sea of bones still fresh in his mind, Steve found it all too easy to believe that monster was tethered to his soul.

He also knew he didn't have much time.

JEFF NELSON, a good miner the company should have kept, knew what was happening. He'd heard the yelling out in the streets, he'd made some calls, he'd loaded his guns, and he was ready to protect his home and his family. Andy Schuller didn't even have to bang on his door before Jeff threw it open and aimed his hunting rifle right in Andy's face. "Back up, Andy!" Andy had five armed men behind him, and Jeff hesitated. "I said back up!"

"Jeff," Andy started to say, "listen—"

A gunshot made them all duck.

The shot had come from Abel Hoffmeier, one of Andy's group, a stubble-faced idler who had borrowed the .45 he held in his hand. Abel was wide-eyed at what he'd just done, but then he started to grin.

Jeff had flinched with the rest of them and didn't realize he'd been shot before his legs buckled under him and he slid down the doorframe to the landing, still clinging to his rifle. The slug that had torn through his heart had left a bloody groove in the doorjamb behind him. His wife Becky started to scream.

Andy and his mob all looked at Abel, then at Jeff, each man sorting out the justice of it.

John Tyler, a trucker, offered a verdict. "He was gonna kill you, Andy."

Andy recovered from his shock, bolstered himself, and ordered, "Okay, boys, clear it out."

With a whoop, they stormed into the house as Becky screamed for mercy and the four children started crying.

DOUG AND KYLE had moved the roadblock, and they watched as the Carlsons and Malones drove through with whatever they could carry in two pickups and a car. They'd left quite a bit behind, hoping to come back for it when it was safe to do so.

"Doug!" yelled Bruce Dilly, a miner on welfare who preferred not to mine. "What about all that stuff they left behind?"

"What about it?"

"Well, are they coming back for it?"

Doug gave him a knowing look. "You see something you want, help yourself."

There was just a moment's hesitation. "What about Harold?"

"What about him?"

Bruce and several friends thought that over, arrived at a conclusion as a body, and with whoops and hollers raced each other to get there first.

STEVE HAD to marvel. "Jules Cryor never knew how close he was."

Steve had gotten his hunch from the mountain peaks across the valley and followed that hunch across the meadow, over a rock outcropping, and to the brink of a cliff where he now lay prone in a niche, looking down at the roof of Jules Cryor's cabin, only two hundred feet below him and not more than half a mile from the dragon's lair. The cabin appeared to be intact and untouched. Cryor must have met his fate while out on the mountainside, perhaps even lured there by the dragon itself.

Steve had no resources, no weapons, no food. He was alone in the dark on the side of a bare mountain, courting the risk of exposure. He had a tenacious beast hunting him down, taking advantage of some intangible—maybe spiritual—link with him. His friend from the sheriff's office had been eaten before his eyes. The friend he recognized too late had been shot dead.

With no other resources, Steve found that praying to God was taking on great importance.

"Now, Lord, You've helped me so far . . ."

Maybe God had. It seemed reasonable that the dragon would have located and killed him by now, Steve thought, and yet, as long as he kept calling on God, the dragon couldn't seem to get a fix on him. With the acknowledgment of God came a sense that somehow the order of things could be reversed, that destiny could be changed. For the first time, Steve felt a sense of hope.

Hope made fighting for his life worthwhile. It made formulating a plan worthwhile. It made climbing down to Jules Cryor's cabin to carry out that plan worthwhile.

With careful, stealthy moves, Steve started working his way down to the cabin, keeping his eyes open, watching the sky and surrounding terrain, monitoring the pain in and over his heart.

SHERIFF COLLINS's wife Francie was worried enough when the phone rang. Hearing the official-sounding voice on the other end didn't make her feel any better.

"Mrs. Collins?"

"Yes."

"Mrs. Collins, this is Lieutenant Barnard with the State Patrol, Oak Springs Precinct. May I speak with Sheriff Collins?"

Mrs. Collins made no effort to hide her concern. "He's not here, Lieutenant. I don't know where he is, and I'm worried about him."

"You have no idea where he is?"

"No. He should have been home two hours ago. He hasn't called. I called the station but the calls are all forwarded—"

"So you talked to the dispatcher?"

"I didn't want to bother the dispatcher. Lester says that number's only for emergencies."

"Okay. Well, listen, we'll see if we can track him down for you."

"Thank you," Francie said. "And will you hurry, please?"

"Will do. Thank you, Mrs. Collins."

Barnard hung up and looked across his desk at Evelyn Benson. "Now do you believe me?" she asked.

At least he was ready to hear more.

STEVE CAREFULLY eyed the distance across the deep crevasse and then jumped it, landing on a narrow ledge. Success.

Well, one step at a time, he told himself.

He hurried along, mentally talking to God. "I think You understand. I mean, it was a mutual thing. She wanted me, I wanted her . . ."

He was carrying a box of necessities he'd gathered from Jules Cryor's cabin, wrapped up in a dark flannel shirt to keep the white box from standing out in the moonlight. Carefully, he stole from rock to bush to niche to rock, then to a lone, struggling pine, making his way back to the dragon's cavern, constantly checking the sky and surrounding terrain for any telltale movement. And all the while he was moving, he kept talking to God.

But talking to God presented one problem: He could only talk to God for so long before he had to be honest, not only with God but with himself. In some areas, that was a new and difficult experience. "Okay, I'm not saying it was a smart thing to do."

He reached the meadow just below the cavern entrance, hid among a cluster of small pines, and studied the sky again, then the surrounding terrain. "Lord, if he's there, help me to see him."

Steve didn't intend for that prayer to have a double meaning, but God answered it that way. He didn't see the dragon anywhere but did hear a little voice in his mind saying, Look inside, look inside.

Sounded like Levi. Same sermon. Same pointing finger.

Maybe he was overdoing the prayer stuff, Steve thought. He shifted his focus toward the rock formations that hid the cavern entrance, then with one mad dash he crossed the meadow and ducked behind the rocks.

"LEGGO, I saw it first!"

"Get real! You don't even play!"

Bruce Dilly and Clayton Gentry had both come upon a fine Martin steel-string guitar while ransacking Jeff Nelson's home, and neither could pass it up or give it up. They were out in front of the house tugging at opposite ends of the black guitar case and about to kill each other for possession.

Another gunshot broke the stalemate. Bruce saw what happened and let go of the guitar. Clayton didn't see what happened until he turned to run, the guitar under his arm.

A block away, a man lay in the street clutching his side, a pool of blood widening on the pavement beneath him. The television he'd been carrying was now being scooped up by the man who'd shot him.

Bruce was stunned enough to forget the guitar.

Clayton had the guitar and a chance to get away with it, so he ran.

Then Bruce ran—down the street to the next vacated house. He wanted to get there before Clayton or anyone else did.

STEVE HAD only worked with explosives once before, trying to get some stumps out of a small pasture back home. This dynamite Jules Cryor had been using was a little different, but the setup procedure was easy enough to figure out. With the welcome help of a flashlight from Cryor's cabin, Steve hastily set a charge in the cavern entrance and strung the fuse out for about thirty seconds of burn, hoping that would be enough for him but not enough for the dragon. It was only a guess and nothing better.

Then came another action based on a guess. He jammed a stick in the floor of the cavern and then pulled a piece of toilet paper, courtesy of Cryor's outhouse, from his shirt pocket. He tore off a narrow strip of the paper and stuck it on the end of the stick, letting it hang down like a flag.

Then—okay. It was working. His hunch was right. The little flag was waving, wiggling toward the cavern. Air was moving into the cavern at this end and apparently flowing out through that other tunnel he'd passed. So this little warning flag might work, if he was lucky and if there was a God and if, in the whole cosmic scheme of things, he was meant to survive this night.

There remained one last thing to double-check. He pulled the lighter from his pocket and flicked it. It worked the first time.

Okay. All set.

"CAR THIRTY, car thirty, West Fork Central . . ."

It was Julie the dispatcher, calling from Central Dispatch in West Fork, the hub office that received all the 911 calls for Clark County and then notified the appropriate authorities. Deputy Brad Johanson grabbed the mike from the dash of the patrol car. "Car thirty."

"Brad?"

"Yeah."

"Have you seen Sheriff Collins tonight?"

"No. When I clocked in at the office, nobody was there."

"Where are you now?"

"About eight miles out of West Fork on 209."

"We got a call from the state patrol. Collins's wife hasn't seen him either, and she's worried."

Johanson sneered a bit. He was getting a call from dispatch because Francie Collins was worried? Johanson wasn't worried at all. Collins was a big boy and could have been sidetracked by any number of things that can come up when you're a cop. "So what do you want me to do?"

"Go back to the office and see if you can find out anything."

And interrupt my rounds? "Like what? The sheriff probably got sidetracked. It happens."

"The state patrol wants to know if there are any signs of foul play."

"What?"

Julie said it again, slowly and clearly. "The state patrol wants to know if there are any signs of foul play."

Now that was weird.

"Okay, I copy. I'll head there right now. Car thirty is clear."

He found a wide shoulder, made a U-turn, and headed back toward West Fork.

WHEN JOHANSON had clocked in, the office had been quiet, deserted, and clean. Finding no one there was a little odd, but he didn't give it a lot of thought. Things got quiet around there at night with the phones forwarded. Tracy Ellis, the officer he was to relieve, could have been out on a call. Already in a hurry, he'd signed out car thirty and left to do his rounds.

Now, taking a second, careful look at the place, things did seem a little strange. For one thing, Sheriff Collins's patrol car was still in its parking slot, and yet he was nowhere around. He always drove that car to and from work, so obviously, he hadn't driven home. But that being the case, where was he?

The door to Collins's office was ajar. Johanson nudged it open with his nightstick, used the nightstick to flip the light on, and looked around inside. Nothing looked out of place. There were no notes or appointments scribbled anywhere that might say where Collins was.

Johanson went out to the counter and checked the sign-out sheet for the day. Both Collins and Ellis had signed in that morning, but neither had signed out.

He grabbed the key to the cell block, opened the metal door, and walked down the narrow corridor to the three cells. He could smell a faint trace of bleach and detergent, but couldn't tell where it was coming from until he got to cell number three. The floor, walls, ceiling, and bars of the cell had been scrubbed clean.

Well, that wasn't unusual, considering the prisoner they were keeping in here the night before. But he kept it in mind.

He went through the rest of the office and found nothing unusual. The Department of Motor Vehicles testing area looked the same, and so did the office area, the conference room, and the coffee room. Yet his instincts told him something was wrong.

He went back to the counter and leaned on it, thinking. Collins had signed in but didn't sign out, his car was still here, his office was clean and neat, cell three was scrubbed clean, the other rooms looked undisturbed—

His office was clean and neat?

Johanson went to Collins's office door again and poked his head in. It did smell rather clean in there. He knelt and sniffed the floor. Yeah. Floor cleaner—a little bit of bleach, too. Somebody had scrubbed this floor just like they scrubbed the floor of cell three.

Why only this office? Why only that cell?

So maybe he wasn't looking for signs of foul play. Maybe he was looking for the obvious lack of them.

Then he spotted Collins's jacket on the coat rack and went over for a closer look. The moment he touched it he noticed black smears all over the back, as if someone had used the jacket for a shop towel. He sniffed it and wrinkled his nose at the smell. Where had Collins been to pick up this stuff?

From this corner, he could see behind the open door. And now he saw something.

He used his nightstick to swing the door aside and knelt down to examine a stain on the floor that whoever had done the scrubbing had missed.

He grabbed his handheld radio. "West Fork Central, car thirty, Johanson."

"West Fork Central," came Julie's voice. "Go ahead, Brad."

"Call the state patrol. I might have something."

STEVE WAS out in front of the cavern entrance, plainly visible, scanning the sky and the flanks of the mountain, walking nonchalantly back and forth—and talking. Loudly.

"I guess Jennifer needed a gentler hand. You know women, the way they are, you have to make them feel loved and give them flowers and all that garbage. I mean, what did she expect, like I've got time for that kind of thing? I earned a living, didn't I? That should've been enough."

He kept his eyes open, but so far nothing looked out of place.

"I mean, a man's got to do what a man's got to do. I've got my life, my career, I've got bears to track and tag, papers to write, classes to teach. The very fate of nature itself hinges on my involvement. Jennifer never understood that."

He paused to listen. No sounds yet.

"And she should have. She was the problem, not me. Hey, if our marriage fell apart, it wasn't my fault."

Far to the east, a star wiggled. Then another.

How long should he keep this up? Steve wondered.

"Anyway, maybe it was all for the best. It made me available again, and I can't knock that. When Tracy came along, I could—" He should have known this part would hurt. "I could—"

Maybe now would be a good time to quit. He couldn't help thinking of Cliff. It had been so easy to blame him, to be angry with him, to marvel at his impulsiveness, his stupidity . . .

Well, Cliff, better move over, bro, I'm standing in the same place. Guess I didn't learn much from what happened to you. Maybe, as Harold Bly had said, Steve had just preferred not to think about it.

The wrinkle in the sky was coming his way across the valley. He could see it widening, growing.

Time to get inside. He dashed through the crooked blind of rocks to the cavern entrance then looked up in time to see a definite shape descending. He could hear the rush of wind over the wings.

He ducked into the cavern and around the first corner. Then he waited, his back tight against the wall, every nerve on edge, the lighter ready in his clenched fist.

A puff of wind whistled through the cavern entrance, and the little flag of toilet paper fluttered straight out from the stick. Then the flag settled back into a slow, lazy waving in the incoming current of air.

Steve held his breath and remained motionless, watching, listening for the barely audible sound of the dragon moving over the ground.

A claw clicked against a stone. A wing rustled as it folded. There was a long, even, scraping sound over the gravel on the mountain slope.

Steve remained rooted to the cave floor, fighting terror, fighting the impulse to flee.

He heard a quick, quiet huff of air through huge nostrils.

A pebble fell from somewhere and plinked on the ground.

Steve craned his neck just enough to check the dynamite placed against the wall of the entrance. A shaft of moonlight had found a path through the rock blind and washed the cavern wall silvery gray.

No sound. No movement. Nothing but waiting.

Come on, come on, Steve thought, his thumb on the lighter's flint wheel. Stick your big ugly head in here!

A shadow appeared, an indefinite shape along the upper reaches of the cavern wall. The dragon was breathing in amazingly slow, prolonged breaths, and then releasing them in a stream that seemed to last for minutes. From the sound it had to be just outside the entrance.

Come on!

The shadow on the cavern wall grew, descending downward, dropping like a veil over the rough surface.

A long, steady breath made the paper flag flutter.

Then the flag drooped, and the tunnel entrance went black. Silence. No motion. No sound.

The big lizard was thinking about it, Steve thought. Perhaps he could smell a trap. Perhaps he knew what dynamite was.

The moonlight returned like a flash. The flag fluttered toward the entrance. Only one footstep fell hard enough to make a grating sound on some rocks, and then there was no sound at all.

The thing was gone.

Or was it? Steve remained where he was, waiting. He craned his neck around the corner to check the dynamite again.

Now for the biggest wait, the biggest gamble.

He stood motionless in the cold dark. It was so quiet he could hear the rumble of blood flowing through his ears. He allowed himself some slow, deep breaths and then waited some more, willing himself to remain there, watching the little paper flag in the moonlight. It stirred lazily, occasionally rippling as the air moved past it on its journey through the mountain.

Then the flag drooped.

Steve stopped breathing. He watched.

The flag hung motionless.

The dragon had reached the other entrance.

Now for the timing. How long to wait? Just how long would it take for that thing to sneak up from behind?

The flag began to wiggle slightly, but the direction of flow was uncertain.

Steve tried to count, to guess the number of seconds that had passed, were passing right now, should pass before he lit the fuse.

The flag began to drift toward the cavern entrance. Then it

started to wave. Then it rose from the stick and began to flutter. Steve stepped out from the wall and could feel the air moving up out of the tunnel.

He's on his way!

Steve flicked the lighter, wincing at the sudden light. He went to the fuse, set the flame to it, and the fuse erupted in red sparks and a plume of smoke.

He could feel wind at his back. He could sense a vibration, a quivering in the floor.

He dashed out the cavern entrance, zigzagged through the rock formations, and bounded across the meadow, counting silently, then in a whisper, then out loud, " . . .twenty-one, twenty-two, twenty-three . . ."

Halfway across the meadow he looked over his shoulder and saw nothing happening.

"Thirty, thirty-one, thirty-two . . ."

BOOM! The sound hit Steve's ears like a thunderclap, then returned from across the valley and hit them again, then rumbled, rumbled, rumbled down the valley like a hundred bowling balls down a stairway.

He stopped, looked back, and saw a cloud of dust rising and rocks falling back to earth where the cavern entrance had been. All he could do now was wait, listen, and watch for the verdict as the rocks settled, the pebbles quit rolling, and the dust drifted slowly away.

Now there was nothing but torturous, taunting silence.

Steve crouched in the grass and remained still. Depending on where the dragon was at the time of the explosion, it could be trapped, or crushed and dying, or dead, or safely on its way out of the cavern by another route. Steve could only hope for the best result, but there was no way to know until—

A rock wiggled, scraped, then tumbled away from the entrance. Then another. Then several went tumbling aside as dust went up again and dirt hissed through the rubble.

Steve felt sick with disappointment. He'd trapped the dragon—for a few moments—but he hadn't killed it. The game wasn't over, and he doubted this little time-out would last very long.

Steve looked ahead. Jules Cryor's cabin was over the rocky bluff, out of sight. If he ran, he could get there in just a few minutes, if he had a few minutes. But he couldn't run, not yet. He had to let the dragon see where he was going.

It's crazy, he heard himself thinking. Run now, you idiot! But he couldn't do it. If he really expected to end this thing, he needed the dragon to follow him.

Against the terror that urged him to run, he stood in place and watched while the creature clawed and scraped his way out of the mountain, casting boulders away as if they weighed nothing.

Long claws appeared through the rocks, groping about. Now Steve could hear the thing huffing and chugging. He could see the dust blasted away in small clouds by the angry breath.

"Aw, you're beautiful when you're angry!" Steve taunted.

The head appeared, the silver horns glistening in the moonlight, as the creature stretched and strained to see over the rocks, scanning, searching. Then the golden eyes locked on Steve. The dragon's head lunged in Steve's direction like a rattlesnake trying to strike, but the body was still held fast in the fallen debris. The creature was incensed!

Steve took off, running for Cryor's cabin as he heard the rocks flying and cascading from the cavern entrance, the huffing of that thing's angry breath, the beating and bashing of its claws against the debris.

Steve ran over the rocks, along the cliff, up to the crevasse. He jumped it, landing on the precarious ledge on the other side. He lost his balance, fell forward to his hands, then got up again and ran. He could see the cabin below.

From far away he heard a sound like the world's biggest parachute snapping open. The dragon was free and had taken to the air.

Just another few seconds now: down a trail, over and around a pile of mine waste, and he'd be at the cabin's front door.

He heard the rushing and beating of the monstrous wings above him and looked up.

No camouflage this time. The dragon was a clear, silvery

shadow in the sky, its eyes like the landing lights of an aircraft, locking onto him like lasers.

Steve ran, leaping over the rocks, stumbling over a boulder, bounding ahead. The cabin was close, but not close enough, not close enough!

The dragon swept its wings back and began to drop toward the earth, its image growing, stretching, filling more and more of the sky. Its shadow swept over the cabin as Steve reached the front door and clambered inside, slamming and bolting the door behind him.

CRASH! Three silver claws pierced through the ceiling, then twisted, yanked, and withdrew. Steve hit the floor against the rear wall, his body curled, his arms upraised for protection.

The golden eyes appeared at the window. They saw him. The claws crashed through the window and groped about the cabin, throwing the table against the wall like a toy, breaking out the opposite window, hooking the bed and flinging it across the room. Steve wriggled on his belly, rolled like a log, scurried this way, then that, too busy dodging death to fear it, the razor-tipped claws whistling over his head, impaling the log walls, wrenching free, then groping again.

One huge golden eye spotted him through a window. Steve leapt aside as the claws drove into the plank floor like spikes. The dragon pulled, yanked, wrenched all but one claw free. The last claw pulled up a floorboard, which remained impaled on it, and now the board flew and flipped about the room with the hand, smashing and shattering everything in sight. The shovels, picks, and drills went flying, the bookshelf disintegrated, the books and papers filled the room like feathers from a burst pillow.

The thing was huffing, in fierce anger. Steve expected to see flames any moment.

As the claws withdrew through the window, they pulled out the window frame.

CHUNG! The silvery claws punched like spears through the metal roofing again, jutted into the room, and then curled inward as the dragon crumpled the metal, the planks, the plywood. The dragon tore at the cabin roof, ripping away the sheet metal, yanking the rafters loose and pulling them up like toothpicks.

Steve remained tightly curled in a corner of the cabin, watching his little fortress disappear in flying shreds and wondering how long he should wait.

Now the cabin was open to the sky, and the huge head punched through with scarcely room to turn and twist, the eyes like burning lamps, the nostrils flared, the teeth bared, snorting and snuffing after its prey.

It's time, Steve thought. He ducked through the thick wooden door in the back of the cabin. One huge, golden eye was only inches from him when he slammed the door shut and bolted it. He hurried down the access tunnel to Cryor's mine, hoping the dragon would try to tear the door open, hoping the beast wouldn't notice the—

The dragon noticed an entire row of explosives set along the back wall of the cabin.

BOOM!

The mountainside erupted in a ball of fire as logs, furniture, roofing, blankets, canned food, planks, rafters, and picks and shovels soared into the sky, borne aloft on a plume of flame and smoke.

The dragon, limp and aflame, its wings shredded and burning, floated upward, then backward in a long, slow arc, then dropped like a flaming aircraft down, down, down the mountainside, until it landed on its back in the low, scrubby pines just above the treeline. It rolled one, two, and finally three slow turns down the hill before it came to rest against a stand of firs.

DEEP INSIDE the tunnel leading from Cryor's cabin to his mine, Steve cowered in a tight corner, his fist wrapped in a death grip around the detonator.

TWENTY-ONE

Havoc

LIEUTENANT BARNARD went into the central office area of the precinct and found Evelyn seated at the desk he'd offered her. She was just hanging up the telephone.

"Any word?" he asked.

She shook her head. "No, Travis has been sitting by the phone all night, but Steve hasn't called, and neither has Deputy Ellis."

He pulled over a chair from the next desk and sat down. "When did you last hear from your brother-in-law?"

She was dismayed at how long it had been. "Last Sunday night, I think. Tracy—Deputy Ellis—was with him since then, but..." Her voice choked with emotion. "Sorry."

Barnard leaned forward and spoke gently. "Listen, I just heard back from the county sheriff's office."

Then there was that tight little moment that could seem like an eternity as Evelyn waited to hear the news.

Barnard chose his words carefully. "Do you think you could stick around just a little longer? We might have a few more questions after our people have a look."

Evelyn was instantly alert. "What have you heard?"

His eyes revealed a trust toward her he'd not shown before. "A sheriff's deputy checked around the sheriff's office, and . . . well, we've decided to look into it."

She agreed to stay and called Travis to let him know.

And then she prayed. Oh Lord, have mercy on Steve—wherever he is.

THE TUNNEL to Jules Cryor's cabin was blocked and useless now. Steve ran down the access tunnel to the mine itself, then ran up the main tunnel to the entrance, about a hundred feet below and to the side of where the cabin used to be.

The air outside the mine was still choked with dust. Burning embers and bits of cabin lay on the mine waste. Judging from the scattered logs, boards, and pieces of furniture he had to climb over to get out, he'd succeeded in wiping the cabin off the face of the earth. As for the dragon . . .

He carried Jules Cryor's shotgun as he stole carefully down the ore-car tracks, stepping over fallen boulders and shreds of metal roofing, coming around the bend to the area immediately below the cabin site. Above, he saw only a crater with not a board left standing. Below, he saw smoke, dust, and small, flickering flames. The dust was still clearing away, drifting like a cloud down the mountainside, down the valley.

He maintained the same careful search pattern he'd always used, scanning the sky, then the surrounding terrain, looking for anything unusual or out of place, any broken lines, any—

Oh, no. Dared he believe it? He looked all around in case he was mistaken, and then looked far down the mountainside again.

There was the dragon, at least two hundred feet below, lying against the treeline like a long, twisted tree trunk, not moving, one wing sticking up like a broken and torn umbrella. A front leg, half blown away, poked into the sky like a dead snag, the jagged tip still smoldering. Here and there on its body, scales dimly flickered in green, red, white, brown, then blinked out, then blinked on again, with no pattern. The dragon's entire body was sending up thin wisps of smoke.

Cautiously, Steve made sure the shotgun had a round in the chamber, then he started down the steep, rocky slope. If this thing wasn't dead yet, he was going to finish it. He was going to make sure.

At least he could see it. At least he could walk in the open and not have to search everything around him in a constant, nerve-grinding struggle to stay alive. His mortal enemy was right there, right in front of him, clearly visible at last.

Finally! Finally, I got you!

He hurried. He had to get a final shot before that thing revived or recharged or whatever it did.

He looked down at the black stain on his chest. It seemed to be drying. He touched it. Nothing came off on his fingers. The slime had turned to a dry crust.

Ohhh, the feeling! After such darkness, such oppression and despair, he could feel hope returning. He didn't want to get too optimistic too soon, but he felt such a release, such a lightness of spirit, that he couldn't help laughing out loud.

"Gotcha!" he cried.

Maybe, he had to remind himself. Thirty feet above the fallen carcass, he slowed his pace, stepping carefully down over the rocks, drawing closer, the shotgun ready, his eyes glued on that beast, looking for the slightest stirring. Small fires flickered all around him, and the stench of smoke stung his nostrils and occasionally blocked his vision. He took each step only when he could see the dragon clearly. He couldn't afford to get careless.

The monster's tail extended up the mountainside to Steve's right. The huge, scaled body stretched along the rocks and trees directly in front of him, the heavily plated belly toward the sky. The neck and head were out of sight in the trees lower down. Steve clicked on his flashlight and caught the right rear leg in the beam. The claws, now clutching at the air, shined silver in the light; some of the scales awakened and tried to mimic the terrain, one here, one there. Other than that, there was no movement.

Steve wanted to get closer. He wanted to find a vulnerable point somewhere to fire the finishing shot. Perhaps the belly, maybe the neck . . .

Then he hesitated. For some reason, without warning, he felt a sickening pain in his stomach, an anguish in his soul. This he didn't need, not now. He took some deep breaths and even lowered his head a little, but it didn't help.

He didn't dare lose this opportunity. He prodded himself to keep approaching.

About ten feet away, he paralleled the dragon's flank, surveying the thick scales, trying to locate the vital organs and some way to put a shot through them. Even as he did, it occurred to him that he didn't feel good about it. The more he tried to find a point of vulnerability, the more ambivalent he became.

He shook away a cloud of doubt and forced himself to study the dragon's anatomy as best he could. With effort, he located the rib cage and the most likely location of the heart and lungs. If he could get the shotgun barrel jammed between some scales somewhere—

He didn't want to do it.

He focused on the shotgun in his hands. It was ready. All he needed was that final shot.

He couldn't do it.

Stupid thought! He shook it off. He had to do it. This thing was a killer and would kill again if he didn't kill it first. Steve forced himself to approach the chest cavity and rib cage, just below the shoulder. The jagged stump of the right foreleg hung in the air above him, the bone and torn flesh smoldering and smoking.

All right. Now to get that shot through the heart and lungs. He had to find a chink, a crack, a gap.

He couldn't do it.

He forced himself to aim the shotgun at the massive, scaled flank. The barrel began to waver; his hands were shaking. With a frustrated sigh, he let his arm go slack. The gun barrel sank toward the ground.

There was just something about this creature, about this whole situation. He couldn't go through with it.

"Come on," he told himself out loud, "let's get this done. This monster's out to kill you, to kill everybody!"

He tried to raise the shotgun again. His hands shook, the barrel wiggled crazily, and he lowered the gun. He couldn't kill this thing. Against all logic, all common sense, he couldn't kill it.

He couldn't kill this thing because this thing was—this thing was—

He couldn't explain it, and he couldn't shake it, but as he looked at that long, serpentine body spread out before him, he felt he was looking at a part of his own body, no different from his arm, his leg, his hand.

Yes. That was it. As strange as it seemed, he felt like he'd be killing himself.

I can't kill it. It's mine. It's me.

He teetered forward, put a foot out to regain his balance, then the other foot, then stepped again. He couldn't stand still, and it was more than just the slope of the mountain: that huge, scaled body seemed to be drawing him. He wanted to touch the creature. He wanted to feel those cold scales under his fingers. He knew better. He knew he shouldn't. He knew it would be dangerous.

But he just had to . . .

The shotgun dropped from his hands. He reached out toward the scales, and his hand came to rest on the thick belly plating. It felt like ceramic tile, cool, hard, and impenetrable. A marvelous creature! Unbelievable. Beautiful in design!

Oh, man, I hope I haven't killed it.

He ran his hand along the scales. The power in this thing! The incredible strength and beauty! Like nothing else in the world!

And he could sense it so clearly now as he touched it: It was a part of him; he was a part of it. He owned it. It was all his . . .

He loved this beast!

Something dribbled down his chest, and he looked in time to see a black stream soaking his shirt, dripping over his belt, spreading in a pool across the dragon's scales.

For some reason, he thought of Tracy.

The scales under his hands quivered. Was this creature moving, or was it the ground?

He looked up, and saw the huge jaws of the creature opening.

He lurched backward, falling onto the rocks just as the monster's snout fell like a tree on its own belly and the jaws clamped shut with a metallic grating.

Steve scrambled up the hill, his chest, hands, and arms spattered and slick, the dust sticking and caking on the slime. He looked back to see the long neck curled in a near circle, the head suspended just above the prone body, swaying, rubbery, weak. The eyes were half open. The dragon was trying to recover, trying to see.

He loved to look at the dragon, to watch it. He wanted to stay there forever and be a part of it.

It was trying to eat him.

He wanted to keep it.

It was trying to eat him.

He didn't want to leave.

IT WAS TRYING TO EAT HIM!

Something in his spirit, some deeply buried sense of conscience finally prevailed, and he began to inch, then stumble, then run across the mountain slope as the beast awakened, coiled, and twisted. The tail lay across Steve's path. He tried to work his way around it. It came alive, twisted, curled, rose into the air and then whipped, the tip just missing his head. He ducked under it, got by it.

The stupor was gone. Now his eyes were open, and all he could see was Evil. He turned and fled downhill.

HAROLD BLY wasn't getting any reports. He could hear screams, shouting, even gunshots out in the streets of Hyde River, but Andy wasn't keeping him informed, and neither was Carl, and he hadn't seen Doug in over an hour. He didn't want his face identified with what was going on out there, and yet he was beginning to wonder if he had trusted the others a little too much. He looked at his watch. If he didn't get a report from somebody in ten minutes . . .

ANDY SCHULLER's mob had broken up, each man looking after his own whims and desires. Andy and John Tyler were going through the Hazelett home, pawing through the handmade jewelry. Abel Hoffmeier felt entitled to a chain-saw in the front window of the hardware store and kicked the glass out to get it. The crash got people's attention, the idea caught on, and soon the power and garden tools, housewares, and tape players started going out the door.

Kyle Figgin's neighbor, Deke Schonley, always thought the property line was more in his favor than Kyle would admit. Well, tonight Kyle was gone, so Deke took the opportunity to sledgehammer every slat out of Kyle's wooden fence.

Someone had stolen their car, so Becky Nelson and her four children fled on foot from their home, past Jeff's dead and bloody body, and down the street, looking for any friendly face, any avenue of escape, the two boys running with their little sister between them and Becky carrying the baby.

"Bigots! Get out of here!" people yelled from their yards as some threw stones at them.

All Becky could do was scream at her children, "Run! Run!" as they fled south with nowhere to go but away. Ken and Cherry Hazelett came by in their pickup and stopped to help them into the truck bed. Then the Hazeletts and Nelsons fled through the opened roadblock and out of town.

Henry Gorst heard what was happening to his hardware store and finally got there, armed with a shotgun. "What do you people think you're doing? Put that stuff down!"

No one listened.

"I'm not on the list!"

That didn't seem to matter.

He fired into the air. Someone felt threatened and fired back. Gorst fell to the street, a bullet in his shoulder.

STEVE WAS using Cryor's flashlight to warn him of branches, briars, and brush, but he was driven now by enough fear that it mattered little what might be in front of him. He just kept crashing, slashing, and pushing his way downhill through the undergrowth.

He didn't feel much pain from the wound over his heart, but it was dripping all over him as if he'd severed a black artery. His clothes were spattered with the black slime. He was leaving black handprints on the trunks of the trees. With one remaining sliver of sanity he thought, This is it, the final stage.

What had that creature done to him? He was terrified of dying but felt no fear of the dragon. He loved that beast while knowing would eat him. He didn't want to run even as he ran.

Ridiculous thoughts cascaded through his mind, and every one of them seemed so true and practical: Maybe there's a way to tame it. Maybe it won't really eat me. If I ignore it it'll leave me alone. This mark doesn't hurt that much, I can live with it. Maybe the dragon won't eat me until tomorrow . . .

I want to keep it! It's mine!

I want to live, too, said a small but powerful voice from a corner of his mind. That one little voice was enough to keep him fleeing down the mountainside.

HIGH ABOVE, on the rocky slope of Saddlehorse, the dragon was reviving. It twisted, curled, clawed the air, and finally, with some leverage from its tail, rolled over on its belly, pushing over some small trees in the process. Then it rested, the glow returning to its eyes, the claws moving, the nostrils sampling the wind. It was drawing strength from hearts and spirits now in chaos below—from the town of Hyde River, from scattered souls up and down the valley, and from that little man now scrambling down the mountainside. It knew, it could feel, it could hear the cries, the shouts, the pain.

It raised its head high, its neck a stunning question mark against the sky, and inhaled a long breath that swelled its chest. Then it raised itself on its left foreleg and the stump of its right, and peered into the valley.

It couldn't see the little man, but it knew where he was. It knew where he was going.

HAROLD BLY looked at his watch. The ten minutes were up, and the noise outside was getting worse. Like it or not, he had to get out there and take control. This was going to be his town, run his way. With the town cleared out, the dragon would be on his side again. With the hearts of the town in his pocket, the land and wealth would follow, pure and simple.

But he had to make that clear to everyone. He had to get out there.

He'd been holding a towel to his chest. He pulled it away to take a look. The wound was oozing black slime, soaking the towel, fouling the air. Well, no matter. It didn't hurt a bit, and soon it would clear up. He threw the towel aside.

"I'm going to live forever!" he proclaimed to the empty tavern. "No rules but my rules!"

He ran out the back door to his car.

STEVE STOPPED to rest, to get his bearings, and to listen. He couldn't hear that thing coming after him, but right now the blood pounding in his ears and his own gasping for breath made hearing impossible.

So okay, Benson, he thought, what's your strategy now?

The Hyde River flowed placidly below him, a black ribbon with silver sparkles of moonlight, only a few more minutes through the woods. He could follow it downstream until he found the Hyde River Road, and from there get back to town.

Yeah. Town. Hyde River, where all the dragon's biggest defenders and concealers were, probably the least safe place on earth for a Steve Benson or any meddling outsider. But it was where this whole nightmare started, and he knew it was where it would have to end. Levi Cobb had been right about everything else. Now, having touched the beast, Steve believed. He could never run far enough to escape the dragon because it was a part of him; wherever he went he would carry the dragon with him like latent death buried in his soul. Someday, the dragon would win. It would take him and destroy him—unless he destroyed the dragon first, and now Steve knew there was only one way to do that.

So, okay. If those people loved the dragon so much, they might as well meet it face to face.

Steve started climbing down the steep slope, through the trees and brush, heading for the river. Here come your two greatest enemies, folks: the dragon you love and the man who's trying to kill it.

THE DRAGON carefully inspected the damage to its wings. They were broken, torn, and useless. Quickly but gingerly, it gathered the snapped bones and tattered membranes together with its mouth and folded them neatly into a close-fitting but ragged cape along its back.

Then it folded its forelegs along its side, pushed with its hind legs, and slid forward over the rocks, gliding like a serpent, its feather-light touch returning. With motion established, it folded its hind legs as well and began to slither. It wove through the trees, arcing over fallen logs, pushing with its coils against the tree trunks, moving like a sled over snow, smoothly, almost silently, picking up speed. It was following the little man who had tried to kill it.

PAUL HAD been looking all over town for his former partner and finally found Jimmy Yates in, of all places, Paul's own living room, going through Paul's desk!

"I hid the checkbook, Jimmy."

Jimmy spun around, surprised, but then bold. "Hey, Paul! How's it going?"

"Where's that pumper truck?"

Jimmy only smiled. "Somewhere."

"I want it back!"

"What's it worth to you?"

"Don't push me!"

"Hey, I'll make you a deal," Jimmy said. "You give me the company checkbook, I'll give you the truck."

Paul smirked at that. "So you can cash out the account? You think I'm crazy?"

"Hey, you want the pumper back, you give me the money. Simple!"

"You want simple?" Paul answered, pulling a pistol from his belt.

Jimmy looked down the barrel, hands outstretched pleadingly. "Hey, Paul, now come on . . ."

Paul smiled. What a feeling!

STEVE HUNG from some low limbs and groped with his feet until they found a resting place on a large rock just above the river. He let go of the limbs and perched on the rock, looking down at the rippling, moon-dappled water. The river was deeper here, and moving fast. It would be a cold swim, but for now the river would be the easiest way to go until he could find some navigable ground. It was also one way to keep from getting lost out here. The decision made, he slid down the rock and into the water, then pushed himself out into the main stream, where the current carried him away.

KYLE FIGGIN heard the gunshot from Paul's house as he ran by but gave it no thought. There was shooting going on all around him right now, and he was in a hurry.

Doug came out of the Nelson house and blocked his path. "Where are you going?"

Kyle tried to dodge around him. "Out of my way!"

Doug grabbed him by the arm and brought him to a joint-stretching halt. "Where's the flatbed?"

"Who cares?"

Now Doug jerked him close. "I told you to take it back to Elmer's before something happens to it."

"Why don't you do it then?"

"Because I told you to."

Kyle beat Doug's hands off. "Yeah, while you and everybody else get to pick through the houses. Forget it!"

Doug tried to deck him, but Kyle knew it was coming and ducked, then head-butted Doug in the stomach. Doug reached down, grabbed Kyle around the waist, and heaved him through the air.

Kyle rolled in the street, and then his hand went to his gun. Doug's boot went to Kyle's jaw.

Just then, a car horn sounded. It was Harold Bly, pulling up with his head out the window. "Doug!"

Doug was in no mood to talk to anybody. "What?"

Bly was in a mood where he'd better be talked to. "What's going on? Where's Andy?"

Doug was keeping an eye on Kyle in case he got up again. "I don't know."

"What about Carl and Bernie?"

"They're cleaning out the houses."

"I haven't seen any of you guys! Did you get the jobs done?"

"Yeah, we did them all."

Kyle was getting up shakily.

Bly demanded, "What's the matter with him?"

"Nothing."

"What about the Nelsons and the Hazeletts?"

"They're out."

"So why didn't anybody tell me?"

"We're busy!"

"Yeah, we're busy," Kyle agreed, wiping his bleeding jaw.

Bly didn't take that very well. "Yeah? Well, you're not through. Get some men together. Dottie Moore has to go!"

Doug and Kyle looked at each other. Doug said, "Who says?"

Bly repeated his order. "Get some men together! I'll meet you over there!" And with that, Bly drove off.

"Do it yourself," Doug hollered after him.

"CAN YOU SEE ANYTHING?" Susan Woods asked.

Reverend Ron Woods was on the floor, peering over the sill of the front window toward the town below. "I see some people running. I think that was Harold Bly's car that just went by."

Susan was huddled on the floor beside the sofa with their young son and daughter, as far as she could get from the outside walls and windows.

Another gunshot rang out.

"Ron, get away from the window!" He joined her.

"What are we going to do?"

"They won't hurt us."

"But what about the others? Some of our friends, and the Nelsons and the Carlsons . . ."

"It's not our problem."

"Ron," she pleaded, "we've got to do something!"

He shrugged lazily. "All we really have to do is wait. Things will settle down, I'm sure." Susan was about to protest, but he tried to soothe her with, "We can't blame them, you know. They're only doing what they think is best."

DOTTIE MOORE had been hiding as well and feared the worst when she heard a loud banging on her door.

For some reason, when she found out it was Harold Bly, she felt relieved. "Well, hello, Harold. And what brings you out of your shell tonight?"

He looked behind him; the other guys hadn't shown up yet. "Dottie, you may have noticed there are some changes being made."

"Oh, I've noticed, all right."

Now Bly straightened his spine and found a stronger voice. "Well, it's going to apply to you as well. We've asked some families to vacate their homes and take up lodging somewhere else. So unless other arrangements can be made, I'll have to ask you to do the same."

She raised one eyebrow. "Other arrangements?"

Bly nodded. "Sure. Things we've discussed."

Well, she could straighten her spine and speak in a strong voice too. "Harold, I think you have the wrong address. This house doesn't belong to the company. Vic and I bought it eight years ago."

"Well, I'm foreclosing on the mortgage."

"You don't hold the mortgage, remember? We bought it through the bank in West Fork. Sure, the company owned it, but it defaulted. This house was never yours!"

Suddenly, and much too late, he remembered. He tried not to feel stupid but felt stupid anyway. He looked for his men, who still hadn't arrived.

Dottie summarized for him. "So the house isn't yours and never will be. Now, was there anything else?"

He scowled at her. "I want you out of town, Dottie! I can make things really difficult for you."

"Get a job, Harold," she said, and tried to close the door.

He held the door open with his hand. "Dottie, I mean it!"

Her eyes looked beyond him, and she smiled. "Harold, maybe you should worry about the property you do own."

He looked in the same direction, down the street, just in time to see Andy Schuller setting fire to the Carlson house while a cheer went up from Andy's buddies.

"That's my property!" Harold realized.

"Good night, Harold," said Dottie, closing the door on him.

Bly ran down the street as flames engulfed the gasoline-soaked front porch and licked up the siding of the little house.

"What are you doing?" he screamed. "I didn't tell you to burn it down!"

Andy still had the empty gasoline can in his hands and didn't seem a bit sorry as he said, "Gee, sorry, Harold! I thought—"

Bly grabbed Andy by the neck. "You stupid—"

Then Andy's buddies were all over Bly. He kicked and wriggled and shook them loose and then stood there with fists clenched, glaring at the grinning Andy in the light and heat of the growing fire. Andy's shirt was smeared black, and so was Bly's. He looked at every man standing there. All of them were smeared and stained with the stuff, their chests, their arms, their faces.

"Are you all crazy?" he demanded. "That's company property! It belonged to me!"

They just laughed at him. Harold Bly on the losing end! Too much!

"Somebody call the fire department!" Bly shouted, nearly hysterical. Then he realized that most of them were the fire department.

Just then, Carl Ingfeldt's wife came running down the street pushing a brand new lawn mower, the wheels rumbling loudly over the asphalt.

They all cheered. "All right!" "Nice catch!" "Go, baby, go!"

She was followed by her children, each carrying a new toy with the price tag still attached. She and the children were followed by a limping, bleeding Henry Gorst. "Margaret! Stop! Those aren't yours! Please!"

"Henry!" Bly cried in shock.

Henry Gorst only glared at him. "Look what you've done!"

Bly ran toward the center of town in time to see neighbors, friends, and even people he'd never met running into Henry Gorst's hardware store and back out with anything and everything they could carry.

He shouted, he hollered, he protested.
They laughed, they smiled, they kept stealing.

STEVE HAD floated down the river until he saw the old road,
then run down the road until he feared detection, then blazed his
way along the river bank until he was close to town. He'd finally
finished the whole trip in the river again, floating when it was
deep enough and crawling when it was too shallow. Now he
stood in the waist-deep water just under the bridge that connected the four-way stop with the big Hyde Mining Company
complex. He was completely, thoroughly wet and cold enough to
be blue but so pumped with adrenaline he didn't notice. He was
listening to the shouting, the shooting, the screams and jeers. He
could see the glow of fire reflected from the face of the company
building. The town was going nuts, and no doubt some people
were being hurt, maybe even killed. The dragon, though physi-
cally in the mountains, was present everywhere in this place right
now.

He knew his behavior was going to defy all evolutionary explanation. His actions would not be those of any avowed rationalist
college professor. As for the rules of self-preservation, he was about
to defy them. But he'd spent the whole trip down the river from
Saddlehorse thinking about it, and now he intended to do something distinctly and oddly human: He intended to stick around,
risk his life, and complete Levi Cobb's plan.

He waded to the concrete bulkhead, reached up to the ledge,
found some footholds, and clambered up out of the river to a grav-
eled alley that ran behind a row of houses. He kept low and got
moving. The water in his shoes squished between his toes, but he
gave it no mind.

The action in town seemed concentrated around the four-way
stop: he heard shouting, screeching tires, breaking glass. He
headed south, ducking past the small houses and closed businesses
until he found the street that would take him up the hill into the

older part of town, the quieter part where the old church was still standing.

He felt as though he were still in the woods, stealing and stalking about to preserve his own life. Only this time the hiding places were of stone, steel, and concrete. Part animal, part commando, his nerves primed and his muscles taut, he stole from old car to oil-drum fence to concrete retaining wall, hearing, seeing, sensing.

He came to the main street and peered around the corner of a windowless grocery store. A house was going up in flames, and no one was doing a thing about it. People were scurrying like ants, each loaded down with something stolen. Prone bodies lay in the street, ignored and unaided. Some teenagers were out breaking windows, and some men were firing guns at buildings, cars, and road signs.

They've all lost it, he thought. Like Charlie, like Tracy, like all the others.

That could only mean the dragon was on its way to collect.

So where did that put him? Through all the running, climbing, and crawling he'd done, he'd managed to get black stuff on just about every part of himself, and swimming in the river had removed only some of it. He rubbed his fingers over his chest. His shirt had been saturated with it before, but right now there didn't seem to be anything fresh. If he could just stay ahead of that beast, if he could just keep hating it . .

Okay, God. It's Your show now. You call it.

He made a mad dash across the Hyde River Road and up the hill beyond, unnoticed.

THE CARLSON house was burning down to a blackened skeleton, the hardware store was nearly empty, the homes of the evicted had been picked clean, but the appetites of the town had not diminished. The two-pump Chevron station offered little, but across the street, Charlie's Tavern and Mercantile, recently renovated, fully stocked, and newly reopened for business, called to the crowds like an irresistible promised land.

Andy Schuller was the first to burst into Charlie's. "Beer! Free beer! We've earned it!"

Paul Myers and Carl Ingfeldt were right behind him in full agreement. Paul hollered to Carl, "Carl, man the pumps!"

Carl leapt over the bar and started pulling the handles, setting the suds in motion and leaving black handprints on everything.

The cowbell over the door rang nonstop as the place filled up. Beer, whiskey, and wine couldn't flow fast enough. Bottles flew across the room to waiting hands, bottle tops twisted, corks popped, and foam sprayed. The cash register rang as it gave away money, folks spat on the floor because it wasn't allowed, and somewhere under all the noise, Harold Bly screamed while nobody listened.

SMOOTHLY, SILENTLY, black as night, cold as the river in which it slithered and swam, the creature slipped into the raucous, noisily preoccupied town, passing under the bridge, low in the water like a crocodile, hearing the sounds, sniffing the stench of its own handiwork. It lowered its three good feet into the rocky river bed and halted just past the bridge.

STEVE FOUND the church door unlocked. He opened it, stepped through into the dark foyer, and closed the door behind him as quietly as possible. He didn't look for the light switch. Lights would attract attention. He needed time, quiet, and privacy.

The church had a warm and intimate little sanctuary with short, rustic pews, a carpeted center aisle, a sturdy pulpit of varnished planks, and a large, stained-glass window above the choir loft. Steve hurried up to the front, looked around for a place that would be appropriate, and finally knelt in front of the platform. He realized his shoes and knees were going to leave muddy circles on the carpet, but that was unimportant at the moment.

Now to pray. Except . . . was there a proper way to do it? Well, he was kneeling, and maybe he'd fold his hands; he'd seen that done.

Should he close his eyes too? No way, not tonight.

He began. At least, he tried to begin. But no words came to mind.

Get on with it, Steve, there's a dragon out there!

"Lord God," he blurted out loud, his eyes looking about warily, "as You know, I am not a religious person. I've seldom if ever entered a church. But I'm a believer now. I believe what Levi said. I'm willing to accept Your existence and the rightness of Your commandments, Your truth, the Ten Commandments, and whatever else there is. We'll just have to make this all-inclusive, all right?

"So Lord God, having established that, I also need to admit, to confess, that—" He hesitated, then continued. "I admit, Lord, that—I have not lived my life in such a way that would be totally pleasing to You. I'm sure You're aware of that."

Behind him, the church door opened silently then closed again.

He was trying to get this task completed as quickly as possible but as thoroughly as required. "Lord, I'm a—well, I'm a sinner. It's that simple. I admit it. I've got this black stuff all over me; I'm being hunted by a tenacious monster—" He stopped. He was talking to God; he'd have to be honest again. "Okay, I'm a very proud man, very self-serving, I suppose—and, uh, quite individualistic, sort of the center of my universe. So consequently, I've violated your moral laws. I've not been honest and faithful in my relationships, and I've caused someone else to not be honest and faithful in hers. I've—"

Oh, brother! Emotion at a time like this? His voice quavered, and his eyes filled with tears. He pushed ahead. "Lord God, Levi asked me how many other Tracys there have been. Well, I've only truly loved one woman, and that was Jennifer. But I failed her—and so I lost her. I didn't deserve her."

This could take all night, and he didn't have all night. "Lord, I do apologize for hurrying through this, but the dragon could be on its way here right now, and I have a lot to do. So let me get to the bottom line if I may. Lord God, if I'm to prevail against that dragon tonight—" His hand went to his heart "—I need to win a victory here first. So, Lord, I'm bringing it to you. All the sin. Every evil thing that's inside me. The—the dragon that's living in there, whatever it is, however it works. And I'm asking you, Lord, to take it away. Please. Unhook me. Set me free."

He looked up through the window as if God was looking down. "Jesus, forgive me. Please forgive me."

"Steve," came a quiet voice behind him. He spun around, startled.

It was Reverend Ron Woods, sitting in the front pew, in the dark. "Sorry. I didn't mean to startle you."

Steve stood. "That's okay."

"I was standing at my window, and I saw you go into the church. I thought I could be of some help."

How nice. Bad timing, though. "Well, Reverend, I may not have time right now."

"But I heard you asking for forgiveness." Steve noticed that Woods's eyes seemed strangely vacant. "Steve, you don't need forgiveness. If anything, you need to forgive yourself."

A counseling session on a night like this? "I'm sure we can talk about this later."

Woods got to his feet. "Steve, listen to me. This town is coming apart because of guilt. We don't need any more of it around here. You don't need it."

Steve tried to push past him. "And that's why I'm getting rid of it!"

Woods blocked his path. "But I'm trying to tell you, you don't have it to begin with! Steve, guilt is a relative term. It's something we foist on ourselves."

"What?"

"Why do you think those people down there are looting and fighting and destroying? It's because they've been deprived for so long and they can't feel good about themselves!"

Steve began to smell an all-too-familiar stench, and he could discern a haunting tone in Woods's voice. "Reverend, I don't think that's the reason."

The Reverend just kept going. "Of course it is. That's what I kept trying to tell Levi, bless his heart. People act guilty because they feel guilty, so it's not what you do; it's how you feel about yourself. If you're true to yourself, if you love yourself, you won't hurt others."

Steve absolutely had to get going. "Reverend, listen, I've been—I've been totally devoted to myself, okay? I've been absolutely nuts about myself. But let me tell you, I've hurt other people a lot!"

"And now you feel guilty, right? Well, I used to feel guilty, did you know that? I was bitter, and I was envious of other ministers who were successful. But now I know, there is no guilt after all. It's all in your head."

Steve noticed the Reverend's hand had remained over his heart. He reached over and pulled the hand away. The black slime stretched in strings from Woods's fingers to his chest. "Not quite, Reverend. Not quite."

Woods just looked down at himself dumbly. "You don't need forgiveness from God. You can change yourself. There's no right or wrong except what we make up for ourselves."

Now, with horror, Steve could see it plainly. "You're hooked . . ."

"Just feel good about yourself, that's all."

"You're hooked and you're losing it."

Woods looked at Steve, his eyes glimmering in the dark and a smile widening on his face. "Steve, there isn't any dragon. That's just a superstition, a tool some people use to manipulate others."

Enough of this! Steve edged toward the door. "I have to go."

Woods blocked his way. "You don't have to go. Please, stay and talk awhile."

"Sorry."

Woods's blackened hand shot out like a trap and locked onto Steve's arm. "Please! Stay! It would be time well spent."

Steve tried to pull away. The Reverend hung on. "Reverend, I've got things to do. Now let go."

But Woods would not relax his grip. "Don't worry about the dragon. Really, there is no such thing."

I've danced to this tune before, Steve thought, and forcefully yanked his arm away.

Woods clamped onto his arm again! "There is no dragon!!"

The stained-glass window exploded in a shower of glass, and Steve saw the golden eyes, the gleaming teeth, and the groping, silver claws. He yanked himself loose and dashed down the center aisle.

Oof! Steve hit the ground with a thud. Woods had tackled him, bringing him down

Steve kicked and twisted, trying to get free. Woods hung on like a wild man, his blackened hands streaking Steve's clothing.

The dragon's neck flowed through the window as the golden retinas once again locked on their target. The left paw came through the opening and crunched a pew in the choir loft; the right stump groped and thumped against the window frame, try-ing to fit through.

Steve got one leg loose, kicked Woods in the head, and broke free. He got to his feet and could hear the dragon inhaling as he reached the rear of the sanctuary.

"Yaaaa!" With a maniacal cry, Woods leapt on Steve from be-hind, arms and legs clamping around him.

CRASH! The dragon smashed the pulpit aside with its flailing head as it continued to work itself through the opening, shaking the whole building. The right leg stump came through the window and slammed into the choir loft. The dragon raised its head until it crunched into the ceiling, the horns splintering a rafter.

Woods himself was like a wild beast, growling, grunting, teeth bared, trying to wrestle Steve backward, trying to pull him toward those jaws and claws and teeth. Steve kicked and punched, trying to knock Woods loose. He was losing.

Steve finally lurched sideways, slamming the pastor's head

against the end of a pew. With a cry of pain, Woods dropped away, grabbed for Steve's leg, and missed.

The dragon's head pitched forward, the jaws opened.

Steve dashed through the foyer and out the front door just as yellow flames exploded out the side windows of the church. A wall of fire blew the front doors open and rolled down the front steps.

Steve ran, feeling the rolling wave of heat at his heels, seeing light like a sunrise washing over the buildings ahead of him He could hear the church coming apart. He looked back.

The dragon had burned a hole through the church roof. Now the head appeared, slashing and biting, ducking under and then lurching up and back, the horns hooking and ripping out the rafters. Burning boards and shingles were flying everywhere.

Then the roof, the brand-new roof, ignited like a torch, and a flurry of sparks and embers shot skyward. The jaws closed on the rafters, then tore them loose.

Steve raced down the hill, heading for Levi Cobb's garage. That thing would be out of the church building any moment and looking for him, flames blasting and fangs ready. Whatever Levi had planned, now was the time to figure it out.

"Okay, Lord," Steve huffed as he fled down the street, "it's all Yours!"

TWENTY-TWO

Free

CHARLIE'S was a beehive gone mad, with people helping themselves to beer and wine, playing video games on stolen quarters, and frying burgers on the grill. A number of men and women had forgotten who was married to whom. They were dancing, flirting, and laughing. One drunken couple banged into a wall, and an elk head came down off its bracket; the elk started dancing on the legs of a drunken man.

The black stuff—the slime—was everywhere. From shirts and blouses it went to hands, and from hands it went to other hands and to faces and to objects. It was on the floor, causing people to slip. It was on doorknobs, on handles, on chair backs, chair seats, tabletops. It got passed around on the sides of beer bottles and edges of plates. It went down hungry mouths with the potato chips, the french fries, the microwaved sandwiches.

It was all over the knob on the door that led to the mercantile, and Carl was getting frustrated, trying to get the knob to turn.

"Hey!" he hollered. "Someone help me over here."

That knob wouldn't turn, however. Not because of the slime but because it was locked—by Harold Bly, the owner.

But Carl wanted in, as did Andy. Then more and more of the folks in the tavern decided they wanted in, and before long there was a crash as the mercantile's front window came out, an advance party climbed in, and the door was swung open from the inside.

There was so much good stuff to steal in that mercantile that it was impossible to carry it all away. But some people had thought ahead: They had cars and trucks outside, ready to load up.

THE CHURCH was engulfed in consuming fire as the dragon climbed out through the roof, slid down the steep pitch, and rolled gently onto the gravel parking lot in a shower of cinders and sparks. Now it crouched, wary, fevered with malice, only half-camouflaged in the dark. It could hear the ballyhoo down at Charlie's, and it could sense other souls engaged in mischief, dashing and hiding throughout the town.

But it had lost connection with the Hunter, and right now, the Hunter was the first victim it wanted.

RAISING A clanging, bashing, metallic racket, Steve frantically searched Levi's workbench, rummaged behind the backhoe, and groped among the scrap metal and heavy machine parts out behind the garage. That spear, that lance, that whatever-it-was, had to be here somewhere.

Unless someone had stolen it or unless Levi had hidden it.

Oh, Lord, where is it? Don't bring me this far and not let me find it!

He ran back inside, frantically scanning the walls, the ceiling, the cluttered floor It wasn't among the hydraulic hoses or leaning against the wall with the dismembered backhoe arm, it wasn't sitting on or behind the oil drums, it wasn't stowed in the overhead rack with the old exhaust systems

That stupid truck! The telephone company's big ladder truck took up half the garage, and Steve kept having to run around it to search. He came around one more time, for one more look. He knew Levi had been working back there on something.

One look up and he found it. The sight stopped him in his tracks. No. He couldn't believe it.

Steve grabbed a wooden stepladder sitting right next to the truck and climbed up for a close look.

Levi had welded the lance to the powered extension ladder atop the truck, and now the lance jutted out beyond the ladder and over the cab. The broad tip had been honed and oiled. You could shave with it.

What was Levi thinking?

"This tip here can slide between the scales, knife up under 'em . . . Once you get through those scales, you just keep shoving 'til you hit something vital . . ."

Yeah, yeah, he knew that part. The part that always puzzled him, which he hadn't figured out even yet, was How?

"You'd have to get up under the dragon to use it . . "

Steve looked up and down that ladder, taking careful note of the truck's size. He tried to think like Levi. Get up under the dragon. Yeah, sure! Sneak up behind him with this big rig?

"I was thinking one way would be to get the dragon to back over it, you know? Just have it propped up somewhere and get the dragon to back up and stab himself . . ."

Another impossibility, Steve thought. The dragon always stayed low to the ground.

And yet, Levi's plan must not be impossible; he must have thought of a way . . .

It hit him. Levi's dying words. "The tunnel. Use the tunnel. Jesus will take care of the rest."

Steve thought it over. He envisioned it; he played it out, and considered the odds.

Yeah, Jesus better take care of the rest . . . because Steve was going to try it.

WHILE STATE TROOPERS combed through the Clark County Sheriff's Office for clues and evidence, Lieutenant Barnard and Evelyn Benson stood in Collins's office with Deputy Johanson; Barnard to view things firsthand and Evelyn to clarify what she'd seen.

"He was sitting right there, propped against the door," Evelyn indicated, pointing at the doorway to the sheriff's office. "And Tracy was over there, near the coat rack."

"Yeah," said Johanson. "The bloodstains were just behind the door. Take a look at that jacket. It has some kind of black scuzz all over it."

Barnard took a look, sniffed it, and shot a look at Evelyn. "What is this stuff? Do you have any idea?"

"It's something they all seem to have in common," she answered.

"And Deputy Ellis was going back to Hyde River?"

"She was going after Steve. They could both be in danger."

Suddenly Barnard's mobile radio squawked, "Car one-eighteen, car one-eighteen."

Barnard grabbed the radio off his belt and spoke into it. "One-eighteen."

Julie the dispatcher's voice crackled out of the radio. "We have reports from Hyde River: full-scale rioting, looting, gunfire. One man down with a gunshot wound. Aid crew is en route."

"What in the—" He looked at Evelyn then replied to the dispatcher, "one-eighteen responding."

"I'll bet Harold Bly's behind this," Johanson said.

Barnard hurried into the hall, barking orders to one of the troopers. "Tape off the whole building. Seal it up."

His radio squawked, "One-oh-nine, two-twenty, two-twenty-five, one-sixteen, respond Hyde River."

All the patrol cars acknowledged.

"They're sending an army out there," Barnard said as he headed for the door.

Evelyn was right behind him. He stopped and asked her, "What if I told you to stay put?"

"I'd drive out there anyway," she answered.

He nodded. "That's what I thought. Come with me. At least then I can keep an eye on you." They went out the door to the patrol car. "Bly's crazy if he thinks he can hide this one."

THE CHURCH ROOF was falling in. Flames licked skyward through every window and every door, and now the flames were eating out gaps between the logs. The fire lit up the whole neighborhood, and people had gathered to see the spectacle.

Somewhere up the hill, some caring folks found the pastor's wife out in the street, screaming and hysterical, and took her and her children away to safety.

By that time the Carlson house had just about burned to the ground and was not that exciting to watch, so the big church fire came just in time for three of Andy Schuller's buddies, all volunteer firemen. With whoops and hollers and a beer in each hand, they came running up the hill to watch the church burn down.

But they never got there. Halfway up the hill, all three had the same hallucination: a freight train with big golden headlights pulling right out in front of them. They were dead, reduced to a cinder before they ever knew what it was.

The flames were still blasting from the dragon's nostrils and scorching the street as the dragon swung his gaze downhill, sensing the Hunter had to have gone that way.

Just then, a vehicle roared up the hill, its lights on high beam. The dragon crouched.

STEVE SAW the golden retinas in his headlights, the pupils contracting when the light hit them. The dragon was unable to fully camouflage itself anymore. Most of the neck and body were out in the street, the neck coiled, the head close to the pavement like a rattlesnake ready to strike. It was leaning on that stumped leg. Hopefully it would move a little slower because of it, Steve thought. This ladder truck was no hot rod.

He drove straight for the dragon's flank, the transmission in second, the engine racing, until the silvery scales filled his windshield. He cranked the wheel hard to the right, and the scales raced across his vision like a flurry of rainbows.

The dragon immediately lurched at him. If not for that shattered leg the contest would have been over.

Steve ducked down a side road that paralleled the highway. He shifted to third and took a quick look in the rearview mirror.

He saw golden eyes and then nothing but flames.

The truck lurched forward as if hit from behind. Steve could smell the paint blistering.

With a tight right turn, tires screeching, the truck leaning, Steve drove back down the hill toward the highway. There were people in the street, standing in his path! He blew the horn. He was going too fast!

The dragon was hobbling only a few yards behind him, running on hind legs, hopping on its foreleg, the wings dragging in tatters on the street, the neck reaching, the teeth bared.

Kawump! Steve hit the bottom of the hill, and the shocks bottomed out as screaming people leapt aside.

Tires squealing, Steve made a left turn. The truck reeled and fishtailed up the main road toward the four-way stop, the Carlson house a smoldering ruin on the right.

Suddenly he saw a pickup truck coming straight toward him.

Steve swerved left, missed it, and kept going—

He looked in the rearview mirror and saw the dragon hobbling, stumbling, then sliding down the steep grade into the intersection. A moment later the pickup plowed into its belly, and both went skidding over the curb and into a boarded-up cafe, the dragon's head trailing on one side of the truck, its tail on the other, its body halfway into the building.

Well, Steve thought, this would buy me some distance.

WEDGED BETWEEN the pickup and the building, the dragon coiled, twisted, and pushed to get free, to back the truck off. The claws found a man inside the cab and crushed him. A woman escaped through the passenger door and ran, screaming.

The dragon could see the ladder truck nearing the four-way stop.

The sinister eyes narrowed, piercing into the souls in the street. The souls in the street heard the call.

STEVE SAW trouble. A man pushing a new wheelbarrow, then a woman carrying a stolen television, then two youths, each with a portable tape player, suddenly turned into the street and into his path. He jammed on his brakes, sounded his horn, swerved around the man, almost hit the woman, then came so close to one of the teenagers that the truck knocked the tape deck out of his hands. What did these people think they were doing? Didn't they know what was back there?

Maybe they did, and that was why they stood in his way.

THE DRAGON hooked the cab of the truck with one toe, shoved it backward into the street, then wriggled free of the building. The head rose high above the truck, found three more people huddling in the truck bed with loot from the mercantile, and with one fiery blast incinerated them all.

THE MINING COMPLEX! Steve had to get to the mining complex! But there were some more people meandering through the four-way stop, blocking off the bridge across the river. Steve jammed on the brakes, and the truck started a side skid.

It slowed enough to turn.

The road going up the hill was clear enough. He cranked the wheel to the left, ground the gears into second, dodged past some blurred bodies and waving arms and headed up the hill again. He didn't know where this street went; he only knew there was a very angry lizard behind him. How he'd ever get back to cross that bridge to the mining complex he had no idea.

Suddenly a man's face appeared right outside Steve's window, which was down. Before he could roll it up, the man grabbed the wheel, and the truck lurched to the left. Steve pulled it to the right.

A tug-of-war ensued as the man pulled to the left and Steve steered to the right. Then the man grabbed a fistful of Steve's hair. Steve took one hand from the wheel to fight him off.

Steve got a good look at the man: it was Clayton Gentry, the young logger. The guy was crazed, maniacal, and smeared with black ooze.

The truck kept rumbling up the hill, swerving and rocking.

"Clayton, let go!" he cried.

Clayton growled and punched Steve in the side of the head.

Steve wrenched the wheel, and the truck swerved across the street to the left. Steve saw a utility pole coming up. He cut the wheel, veering in close.

The pole took off the left-side mirror—and Clayton Gentry.

THE PICKUP was engulfed in flames and black smoke. The gas tank blew and the ball of flame ignited the old cafe. The dragon's neck reached above the inferno, and it saw where Steve had gone. It leapt over the burning pickup, through the tower of flame, and headed up the hill again, steam and smoke wisping from its nostrils.

It probed for souls with its mind, its essence. It reached for hearts it could herd.

BOOM! The shotgun blast got the crowd's attention. They froze, the canned goods, wool socks, clothing, and garden supplies still in their hands.

Harold Bly chambered another round and aimed the gun toward the ceiling. "All right now. Hold it!"

Click-click. Click. Click-click-click. Pistols, revolvers, rifles aimed at him from every direction. It appeared that his power was eroding.

At that moment Carl burst in the front door. "I just saw the professor drive by!"

As everyone stood frozen, Carl gushed something about a phone company truck and the hill above the town and lots of fire up the street. United again, everybody headed for the door.

"Block the roads!" Bly shouted, in charge again. "Block the roads! Andy, take the north end! Carl take the south! Doug, take the four-way stop, don't let him across the bridge!"

They ran for their vehicles.

"I saw him go up there!" Carl shouted, pointing up the hill. "Paul!" shouted Bly. "You and Kyle go after him, flush him out. The rest of you block the roads!"

Trucks and cars roared to life and raced off.

STEVE REACHED the crest of the hill and came to a T in the road. He looked both ways and decided to go right, up a narrow road past some old frame houses. He drove a block and came to a fork in the road, the left climbing the hill, the right descending.

He was as good as lost. He had to find a way back to the highway, back to the four-way stop and across that river. He thought he'd take the right—

He spotted a black shadow leaping out from behind a house and across that road. His headlights caught the flicker of silver scales and a stringy wisp of gray smoke.

There was a driveway on the right. He took it, then drove right through the yard, hooking and dragging a swing set for several yards and then crashing through a split-rail fence. Now he was in another yard, where he dodged a laundry tree but gave it a spin, then rammed a raised planting bed with such force that his head hit the ceiling. When the headlights came down to ground level again, he was in a narrow alley. He screeched to the right again, trying to double back the way he had come, back to the four-way and that bridge.

THE DRAGON clattered and clawed up one side of a house, roosted for only an instant on the peak of the roof, and then came crashing down into the alley, its tail smashing a small porch and a row of garbage cans. It didn't run down the alley, but leapt atop another house, slipping and clawing on the steep metal roof until it hooked its claws on the ridge and pulled itself over. It caught sight of the truck going back down the hill, then it slid and rolled off the roof and landed in the yard. As it lunged into the street again, it caved in the roof of a car. It could see one remaining taillight—the other had melted—on that lumbering truck just above the four-way.

But the dragon's net was closing.

PAUL AND KYLE came barreling up the hill in Kyle's off-road pickup just in time to play chicken with the telephone truck coming the other way.

Steve saw them coming, their headlights and amber foglights in his eyes.

Oh-man-oh-man-oh-man—GET OUT OF THE WAY!

Kyle veered to the right. So did the telephone truck. They barely missed each other. Kyle jammed on the brakes. He was about to turn around when a silvery, glittery freight train roared by the windshield.

"Aaawww!" Kyle screamed. "What was that?"

They both knew. Neither could say it.

STEVE WAS building up speed again, diving down into that four-way with little chance of stopping. The four-way was more solidly blocked than before. Two cars were parked bumper to bumper across the bridge. Some men with rifles were standing beside them.

Well, it was all or nothing now, Steve thought. He kept going hit the horn and held it there.

He only had fifty feet to go now. People darted sideways out of his path. He could see Doug Ellis by the roadblock aiming a rifle.

Twenty. He ducked down, just barely able to see over the steering wheel.

Crash! The truck struck both cars and spun them aside, opening the roadblock like a gate. He hit the gas and headed over the bridge.

Steve took one quick look in the mirror. There was Doug Ellis, aiming at him. A bullet ripped through the back door and several tool racks. Then another. Steve ducked, and the truck swerved.

NOW THE dragon's way was blocked by its own net. The four-way was full of people, trucks, cars, and loot thrown everywhere. It filled its lungs as it galloped down the hill, step-thump, step-thump, step-thump.

Bernie and Melinda saw it. Joe and Elmer saw it.

Harold Bly saw it.

Everyone screamed and ducked behind cars, trucks, utility poles and one another.

Doug Ellis stepped out and aimed his rifle at the dragon.

The dragon expelled a ball of fire that engulfed the four-way, igniting cars, buildings, and littered loot. The hill was steep, and the dragon stumbled, then slid, then tumbled over the burning cars and through the four-way into the clear on the other side. It righted itself and bounded toward the bridge.

Bly and the others were awestruck. They'd never seen it before.

"Did you—" Bernie stammered. "Did you see that?"

"It's after the professor," Elmer said.

Paul and Kyle came to a screeching halt in the middle of the four-way. "Did you see that?" Kyle screamed, his voice a terrified falsetto.

"It's going after the professor!" Bly hollered, wielding his shotgun. "It wants him!" He laughed with delight. "See? What'd I tell you?"

Nobody moved.

The dragon was real. They'd seen it. Buildings and vehicles were burning all around them, as further proof. And Doug Ellis was dead—burned and crushed.

They were stunned, mesmerized.

Meanwhile, Steve roared along the narrow ramp that paralleled the river, hoping this route would take him to the tunnel. The last time he had gone this way he was drugged out of his skull.

Oh Lord, make this work even if it is crazy!

BLY HAD to goad the people to get them moving again. "Joe and Elmer! Get those cars across the road again! Kyle! Get your truck over there!"

Kyle was looking at Doug's charred body and the two rammed cars. "But—"

"Do it! Benson's trapped. There's no way out of there."

They couldn't move. All they could do was stare across the bridge and then at each other.

Bly shoved them and slapped them to get them moving. "Come on. The dragon's on our side! Let's help him out!"

Joe got into one car, Elmer into the other, and they jockeyed them into position so that they blocked the road again.

Melinda was cowering by the corner of the ransacked hardware store. "The dragon's not on our side," she said, her voice quivering with fear. "He's not on anybody's side."

Nobody else seemed to catch her words, but Bly did. He shot her a dirty look and then hollered his rebuttal to the others. "The dragon wants Benson; you all saw it! We gave him Benson and he's taking Benson! He's bought the deal!"

Melinda was silenced, but she did not change her mind. She said nothing more, but only shook her head no.

Bly hollered louder, "The dragon wants Benson, and I want him too! Benson's the cause of it all!"

Kyle nosed his truck up against the two cars. The professor wouldn't bash his way through here next time.

"All right," said Bly, raising and waving his shotgun, "let's go!"

Elmer and Joe took up the call, "Let's go."

Bernie was ready and stepped forward. But Paul wasn't sure. "What for? You want to help that thing?"

Melinda found her voice again and shouted defiantly, "I'm not!" She pointed to Doug's charred body. "The dragon wants all of us; can't you see that?"

Kyle wasn't sure about anything, but he was a great follower; he followed.

Andy had seen the ruckus and the fire from the north roadblock and come back to be a part of it. He was armed and ready. He was ready to follow Bly, and Andy's buddies—tnose wno were left— went where he went.

Then Carl came running from the south, his eyes popping out. "What'd I miss?"

"Come on," Bly said. "The action's this way."

They were a fresh mob now, an armed gang ready to side with the dragon and erase the last vestige of the Trouble. They squeezed around the roadblock and headed across the bridge toward the towering, tangled mine complex.

STEVE'S HEADLIGHTS illuminated a tunnel running under the huge company building. Was this the one? No. He remembered another . . .

He slowed just a little, looking back. Was the dragon following him? No sign of it.

His eyes came forward in time to see silver claws come over the wall up ahead on the right, up from the river below.

Steve hit the gas, hoping he could get past it in time. He had to keep that thing behind him.

Silver horns appeared, then the head came over the wall, the eyes blazing, the teeth bared, smoke puffing from the nostrils.

Claws burst through the windshield in a shower of glass and grabbed hold of the cab frame. The truck lurched and leaned to the right. Steve shifted down and floored the accelerator, steering left, dragging the beast along the wall as he headed for the tunnel. One huge eye glared through the window, and stinging smoke came through the windshield.

Thirty miles per hour, slowing, slowing; twenty miles per hour . . . The beast was dragging the truck to a stop.

The tunnel was coming up. Come on. Come on!

The truck reached the tunnel and squeezed in. The dragon held on, its arm going into the tunnel, until its body struck against the company building with a heavy thud.

The truck lurched to a stop, then went crooked in the tunnel, the tires spinning, shrieking, smoking.

The claws began to uncurl.

Steve let off the accelerator, then hit it again. The truck lurched forward, the claws slipped out, and the truck surged ahead down the dark tunnel, the roar of the engine resounding off the water-streaked walls.

Steve looked in the rearview mirror. A ball of fire filled the tunnel and then a horned, golden-eyed face came through it, closing the distance.

The truck shot out of the tunnel like a torpedo and into a wide expanse where Steve saw loading chutes, piles of ore, an old rail-road bed. Now he remembered: This was the old railroad loading yard. There was a huge articulated loader parked at one end, a pile of rubble, and a slightly bent sheriff's patrol car lying in a heap before the big bucket—Yes! Steve remembered Levi driving that thing through the pile of debris, clearing away the barricade that blocked the tunnel!

Yes, there was the old railroad tunnel. He circled the loading area in a wide left turn, looking for it.

Over his left shoulder Steve saw the dragon burst from the passage he'd just come through. The glowing retinas locked on him.

There was Levi's tunnel! Steve drove just past it. He slammed on the brakes and ground to a halt in the gravel.

The dragon was coming at him, flames already huffing in small billows before its jaws, the orange light reflecting from the scales on its face.

He slammed the truck into reverse, stuck his head out the window to look behind, and backed into the tunnel. Faster, faster. He was barely able to see in the dark with only a half-melted taillight. He flipped on the left turn signal, and it flashed against the tunnel walls, giving him intermittent glimpses of where he was going.

He looked ahead, through the shattered windshield. No dragon. He looked behind and saw only the endless black tube of that tunnel.

Try and trap me again, come on. Let's see you sneak up from behind!

How long was this tunnel? He didn't want to go too far, but he had to go far enough—

There! Far down the tunnel he caught the weakest glint of silver scales blinking back the light from his turn signal.

He hit the brakes. The golden eyes reflected back the glare of his one remaining brake light.

First gear. The truck eased forward. Steady, steady. Steve kept his eyes on the rearview mirror. You coming, big guy?

In the weird stroboscopic effect of the turn signal, the golden eyes and glimmering scales seemed to gallop forward in violent lurches, closer and closer with each flash of light.

Steve hit the gas and shot forward, keeping an eye ahead and an eye on the mirror. Now he was just about matching the dragon's speed. Good. He needed the time.

He hit the brakes and brought the truck to a stop just ten feet inside the tunnel entrance. He cranked the wheel, backed up, shifted into first, cranked the other way, lurched forward.

Now the truck sat crooked, totally blocking the tunnel.

The only way out was over the top.

He leapt from the cab.

Now the dragon was huffing fire with every breath as it ran up the tunnel, step-thump, step-thump, step-thump!

Steve ran back to the ladder control and could see the control lever in the pulsing light of the dragon's flames. With the slithering, stomping sound of the beast echoing all around him, he grabbed the lever and threw it forward. The hydraulic pump came to life with a whirrrr, and the ladder started to raise toward the ceiling. He eased the lever sideways and swung the ladder around, aiming it straight out the tunnel, then raised it some more, just high enough and no higher. Now the lance angled upward, the edge of the blade reflecting the flashes of flame from behind.

STEP-THUMP, STEP-THUMP, STEP-THUMP!

All set. Steve ran forward, squeezed around the truck's fender, and ran into the loading yard just as flashlights, shouts, and guns came pouring out of the opposite tunnel. The light beams caught him.

"There he is!" somebody yelled.

"Benson!" came the voice of Harold Bly.

Andy Schuller, Kyle Figgin, Carl Ingfeldt, Elmer and Joe, Bernie, and Harold Bly fanned out to block all paths of escape, their guns and rifles clacking as they each chambered a round. Steve came to a halt. There was nowhere to go.

Then came a crashing and creaking of metal behind him. Bly and his mob were now looking past Steve, their eyes wide and white in the dim light.

Steve shot a glance backward and saw the dragon's head lunge over the top of the ladder truck as the truck creaked and rocked under its weight. The front leg groped for a foothold; the stump banged and scraped on the cab. The scaled neck slid over that lance like a creeping python, the lance tip clicking over each scale like a stick on a picket fence.

Steve's eyes went from the dragon back to Bly and his mob. They were frozen in a bizarre, silent tableau, their flashlight beams all focused on the huge beast trapped between that truck and the tunnel ceiling.

And here I am in the middle, Steve thought.

The dragon was incensed. It struggled and pushed to get over the truck. Clack, clack, clack-clack-clack, the scales passed over the tip of the lance as the dragon slid by, inch by inch.

Okay, Lord. What now? Steve asked.

The dragon got its shoulders through, past the truck, past the lance. In only a moment it would be free of the truck altogether. It would be out of the tunnel, into the open, ready to take its pick of the souls at its mercy. The lance was clicking over the scales just below the rib cage. A rear foot was on the truck cab.

Harold Bly found his voice, and it was shaking. "Don't be afraid, boys. He's ours . . . he's nothing to be afraid of . . ."

By the way they were backing away and trying to remember what their guns were for, Steve sensed Bly's words weren't helping much.

Then Steve recalled Levi's words: "When the dragon sees Jesus in you, he'll back up. You'll scare him . . ."

But is Jesus in me?

Clack-clack-clack, the scales moved over the lance. There was no time to wonder.

"Jesus . . ." Steve prayed as he turned and faced the dragon head-on. "Please be in me."

Against all common sense, against an all-consuming terror, needing all the strength he could muster, Steve took a small, trial step of faith—toward the dragon. He planted his foot down—and waited. He remained alive, and strangely, he now found he had just enough faith to take the next step, so he did. Then he took another step toward the dragon. Then another.

There wasn't time to analyze or understand it, but his fear was gone now. He was looking that beast right in the eyes, and for the first time, he was not afraid.

The dragon was pushing, clawing, trying to get around and over that ladder truck, spitting and huffing fire in its intense anger.

With reckless abandon and a cry of war, Steve broke into a run, charging right under the open jaws of the dragon.

The dragon inhaled deeply, and then a blinding wall of flame blasted Steve off his feet, tossing him with the force of an ocean wave, carrying him along as he tumbled over and over and over.

He could feel his arms, legs, every square inch of his body contacting the sharp edges of the mine waste and spilled ore as he landed and bounced and rolled in the fire.

Even Harold Bly ran for cover, joining his mob behind the big loader, cowering behind the huge tires and the monstrous front bucket.

The dragon clapped its jaws shut, cutting off the flame, and then it raised its head to survey its work. Small fires flickered and licked in a long, blackened streak on the ground. The air was murky with smoke.

Bly gathered the fortitude to snicker. "Heh, man, what a show! That Benson's done for. He's gone."

Not quite. As they watched in amazement, a shadow emerged through the red glowing smoke in the middle of the yard. Steve Benson, dizzy and battered, struggled to his feet and looked around to get his bearings.

Before he knew where he was or how he was, flames hit him again, knocking him down. Head over heels, he tumbled then slammed flat into a wall as fingers of fire washed over him, scorching the wall black.

The dragon rested, the fire receded.

Steve flopped from the wall to the ground, flat on his back, feeling pulverized. All he could see was smoke.

Man, what a slow way to die! he thought. But I have to get up.

Slowly, deliberately, he got to his feet. Then he wandered, lost and blinded through the smoke.

Where's the dragon? Gotta make that lizard back up . . . Jesus'll take care of the rest . . .

Before he even knew where he was, flames hit him again, and again he went flying into the wall.

Just how long was this going to go on? he wondered.

He thought about Harold Bly, Andy Schuller, and all the others who had followed him. Weird. They tried to throw me to the dragon, and now what am I doing?

Slowly, painfully, like a boxer at the count of nine, he got his legs under him, straightened his knees, and stood up. Some of Bly's men, wherever they were, shouted to one another in amazement. He hurt all over. He rubbed his eyes, his face.

He thought he heard sirens in the distance. Cops? Fire trucks? That would help.

The dragon's eyes were watching him through the smoke. He stumbled forward, toward those eyes. Forward. Just forward.

The eyes were widening. The nostrils were flaring. That thing was sucking in air, building up for another blast.

Flames hit him again, and he lost sight of the world, lost feeling, lost awareness.

He woke up on his back in the hard, sharp-edged mine waste, the ground like a reeling turntable beneath him. One more time he found the strength to get to his feet, then turned right and left, looking for those eyes, those smoking, flaming nostrils.

There they were, clear across the loading yard.

He took a step forward, then he took another.

The eyes were locked on him. They seemed surprised.

Steve was surprised. He was still alive, on his feet, and—he looked at his arms, his body—he wasn't burned! Not even singed! He looked up at the dragon looking back. He thought the dragon looked as stunned as he was.

Andy Schuller couldn't believe his eyes. Nor could Kyle Figgin. Carl Ingfeldt squeaked, "How'd he do that?" but Joe and Elmer only looked at each other dumbly; they hadn't a clue.

Bly was cursing under his breath, fingering his shotgun.

For a man who'd been dashed across a bed of rough gravel time after time and should have been a black cinder by now, Steve was feeling remarkably calm and resolute as he kept walking right toward that hideous beast. More of Levi's words came to mind. Well, they had worked for Levi . . .

"GO ON! GET! GET OUT OF HERE!!"

That big head jerked backward, and the evil eyes widened with—

No. Come on. Really? Did he actually see fear in those eyes?

Steve wondered. That huge, slithering, devouring monster was afraid?

So try it again, Steve! "GO ON! GET BACK!"

Steve didn't realize how weak he was. Without warning his legs buckled, and he went down on his knees. Nope. No way. He'd been on his knees in front of this beast before, and he wasn't going to do that again. He mustered his strength and got back on his feet, staggering, his legs like rubber.

The moment he rose to full height, the dragon shied back. It was a small, almost imperceptible move—but it was backward.

Steve raised a hand and gestured a push-back as he said quietly but firmly, "I won't bow to you. You don't own me, not anymore."

He could see the front foot push into the dirt, the stump gouging in. The head shied back as the neck curled.

That move was obvious enough for Harold Bly to see it. He came out from behind the loader, shotgun in hand, his indignity far outweighing his fear. "What's going on there? Why doesn't it take him?"

"Harold!" Bernie cried from behind the wrecked patrol car. "Harold, don't go out there!"

"Shut up!" Harold snapped back. Then he turned to the dragon. "Take him! He's the one you want, we brought him to you. Kill him. What're you waiting for?"

The dragon inched forward, the head lowering, the eyes glaring at Steve, staring him down. Clack. The belly moved over the lance just one more scale and stayed there.

Steve stood his ground and glared right back. "You see Jesus in me, don't you?"

The dragon started backing up.

All right! We need more of that. Steve started forward with bold, deliberate steps, staring the dragon down. "GO ON! I'M THROUGH WITH YOU! YOU'VE GOT NOTHING ON ME!"

The rear foot stepped back off the truck cab. The dragon

pushed with its front leg and stump. The head turned far away from the little man coming at him.

Steve felt a thrill course through him. This was working! There was a God! He started taking big, determined steps to be sure the dragon could see each one.

The dragon saw them, all right, and slid backward over the lance. The lance was slightly crooked; it jumped a scale, then another.

Steve kept coming. "YOU'RE WASHED OUT OF MY LIFE, AND YOU KNOW IT. NOW BEAT IT!"

The dragon lunged backward. The lance jumped a scale, jumped a scale, jumped a scale—

Caught!

Steve could see the broad tip slide up under a scale just below the rib cage.

Okay. Now to settle accounts. "CLIFF BENSON!" Steve shouted into the lizard's face. "TRACY ELLIS! LEVI COBB!" The dragon cringed at the sound. "MAGGIE BLY! CHARLIE MACK! VIC MOORE!" The dragon would not look at him.

Okay, Cliff, this one's for you. With a new rage giving him strength, he ran forward in a suicide charge, hollering like a madman, "YAAAAAAHHHH!"

The dragon jerked its head in and wriggled backward over the truck.

The lance went in.

Fireworks! Lightning! The scales flashed and rippled like a neon display as the dragon's neck shot skyward and its lungs emptied an agonized gush of air. It groped about its belly, the truck, the ladder, then curled its head down and back under, looking for the wound, trying to see what had happened.

Harold Bly ran forward, horrified, incredulous. This couldn't be happening!

Andy Schuller stayed behind the loader, peering from around a big tire. Kyle Figgin ran back as far as the entry tunnel and peeked from inside. Carl, Bernie, Elmer, and Joe didn't know what

to do or where to go, so they just ran back and forth in little pan-
icky circles until they finally returned to cower and cling to the
loader. They were spellbound, their eyes blinking and squinting at
the flash of the scales, and the dragon's rumbling, crashing struggle
with the ladder truck the only sound they heard.

They didn't hear the approaching sirens or see the flashing
lights coming through town.

The dragon heaved its body forward, pushing with its forelegs
against the truck, trying to get loose.

The lance wouldn't budge.

The dragon rocked to one side, then the other, pushed with its
hind legs, slammed its head against the ground and pushed with its
neck. The truck bounced on its springs, rocked, skidded sideways.

He's going to tear up his insides, Steve thought.

"You dirty dog! You've killed my dragon!" Bly screamed, raising his shotgun with shaking, fumbling hands.

The gun discharged, almost leaping from Bly's hands, before he
could aim. Some of the shot pelted the dragon's neck and head, and
it flinched in pain as sparks flew from its scales. Hopelessly impaled, the dragon shifted its gaze toward the screaming, fumbling
Harold Bly. The eyes of the creature narrowed, the breath hissed
through clenched teeth.

Bly was still holding the gun when he caught sight of the
dragon's hateful glare. He took a step backward. He started to
tremble.

"H-Hey now," he stammered. "It wasn't me. I'm on your side!"
Bly pointed toward Steve. "He's over there! Over there!"

The dragon seemed to gain strength from its boiling rage. Its
eyes locked on the bold, loudmouthed ruler of Hyde River as it
pulled at the lance.

The truck rolled, bounced, and screeched forward out of the
tunnel. The dragon's body cascaded over the top of it and to the
ground, twisting and finally snapping the ladder off.

As the dragon lay on its side, it craned its neck to and fro in
search of Harold Bly. When it spotted him, the neck reached like

a serpent, the head moved low to the ground, the breath sucked in, the left front leg reached out, claws extended.

Bly started backing away, his face contorted with horror and disbelief, his hands chambering another round in the shotgun. "No! Now come on, you don't want me . . ."

The dragon's burning eyes said otherwise as it slowly inched and slithered toward him.

Andy and his buddies fled in terror back through the first tunnel, followed by Kyle, Carl, Bernie, Elmer, and Joe.

The dragon pulled itself closer to Bly, its chin only inches from the ground.

Bly aimed the shotgun directly at the dragon's face and fired. A myriad of sparks and flashes exploded from the dragon's face, but it didn't flinch this time, and it didn't turn away.

The head rose from the ground; the dragon gasped a short breath.

Bly's hands were shaking as he chambered another round. "Get back . . . get BACK!" He aimed the gun and fired.

The dragon's face lit up like a fireworks display, but it kept crawling, clawing, slithering toward him. It opened its mouth and exhaled a blast of air, but there was no flame.

Bly prepared to fire again, chambering a round, aiming the shotgun. He waited this time, feeling some confidence. He could see the dragon was fading.

As if spurred on by Bly's cockiness, the dragon gathered its strength, raised its head high, and drew in air for one more try.

It couldn't hold the air in. Its last breath escaped, and a very small flame appeared but quickly burned itself out. The beast stared at Bly, its neck swaying like a tree in the wind.

Bly started to chuckle as he looked up at the gnarled face. "Not today, buddy. You're finished. You can't touch me!"

The dragon's fiery eyes dimmed, flickered, then went dark. Slowly, the neck went limp, began to sink—and then, in a long, slow arc, it flopped to the rocky ground with an earthshaking thud as Bly leapt and stumbled out of the way.

Bly recovered his balance, ready to run, but then saw no need. The big, scaly head was flat upon the ground; the eyes still looked his way, but no longer saw him. There was a long, silent, motionless moment in which Bly stared into the dragon's face, breathing hard, shotgun aimed, still shaking, needing time to believe the dragon was dead. Then a grin spread over his face, and he began to laugh defiantly. "There! There now!" He looked around for any witnesses to his triumph. "You see? You see that? This is Harold Bly we're talking about! I'm still on top! Still on top!"

He looked everywhere, wondering what had become of his followers. "Hey! Hey! Where'd you all go?" But no one remained in that vast, empty place except Steve Benson, battered, bruised, and exhausted, standing very still among the small fires and lingering smoke. It was just the two of them now, and Benson had to have seen everything.

Bly's jubilation soured into pure malice. "You!" He raised the shotgun. "Guess I still have one piece of unfinished business."

Steve sighed, his shoulders drooping with dismay. He'd survived so much. Would it all end this way? "Mr. Bly." He knew his argument would sound weak. "I did save your life."

Bly sneered and shook his head as if he'd just heard the dumbest statement ever made. "Weren't you watching?"

Steve could look past Bly and see the lance rammed up the dragon's belly. He'd fired enough rounds at the dragon to know a shotgun would never kill it. But Bly saw only what he wanted to see; it was that way with this town.

Bly raised the shotgun and sighted down the barrel at Steve's heart. "I don't owe you a thing, Benson, except what you've got coming, right now. Nothing's ever gonna kill Harold Bly—"

THUNK! Three silver spikes skewered Bly from behind and sprouted from his chest with a spattering of blood. He quivered, his face contorted with shock, pain, disbelief. The shotgun fell from his hands.

The dragon lifted Bly from the ground. His body hung on the claws like meat on a fork, his legs dangling. Then a claw sank like a needle through the black stain and into Bly's heart.

Through the wisps of smoke drifting over the rocky ground, Steve could see a slight, yellow glow from one half-open eye. The beast was alive, if only to finish the work the Hydes had begun so long ago. Slowly, mechanically, the dragon opened its jaws, flipped Bly's body across the rows of teeth, and bit down.

Then Steve was blinded by a sudden, unexpected flash of light. He turned away, his eyes tightly shut, expecting an explosion, but none came. He opened his eyes and slowly turned back toward the dragon and Harold Bly. He was still blinded. All he could see was a vague, serpentine spot in front of his eyes. He could hear no sound except sirens approaching from across the river and far down the valley.

Finally his vision began to clear, and he could vaguely see the corpse of Harold Bly lying crooked and mangled on the rough stones. He could make out the wide, empty expanse of the old loading yard and the last, dying remnants of the dragon's fires. The huge articulated loader was still sitting where Levi had parked it.

But the dragon was gone without a trace. It had vanished as if it never existed.

Gone.

Steve's knees buckled, and he sank to the ground, his strength gone. He was lying on hard, broken ore, but he didn't feel it. He was slipping away, falling into the sweet oblivion of a dead faint.

HE FELT a hand on his shoulder, gently shaking him, waking him up. He stirred and tried to open his eyes. How long had he been out? Where was he? Was the nightmare over?

He looked up and saw Evelyn staring down at him. The pink light of dawn was just over her shoulder.

There were other lights, too: headlights, flashing blue lights, flashing red.

"Steve? Are you all right?"

He sat up slowly. The world began to spin, and he lay back down. Evelyn was instantly beside him. She cradled his head in her arms. "Take it easy." Now he could see the police cars that had come through the access tunnel, and an aid car. Cops. Badges. Paramedics. Flashlights and headlights and people moving around shouting orders, questions, answers.

He tried to sit up again, and this time he made it.

"So how're you doing?" she asked.

"I—I'm not sure."

"Where's Tracy?"

Steve was sitting, but as he probed his beleaguered mind for an answer to Evelyn's question, the thought of Tracy pierced his soul, and he felt he would collapse again. He could see her face, young, pretty, and so intense at times. He loathed the sound of his words. "Tracy . . . is dead."

Evelyn looked so tired, so beaten down, and this news was one more cruel blow. He touched her shoulder to steady her.

"Was it the dragon?" she asked.

He nodded and knew he could say no more. He could not bear to recount or describe that horrible scene. But of course Evelyn had been there herself, was still there. She understood.

Steve looked across the loading yard and saw state troopers and fire fighters examining Harold Bly's body with their flashlights, muttering to one another in amazement. Bly appeared to be in two halves. From up here Steve could see the town and thought he'd never seen so many flashing lights in one place. Fire trucks, patrol cars, aid cars, private vehicles with emergency flashers. The whole valley had turned out, maybe the whole county.

"Where's the dragon now?" she asked.

"It's dead," he said simply, noticing how different it felt to share some good news for a change.

Good news had been in short supply for Evelyn as well, and she was glad to receive it. "Are you sure? Did you kill it?"

He looked across the yard at the nearly demolished telephone truck and the broken, mangled ladder. "No. I would say God did that—God and Levi Cobb. I just helped." He struggled to his feet with her assistance. "It died—it died with Harold Bly in its mouth, right over there . . ."

Evelyn was puzzled. "Where?"

The area Steve indicated was empty except for the police and medics now bagging up Bly's body. They walked over for a closer look, Steve leaning on Evelyn for support.

They found Levi's lance, still welded to the end of the ladder but now bent several ways in several places. The tip was intact, razor-edged, and clean—no trace of blood or flesh or scales. "Heh—look at that. Levi was right. He was the last one anyone wanted to listen to, but the old fanatic was right."

"Who is Levi?" Evelyn asked.

Steve didn't want to share more bad news. "A good friend. He saved my life. He built this lance—"

"Where is he?"

Steve knew he was telling the truth. "He's safe. He's out of harm's way for sure."

He carefully retraced where he remembered the neck had fallen. He didn't expect to find what he was looking for, but was pleasantly surprised when he did.

"Here," he said, stooping down. "Recognize this?" He picked up a piece of metal, sharp-tipped, sharp on one edge, and broken off. It was the tip of Evelyn's hunting knife. He handed it to her. "In case you ever have any doubts . . . you were there, all right. You stood up to the dragon, and he couldn't whip you."

They would never have to prove to themselves what they'd been through, but this special token brought Evelyn such assurance that tears came to her eyes.

A trooper asked, "Excuse me. Did either of you see what happened here?"

Evelyn looked at Steve, and Steve looked at the trooper, unable to think of any answer that would not take several days.

"Yes, officer," he answered after a futile attempt to think of something. "I saw what happened."

"Well," the officer said, "I'll need to get a statement—"

Oh sure, Steve thought, like you're going to believe it?

Evelyn cut in, "Sir, this man is injured, and I'd like to get him out of here."

He nodded toward the access tunnel and let them pass but reminded them, "We'll need a statement."

Then someone shouted from the tunnel, "It's all his fault! Arrest him, you hear me?" It was Carl Ingfeldt, tugging at two burly troopers and pointing in Steve's direction. "Benson! You killed our dragon!" He yelled up at a trooper, "He killed our dragon! It was our dragon, and he killed it!"

Steve approached and noticed the black stain was still there on Carl's shirt. "Carl, calm down."

"We'll sue you, Benson!"

One of the troopers asked Steve, "Do you know what he's talking about?"

Steve gave the trooper an apologetic look. "He's beside himself."

Both troopers nodded in agreement.

Steve looked at Carl curiously. "You're going to go into a court of law and testify that I killed your dragon? What dragon?"

Carl became flustered and couldn't answer.

Steve pointed to the black stain and lowered his voice to share a secret. "You still have him in there, Carl. You haven't lost a thing."

"Okay, fella," muttered one of the troopers, "clear the area. Go home."

Carl didn't change his tune as the troopers prodded him along. "You killed our dragon, Benson! We'll get you for that!"

"Move!" a trooper warned.

Steve and Evelyn could hear him arguing with the troopers, his voice a faint echo, long after they disappeared down the tunnel that led out of the complex.

Evelyn was considering Carl's ravings. "So now we have a witness in case you ever have any doubts. You really did kill the dragon."

Steve needed to check out one more thing to prove to himself that he had, indeed, killed the dragon. He looked down at his torn shirt. The black slime had turned to an ash gray dust he could easily brush off. He unbuttoned his shirt. Over his heart there was no wound, no pain. "I'm free," he said simply.

Evelyn gave him a hug, and then they turned and walked arm-in-arm through the tunnel, down the long ramp, over the bridge, and finally to Steve's camper, still parked in front of Charlie's Tavern and Mercantile. The camper's tires were flat, of course, but now the windows were all broken out as well and the inside stripped clean of Steve's gear, clothing, and guns.

Oh, well, he thought. The bunk was still intact. At least there was still a mattress on it.

Steve climbed in, his feet crunching on broken glass, and flopped on the bunk, dazed and exhausted.

"I'll see if I can find Lieutenant Barnard," Evelyn said. "You going to be okay?"

She got an unintelligible noise spoken into the mattress for a reply. She closed the door gently. One remaining shard of glass fell from the empty window frame and tinkled to the floor.

Steve lay limp on the mattress and just let his mind wonder.

He saw Cliff again, much younger, holding Evelyn by the hand and holding up a huge cutthroat trout, bigger than he'd ever caught before, and, he was careful to point out, bigger than Steve had ever caught before . . .

Aw, c'mon, Cliff, it wasn't that big . . .

He could see Tracy up in Homer's cabin, looking strangely at home in that little place, living in a part of her past when life was so much simpler and mistakes were not so costly . . .

She wasn't just beautiful on the outside.

He dwelt a moment on the last sight he'd ever had of Levi Cobb, lying on the ground, slipping into death as peacefully as slipping into a sleeping bag.

You weren't crazy, old buddy. You had your quirks, but one thing you had that nobody else had was peace. That says a lot.

He even considered Harold Bly for a moment, perhaps the best embodiment Steve had ever seen of all that could go wrong in a man. Harold was the very last of the Hyde family, and maybe that was just as well. The dragon came in with Benjamin Hyde, filled its cave with bones over the years, and finally went out with

Harold. "If This Be Sin, Let Sin Be Served," they had said. Not such a great idea after all.

So count me out, he thought.

With enough sorrow to last him for years, Steve just wanted to get out of Hyde River, away from this mess, these people, these patrol cars and cops and questions. He needed a shower, he needed some sleep, he ached all over, he was tired, he was filthy . . .

But he wasn't burned. That thought occurred to him again. He should have been a black cinder by now, deader than dead, gone from this world, pure history.

But he wasn't. He'd fought the dragon too, just like Evelyn. And just like Evelyn, he'd come out a winner.

Which brought another thought, a thought that had been so far away for so long: "Hey, I'm not going to die today. I get to live. I don't have to be dragon manure; I don't have to end up a pile of bones in that cave." He couldn't quite believe it, so he told himself again, "You get to live, Benson. You're free."

The sun would be up in just a few minutes. Wow. He'd be alive to see it.

Flashing lights filled the camper for just a moment as an aid car roared by, heading for West Fork. He figured there'd be more of that kind of noise but decided he could sleep through it.

He felt at peace; that was the main thing. Even in sorrow, while the fire crews mopped up the fires and the police rounded up the looters, while investigators asked their questions and the rioters slinked back to their homes, he felt so much at peace that he fell asleep right there—kind of like Levi—in his battered and broken camper, and slept until Evelyn and Lieutenant Barnard finally woke him and offered him a lift out of the valley.

THE END

THE MEDIA carried the story of the Hyde River riot for a day or two, blaming poverty, unemployment, and labor/management disputes for the sudden outburst of destruction and violence.

The police concluded that Harold Bly had been torn in two—accidentally or intentionally they could not determine—by an articulated loader they found parked near his body. They determined that the fires around town were set by rioters and the burned corpses were victims of those fires. Because no witnesses came forward, there were few arrests other than looters caught in the act. The only persons regarded as missing were Charlie Mack, Phil Garrett, Sheriff Lester Collins, and Sheriff's Deputy Tracy Ellis. Anyone else not found, either dead or alive, was accounted for by friends and relatives and crossed off the list.

The people who were driven out of Hyde River have left for good; those still living there have had nothing to say.

Levi Cobb is dead; the binder he had me read is gone and most likely destroyed. His killer, Harold Bly, is dead as well, so that case was summarily closed. Levi's body was released to his sister, who with power of attorney and the key Levi gave me opened Levi's safe-deposit box and recovered the original diary of Holly Ann Mayfield, the Hyde River Charter, and the other documents Levi had collected. Levi's legacy remains.

THE OATH also remains.

Last month, if only to resolve the matter in my own mind, I slipped surreptitiously through the town of Hyde River and once again climbed Saddlehorse. What I expected, I found: the cavern where the dragon had made its lair was blasted shut.

I looked all through my camper and whatever gear I had left after the looting, trying to find that small dragon scale I'd found the day the dragon trapped me. I suppose it vanished, simply ceased to exist, the moment the dragon vanished.

So all the evidence is gone, and the dragon is once again a myth, guarded by believers and ignored by skeptics.

To keep the memory vivid—and to be sure I didn't dream the whole thing—I still make frequent trips back to Oak Springs to visit Evelyn and her boys, and to visit Levi's grave—yes, he really is buried in the family plot near West Fork. Up the road from the cemetery I always pull off at a popular viewpoint and gaze upon the Hyde River Valley as it stretches and winds far to the north. I've viewed the lazy river and the steep, tree laden mountains in all four seasons now, and even photographed them with one of Cliff's cameras.

It's not that I'm enthralled by one view, majestic as it is. It's because I'm haunted by the possibility that one day, though I hope it never happens, I might detect an unnatural ripple in the clouds that gather over Saddlehorse, or a delicate, serpentine window of silver flickering for only an instant against the pink sky of sunset. It happened, and I want to remember; if it happens again, I want to know.

Because others must be told, I now add this, my own account, to the letters, cryptic notes, diaries, and press accounts gleaned by Levi Cobb from the past century. I expect my story will be largely ignored by those who come after me, but who knows? It just might prove useful to the next hapless soul who suspects he is being followed, marked, and hunted by those insidious, golden eyes. After all, we all live in Hyde River. We all have our dragon.

The epilogue from an account of the Hyde River phenomenon by Steven Clive Benson, Ph.D.

ABOUT THE AUTHOR

FRANK PERETTI, whose books have sold almost five million copies worldwide, is the author of *This Present Darkness* which has been translated into several languages and released on audio tape, as well as *Piercing the Darkness* and *Prophet*. His children's stories include *Trapped at the Bottom of the Sea*, *The Tombs of Anak*, *Escape from the Island of Aquarius*, and *The Door in the Dragon's Throat*. He lives with his wife Barbara in the Pacific Northwest.